YOUNG
ERIC
MALONE

YOUNG ERIC MALONE

New England Stories, 1950-67

ED MAHONEY

MILL CITY PRESS | MINNEAPOLIS, MN

Mill City Press, Inc.
322 First Avenue N, 5th floor
Minneapolis, MN 55401
612.455.2293
www.millcitypublishing.com

Cover Photo--This picture of me, my father Vin Mahoney, and my sister Mary Beth was taken by our mother Mary Mahoney in July1950 on the dunes at Plum Island, Massachusetts.

ISBN-13: 978-1-63413-845-1
LCCN: 2015916402

Cover Design by Alan Pranke
Typeset by B. Cook

Printed in the United States of America

To my parents,
Vincent W. Mahoney (1913–67)
Mary E. (Hodnett) Mahoney (1913–2000)
who earned their own highest compliment,
"the salt of the earth"

CONTENTS

INTRODUCTION

These stories have been brewing in my imagination for more than thirty years. In September of 2006, I was finally able to return to Lowell and begin writing them. While the stories come *from* my life, they reach for the larger truths of fiction beyond the limitations of fact. If they didn't exactly "happen," they are still as true as I can make them. What finally matters is how authentic they feel to the reader.

While I hope that each story stands on its own, taken together they tell how a New England boy grew up in the 1950s and '60s. They are a fictional memoir in chronological episodes rather than a collection of independent tales. They are not a novel or an autobiography. Some stories are almost entirely narrative while others mix Eric's story with expository passages about his intellectual growth, especially through his reading and his experiences as a debater and debate coach. So the reader should expect shifts in the writing style between "showing" and "telling," particularly in the later stories. I understand the risks of such variations, but I hope the result is a multi-level portrait of Eric within the New England culture and the various subcultures that shaped him. These include family, church, school, baseball, and the specialized world of high school and college debating. If this collection recalls the flavor of those receding decades for readers who were there, I am glad. For younger readers, I hope that it offers a convincing glimpse of a different time that still resonates today. When these stories show the flaws of people and institutions, I speak only with candid affection. YEM includes conflicts and mistaken judgments (Eric's especially), but this book has no villains (not even Gilly Dennis). No pleasure from reading this collection will approach the joy of writing it. Whatever shortcomings the reader finds here are, of course, my responsibility.

Several readers were kind enough to look at individual stories and give me interesting feedback. I thank my friends Jan Mahoney and Nancy Norton, fellow teacher Katie DiMarca, and my daughter Briana Mahoney for their comments. Five readers surveyed the entire text and helped make it more consistent and unified. Thanks to Tim Stevens, K.A. '65 and a great debater; LCHS teacher John Pawlak; my sister Mary Plouffe; and two lifetime friends Robert Bourgeois and Richard Pierce. Richard even helped me to discover the "missing story" which became "Belvidere."

From the Lowell Catholic High School staff, I thank my teaching colleague Kyle Fuller, IT specialist Donna Boucher, English teacher and coach Tom Varnum, and registrar LeeAnn Varnum, whose *essential* computer assistance helped me with the preparation of this manuscript. Also, Patricia Ducey, Steve Rossi, and Beth Noel of Middlesex Community College have aided at various points in the preparation of the cover image, as has the staff of the Staples store in Chelmsford, Massachusetts. The editors at Mill City Press have patiently guided me through the intricacies of the publication process.

—Ed Mahoney
Lowell, Massachusetts
October 2015

PLUM ISLAND

I

The new-car scent lingered in their '50 Ford Custom on a hot July morning as the Malones rode east on 133 toward Plum Island. Beside him, Betty, not quite three, slept on a pillow wedged between the seat and the locked door. Up front, Grampa Harrigan sat quietly by the passenger door, and Mom and Dad talked of places along the road where friends lived or where Dad could imagine living—Andover and Shawsheen Village, Boxford and Georgetown and Byfield, Groveland and Marlboro and the funny one, Ipswich. Eric played with their names through the road-drowsy miles. *Shawsheen, land of green. The clean village green of Shawsheen. Ipswich-whipstitch. Don't slip in the Ipswich ditch. Who lives in Ipswich? The Ipswich witch. Good-bye to Byfield by the field. Where were Boxford's boxed Fords? Was their Ford boxed in Boxford? Daddy smokes Marlboros. Do they make them all in Marlboro? No sign of the Ipswich witch. She wouldn't be out in the morning.*

Betty turned in her pillow and seemed almost awake, then curled up again with her blanket and was gone. Eric yawned, stretched his legs toward her along the seat, and then drew them up to his chin and leaned forward, hoping for a glimpse of water. No water yet.

"Are we almost there?" he asked lazily, knowing the answer.

"Not yet, Eric," Mom said. "We'll be in Newbury soon. Then you'll see the water and the bridge to Plum Island."

He lay back and closed his eyes. *He'd like some new blueberries in Newbury, but not if they're Shawsheen green.* Soon he was asleep and

1

saw nothing of Plum Island's odd little airport or the drawbridge. He awoke only when seagulls cawed loudly and circled the dank inlet for fish. The mud-yucky tidal flats stunk, but the ducks and gulls never cared. Birds liked strange places, Eric decided. Between clumps of reedy dune grass, he finally saw the silver-blue water glisten and roll.

Soon they turned onto Northern Boulevard and rode by the familiar neighbors' cottages to the Bethmere. The salt air swept through the open windows and Betty awoke.

"Is it Plum Island?" she asked suddenly.

"That's right, Betty. Here's our cottage," Daddy assured her. A gust blew a thin plume of sand along the edge of the road and into their short driveway as they stopped. Another Plum Island summer. This year they would spend nearly all of July here, Dad promised, more than the two weeks of earlier summers. So many beach days all together were more than Eric could imagine as he watched the dune grass sway. He opened the door with both hands and stepped down onto the sandy driveway. Betty did a quick jump to the pavement after him.

Mom and Dad took a long look around, so Eric and Betty did, too. The cottage needed paint. Sand had collected on the old wooden steps leading up to the screened-in porch around two sides of the Bethmere. Eric remembered nights last summer when he had slept on the porch and thought how the waves never slept. Mom lifted Betty onto the porch while Dad placed their bags and a large beach umbrella by the kitchen wall. Betty trundled over to the shore side of the porch to stand by Eric and look out at the ocean with him. He saw how much closer the ocean was compared to last year. Or was that just high tide? The year before, Mr. McGreavy, who rented this cottage to the Malones, actually had the house moved back from the sea and nearer to the road. *They . . . moved . . . a . . . whole . . . house,* Eric thought slowly. *How did they do that?* Even after Daddy had explained, Eric wasn't sure it was possible. Why didn't the Bethmere just break into pieces? And how did they keep those cinder block posts firm in all that sand? Grown-ups did amazing things.

"Janie, Janie," Betty shouted. She pointed to a little girl who was digging a hole in the sand by the next-door porch. Her friend from last year was back. Janie came running to the Bethmere and climbed deliberately up the four big steps till she could push open the creaky screen door and run to hug Betty. Eric said "Hi" and stepped slightly away as Betty and Janie went into the kitchen where Mom had some lemonade ready for them.

"Do you want some, Eric?" she called.

"No thanks."

He'd rather stare some more at the ocean and the clouds above it, golden in the late-morning sun. The surf crashed and rolled up the slope of the beach, then retreated in swirls of foam. He remembered when waves sometimes criss-crossed each other and formed little pockets that sucked his feet into the mushy sand. He'd pull them out slowly one at a time and then run higher before the next wave. Toward the horizon he saw three fishing boats far apart. Anglers with bamboo poles leaned over the sides of each. A few other figures weren't fishing at all—just waiting for a catch. Daddy had taken him mackerel fishing last summer. Eric could still see the blood, gills, and fish eyes and hear the flapping of the fresh-caught victims. Eating fish was less troubling than catching them. He looked again at the swelling blue waves that rose and crashed and rose. He might have stood there for an hour if Mom had not broken the spell. "Lunch time."

* * *

"Bethmere," the sign on the porch wall said. White letters on a black-board hanging from iron hooks on old nails that streaked a little rust onto the yellow wall. Bethmere. Like Betty's real name backward: Mary Elizabeth. Should he tell Betty that this cottage was really named for her? No, he would keep that strange discovery to himself. Did Mr. McGreavy know Betty's name? He didn't think so.

"Eric."

"Yes, Mom."

"Bring your tube and that blue-and-white towel with you."

"OK."

He walked off behind his parents down the short path through the dune grass to the sloping beach. Janie sat down with Mom on their blanket as Dad slowly twisted their beach umbrella into the sand, then tilted it against the wind. Johnny Onslow had come to play with Eric and wore his own black tube over his shoulders. Maybe they'd see his mom on the beach later. Daddy was off work all day today and might play catch in a while with Eric and "Johnny Onnie," as Daddy called him, but first everyone would test the ocean to see how cold their ankles got. Only Grampa Harrigan never worried about the water temperature. He liked to tease Eric and Betty about their shivery approaches to the wave ends. Sure enough, as Eric and his mom arranged the towels, sandals, and snack basket on their blanket, Grampa Harrigan walked steadily down to the sea and straight into the waves up to his shoulders before ducking his head and coming up for air. He swam a few quick strokes and waded in closer to the beach. Then he sat where each new wave could wet his feet on its way. Dad had taken Betty and Janie by the hand and walked them carefully down to the wave edges. Eric sat by his mother while she firmed her beach hat against her head to resist the steady breeze.

"How come Grampa never minds cold water?" Eric asked. His mom smiled.

"Well, Grampa grew up in Ireland near a city called Cork. The family farm went right down to the beach, and the water there was colder than here, so he just got used to it as a boy."

"Why did Grampa leave Ireland?"

"Now there's a question with a long answer. Why don't you and Johnny try the water and we'll talk about that later? OK?"

"Yeah," Eric agreed, still curious but happy enough to avoid long answers. Eric and Johnny stepped slowly into the water and found it as cold as ever. Their ankles gradually numbed, but soon their calves and the backs of their knees ached. Janie and Betty had retreated from the waves to build sand castles. Giving up on the water, the boys had a couple of disputed races with each other toward lines they drew in the sand before Eric's dad took them for a long walk down the beach and back. As the afternoon passed, a few more bloodless souls conquered the surf, and a couple of teenagers were even trying to ride small surfboards with brief success. The wind slowly died and the day got hotter.

Then Dad pulled out the gloves and a baseball from his bag of sports gear and set up a three-way game of catch. He lobbed little fly balls to the boys, who tried to catch them away from their bodies and missed as many as they grabbed. Then Eric threw one overhand to Johnny, who couldn't handle the ball and didn't run fast enough to save it from rolling slowly toward the surf. Dad came rushing over to pick up the ball before a large wave could take it away.

"Let's try to keep the ball dry, boys," he advised.

They moved higher up on the sand and continued their game for a few minutes more until the boys grew restless at their uneven skills. Eric finally yelled at Johnny to throw better, and Dad intervened.

"That's enough, Eric. I think maybe we've had enough catch for now. How about a snack?"

As they ate tuna sandwiches and chips and drank cokes and ginger ale, Eric noticed some odd shapes in the water. Filmy blobs had clustered in one quieter section of the surf. "What's that, Dad?"

"Where, Eric?" The boys pointed.

"Oh, they're jellyfish. You should stay away from them because they can sting pretty badly sometimes."

Grampa had moved to a small beach chair in the sand near the family blanket and was talking quietly with Betty and Janie about the castle they had built. Mom gathered up the lunch leftovers and repacked the basket. When clouds thickened rather quickly along the shore to the south and the wind picked up, Mom said, "Well, kids, I think that's enough beach time for the first day. Let's go in, and I'll see if anyone needs a little Noxzema for sunburn. Eric, your back is a bit red."

Eric tried to look over his shoulder but couldn't see much. When he touched his back, though, he felt the tingle of raw skin, and he carefully put a towel around himself. They all took things to carry as Janie said "Bye" and went off with her parents. Since Mrs. Onslow had never appeared, Dad and Eric watched Johnny walk carefully along the road edge about six houses down toward his cottage and safely up his porch stairs.

The evening came quickly after a light supper, and the sea reflected the half-moon in a rippling trail of light. Dad read a newspaper, and

Mom searched radio stations to get a weather report, but she found none and finally turned it off. Grampa settled into a chair and closed his eyes. When he opened them, Eric was standing near and looking at Grampa's left thumb as closely as he dared. He drew back quickly when the old man looked right at him and smiled.

"Oh, lad, you're wondering about my thumb, are ya?" Eric nodded.

"Well," Grampa began, lifting Eric onto his lap for a little chat, "that happened a long time ago. I was working in the railroad machine shop and I wasn't paying attention." Eric waited as his grandfather paused, deciding how much detail Eric needed. "Well, my thumb got caught in a . . . a machine," Grampa said with careful vagueness, "and then I lost the nail."

"Did it hurt, Grampa?"

"Oh yes, lad. It hurt like . . . for quite a while. But then it was all right. Only the nail never grew back, so now I just have this knobby old thumb. But at least it's good for one thing."

"What's that?"

"Well . . . THIS," Grampa said suddenly as he poked the thumb around Eric's ribs till the boy laughed at being tickled and squirmed to get free. Soon Grampa relented and let Eric go.

In the early evening Mom had Eric and Betty change into their pajamas, and Dad took them one by one on his back for the good-nights. At the Bethmere they had a whole new set of good-nights to give. While Dad did a slow trot around the kitchen, Eric began: "Good night, stove . . . good night, breadbox . . . good night, cabinets . . . good night, glasses . . . good night, kitchen sink." Betty moved impatiently in Mom's lap for her turn, but Eric's inventiveness kept Dad trotting off this way and that through the living room and into the bathroom. "Good night, toilet." Betty and her mom laughed. "Good night, toilet paper," Eric carried on. "Good night, wastebasket."

"OK, Eric," Dad finally intervened. "I think everything is ready for sleep, including the horse."

"Me, Daddy," Betty piped up. Reluctantly Eric dismounted and watched as Mom lifted Betty carefully onto her dad's back. With her arms securely around his neck, Dad once more circled the cottage as Betty tried to think of "good-nights" that Eric had missed. When Dad helpfully opened the old icebox door, Betty had new possibilities. "Good night, milk . . . ," she squealed. "Good night, butter . . . good night, corn . . . good night, peaches." As Dad started closing the door, she looked quickly around for her final target. At last, in her high-pitched voice, she yelled, "Good night, hotdogs." Everyone broke into laughter.

"Good one, Betty," Mom praised her as she lifted the triumphant little rider from her steed. Dad slumped into the nearest chair, and Mom tucked Betty into bed and mumbled a little prayer with her. Overhearing them, Eric knew to kneel quickly by his bed on the porch and recite the family litany of living relatives that Mom had taught him.

"God bless Grampa Malone and Grampa Harrigan and Mommy and Daddy and Betty. God bless Uncle Bill and Aunt Bob (Eric tried to remember again why he had an Aunt Bob but couldn't) and Uncle Ben and Aunt Stella and Aunt Emma and Fr. Eric. God bless Uncle Ted and Aunt Sarah and the Harrigans and all my cousins. And . . ." Eric always tried to end inventively, "God bless Grampa Harrigan's thumb and let the nail grow back again. Amen." Into bed Eric went, happy once more to be sleeping on the porch as long as the wind was calm and the two blankets were enough to keep him warm. From his bed tonight he could see many stars and the moon shining on the water close to the horizon. Soon the slow roar of the endless waves faded into the night, and the first day of Plum Island in July was done.

11

The summer days quickened their pace with beach time and cookouts and games with familiar and new friends. The cottage was now so close to the road that Mom and Dad often cautioned Eric and Betty about staying off the pavement without a parent there.

On the first Sunday morning of the vacation, the Malones dressed in the casual church attire of summer and drove the few blocks up the street to the little stucco church on the inside of the island. "Star of the Sea" it was called, and Mom explained that that was one of the Blessed Mother's titles, though how she had become the star of the sea Eric never quite understood. Anyway, Plum Island seemed a good place for it. The thirty or so Catholics at the ten o'clock mass waved or shook hands with those they knew. Parents did quick catching up on family lives since last summer, and kids scanned the pews for last summer's friends and potential new playmates.

Eric knew that during July certain family friends and relatives would visit. Their cottage had two unused bedrooms upstairs, so Aunt Emma would come for a weekend with Jerry and Theresa—about fifteen and thirteen, Eric guessed—and the Reillys from across Medford street in Lowell would bring as many of their kids as might use the available beds, with maybe an extra mattress on the floor. Mom's unmarried cousins the Harrigans (Mildred, Ralph, and George) might also visit for a few days in late July, though they were very neat adults who didn't like sand on their feet, damp bathing suits, or salty hair. They did more sitting and chatting on the porch than anything else. A fishing trip or two with Dad and a couple of hours at the rides in Newburyport were also likely, especially with their longer stay. In Eric's mind the summer took shape. He liked what he saw. Yet the sea and the weather could always surprise, and moments of boredom still crept into the best-planned summer days.

In the years before the Malones had cautiously yielded to the new invention called television, they read the local paper more often and got news and weather reports from the radio, a brown box with black tuning nobs that Eric didn't quite know how to use. Where were the stations exactly, and how come they faded in and out sometimes? The Malones' new car even had an antenna on the driver's side of the hood. It looked strange to Eric, like something on a spaceship. When no one saw, he would bend it back as much as he dared and watch it wobble back into place, but he gave that up on his own when he realized that a loose antenna might mean more static on the radio.

One Thursday afternoon after the McCarrons had arrived and Aunt Emma and Dad had taken Eric, Betty, and their cousin Theresa to the rides in Newburyport, dark clouds gathered to the west as they rode back to the Bethmere. Dad tried the radio but got only noise and broken-up voices.

"Maybe the weather's interfering," he said.

"Yes," agreed Aunt Emma. "Looks very dark over there," she pointed as they both scanned the sky in all directions. When they turned onto Northern Boulevard and approached the cottage, Eric saw a weather-worn truck at their house.

"That looks like McGreavy," Dad said. "Wonder what he wants."

Once inside, they walked in on the landlord's news that a tropical storm was heading across eastern Massachusetts and would mean high surf that night and into the morning. He didn't know exactly how strong the wind would be, but a captain at the Coast Guard station had told him of small craft warnings and of some voluntary evacuations from the island.

"I guess that's why we saw more cars than usual heading toward the main road," Aunt Emma observed.

"Do you think we are OK here?" Eric's mom asked Mr. McGreavy.

"Well," he cleared his throat, "I know the house is in good shape. Bethmere should do fine, but we should board up the windows anyway. I've got plywood in the storeroom."

Betty walked quietly over to Mom, who picked her up and stroked her hair.

"I've stayed through a lot of these," McGreavy filled the silence as best he could. "Had no problem except once, and that was my own fault." He didn't explain.

"Let's go ahead and board up then," Dad suggested and moved toward the door. In less than an hour, he and Mr. McGreavy had nailed boards across all the windows on both floors, and Grampa and Mom had moved the porch furniture inside. No sleeping outside tonight, Eric knew.

"In case it does get bad," Mom said to Aunt Emma, "we'd better all sleep downstairs. We can put mattresses on the living room floor for one night." They agreed, and Jerry and Theresa joined their mom in rearranging the furniture and securing all the loose items they could. Eric wondered if the upstairs wouldn't be safer from the water, but maybe the wind would be worse up there. Anyway, the adults seemed to know what to do, so he made himself as useful as a little kid could. Excitement and concern mingled in his mind as he thought what the night might be like in their little cottage.

After a quicker than usual supper of corned beef, corn, green beans, and potatoes, Dad turned on the radio to see if he could learn more about the storm. The reception was better than in the car, and through some static and a few station changes, they all gradually learned of a more serious storm than Mr. McGreavy had suggested. Already the winds were at hurricane force over parts of Rhode Island, and they would probably gain strength offshore east of Boston and then veer slightly west across Gloucester and up to Plum Island. Later the storm would weaken as it crossed inland into Maine. *How did they know all that?* Eric wondered.

"Gusts over one hundred miles per hour are forecast. High seas will cause some coastal flooding from Cape Cod to the North Shore," the announcer warned.

"I wonder if we should have left, Vic," Mom said.

"Well, I think it's risky now with sunset so close. Water could flood the road on either side of the bridge anytime."

Everyone thought about that for a moment.

"I agree," Aunt Emma answered. "We're better off here than trying to leave now."

"Yes," added Grampa Harrigan, as much to the children as to the adults. "Them boards are nailed up tight, and the dunes have been shored up over the winter. They'll take most of the waves all right."

Mom made some hot chocolate and popped corn in a large pan over the gas burner. Dad turned off the radio music.

"We'll listen again later," he assured everyone. "Let's check that everything is tight." He, Grampa, and Jerry went out onto the porch in the rising wind and looked at all the reinforcements; then Dad and Jerry climbed the permanent roof ladder to survey the upstairs windows and shutters. Jerry brought in a small porch table they'd forgotten about and wedged it between a living room chair and the wall.

"Everything looks OK to me," he announced with a summary wave toward the outside.

"Good," Aunt Emma responded with a little chuckle that Jerry didn't mind as everyone smiled.

* * *

The darkness came quickly and the wind intensified. The steady rain began to pound the roof, and a few of the shutters rattled despite their hooks. Mom took out four candles and an oil lamp to be ready if the power went out.

While Theresa and Betty played quietly with dolls on the rug, the adults sipped coffee or tea and ate the last of a second batch of popcorn. The lights flickered once but stayed on, and everyone tried to look unworried. Eric was turning a page of his Hopalong Cassidy picture book when a rush of wind and a loud crash upstairs startled everyone.

"Good heavens," Aunt Emma blurted out, then quickly reassured the kids that everything would be fine. Dad went slowly upstairs. The plywood over one of the windows had come loose and slammed down onto the roof. He lifted the stiff window carefully, reached out into the rain for the board, and then angled it slowly back into the bedroom before forcing the window shut again. When he descended the stairs, Mom handed him a towel to dry off. He then got the hammer and some nails from the toolbox and went back upstairs to fasten the board against the inside of the window, which he did amid more wind gusts and the sideways pelting of the rain on the window glass.

Betty began to cry and Mom held her, while Eric put down his book and sat between Grampa and Aunt Emma on the sofa. An hour later, the adults brought down two more small mattresses and piled some linens on the arm of the sofa. Mom tucked in Betty and everyone prepared to sleep on floor mattresses or face-to-face chairs. Dad pulled a mattress to the corner of the living room, added sheets and two pillows with fresh white cases, and motioned for Eric to come to bed with him.

"We'll be fine," he said quietly to Eric, and they both closed their eyes and wished that a quick sleep would get them through till morning. No routine prayers tonight. The wind and the rain continued their steady roar like some relentless engine. Eric put his hands around his pillow and held it. "God bless everyone in the storm," he whispered. He was surprised to hear Daddy say a very clear "Amen." Eric drifted off and had been having oddly happy dreams when he heard a crack and felt an arm lift him up suddenly and move him across the room. Everyone was quickly awake, and Mom lit two candles that revealed some dripping near the wall. The leaves of a tree branch dangled through the ceiling.

"God, that damn old maple tree," Dad said before checking himself. "I should have asked McGreavy to cut it down last summer." The last tree near the cottage had fallen, and a large limb had punctured a foot-long hole in the roof. Mom got a bucket from the kitchen and put three old dust rags in the bottom to muffle the plop of water as it landed. After a quiet discussion, Dad and Grampa Harrigan decided they could nail a piece of canvas from the storeroom against the opening and divert most of the water down along the porch roof. A small piece of board placed between the canvas and the opening helped to block nearly all of the water so that everyone could finally try to get back to sleep with just an occasional plop into the bucket cloths to bother them. But when the repair was done, sleep eluded Eric. He heard Betty being walked by Mom in the kitchen, and Jerry and Theresa both seemed restless. The air was cooler and wind ruffled the canvas patch. The night dragged on in windy desolation. Eric tried not to cry and mostly succeeded. Dad rearranged his blanket a few times and finally went off to sleep himself. His muffled snoring droned on quietly against the living room wall. Without knowing it, Eric finally dozed himself and remembered no dreams when he finally awoke to morning light.

He looked up and saw Dad standing at the porch door, which he slowly opened and stepped into a morning breeze. To the east the sun streaked along jagged clouds and proved that the storm was over.

Mom was already in the kitchen heating some water. Eric looked to the ceiling hole and saw that the nailed canvas had sagged slightly but held. The dripping had stopped. After wiping the floor around the bucket, Mom emptied it into the sink and then mixed a little cereal for Betty. Everyone else stirred drowsily and began to sit up. Aunt Emma gave Theresa a quick hug.

"OK, kiddo. The excitement's over," she said as happily as she could, and her daughter nodded silently.

III

The storm damage was worse for most of the neighbors than for the Malones. Mr. McGreavy had been right about the Bethmere. "A storm-worthy little place," Dad called it as he circled around through the dune grass to look closely. An interesting word, Eric thought. Mom had explained "sea-worthy" from a story she had read to him. How many kinds of "worthies" could there be? Could a car be "crash-worthy"? Would a church be "God-worthy"? That was a tricky one.

Dad and Jerry walked along the beach with Eric to see how other houses had done. The Onslows had lost most of their porch roof, and Johnny's dad and mom were gathering up stray pieces.

"Quite a mess," Mr. Onslow called to them.

"Yes, but we were pretty lucky," Dad answered.

Shingles and stray boards littered the beach, and in the distance a whole cottage had slipped from its foundation and sagged badly in the sand.

"They won't be able to stay there," said Jerry, pointing to the wreckage.

"No," agreed Dad. "That's the Fentons' place. From Manchester. I wonder how much damage I'll hear about in Lowell," Dad said with a roll of his eyes.

Jerry laughed at his uncle's "insurance agent" lament.

"Well, whatever it is, it is," Dad said to no one in particular. Eric played with that phrase in his head for a moment. He wasn't sure what it meant but didn't ask.

From the beach, the three walked out along an access path to the road to see the other side of the oceanfront cottages and those beyond the street. The church looked OK from a distance except for debris all over the parking lot. Damp sand had spilled onto the boulevard everywhere until it was mostly a one-lane road, though no cars were out this soon. When they had looped back to the Bethmere, Mr. McGreavy was there looking over his cottage and talking with Grampa Harrigan about it.

"Thirty-six flood in Lowell was the worst I seen," Grampa recalled. "River went crazy that time."

"Oh, yes," McGreavy remembered. "And everything upriver washed down here. People were salvaging wood and tables and God-knows-what-else from that one."

The two old men nodded and laughed philosophically, and Eric pondered how even a remembered disaster could make old people smile. What he saw all around didn't look too funny. Grown-ups made strange jokes.

Later on the radio, Eric heard that a small plane had crashed at the little Plum Island Airport just before the storm had hit.

"Trying to beat the weather, I suppose," Grampa said.

"Those poor people," Mom added.

Eric learned that the pilot and his twelve-year-old son had been killed in the accident.

"They probably violated instructions not to fly," Dad surmised. "Those private pilots aren't like the airline crews. Some of them think they can get away with anything, like bad drivers."

"Now that's an insurance agent talking," Aunt Emma teased. Dad nodded agreement and shrugged his shoulders as the adults all laughed. But Eric kept thinking of the boy dying in a plane crash and didn't see what was so funny about it.

Within a few days, the storm debris was mostly cleared away and the roads were open. The McCarrons decided it was time to pack up and return to Lowell.

"So long, Eric," Jerry hollered from the car window. Theresa waved to Betty, and the adults all said "Bye."

"I'll give you a damage report from Lowell," Aunt Emma promised Daddy.

"Oh, wonderful," he said in mock gratitude. "Always looking out for your little brother."

Everyone laughed as the McCarrons drove away with their storm story for the Lowell neighbors. Eric smiled too, and thought that he was beginning to understand adult jokes a little better. Dad was Aunt Emma's little brother, and she liked teasing him.

After Daddy had been back to his insurance office for a few days, he and Mom talked about various "claims" that his customers would make. Grampa Harrigan was pleased to hear that his Highlands double-decker, which the Malones shared with him, was OK.

"Yard's a mess," Dad waved his hand, "but everything's all right inside. The Reillys have some water damage, though. Bart said they'd wait a bit before visiting us here so they can clean up everything."

Grampa nodded and seemed to be picturing his neighborhood all around Stimson and Medford Streets. Eric wondered about the very old people who lived on the opposite corner, Mr. and Mrs. Alderson.

"How are the Aldersons?" he suddenly asked, and Betty looked curiously at Daddy.

He smiled to see his kids' concern for the elders of the neighborhood.

"Owned that house since 1912," Grampa Harrigan interjected. Dad waited politely before answering Eric.

"They're fine. Their son came from Lawrence to check on them. The big maple tree on the Stimson Street side came down in their yard but didn't touch the house."

Dad and Mom talked more about various neighbors and Dad's customers in other parts of the city, and Eric realized how important to many people his dad was after a storm. How he could help fix all that damage Eric wasn't quite sure, but he sensed that his dad found amazing ways to get things done for people. He thought of the canvas ceiling patch and all the water that *didn't* get into the Bethmere.

I V

Five days after the hurricane, the Reillys did arrive, at least four of them. The parents, Bart and Phyllis, greeted Mom and Dad and

Grampa Harrigan. Their two teenage daughters, Helen and Jane, were happy to see Betty and Eric. They'd each babysat a few times for the Malones and couldn't wait for some beach days with the kids. And the Reillys never went anywhere empty-handed. Eric look with amazement as they unloaded two cooked chickens, several vegetable plates, and no less than four pies; at least one of them had to be cherry, Eric knew. Mom kept thanking them and lifting her hands in appreciation, and the women made room in the icebox and on the pantry shelves for all the new food.

After a Friday afternoon at the beach and a cookout that featured hot dogs and hamburgers and almost none of the Reillys' food—that must be Sunday dinner, Eric figured—everyone sat on the porch and seemed to talk all at once, though mostly in male and female circles of interest. The women thought that a Saturday drive to the Newburyport amusement park would be fun, especially for Betty. Eric was welcome, of course, except that Dad and Mr. Reilly were thinking about taking a fishing boat out for mackerel and whatever else might be running then. Dad phoned the Fishing Tours office next to the Coast Guard station on the north side of the island and got their schedule.

"How about nine to noon tomorrow?" The men all agreed. When fifteen-year-old Jane looked at Daddy with interest, he said that she could join them if she liked. She nodded eagerly. So Dad phoned again to make the reservation. Fishing on Saturday it was, for Grampa, Mr. Reilly, Daddy, Eric, and Jane. Eric wondered if Jane really knew how to fish. Anyway, the men could help her. And Dad would help Eric hold that long bamboo pole and toss the line out into the water. Since this would be his second fishing trip, Eric knew not to look too much at the dead and dying fish, but to pay close attention to the task of fishing. No easy separation, yet if he sat in the right place, he could see mostly ocean and not the dying fish or the squirming worms in the bait buckets on the deck.

The next morning everyone ate eggs, toast, and bacon for breakfast. All the fishermen were ready just after eight o'clock and said good-bye to the women, who would head for Newburyport rides and a little shopping later in the Reillys' car, which Mr. Reilly laughingly called the best '39 Chrysler still on the road. "Mother-a-God," was all his wife could say with a shake of the head in a Catholic mix of profanity and reverence.

The fishermen all piled into the Ford with Eric trailing behind them. In his rush to join the group, he forgot to shut the screen door behind him. When Dad asked the familiar question, "Were ya brought up in a barn?" Eric turned abruptly and shut the door, then climbed into the back seat with Mr. Reilly and Jane. As they rode to the end of Northern Boulevard and up the parking lot hill toward the tour shop, Eric saw the largest fish of his life. Hanging tail-up from a chain on a crossbar was a gigantic tuna, all the bigger for its position at the crest of the pavement.

"What's that?" was all he could say.

"Looks like the tuna men were out early today," Grampa Harrigan said.

"Yes," said Mr. Reilly. "That one must be—what d'ya think—three hundred pounds?"

"Easily," Dad agreed. "Maybe closer to four."

As they all walked into the shop, Eric made a slow circle around the tuna. Jane was impressed too, and even dared to touch the giant fish quickly, then drew her hand back.

"Feels fishy," she joked to Eric.

Her dad cleared his throat loudly at his daughter's humor. "Well, I suppose it would, Jane," he teased. "Jane has a ready wit, ya know," he went on for the men's amusement. "Let us know when it's ready, Jane." Everyone laughed, but Jane just giggled and didn't mind. She liked being with all these guys, Eric could see, and she was always nice to him, as if he, a few weeks short of five, was also one of the guys.

About twenty others joined them on the fishing boat until the bench around the deck was nearly full. Large buckets of bait, either worms or chunks of fish, were waiting for the fishermen's choice. Dad helped Eric attach a wriggling worm onto his hook, and Mr. Reilly did the same for Jane. Soon everyone was ready as the boat cruised out into an open channel and then anchored at a spot the captain optimistically announced as "Fish Cove," to scattered laughter.

The sun climbed slowly in the midmorning sky, and Eric felt more heat and little sea breeze. The boat rolled on the waves, and Eric tried not to think of the breakfast he'd eaten an hour before. Occasionally someone pulled in a mackerel or a striped bass, sometimes throwing back a small one. The catch began to accumulate in the large fish bin at the center of the deck. Grampa Harrigan was the first of their group to get lucky. He pulled and leaned back as he fought what seemed a pretty large fish until his frustration grew.

"Son of a bitch," he said thoughtfully to himself and prepared for a longer struggle. Others offered free advice, but Grampa was inclined to do it his own way and finally succeeded in lifting about fourteen inches of fish onto the deck. Dad grabbed a knife and cut the hook loose. Mr. Reilly held the wriggling catch until they could drop it into the bin. The captain's mate wiped a mix of water and blood from a spot on the deck and everyone resumed the quest. Three times Eric thought he felt tugs on his line, but no fish had appeared when Dad grabbed the pole to help him.

After a lull in the harvest, Jane, one of three women on the boat, suddenly yelled, "Oh my God, it's a fish!" She grabbed her pole tightly. Her father put one hand over hers to steady her grip.

"Well, that is why we've come, Jane," he said dryly and pretended his eardrum had been damaged. After several minutes of struggles and pauses, punctuated with Jane's abrupt squeals and laughs, she managed to land a mackerel almost as large as Grampa's catch and was nearly jumping with excitement.

"Oh my God, I got it," she exclaimed to the amusement of the whole party. The captain then announced that Jane had just won the "Most Enthusiastic Fisherman" award, and everyone laughed and gave vigorous applause.

The morning wore on with occasional catches and frequent disappointments. Eric's interest began to fade as he realized that fishing was mostly waiting and that sometimes nothing happened. Dad said he could pull his line up for a while and just watch the others if he wanted. He did that, and later he sat on Dad's lap and they held one pole together. Eric wondered how people took their own fish home since everyone's was thrown together into the large tub.

"Well," Dad explained, "people usually remember which ones they've caught, and no one worries too much about the smaller ones anyway. Probably every family group will go home with something, even if they didn't all have a catch."

Eric thought about that and finally declared it "a nice approach," to which Dad for some reason kept chuckling with half-suppressed laughter.

"Yes, it is," he finally agreed and seemed to settle down.

Sometime close to noon when Eric was tired and even Jane had grown quiet, a heavy man with a baseball cap and loose shirttails had a strike and stood up to see it a little too quickly. His friend tried to grab him by the waist but couldn't hold on, and the man fell head-long into the water.

The captain quickly grabbed the tube on a rope and tossed it to the man, who panicked and kept turning the wrong way to get it as it bobbed in the waves.

"Cliff," his friend hollered, "just grab the tube and let go of your fishing pole."

Another man leaned over and managed to snag the top of the pole and drag it aboard and away from the frantic swimmer. Finally, Cliff got one arm securely around the tube as he coughed up water. Dad joined the captain and the mate as they all pulled on the rope and drew the man closer to the boat. Eric and Sue watched intently while the three rescuers got hold of both arms and a leg and finally lifted the exhausted victim back on deck. The captain and mate leaned over him, but the man was breathing steadily now and seemed much calmer.

"Oh, Cliff, I'm so glad you're OK," his friend said at last, and Cliff just nodded.

After a cautionary few minutes of watching Cliff, the captain stepped away from him and addressed everyone. "Folks, we obviously need to be very careful at the edge of the boat. Concentrate on handling your pole before you worry about seeing your catch." Everyone murmured agreement. Cliff was finally able to thank Dad and the crew members for helping him.

"Just happy everything is fine," Dad said with his usual calm.

As the boat sailed back to the dock, several people wished Cliff well again and began claiming their catches. Dad's group came away with six fish, though Eric wasn't sure they'd caught them all; not that it mattered, of course.

"Oh my God, I was so worried," Jane said in the car, and everyone commented on how the man must have fallen and how well the rescue had gone.

"Good job, Vic," Grampa Harrigan finally said, and they all agreed. Dad always knew what to do.

Back home, the fishermen recounted their rescue story and passed their catch along to Mom and Mrs. Reilly, who made room in the icebox for all the fish. The women were amazed that someone had fallen overboard and that he had been so lucky. At last, when the concerned tones subsided, Helen could not resist teasing her sister: "I bet you were a big help, Jane." To which their father responded solemnly, "She alerted the entire boat."

"Now leave Janie alone," her mom countered with a little half smile.

The Reillys served their portable feast on Sunday afternoon after all had sunned themselves and braved the water as much or as little as they dared. Once, when Eric had turned from the waves to call to Johnny Onslow on his front porch, Grampa Harrigan looked beyond him and suddenly yelled, "Watch out, lad." Puzzled for a second, Eric turned toward his grandfather sitting on the beach and then heard loud thuds behind him in the retreating water. He felt an arm lift him at the waist and realized that Dad was heaving him upward just in time to ride with him over the crest of a giant wave that broke violently beyond them at the shore. By now, Grampa Harrigan was standing nearby, and Mom called from the beach blanket, "Eric, are you OK?"

Dad picked Eric up and stood him on the damp sand as he kneeled in front of him.

"You've got to watch those breakers, Eric," he said with deliberate stress on each word.

Eric nodded carefully as Dad tapped him on the head and walked away. An unknown little boy just then was recovering his kite that had landed close by.

"That was my dad," Eric announced to the kid, who hadn't even asked.

V

The Harrigans had called sometime in the middle of the month to say they wouldn't be coming to Plum Island after all. They'd decided on a week at a hotel near Lake Winnipesaukee instead, and they'd see the Malones back in Lowell. Soon it was Eric's much-celebrated birthday on the 20th, complete with cherry pie and vanilla ice cream in addition to a coconut cake with five candles. After that, Eric admitted to himself that the Plum Island vacation was nearly over. Each day Mom and Dad did a little more packing and cleaning. Some toys were stowed away before Betty and Eric were quite through with them. But as other families began to leave, including Janie and her mom and Johnny Onnie's family, Eric and Betty were more reconciled to heading home.

On their final night at the Bethmere, Eric got to sleep on the porch one more time. Mr. McGreavy came by on their last morning to ask how the summer had gone and to have another look at the roof repair he'd arranged after the hurricane damage.

"Well, Vic, I hope to see you back here next summer," the old man said.

"We'll have to see about that," Dad answered, catching both Betty and Eric by surprise. Would they possibly not return?

"You see, Marian and I are expecting again," Dad added. Mr. McGreavy shook Dad's hand vigorously, and Eric thought he knew what "expecting" meant but wasn't completely sure. "The cottage is so close to the road now, and this last storm probably cut away even more beach."

Mr. McGreavy nodded agreement.

"We're thinking about the kids—and a new one—being so close to the road all the time."

"Yes, I see. Can't blame you. Just want you to know that I'd be glad to have you again if that's what you want."

"Thanks very much," Mom said. "If we are back, we'd be happy to rent from you again. I just wish the cottage could be further from the road."

"Nowhere else to move it, I'm afraid," Mr. McGreavy shrugged. "The lots across the road are pretty much taken, and too many moves ain't good for the old place."

"Of course," Dad responded. "We'll let you know how we feel over the winter."

"OK . . . well, good-bye you kids," Mr. McGreavy added without using their names. Eric knew right then that the Bethmere had not been named for his sister.

Mom and Dad loaded the last items into the car as Mr. McGreavy stood by the driveway watching another of his tenants depart. They pulled out on the road and waved good-bye to their white-haired landlord. Then they crossed the drawbridge that sometimes opened for boats, but not today. At the little airport Eric remembered the plane crash and the dead twelve-year-old boy and wondered why people wanted to fly in such small planes. Soon they were onto Route 1A and then 133 (Dad announced the numbers like a tour guide to his kids). They passed the road signs for Ipswich, Byfield, and the Shawsheen green on their way home to Lowell.

THE ARSONIST

I

"You hafta strike it sideways, like this."

Eric took the match from Ricky and scraped it across the matchbox. A spark flew out and died. The broken head dangled from the stick. He grabbed another. *Ffft!* The flame burst and steadied. Between them the ragged yellow peak bobbed slightly left and right. They saw each other through the flame. Then their eyes lost focus in a blur of features distended by the rippling heat. Eric looked away when his eyes teared and stung; he rubbed them with his free hand. Ricky blew out the flame before it reached his friend's fingers.

"Let me—"

"Yeah." Eric still soothed his eyes.

Ffft! "It's easy that way, huh?"

Ricky reached for a leaf by his foot but moved the match too suddenly. The flame died, sending out another smoky trail. Eric looked up at last and let his eyes float gently along the undulating film—a smoky spire twisting in the still October air. He eyes felt relaxed and free, much better than when the flame had drawn them into itself. He sat with his elbows hunched on a large rotting log and said nothing while Ricky carefully dug out another match and slid the box closed. He smiled and assumed a ceremonial pose, arms in front, match poised, awaiting some command.

"Flame, Sidney!" Eric improvised in a British accent. Ricky took his cue, but nothing happened.

"Sidney, I say! Flame!"

"Yes, sir," Ricky snapped. *Ffft!* The fire blossomed and Sidney awaited instructions. Eric rolled a leaf tight and stuck it into the corner of his mouth. Then he softened his voice from lord to lover.

"Ursula, light my fire." Ricky laughed through his nose and held the flame to the rolled leaf end. Eric puffed a smoky billow through the hollow cigar and overwhelmed the small flame at the tip. He spewed smoke in a fit of coughing while Ricky shook out the match and cleared the air with his hand. *Ecth! Pthew!* The smoker spat loudly and cleared his throat to spit again. Ricky said not to breathe in so Eric wouldn't get cancer, and they both tried *not* to inhale, however a smoker did that. But the taste was still bad, and smoke up the nose soon smothered each of their attempted charades. Even their dragon faces lasted only a moment.

"Dragon face!" Each laughed when the Ricky flailed his spiny dragon claws and rolled away from the nasal smoke onto the huge pile of brown leaves against the barn.

I I

The late afternoon sun sank behind the eaves of the old carriage barn and touched the round heap of leaves with soft shadows. From the large mound the boys scanned the mixed row of spruce and elm trees lining the brick barrier of the old Tull Estate. At the southwest corner a rusted gate sagged from one hinge behind a dense forsythia clump that bordered the weedy remnants of a once-contoured flower garden. The caretaker never went back that far to rake leaves or prune the dead plants, so hidden entry was assured. Large, nearly barren trees drew the boys' eyes west from the old garden across a grassy slope toward the giant manor house mostly hidden from them behind the peeling, dingy carriage barn. Beyond, out of sight, a gravel driveway looped through maybe ten maple trees toward the Stimson Street traffic, a distant intruder into the solitude of Randolph Tull.

They looked again at the matches.

Eric struck one and held a burning leaf in his hand. He dropped it just before the flame reached his fingers. One green leaf wouldn't burn, but a few of the dead ones flared quickly and then smoldered. He sampled sizes, colors, and shapes and silently noted the fire's effect and the unique qualities of each new flame. Ricky watched closely and then selected leaves for each new test. A small pile of ashes grew between them. The scent of each little fire drew them closer to the pile by the barn for their samples. Stem-first, tip-first, center-to-edge they burned. Little tepees of leaves mimicked campfires. Strike, flare, contract, crumble—they studied each burnt offering. How easy to strike big matches and light little fires. They struck every match briskly now; they *knew* how to do it. Their fingers dipped alternately into the open matchbox between them. They smiled to each other and prepared unique little pyres for the flame; one stoked, the other lit. They stared at the little holocausts.

From the base of the huge, brownish mound of leaves, Ricky now joined red, yellow, and orange leaves in a colorful, chain-like design that circled up the surface of pile for a few feet and then down to the ground again. Could Eric burn along that arc? He pruned his fingernail and looked from his hand to the neatly circled leaves. He glanced at Ricky and down again to his hand.

"You light the match," he said. "Then hand it to me."

Ricky shook his head slowly and stepped back.

"Light it!" Eric waited.

Ricky lit the match. Eric rolled it firmly between his fingers. He looked at the flame briefly and then lowered his hand to the leaves. Near the ground he touched the last leaf tip with fire. It burned slowly at first, almost expiring in a faint new breeze. Around the arc of that first leaf the flame rose, then down the underside to touch the second leaf in Ricky's chain. A base of well-packed leaves underneath seemed impervious to the rising flame. The fire settled on the first two leaf-links of the chain and burned for a satisfying moment.

When Eric looked back at Ricky now, his eyes were fixed on the leaves just ahead of the flame. How would this fire grow? Along the surface design or down into the matted pile? Or would it leave a blackening trail spreading both ways at once? Ricky looked into the flame and blinked. He stepped back from the rising smoke.

"I'm going home now," he blurted out and walked quickly toward the hidden gate.

Eric turned to him but said nothing. Then he looked back at the fire and watched the shape and tone and texture of the flame. He saw it rise along Ricky's chain of leaves, then yield a widening black line of hot ashes that sank slowly into the pile. He noticed a glow underneath and scrambled away as the flame rippled close to him in a gust of wind. It crackled now. He looked around to the forsythia and waited a long moment before glancing back to the fire and running hard for the gate and down the shrub-lined alley onto Medford Street and into his house by the kitchen door.

I I I

From his bedroom window Eric could see through the Parker and McDermott backyards to Tull's brick wall and the thin line of white smoke rising beside the barn. It didn't seem like much. He couldn't see any fire. He fingered a baseball from his bureau, noting the circle of the seam rise, fall, and disappear around the edges. He rolled it along the windowsill and cupped it with a hand at each end. Now the smoke was thicker, wider, and darker. He stared at the clear column of air between the smoke and the barn. How wide was that? Twenty feet? Maybe ten? Were the leaves piled *against* the barn or just near it? He could only remember the flame rising along Ricky's circle. The distances to the top of the pile and then to the barn were a blur. Why hadn't he noticed them exactly?

When he lay down on his bed, leaves crumpled between his dungarees and the quilt. He jumped up and picked away the pieces for the wastebasket. He found more on his sleeves and legs. He felt the scratch of a leaf fragment against his big toe in his left sneaker with its hole near the top. He circled his finger around his jersey collar and recovered more remnants. Leaf fragments stuck to the sweat on his hands, so he carefully picked them off. He looked out the window again and sat hard on his bed when he heard the sirens. His kept wiping bits of leaves from his hands.

The smoke spread when the water arched onto the leaves. He saw a ladder against the barn and a fireman climbing into the loft.

Then someone knocked at his door.

He stiffened. Slowly he got up and put his hand to the knob. He gripped it tight and opened it carefully. Mom stood near him. She stepped into his room and bent down on one knee in front of him. Her hand picked a small leaf fragment from his shoulder.

"Eric, did you set that fire?" She looked right at him, gentle and steady-eyed. He noticed the curl of her black hair nearly touching her shoulder.

His eyes widened, returning her look. Quietly, simply, he answered no.

"No, I was out playing," he said.

She smiled. "OK. Wash your hands for supper, will you?"

"Yes, Mom."

He waited till she took down supper dishes from the pantry shelf before soundlessly closing his door. Now the smoke rose slow, wide, and pale, just steam from all the water. It was over. The fire had never touched the barn. He picked some last stubborn leaf specks from his right sleeve and brushed vigorously all over.

Looking out again, he remembered the sound of the matches and Ricky's bizarre dragon face. Would the flame burn along the circle of leaves or would it spread wider and deeper into the pile? He remembered demanding that Ricky light the match. He saw the flame rising slowly again from that first leaf.

And it seemed, as far as he could tell, that he had *not* set that fire, not really.

A SUMMER AT THE LAKE

I

On a muggy July 4, the lake still cooled the skin enough to justify swimming all afternoon—or ducking and sunning a half-dozen times in the lazy freedom of summer. Yet the holiday also included these obligatory swimming races, and here he was again at the starting line of the ten- to twelve-year-old boys' crawl. His stick-like frame moved well enough through still water, but his thin arms lacked power and his strong leg kicks were never enough.

"Go," shouted Mrs. Sanderson, and eleven boys pushed off from a standing crouch into rib-high water and scrambled toward the measuring tape that Dad and Phineas Hurley held for a finish line, about eighty feet away.

"C'mon, Eric," Dad shouted, abandoning impartiality even as a keeper of the finish line.

Eric started well and kept a pretty good breathing rhythm. He raised and lowered his head and forced his arms as far into the water as he could. For several strokes he stayed almost even with the bodies at his side, Brad Hendrickson on the left and "Dynamite" Dudley on the right. Where everyone else was, he couldn't tell and tried not to care. Just breathe, pull, and kick. "Let the water do the work," he recalled Mrs. Sanderson's mysterious advice and almost laughed in mid-breath.

A small cluster of relatives and neighbors shouted from either side of the imaginary lanes as eleven boys tried to swim straight, but they couldn't for long.

About halfway through the race, Eric noticed that in the lanes beside him, the heads became shoulders, then chests, then bathing suits, thighs, and finally feet. Just finish, he told himself. It will all be over soon. And it was. With a final few breaths, he knew that he was done, not because he touched the finishing tape that the holders raised above each racer as he crossed it, but because several rivals were already shaking hands and waving to little pockets of happy parents or avoiding their ruthless peers.

"That's OK, Doug. Good effort."

"Wayda go, Jackie. Ya almos' beat ya brothah."

"Get the lead out, Brannigan."

When Eric stood up and cleared his eyes, he saw Dad's broad smile and happy nod. Then Mrs. Sanderson, the phys. ed. teacher from Dracut High who always ran these games and never needed a megaphone, announced the three "medalists." They would get extra time in the sawdust pile and a free bathing suit donated by Hurley's Sports Shop in Nashua.

"In third place, thanks to his wild leg kicks, Dan-ny Broc-ton!" Cheers.

"The second place winner, who came from behind and almost caught his brother"—laughter—"Jack-ie Va-chin-ski!" More cheering.

"And the winner and boy's champion crawler for the second straight year, Frank-ie Va-chin-ski!" Everyone applauded, and Jackie and Frankie gave each other as quick a brotherly hug as they dared in public.

"That concludes the swimming races," Mrs. Sanderson boomed. "The cookout will start in half an hour on the McMennimans' side lot, followed by the sawdust pile scrambles and then the running races by the softball field. And all you adults, start picking your partners for the three-legged race." Mocking teenage laughter and shouts of improbable pairings resounded as the crowd headed back to their cottages to bring hot dogs, hamburgers, salads, and desserts to the holiday cookout.

Eric walked quietly over to Jeff Healey, a muscular Lowell High senior who had the job of recording each racer's finish and approximate time, though only the "medalists" really mattered. Without a word from Eric, Jeff looked at his handwritten race chart.

"Ninth, Eric. Just ahead of Buzz Brannigan and the Jacobellis kid, ah, Dickie."

Eric nodded. Ninth ahead of two barely ten-year-olds and he was almost eleven. Well, that was two places better than last year.

"OK, Eric. You hung in there, kid," Dad said generously as they walked back up the dirt road past McMennimans' and through Aunt Emma's yard to their "camp"—everyone's word for these summer cottages of Pine Terrace, their little tree-shaded neighborhood between the lake and the old cemetery opposite Judd's Corner, a snack bar and teenage hangout.

* * *

The Malones had been coming to Cobbetts Pond for four summers now, ever since Eric's parents had decided that their Plum Island cottage was too close to the road for his little sister Marsha. Dad had bought a piece of land adjacent to Grampa Malone's camp and had a cottage build there in the summer of '52. Each summer since, they had spent nearly three months at Pine Terrace, from mid-June to just after Labor Day. What a time it was each year, and so much longer than they used to have at Plum Island. Still, the lake was not the ocean, and moving surf always excited Eric more than lightly rippling waters. Funny how the name never seemed quite right to him—Cobbetts Pond. It was too big to be a "pond," he thought, with its several miles of shoreline and ample room for sailing, water skiing, and even crazy teenage speedboat races sometimes. At one end was Hendleys' Sandy Beach, a family business. Sandra Hendley, about seven, often played with Betty there or at Pine Terrace. From other little coves straight across the water a dozen or so softball players (with occasional ringers from nearby towns, Eric was sure) came to battle the best team that Pine Terrace could assemble each Sunday afternoon.

Coach Sanderson and Jeff Healey managed the team and put together some motley lineups, from speedsters in their teens to a few old sluggers on the far side of fifty. Eric had pinch-run a few times but was too young yet to make the game lineup, though he played pickup games with other kids on weekdays. He could already hit much better than he could field. His light frame and long legs let him outrun many better players, but his game sense still failed at times, like the Sunday when he pinch-ran for fifty-five-year-old Vic Hadley after his double in the eleventh. Eric advanced to third on a grounder. Then, for some insane reason, he danced off third like Jackie Robinson and into a game-ending pickoff.

"Eric," his friend Dutch had moaned, "why did you do that? Ya shoulda just waited for a hit ta scoah. You coulda tied the game."

"I know. I know. What was I thinkin'? I shoulda *sat* on that base."

That was three endless weeks ago, and still as raw in Eric's mind as he was sure it was for all of Pine Terrace. But now he just tried to think about the afternoon running races (far better for him than swimming) and wished beyond all these contests for the end of holiday competition and the fireworks that night.

Why did adults need to organize everything and force reluctant competitors into self-conscious defeats? This was his dad's year as president of the Pine Terrace Association, so Eric felt even more pressure to be a visible part of the July 4 and Labor Day games. Mostly they were fun, of course, and sometimes kids did amazing things, but "filling out a field" often meant watching the less talented go through the quiet ordeal of being good losers year after year until winning was either finally possible or no longer mattered. Eric didn't like himself when he thought this way. Dad wouldn't like it either, though he never directly asked Eric to do anything. He just hoped that his son wanted to be "a good sport." And with so many free days to roam around the lake and play horseshoes and badminton and swim with his friends, how could he complain about two sets of holiday "Olympics" that Coach Sanderson seemed to live for?

Meanwhile, he ate eagerly at the cookout—three hot dogs, some salad, and apple pie with vanilla ice cream—and then came up with $2.25 in the chaos of the sawdust pile scramble. He brushed the wood chips from his hair and clothes and then rested a little at home before the running races started at three o'clock. This year, Sanderson and Healey had "filled out more fields" than ever: boys' and girls' races from ages six to eight, nine to twelve, and thirteen to fifteen; relay races for the thirteen to fifteen groups; and the comic climax of the three-legged races for the over-twenties and then, most hilarious of all, for the over-forty husband-and-wife-only teams. By then, Eric figured, the idea was to let all the young ones laugh at their elders, who'd been cheering and teasing the kids for most of the day. It worked pretty well, he had to admit.

In the boys' nine to twelve sprint, Eric knew he could outrun many of the older guys because he was already as tall as most of them. This time, twelve guys lined up for the race, and Eric breathed in and out slowly and closed his eyes for a moment. "On your mark . . . get set . . . go," Mrs. Sanderson shouted at the starting line. Her games committee of Jeff Healey, Phineas Hurley, Debbie Robideaux, and Dad waited at the finish line. After a burst of cheering as the race began, the neighbors all got suddenly quiet. Everyone watched the faces and legs of the runners with more attention than they gave to the splashing confusion of the swimming races. Eric stretched his legs in long strides and stayed near the lead all the way through the 150-foot "track" of dusty road and open field. The committee had tried to rake the course clean of pebbles and to level the deeper holes, but the course was neither clean nor level. With twelve across in this race, the runners at either end had more grass underfoot than the others. His legs straining, Eric pounded to the finish and leaned forward to take third place and a $5 prize. He bent over, hands on knees, and puffed heavily as both Betty and Marsha came to him for quick hugs. The older runners took notice that Eric Malone could be a threat by Labor Day, or at least on the Fourth next summer.

Finally, prize or not, it was done. His competitive nerves slackened, and he watched the fireworks in Pelham Center with a big crowd from the lake and the town. They even saw the tops of much bigger explosions from Canobie Lake Park several miles away.

1 1

Vic lingered over his breakfast longer than usual and swallowed an extra glass of milk after his coffee.

"Not so good, Vic?" Marian asked. Eric caught Mom's eye and quickly looked away.

"It'll be OK," he answered and kissed her on the cheek before giving a good-bye wave to Eric and Betty and a brief hug to five-year-old Marsha. "You all be good today," he called from the car window as he backed out onto the dirt road and was gone in the dust. Mom cleared away the leftovers and piled the dishes in the sink. The girls went off to their bedroom to put on bathing suits for a beach morning with her.

"What's up for you, Eric?"

"Dutch and I'll play some horseshoes for a while and then, I don't know, maybe walk out to Caldwell Point."

"OK. How about drying these dishes for me now?" Eric hesitated for a second until she gave him a direct look. Then he grabbed a towel and worked through the stack with her.

"Thanks," she said, emptying the dishwater.

"OK," Eric nodded.

"You and Dutch be careful if you go to the Point. Give a wave when I'm on the beach with the girls if you see me."

Eric agreed and went off to decide if dungarees or shorts were a better choice for the morning. He chose the dungarees, changed from his pajamas, and slipped out of his camp and off to Dutch's along their unnamed dirt road.

As she gathered beach things together, Marian looked along the pine beams and roof boards and took in their scent with a deep breath. Their camp smelled the same inside or out, she thought. Pine everywhere. What a good decision they had made to buy this lot and build here. The kids loved it and so did she—and Vic had a quick ride home from the office every day. Much easier than staying at Plum Island.

"Let's go, girls," she called, and Betty and Marsha walked with her through Aunt Emma's backyard and over to the next dirt road that led to the Pine Terrace beach archway. Beyond it, a thirty-foot strip of sand shaded by four large pines sloped down about two hundred feet to the lake and the little bench-lined shelter where

Marian could sit if the sun got too warm.

Betty and Marsha walked to the water and waded in slowly. Then Marsha came out and played with a pail and shovel in the sand while Betty did short strokes and little dives into waist-level water. Marian watched them both from a large towel on the sand and then scanned yesterday's *Lowell Star* again. Soon she put it down and glanced at the girls, who seemed content playing separately for now.

She remembered the odd look on Vic's face at breakfast, as if he might be trying to imagine the source of his pain somewhere in the lining of his stomach that the ulcer surgery had contracted. How well had he healed? These bouts of stomach pain never quite went away. He was eating more, taking occasional antacid pills, and when necessary, going out for a milkshake to settle his stomach. He'd gained some weight lately, and she was sure that some other solutions must be better. But Dr. Boudreau didn't seem to have any ideas. A few tablets, more liquids, no spicy foods, limited alcohol. A little of this and a little of that and not much relief, she parodied his advice to herself. Could a second ulcer occur despite the odds against it? Should he have agreed to be president of the association so soon after his surgery?

"Betty, come back in a little," she called, and Betty obeyed. Marsha had lost interest in the sand and now played with a doll on the towel next to her mother.

Marian thought of three or four Pine Terrace folks who could have taken their turn as president this year but had not volunteered. Perhaps Vic had been too willing. He should say no more often. A tingle of resentment passed through her as she considered how quickly most people seemed to forget how sick he had been, not even two years ago. Helping the association was all well and good, but he could have delayed it a year or two. Then she realized that as renters at Plum Island they had no association to worry about and not even house repairs to pay for. But when their Pine Terrace neighbors, the McArdles and the Jacksons, proclaimed Vic's ability to get along with everyone and to ease all the little tensions among the campers, he didn't have the heart to turn them down. What about *the stomach*? She smiled at her joke. Should everything be decided by the heart?

"Are you all right, Marian?" she heard Hazel Lewitski say as she spread a small blanket beside her.

"Oh, Hazel. I didn't see you." Marian reached into her beach bag for a tissue and busily cleaned her sunglasses. "I'm just sitting here worrying about nothing."

Hazel laughed. "We all do our share of that, don't we? If it's not one thing, it's another."

Louise and Phyllis Lewitski had arrived with their mom and quickly joined Betty. Then Sandra Henley and her mom showed up, and Sandra went over to the other three girls, who all started a game of water tag.

"Want to play, Marsha?" Betty called out, and Marsha looked up at her mom.

"That's all right, dear," she said, and then to Betty, "Just be sure you girls don't go out too deep for Marsha."

"OK," agreed Betty, and Marsha joined the game.

After a quiet minute, Hazel said that her older sister Agnes was having a biopsy to check for breast cancer.

"Oh, I am sorry to hear that."

"Well, let's hope it will be all right. Agnes can be a bit of a hypochondriac," Hazel sighed, "but she has complained of some discomfort lately on the left side of her chest."

Marian nodded. "Let me know what she learns. I'll be glad to help if I can."

"Oh, that's thoughtful. I don't know how much Agnes will let anyone do for her. You know, she's always got a problem but rejects all solutions." Both women laughed at the behavior type they understood too well.

"How's Vic feeling?" Hazel asked gently.

"Oh . . . well enough," Marian hesitated. "Stomach troubles never quite go away. He still has some pain now and then."

"Yes," Hazel responded.

"He's always got so much to do between the business and the association here. And *his father* hasn't been himself lately."

"How old is Mr. Malone?" Hazel asked directly.

Marian thought. "Eighty-four, I believe. His children had a party for him last February. Emma says he's been moody and a bit abrupt sometimes. Not like him. Vic's wondering if he's feeling all right, though nothing physical seems to be wrong."

Hazel nodded. Both women looked out at the lake in the late morning sun. The girls' game ended, and Marsha came back to her mom while the other girls chatted in a circle on the beach. More families had arrived and spread blankets nearby. A couple of teenage boys ran noisily by the adults and into the water, and Marsha leaned against her mom to avoid them.

"Want to go in with Mrs. Lewitski and me?" Mom asked.

"OK, Mommy."

"What a big girl you are getting to be," Hazel said to Marsha, who smiled and hid her face in her mother's shoulder.

The women walked into the water. Mrs. Lewitski dipped her hand and blessed herself in her familiar piety and then dove in and bobbed up again. Mom stroked some water over Marsha's back and looked across the west side of the lake toward Caldwell Point. Seeing two boys there partly obscured by a boulder and a large pine, she waved and called out, "Eric, Eric." Marsha added her tiny voice as well, and the two women smiled.

"Eric," his mom tried again, and the boys looked in their direction. At last Eric saw them and waved.

"OK," Mom called back to them, completing the "check-in."

"I noticed that Eric finished third in his race last week," Hazel said. "He is quite tall now, and fast," she added.

"Yes, he did well. He seems to like the competition, though he never exactly says that." Marian smiled.

Hazel nodded. "He is a pretty quiet one, but I guess most boys are like that at that age, not that I would really know," she added with a reference to her three daughters.

Marian laughed with her over the various moods of their five girls and one boy until Hazel called to Louise and Phyllis to come home with her for some lunch.

"See you later," Hazel said with a quick wave. "Hope everything is OK with Vic and his father."

"Thank you," Marian said with a squeeze of Hazel's hand. The Lewitskis gathered up their things and departed, and Marian scanned the paper once more. She read quickly through an article about two Lowell city councilors who proclaimed themselves "innocent of all charges" and then folded the paper into her beach bag.

"Pols," she said to herself with heavy sarcasm and then picked up her towel and put away her sunglasses.

"Girls, let's go have some lunch," she offered, and Betty and Marsha started with her toward the beach exit. A few hundred feet from Aunt Emma's camp, where the three would cut through her yard to their cottage, Marian saw her sister-in-law closing the passenger door of her car. Soon she recognized Emma's dad in the passenger seat. Emma seemed to be in a hurry and was startled to see Marian and her daughters approach.

"Hi, Aunt Emma," Marsha said happily.

"Hello, dear," Emma responded in a subdued voice that caught Marian's attention.

"Is everything all right, Em?" Marian asked.

"Well, Pa is feeling very weak this morning. He's . . . unsteady on his feet," she said, choosing her words carefully in front of the two girls. "I'm going to take him to the Pelham Clinic to see what they think."

"Should I go with you?" Marian asked. At last the old man seemed to hear them and gave a feeble wave, which Marian returned.

"Let's go if we're goin'," he then snapped at his daughter.

"OK, Pa."

Emma nodded good-bye to her sister-in-law and the girls and then started up the car. As she drove carefully along the bumpy dirt road toward the paved one near the cemetery, Marian led her silent daughters home.

"Is Grampa Malone sick?" Betty asked at last.

"Well, let's just say he's not himself lately," Mom answered. "Let's hope the doctor at the clinic can help."

"Mommy, if Grampa's not himself, who is he?" Marsha asked. Marian and Betty laughed out loud until Marsha's hurt expression stopped them.

"Oh, sweetie, that's just a way of saying he's not feeling well." Marsha nodded and sat down at the kitchen table. Marian fixed sandwiches for the girls and then made two more to be ready when Eric's hunger would drive him home. She sipped some ice tea, ate a little salad, and thought about her father-in-law and her husband, who were not having such a good summer of '56 at the lake.

III

"Mr. Malone," his new, young secretary called from the outer office.

"Please, Janet. Call me Vic."

"Well, all right. It just feels . . . well . . . Vic," she forced herself, "your sister Emma called while you were at lunch. She'd like you to call her."

"Thank you."

He picked up the receiver and started to dial, then put down the phone and walked over to his office window. The traffic was picking up at just after four o'clock. An old couple walked slowly out of Bridgewell Drug Store at the opposite corner and made ready for the ordeal of crossing the intersection toward his office building. How good it would feel to get back to Cobbetts in an hour and take a duck. He turned back to his desk and scanned the pictures of Eric, Betty, and Marsha. Imagine Marsha already five. Seemed like no time since he'd decided not to return to Plum Island because the cottage was too close to the road. The privacy of Cobbetts was surely better that way, though his father-in-law had never warmed up to it. He mostly stayed in Lowell alone on these hot summer days instead of joining them at the lake. Marian was annoyed at him, but he would not be persuaded. *Better check up on him before I leave*, Vic thought. Then he remembered the phone message and thought again about his own father. Dr. Broglio in Pelham hadn't been very helpful when Em had taken Pa there last week. Of course, Pa had hardly spoken. For years he had teased doctors about how little he needed them and how most medicines were devious moneymakers. Now he was silent—or testy when he did speak. Maybe he was afraid. Was his independence of doctors ending at last? Why couldn't they give some sort of diagnosis? Surely his mood change had some physical causes. Well, make the call, he thought, and hear the latest. So he rang his sister.

"How is it going, Em?"

"They kept him at St. Benedict's last night for observation. Dr. Flanagan told me that his blood pressure is a bit low and that he needs to eat more, but Pa has lost his appetite. They gave me a prescription for sleeping pills so he will rest better if he will take them," she added pointedly.

"Should I say something to him?" he asked.

"I wouldn't just yet. Let's see if I can get more food and the prescription into him back at camp. I'm sure he'll be happier just to get away from the hospital."

"OK. Let me know what I should do and when."

"Yes. If I don't succeed, I'll see if another voice might work."

"OK. Are you bringing him back to camp tonight?"

"Yes. I pick him up at six o'clock."

"All right. See you tonight."

"Bye." He looked out of the office window again and rubbed his hands back across his bald head and over the rim of hair in back. At least his stomach had been good today. No need for that trouble on top of everything else.

At five, he said good-bye to Janet, who managed to say, "Goodnight, Vic," and drove with surprising ease through the downtown, along Chelmsford Street, and then right onto Medford Street and to their house at the corner of Stimson.

He knocked at the upstairs flat. "Mr. Harrigan," he called. His father-in-law opened the door and assured him that everything was fine. He was heating some stew for supper and would listen to the Red Sox on the radio later.

"OK," Vic answered. Then he took a deep breath and asked, "Would you want to spend the weekend with us at Cobbetts, and I could bring you back here Sunday night?"

To Vic's surprise, his father-in-law agreed. "Well, yes, that would be all right."

"OK, then. I'll pick you up after five o'clock tomorrow and you can have supper with us."

Marian will be glad to hear that, he thought as he started the car again. Now if Pa can start feeling a little better . . . He turned toward the bridge at Pawtucket Falls just beyond the Franco American Orphanage and then started out Mammoth Road on the familiar route toward New Hampshire. Despite an occasional new home, the road quickly turned rural through farmland that reminded him of the little farm his father had bought in the late twenties as a getaway from the city. No one in the family was much of a farmer, he smiled to recall, but they had some fun pretending for a while. He rode over the small bridge by a stream where two boys were swinging into the water on a rope from a large overhanging tree limb. Norman Rockwell must have painted that one already. His mind wandered with the curve of the road and the summer green of the large oaks and maples until he turned among more pines onto Cobbetts Pond Road and then took a left at Judd's Corner. Not even supper time and several teens were already hanging out there! Many more would arrive with the night. He'd even seen them all around the parking lot and sitting along the cemetery wall. How many more were in the cemetery doing who-knows-what? Would he stay at Cobbetts until his own kids were asking for trouble at Judd's Corner after dark? Then he laughed at his paternal severity. Where were kids supposed to go on warm summer nights at a rural lake with no night life? Where would he have gone thirty years ago? Better here for his kids than running off to Hampton Beach.

As he pulled up to the cottage, Eric and Dutch stopped their badminton game to wave.

"Who's winning?" he asked with a grin.

"Dutch, 14–12," Eric admitted, "but not for long."

"We'll see," Dutch countered calmly.

Vic laughed and told the boys to finish their game and then come in for supper. Dutch could stay, too, if he wanted, but Dutch said his cousins from Nashua were coming soon, so he had to be home. Vic brought Marian up to date on their fathers. She was happy that her dad would be joining them that weekend for only the second time this summer.

"Yes, he fooled me," Vic said. "Maybe he likes us after all." Marian laughed, and Vic called to Eric to "take a duck" with him before supper. Eric smiled at his father's inevitable phrase, put on his bathing suit, and walked with him toward the water.

That night Aunt Emma arrived with her father at their cottage and spoke briefly to Vic before encouraging Pa to take his new prescription and retire early. After a little grumbling, he did.

In the morning, Eric learned that Grampa Malone was feeling better and had suggested that Eric and his dad might want to watch the Red Sox with him on Saturday. The team was playing Chicago, and Mel Parnell was pitching. So, with Grampa Harrigan joining them, they did.

"Parnell was quite a pitcher years ago," Grampa Harrigan remembered.

"Yes," added Dad, "I think he won twenty-four or twenty-five games one year." Eric was impressed. A Red Sox pitcher could win that many games?

Grampa Malone sat quietly watching the screen without adding to the baseball wisdom. Dad and Eric talked about certain pitchers and why some hitters were tougher on them than others.

"Them White Sox have speed," Grampa Harrigan noted.

"Yes. Minoso and this new shortstop—ah, Aparicio. Of course, Eric, they don't have anyone like Ted Williams." Eric smiled because he understood already that there wasn't anyone else like Ted Williams.

By about the sixth inning, Eric and the others realized that Parnell was not only pitching a shutout but a no-hitter, too. Without exactly saying so to jinx the effort, they commented on his pitches and on the hitters still likely to be the most trouble. The eighth inning gave way to the ninth and still the spell continued. With a 4-0 lead, Parnell bore down on the final three hitters. Eric's feet jiggled with tension as Dad smiled at him but said nothing. Grampa Harrigan leaned forward, elbows on his knees, and seemed deep in thought. *Had he ever heard a no-hit game on the radio?* Eric wondered. He felt sure that no one in his family had seen one yet on television. He was so glad that Grampa Malone had invited them to watch the game with him. Then, as Eric glanced at the old man, he saw moisture in his eyes, not tears exactly but the silent emotion of the moment.

When Parnell got the final out, everyone felt relief. Grampa Harrigan clapped his hands once in celebration. "Well, he did it. That is somethin' ta see." Dad patted Eric on the knee. "I can't remember when a Red Sox pitcher last did that," he added.

"Too bad it's only one game in the standings," Eric observed.

"That's true," agreed Dad. "Be nice to count this one several times."

As the guests got up to leave, Vic took a quick look at his still-silent father, who rose very slowly to see them all out. The old man had moist eyes and a look that his son had not seen in a long time, the glow of some nameless happiness that had nothing to do with baseball.

IV

By late July, Eric was dividing his time, and some of his loyalty, between Dutch Saulnier and Danny Wallenz. Both were from Nashua, but they didn't get along at all and each appealed to different sides of Eric. Dutch was funny and easy to be with. Horseshoes, badminton, and softball kept them both amused. While Eric was taller and ran faster, Dutch had quick reflexes and fast thinking that kept their badminton games unpredictable. Eric was better at horseshoes and Dutch tried to learn from him, but he could not throw the shoes in Eric's end-over-end spiral. Instead, he gripped them on the side and spun them toward the post.

"I can't do it that way," Eric explained. "How can you make the open end catch the post if you can't control the spin?"

"Yeah, Eric, but the shoe wobbles if I throw your way. I can't throw it straight."

So each player worked on his separate technique.

At random moments, Dutch had a funny way of clapping the edges of his hands vertically while snapping each thumb and middle finger all at once. Eric could never get the rhythm of it, and Dutch laughed at the confusion of fingers and wrists that always ended Eric's attempts. Both liked word games and baseball, and Dutch created little absurdities joining the two. About two players, for instance, Dutch never tired of reminding Eric that if Bubba Phillips and Sherm Lollar ever became the same person, that would be "Bubba Lollah." Then they would stare dumbly at each other until both ended up laughing again.

"Clutch Dutch," his friend liked to call himself. Or when they considered which amusement to pursue next, Dutch inevitably asked. "You want I should? I want I should."

"Yes, Dutch, I want you should," Eric would sigh finally just to get the nutty question answered.

Dutch's quirky little absurdities kept Eric laughing or groaning or occasionally trying to top the zaniness, which rarely happened. Danny Wallenz, however, never warmed up to Dutch's endless jokes. He'd get quickly sarcastic about "idiot boy" or "space invader." So when Eric tired of Dutch's chatter or when family events separated them, Eric would wander off with Danny, who didn't much care for camper games but preferred to explore the woods or roam to the far side of the lake. He knew quite a bit about plants like mushrooms and poison ivy and about various types of insects. Eric found Danny's exotic interests oddly appealing, even though he didn't share them. And Danny was a bit of a daredevil always on the edge of trouble, which fascinated Eric and sometimes tested his judgment.

One afternoon Eric and Danny hiked beyond Caldwell Point to the west edge of the lake and into a thick part of the forest. They climbed an old, angular tree and tried their jumping skills from a large limb onto beds of pines. Later, Danny pried under one matted clump of needles with a stick and uncovered a colony of large red ants, whose movements he watched intently. Eric looked over Danny's shoulder for a minute before walking off toward a small cluster of low pines. Behind them he saw what looked like a fur ball. He walked around it until the eyes and open mouth of a large dead rabbit became obvious.

"Danny, look at this," he called.

Danny used his stick to probe the skin and skeleton of the animal until he found a short arrow point in the animal's left side. The rest of the arrow was gone. Chewed away, it looked like.

"Someone shot it and left it here. Pretty dumb. They could have had a nice dinner."

"How long do you think it's been here?"

"Umm," Danny thought, "several days anyway. Maybe the hunter couldn't find it or thought he'd missed. Ever go hunting, Eric?"

"No."

"It's amazing sometimes, trying to figure out how an animal thinks. Then zap with an arrow or bam with a rifle and it doesn't matter how it thought." Danny laughed and Eric looked a little put off with this ruthless picture of the hunt.

"Well, anyway . . . I'm sure you don't mind eating the results." Eric nodded but didn't want to pursue this hard topic of his confusion about fishing and hunting. They wandered a little farther into the woods until Danny sat on a low rock and pulled some kind of pouch from his back pocket. Eric watched as he unfolded it.

"What's that?" he asked reluctantly.

"Feel it," Danny held it up.

Eric stroked the thin fibers but didn't recognize them. Danny had a large wad of whatever it was, maybe an inch think, five or six inches long, and browner at the ends. Many thin fibers were more or less wound together. Then Danny stuck two fingers to the bottom of the pouch and pulled out small sheets of paper and a pack of matches.

"Still no clue, Eric? You've seen these things quite often. They're part of something you eat almost every day."

A look of recognition crossed Eric's face. "Is that corn silk?"

"Bingo."

"How did you get that much of it?"

"Whenever we have corn, I remove the fibers and save them."

"So now you're going to smoke them?"

"Yeah. Ever try it? Never mind. Of course you haven't." Danny shrugged at his hopeless, straight-arrow friend. Eric looked annoyed at the dismissal until Danny stared straight back at him and said, "Well then, try it."

"All right," Eric agreed stiffly, and Danny rolled two corn silk cigarettes and licked them shut. He smoothed the surfaces and took out a match.

"I'll light it," Eric offered, and Danny laughed at his friend's guarded participation. Eric struck the match and held it to the tip of the paper.

Danny puffed lightly until the flame settled into a red glow. He blew a couple of smoke rings and held the cigarette between his fingers like someone in the movies.

"Tastes all right," Danny offered. "Not as much bite to it as tobacco. I think even you can handle this, man."

Eric picked up the other cigarette and let Danny light it. At first, he just held the paper in his lips to get used to the feeling.

"OK, now breathe in slowly," Danny coached. Eric did and felt the rough texture of the heavy air against his throat. Suddenly he choked up, took the cigarette quickly from his mouth, and coughed loudly as Danny laughed. Eric waved away all the smoke and backed up several feet to get some clear air.

"You can have the rest of mine," he said at last.

"OK, at least you gave it a shot, man." Danny took Eric's smoke and snuffed it out with his fingers, then stored the rest of it in his pouch. As he relit his own to smoke some more, the boys heard a rustling in the trees. They looked toward the sound and then crouched behind a fallen log. Someone was walking in the distance. Danny snuffed out his cigarette.

"Let's get going," Eric whispered. "If someone sees the smoke, they'll think we're starting a fire." For once, Danny agreed, and the boys crept quietly back along the path until they were far enough from their little smoke cloud to turn and walk quickly back to Caldwell Point and then along the road toward Pine Terrace. Danny stuffed the pouch away, and the smokers cleared their throats and spat a few times to rid their mouths of the filmy residue and to hide the scent as much as they could.

"See you later, man." Danny waved quickly to Eric as they separated, each knowing that neither would speak about their little experiment to anyone.

When Eric walked toward his camp, he was surprised to see Dad's car there at just after noontime. Then he noticed the flashing lights of an ambulance, but with no siren, waiting by Aunt Emma's cottage. Slowly as he watched it, the vehicle backed away into the road.

"Grampa Malone is very sick," Mom said quietly from the porch steps. "Daddy's going to follow the ambulance back into Lowell so they can get him to St. Benedict's."

"I never heard a siren," Eric said.

"No. Aunt Emma asked if they could not sound it near the cottage so that Grampa wouldn't get upset. He's never liked doctors or hospitals much," Mom added.

Marsha held Betty's hand quietly as Dad pulled his car away and drove up the dirt road to meet the ambulance at the paved street along the cemetery. Once the vehicles were together, they rode away with only an occasional beep of the alarm to warn traffic.

"Well, let's have some lunch," Mom said to the three kids, and they all walked into the cottage after her. Three days later, Grampa Malone was dead.

V

Eric had only been to two wakes before, and Betty and Marsha had never been. Mom explained what would happen and how Grampa Malone would be all dressed up and look asleep. They should give Aunt Emma a hug and then kneel in front of Grampa and say a prayer. Then they would all go into the backroom where people would be talking quietly; Mom would take them home soon after.

Uncle Bill was Grampa's oldest son and also the funeral director of this business that Grampa had begun decades earlier for two of his sons. So Dad had explained to Eric. Uncle Bill greeted many of the visitors who had come to "pay their respects" to Grampa Malone. Quickly a line formed at the Malone Funeral Parlor door and out onto the sidewalk. Fifteen minutes later, Eric saw that the line had grown across the parking lot entrance and beyond the next two houses.

"How long does a wake last?" he whispered to Dad as they stood in the receiving line.

"People will come until eight o'clock tonight, and then we have more visiting hours tomorrow from three to eight."

"How many people will be here?" Eric asked with growing amazement at such a crowd, most of whom he had never seen before. Dad smiled. "Well, many people knew Grampa Malone over a long time. He helped a lot of people and had many friends in the city, even before I was born." Eric tried to imagine a time before his father had been born, as if old photos in the family album might suddenly come to life.

"How did all these people know Grampa?"

Dad turned from Eric to greet several more visitors and shake their hands. Sometimes he introduced Eric, but more often people just nodded to him and moved up the line toward the casket.

"Let's go into the backroom for a few minutes and I'll answer that question," Dad said and excused himself from the receiving line. They walked back into the sitting room and found a couple of empty chairs in the far corner away from the flow of visitors who filed through, talked briefly with anyone near them, and left by the back door.

Dad leaned toward Eric and spoke quietly. "Grampa's parents came to America in 1870. Life was hard for many people in Ireland and they felt they would have more opportunities here. He . . . well, he owned a bar for a while and then he . . ."

"Grampa was a bartender?" Eric asked a bit too loudly, and Mom, sitting nearby with the girls, glanced at Dad.

"I'll tell you what, Eric," his father reconsidered. "This is not the best time or place to tell you all about your grandfather, but I will get back to that another time, OK?" Eric nodded and pretty well understood. Maybe he should have saved the question for later. After a few minutes of watching darkly clothed people move around little circles of conversation toward quick departures, Eric saw an old woman approach Dad. She touched her wet eyes with a handkerchief and reached out her other hand to Dad, who took it in both of his. Eric thought she was shaking a little as she walked.

"Aunt Lilly," Dad said softly.

"I never wanted this day to come," Eric heard her say.

"I know," Dad answered, "but he had a good, long life. We can't ask for more than that."

"Yes, yes," her voice trailed off for a moment, "but there was no one like him. When many of us thought we couldn't make it, he kept us going. I couldn't tell you all the help he gave people. Money, jobs, housing—and time, so much of his time. When your Uncle Eamon was let go by the sanitation department that time and had nowhere to turn and three kids, who do you think hired him for a property manager and then gave him a free-rent flat on Donlan Street for nearly a year?"

"Yes . . . ," Dad said with a touch of impatience that his aunt was going on a bit too long and revealing details that should stay in the family.

"Well," she stopped herself, sensing his point, "I just mean to say that he was"—she paused, seeking the right word—"a tower. Your father . . . was a tower . . . for us all." As Aunt Lilly stepped back to sit with her daughter, Eric could see emotion all over Dad's face. It reminded him somehow of Grampa Malone's expression at the end of Parnell's no-hitter, though it wasn't exactly the same. Certain looks, Eric thought, meant more than anyone could explain, or had to.

V I

After the huge wake and funeral for Patrick Aloysius Malone that half of Lowell seemed to attend, the August days slowly found their summer rhythm again. When Eric wasn't off with Dutch or Danny, he might join in skits that the three Lewitski sisters—Louise, Phyllis, and their older sister Flo—liked to create with great theatrical attention. Anyone might join in, though Danny never would. They used sheets as theater curtains, made cardboard props, and painted characters' faces to present whatever dramas the girls had imagined. Last-minute rescues and sad family misunderstandings were fruitful themes, or the arrival of a crazy relative who left the whole family exhausted when he finally departed. Sometimes the creations even parodied the Pine Terrace parent world, from Coach Sanderson's sports extravaganzas to the righteous indignation of campers at parents who couldn't, or wouldn't, control their wild teenagers. Mostly the girls created the scenes, and any willing boys took their assigned roles. A parent might occasionally overhear one of these productions, but the space among the trees behind Lewitski's storage shed was usually enough protection from prying ears and eyes.

The end of August had Eric thinking again about Coach Sanderson and the coming games of Labor Day. What events would he enter, and could he find a way not to swim in the crawl, breaststroke, and backstroke races? And why couldn't they have badminton or horseshoe competitions, where he'd beat most kids anywhere near his age?

The sunny days and breezes on the lake could bring sweet forgetfulness, but thoughts of competition never left Eric's mind for long. His legs would jiggle as he sat thinking of such challenges, and his nails never got much chance to grow. He was always looking for sharp edges or the least bits of growth to prune away with his teeth. And whatever was left of his fingernails became the tools for toenail work. He'd feel foolish whenever he tore back a nail too far and a finger or toe would hurt until new growth repaired it. Yet days later he'd be back at his habit again, unable to leave a good thing alone.

Picking his nose was even worse, he admitted, but at least it was painless and cleansing, the next best thing to using a tissue or a handkerchief. Anyway, hankies could get pretty unpleasant sitting in his pocket for too long. If he'd just stop biting his nails, he joked to himself, he could pick his nose more efficiently, but like so many of his good ideas, this one never went anywhere for Eric either. He just lacked the resolution to carry it through. Lots of kids, and even adults, did these things, he figured, but no one ever wanted to admit it or to be caught doing such crude grooming in public. What harm was it really? His nose was no worse for his explorations, and his nails always grew back.

"Come home and wash up for dinner," Mom called to Eric on a cloudy, late-August afternoon.

"OK," he yelled back and started one last run around the softball diamond before finishing with a sprint all the way to his door. As he turned at third base, he felt a little twinge inside his sneaker on the left big toe. He kept running but eased the pressure on the left foot a little. That night they cooked out in the yard and sat talking with the McArdles and the Jacksons for a few hours. Finally, Eric went inside to look at pictures and read a little from a baseball magazine his dad had bought him. Getting into bed at last, Eric felt the top sheet rub against his left toes uncomfortably. He sat up and looked at his foot. A puffy, reddish area marked the left side of his big toenail. It was tender when he touched it. He had picked back that nail too far, but he'd leave it alone now and it would soon grow out. It didn't. Within a day, Eric was clearly favoring the left foot until Mom finally noticed.

"Eric, why are you limping?"

"Oh, it's OK."

"Let me see your foot," she pursued the point. "Eric, I think this toe is infected." By now the red area had spread and the puffiness had welled up all around what was left of the visible toenail. "We'd better have Dr. Muldoon take a look at this."

As much as he wanted to resist the suggestion, Eric knew he had no choice. That nail was getting worse, not growing out. Now he couldn't run at all, and walking was uncomfortable as he leaned on the outside of his left foot. Mom cut off the top of an old sneaker for Eric to wear on that foot. She cleaned the toe with hot water and a face cloth and put Mercurochrome over the swelled area, but it was too late. The nail was too deeply in-grown.

When Dr. Muldoon looked over Eric's toe the next morning at his Lowell office, he was typically blunt. "That nail has to come out." Eric panicked a little and teared up for fear of the pain. Muldoon saw his distress and tried to ease it, with limited success. "Eric, I'll give you a shot to numb the toe. You won't feel any pain, just a little scratching when I work on the nail. Then we'll bandage it up. You'll need to stay off it for several days until the healing is done. Understand?"

Eric nodded and said nothing. Mom put her hand on his shoulder.

"Are you hungry, Eric?" the doctor suddenly asked.

Well, actually he was. He nodded.

"All right. Go get him something to eat, Marian. Then come back here in an hour or so and we'll get this done." So Mom took him for a sandwich and ginger ale and returned with him for his toe surgery. When it was all over, the doctor smiled at Eric. "Not so bad, was it?"

"No. You were right. It just felt like something scratching."

"OK, but you need to keep off that foot for several days. When the shot wears off, you will feel some pain." Eric nodded, Mom helped him hop out to the car, and he lifted his left leg up across the backseat.

The toe healed slowly and Eric felt more than a little pain, especially when he tried to sleep and could never get comfortable. And so, with no deliberate plan in mind, Eric found himself completely free from the Labor Day games. He watched the runners from a folding chair by the side of the road and had the most respectable of excuses—"I had surgery on my toe." Exactly how his toe had become "injured" Eric avoided discussing. Within about a week, Eric's foot was fine for walking. Running took a little longer. The nail was not quite all gone, and it was misshapen as well. It grew up from the skin in a thick, curled pattern that eventually left punctures in the top of most of his left socks. Eric still couldn't stop his nail biting and picking, but at least he avoided the most extreme pruning so that no more infections could start.

Two days after Labor Day and a week before school would start, the Malones said good-bye to Aunt Emma. She was still missing her father very much and wasn't sure when she'd close up her camp and move back into Lowell. As the Malones' car pulled away from the cottage, Clutch Dutch announced himself and gave Eric one last finger-popping display that made him laugh. Danny was nowhere to be seen, and the Lewitskis had left the day before. Several miles later, when they passed over the bridge by the little stream along Mammoth Road, no one swung from the rope that still hung from the branch that arched out over the colder September water.

COUNTING COUP,
CHANGING TURF

I

Gilly Dennis throws rocks almost as good as me, Eric sometimes admitted to himself. Once in a rock fight he had hit Gilly in the right calf as his enemy had lunged from the corner of the Jefferson School to the cover of the stone wall circling the school yard. Just a ten-foot dash, but Eric had caught him in flight. Gilly's dungarees showed a tear from the sharp edge of the stone. A dozen or so boys from their two warring packs had fired from along the wall or at the building's edge, but Gilly knew who it was.

A month later, Eric rode his bike alone through the school yard and around the far corner of the building on a grey Wednesday before Thanksgiving, no one in sight. He looped wide swirls around the blacktop on his green-and-white Columbia and savored the maneuvers. Then his right hand shot up to grab the sharp sting that cut into the back of his neck, just under the right ear. He fell to the pavement in a tangle of peddles and legs and felt stunned and then angry, but at last, in a long moment, just amazed. And then, sitting on the blacktop, he knew.

What a shot. He looked around, but Gilly was long gone. *That Gilly Dennis throws rocks almost as good as me*, he conceded again as he touched his wound and rolled his neck slowly back and forth. With blood on his hand, he walked to the grassy slope beyond the pavement. Wiping his fingers in a thick clump of brown November grass, he picked up a stray piece of paper and dabbed his wound again. The cut was drying already. A slight pain still tingled in his neck and upper shoulder when he turned his head left and right, but he was OK. He would just need to clean the cut before Mom noticed it.

What should he do about a solitary attack like this, not in a clear fight? Strike back when he could ambush Gilly alone? Wait till the next time the guys faced Gilly's gang and shout out his payback? Or, he could just let it go. Give Gilly credit for the surprise and skill of the hit. He imagined several moments of revenge, but they didn't interest him for long. The artistry of the strike overcame all bitterness. And the honor of it, he could almost say. Gilly had singled him out, and why not? They understood each other, like Indian braves he'd read about counting coup.

That night before supper, Eric took a tissue to the wound again. No one had noticed it. He'd kept the back of his head safely turned away from everyone's sight, or he stretched his hands behind his neck whenever detection seemed a risk. Maybe a face cloth under his head as he slept would keep any blood stain from the pillow case. By morning the wound would be almost healed and he could pass it off as a clumsy bump if anyone asked. Gilly probably had an even easier time hiding his leg wound.

* * *

The Harrigans arrived in the early afternoon for Thanksgiving dinner. Everyone sat around the living room and talked while the smell of turkey and potatoes slowly filled the house. Mom checked on the oven now and then and sipped her drink near the edge of the conversation. Holidays meant that everyone would have a scotch, but the variations were important. B&B, Dewar's, or Cutty Sark? On the rocks or with water? Stronger or weaker? Would she have another? Was that strong enough for him? Mostly, of course, drinks in hand, Dad and the Harrigans talked, and Eric and Betty listened and smiled at any direct looks. Marsha played with her dolls in the front parlor beyond the living room. Her little family conversations with the doll children blended in Eric's mind with the adults' rhythmic dialogue. He had long noticed how well the Harrigans could finish each other's sentences and fill the silences with "yes-uh-huh-mmm" until, after a suitable pause, someone ventured into a new topic. The traffic, high prices, and cold weather (that might or might not feel like snow) could give way to local politics (which was often "disgraceful, but no surprise there") or larger questions like how Eisenhower should handle Khrushchev (who would "lie as soon as look at you," Ralph observed with disdain) or whether an Oldsmobile was really worth the money (George thought so "if you read up on it before you start talking to a dealer").

"Well," Mildred offered with a smile, "at least you can always rely on the phone company." Everyone laughed at such a self-serving remark, but Mildred stood her ground with mock righteousness. "Never a doubt there, no sirree."

Soon Grampa Harrigan was heard descending from his flat and slowly approaching the Malones' living room. His two nephews and niece stood to greet him with nephews' handshakes and a niece's quick hug.

"Uncle George, you're looking very well," Mildred asserted.

Eric noticed the slight roll of his grandfather's shoulders as he discounted the idea. "I never thought I'd be here this long, but here I am."

"Yes-uh-huh-mmm," the Harrigans seemed to say almost together as Grampa sat down and accepted a light Cutty Sark.

"And how is school, Eric?" Mildred wondered.

"Oh, pretty good," Eric responded vaguely.

"Eric," Mom prompted, "tell everyone what Sister Veronica said last month about your singing."

"Oh." Eric blushed slightly and sat up in his chair, knowing that he must now retell the joke for this new group of curious relatives.

"Quite a compliment, I'd say," Dad primed his son. The Harrigans were ready to be appreciative as soon as Eric gave them the chance.

"Well, sister said she wanted me to try out for the choir because I have a voice like a bird." Everyone laughed and pretended agreement.

"Of course," Eric drew a breath, "she didn't say what kind of a bird." Ralph and George slapped their knees and tossed back their heads, and Mildred's high-pitched laughter filled the room. Dad smiled broadly at Eric's successful delivery of the joke, and then Betty took advantage of the opening.

"Maybe it was a crow."

When Mildred burst into laughter again and nearly spilled her drink onto Grampa Harrigan's sweater, Mom quickly handed her another napkin and placed a larger coaster for her drink on the side table. Everyone applauded Betty's wit. She asked if she could have some ginger ale, and Mom brought in drinks for the three children, who were then allowed to watch a little television in the parlor before dinnertime.

At last everyone took their places at the dinner table, and Marsha sat in her special chair by Mom. Dad said grace with slow reverence: "Bless us, Oh Lord, and these thy gifts, which we are about to receive from thy bounty, through Christ our Lord. Amen." The feast began with rich aromas and the passing of serving plates. Mom or Dad held the heavier ones for the children and gave them suitable portions. A quiet descended on the diners with only an occasional, "Yes, thank you," or "No, I couldn't" to offers of seconds and thirds.

When the plates were cleared away, everyone found the same chairs in the living room for another round of conversation until in an hour or so Dad suggested that maybe they would all like to take a walk before sitting down again to coffee or tea and turkey sandwiches. So everyone did, and the early evening cold felt good after the warmth of dinner, drinks, and talk.

In bed that night, Eric thought how much alike these Thanksgivings all seemed. Oh, there could be some family news. Dad's ulcer might be better or worse. The Harrigans might have decided on a Lincoln this year instead of another Oldsmobile. The kids were now (who could believe it?) a grade higher in school. But mostly the adults liked the familiar routine of it. Would Dad's new idea of a walk around the neighborhood become part of the ritual? Eric thought so. Of course, he liked all the endless good food and he guessed that so much adult contentment had to be a good thing, even if a kid's mind wandered at times. He touched the back of his neck carefully and then removed the face cloth, hidden in his pajama tops, and placed it on the pillow case. Probably he didn't even need it anymore, but why take the chance?

I I

On Saturday after Thanksgiving, the guys gathered after lunch. Ricky waved to Eric from his porch across Stimson Street and said that his brother Eli wanted to come, too.

"OK," Eric hollered from his yard. "We'll get the twins and then go by Jack's. Let's go to Cowboy Rock." Ricky agreed. He had to change clothes and would be at Eric's in a few minutes. Eric went inside to change from light chinos to heavier dungarees.

"Are you boys going hiking in the woods?" Mom asked. She had heard him call Ricky.

"Yes, Mom. Lots of guys are coming."

"Well, be careful out there. And be back here before supper."

"OK," Eric agreed from his bedroom as he decided on a sweater and jacket.

The guys were still friendly and all, but it was different since Tommy Barnes had moved away. He and Tom had been best friends for a long time. Tom was a year older than Eric and knew what to do pretty much all the time. Gilly didn't challenge Tom. Eric was sort of Tom's sidekick, like Hopalong Cassidy had a sidekick who always followed Hoppy's lead and never regretted it. The Barnes family had that huge cherry tree behind their house where he and Tom would climb, pick, eat, and then spit cherry pits at each other until someone surrendered, mostly Eric, or until Mrs. Barnes heard their shouts and said they'd had enough cherries for today. When Eric and Tommy went off to Hale's Brook or out along Chelmsford Street beyond the newest houses and into the woods, they always found something interesting. Tom seemed to have been on every trail before. He told Eric about raccoon holes and a beaver dam on the brook, and he showed him the four pointed stones that he'd found. Indian arrowheads, he thought, though Eric wondered how they could still be here so long after the Indians were gone. And then, last April, the Barnes family had moved. Tommy's dad had a new job somewhere south of Boston, and while Tom said he'd write, no letter ever came. Eric didn't mind. Being together was the fun of knowing Tom. Writing some stuff about his new house or new friends wouldn't make Eric Tom's sidekick again. That was over. He might never see Tommy Barnes again.

"Eric," Ricky called as he knocked on the back door.

"OK," Eric shouted. "Bye, Mom," Eric said as he left. He, Ricky, and Eli started off for the twins' house. Eli was older than them both, but he sometimes tagged along. He never said much, not like chatty Ricky, and Eric often wondered what Eli Farrell was thinking. These Farrell brothers sure were different, but that was OK. Eric realized that now Ricky was actually *his* sidekick, and *he* was Hoppy. He liked that, though he wasn't sure he always knew what to do, like Tom did.

"You guys wanna go to Cowboy Rock?" Eric called to the Rawls twins in their upstairs bedroom. No need to ask really. In a minute the five boys headed down Merchant Street to the house at the dead end where Jack Dixon lived. From the tree in his yard, Jack saw them coming. He yelled Tarzan-like and made a wild jump into a pile of leaves as all the guys laughed.

"Goin' to the Rock?" Jack asked unnecessarily. From Dixon's, a trail led into the woods and along an overgrown, swampy stream that could leave you with wet sneakers if you weren't careful. After a thousand feet following the stream, the woods ended at an unfenced open field that the guys knew as Parker's Pasture, though no farmhouse or cows were visible. The land rose slowly and then descended toward an open-field stream called Wedge Creek. Across it on a slight rise stood Cowboy Rock, a boulder ten feet high and twice as far around. It had several natural chips or steps on one side and was fairly flat at the top. The boys' feet fit the steps well, and three or four guys could sit atop the rock at a time. From there, they could see the houses of the Highlands on one side and the newest Chelmsford neighborhood the other way. The new Route 3 had cut into the open land about a half mile away, but the pasture was still untouched, and the

Rock was their special place in it.

"Who named this Cowboy Rock?" Simon Rawls asked suddenly. "Ain't no cowboys in Lowell." The guys laughed.

"Maybe we did," his twin Jason said. "I mean, it sorta looks like a rock you see on a trail in *Hopalong Cassidy* or *The Lone Ranger*. Maybe some kid just named it." Eric nodded. He didn't know. They'd always called it Cowboy Rock. Even Tom Barnes called it that, and no one had ever asked why till now. The twins decided to wander for a while along Wedge Creek. They'd climb the Rock later. Eli went off by himself to look for animal burrows and snake holes, so Eric, Ricky, and Jack climbed Cowboy Rock and looked around at the bare trees and the low November sun.

"I guess we don't know why this is Pahkah's Paschah, eithah," Jack said. "Who's Pahkah anyway and where's his herd?" Eric and Ricky laughed.

"Seems like everybody wants to be a cowboy," Jack added. "I'd rather be Tarzan or one of those elephant trainers in India."

"We know," Eric said mockingly as he and Ricky laughed again.

"Well, Tarzan, why don't you jump from Cowboy Rock?" Ricky abruptly asked.

"Yeah," Eric teased. "Could you do it?" Jack looked at his taunting friends and then walked slowly in a squatting posture around the edge of their perch. He scanned the grass below and tried to see if any soft spot would do for a landing. Between Wedge Creek and the Rock, about ten feet away, he eyed a mushy patch of grass next to the stream. He looked back at Eric and Ricky and smiled.

"Yeah, I could." He nodded slowly and pointed to the landing patch he'd chosen. Eric and Ricky stared at it and smiled at each other.

"You'd better jump all the way there," Eric advised, "or you'll break a leg on the hard ground."

"I know," Jack agreed. "I know what I hafta do," he said solemnly as Ricky and Eric waited. Jack scanned the Rock closely for the best leaping spot, somewhere with enough room for a short running start. Three or four quick steps. The other two edged out of his way and watched as Jack picked his spot.

"Hey, you guys," Ricky yelled to the twins and Eli, "Jack's gonna jump from the Rock." The boys turned and watched as Jack kept looking over his launching place and landing target and calculated the jump.

"Don't break your neck," Eli called.

"Thanks for the advice." Jack smiled at him. The twins looked at each other and then back at Jack. No turning back now, he realized, with all eyes on him. Jack stepped to the spot where his jump would start. He leaned with his hands on his thighs and swayed slowly back and forth, one foot toward the landing place. He looked around at all the silent faces and then back at his target. Swaying slowly, he started his leaping cry, ran four quick steps, then threw his hands out and jumped. "Ahh-ah-ah-ah-ah-ah," he yelled as he hurled himself off the Rock and into midair before falling toward the hands-and-knees landing he wanted. But as his feet hit the mushy grass, they stuck in the mud and his body jerked awkwardly forward and flat against his elbows and face. His feet came out of his sneakers and his body slid forward and down into the two-foot depth of the stream. For a second, no one spoke until Jack slowly pulled himself out of the water and onto the other side of the creek. Then the boys clapped and yelled. Jack wiped the water from his eyes and brushed back his soaked hair. Slowly he stood up, unsteady at first, but then firmly at full height and bowed to the guys, who cheered all over again.

"You did it," Eric shouted.

"Man, you're a mess," Eli said as he and the twins walked closer to Jack. The drenched leaper shook water from his clothes and stepped away from the damp ground in his stocking feet. He scraped away mud stains from his pants and pried his sneakers loose from the mud.

"Your mom's gonna be mad." Jason shook his head to imagine, and everyone else nodded.

Jack smiled. "I'll just tell her I fell in the creek," Jack said confidently, and everybody laughed at such a lame explanation. Jack cleaned himself awhile longer, took off his shirt and squeezed water from it, then put it on again with a shiver and found some dry grass away from the stream. He lay there awhile to let the sun dry him off as much as it would this late in November. The other boys wandered off again, and Eric and Ricky talked quietly on the Rock.

"Wonder how long Cowboy Rock's been here," Ricky said.

"Maybe thousands of years," Eric offered.

"Might as well be forever," Ricky added.

"Well, it can't be forever. Nothing lasts forever."

"God does," Ricky remembered from religion class at St. Mary Magdalene's where he and Eric were classmates. Eric recalled Sister Agatha's vague explanation of "forever."

"What does forever *really* mean?" he asked as much to himself as to Ricky.

"It's sorta like fire," Ricky reached for a comparison. "You can't hold fire and you can't understand forever." Eric remembered their fire behind Tull's barn and figured Ricky might be thinking of it, too.

"Yeah," Eric said, unsatisfied. He looked around at Jack lying in the grass while the other three still explored the field.

"Or maybe it's just so long they call it forever." Ricky seemed to back away from the edge of the mystery.

"Nope," Eric rejected, "a long time still isn't forever."

"If something lasts forever, it has no beginning, right?"

"Umm," Eric agreed.

"But everything starts someplace. If you go back and back and back, you gotta get to the start. I mean, it wouldn't be here if it didn't start, right? Except God," Ricky allowed himself the catechism's escape.

"But if God never started, how can He exist now?" Eric shrugged.

"It's a mystery, Eric," Ricky said firmly.

"But that's no answer."

"Well, lots of things are mysteries."

"Yeah, but maybe that's cuz we just haven't figured 'em out yet. Like they usta think the earth was round—I mean, flat—but now we know it's round, right?"

"But that's because they *proved* it," Ricky stressed the distinction.

"Who proved it?"

"I don't know. Balboa, I think. One a' those explorahs."

"How do ya prove the earth is round?"

"You *sail* around it." Ricky stood up quickly and swung his hands wide and laughed until, for a second, he almost lost his balance near the edge of the Rock.

"Boy, what a trip, huh? Better than hangin' around Lowell." Eric imagined the voyage.

Ricky hooked his finger into the loop of Eric's sneaker lace and swayed the foot slowly. Two dogs barked far away while Eric studied the growing shadows of the afternoon and felt bored for a moment with the same old houses on the same old streets of his neighborhood. How many years had it been like this? The Indians were all over here once. Their image passed dully away and he looked at Ricky again. Forever. No beginning and no end. It just goes on and on the same.

"Ricky, do you think forever's boring?"

"I don't know. Depends on what you're doin', I guess."

"But if something goes on forever, it's the *same* thing."

"You can't figure it out," Ricky stressed.

"Why not? They proved the earth was round, didn't they?"

"Yeah, but how can ya prove anything about forever? Ya can't *sail* around it."

"I don't know. There must be *some* way."

"There's no way, Eric. Only God understands forever. You just live, and whatever happens happens. It's a mystery." Ricky was calm and conclusive.

Eric lay back on the Rock and swung his arms behind his head again. It felt nice to do that. The stone was almost warm. But soon Eric sat up again. Ricky was pretty decided about forever. He didn't mind that it was a mystery. He just thought it was the same whether you figure it out or not. *Well, maybe that's OK for Ricky, but it's not good enough for me*, Eric thought. Maybe if he just spent time thinking hard enough about it, he *could* figure it out. It might take a few years, but it sure would be worth it. Imagine telling all the guys, and even Sister Agatha. What faces they'd all make when he'd tell them so clear they'd wonder why they hadn't seen it before and that would be the end of the mystery business. Maybe he'd save it for a time at Parker's Pasture or speak it from Cowboy Rock. He'd bring it up slowly and let them in on the biggest secret of all. Wonder what they'd say and how they'd think of him then.

"We want to come up now," Jason said with Simon standing by him at the base of the Rock.

"OK," Eric answered and lowered himself back down the steps. Ricky followed, and then the twins had the Rock to themselves. Eli had drifted over to Jack, and they talked in low voices about Jack's leap and whether Eli would ever try it. Eli said maybe, but he wouldn't say when.

III

After supper that night, Eric watched a little TV, but nothing good was on. The Friday night lineup of *Howdy Doody, Lassie, Superman, Mama,* and *Topper* was the best night for TV, and anyway his parents didn't let them watch more than *Howdy Doody* on school nights. When he grew tired, Eric was happy enough to turn off the television and head up the creaky stairs to his bedroom at the back of Grampa Harrigan's flat. He went in, got his pajamas on, and then waited to hear Grampa's slippers scraping along as he went over to the cast-iron stove and sniffed the steaming pot with an indifferent patience.

Eric came out of the bedroom and sat at the kitchen table behind his grandfather. The old man lifted the cover and peered through thick glasses into the bubbling solution. As he bent softly over, long strands of white hair hung down and hid the faint trace of a smile.

"Is it ready, Grampa?" Eric asked.

Grampa turned to Eric with a curious look. "Not yet, Eric. Would ya like a little taste?"

Eric blushed and said what Grampa already knew. "No, I don't like it very much." Grampa covered the pan and opened his golden pocket watch for the time.

"So what's goin' on at the school?" Grampa asked.

"Oh, nothing much."

Grampa Harrigan sat down at the kitchen table across from Eric and looked out into the night. Alderson's yard was bit overgrown and some new neighbors were building a house on the lot where Grampa once grew tomatoes and squash. Eric watched his grandfather's index finger rub absently over the knob of his left thumb where the nail was gone. Grampa looked at the stove again and then at Eric.

"What have they been larnin' ya lately?"

"Well," Eric started after a thoughtful pause, "we read about Woodrow Wilson, who sent the duff boys to Europe to fight the Germans. Sister said he was a great president and he suffered a lot. And Johnny Stapleton asked if he was a Catholic and she said no, but a very good man just the same." Grampa smiled and went back to the stove to give another few stirs, then returned.

"Do *you* remember Woodrow Wilson, Grampa?"

"I remember 'im, lad," he said slowly. "He was a man for the people and very idealist, too. That was an awful war." His eyes lowered. "They had to fight them Germans, though. They were gettin' too wise."

"Whadaya mean wise, Grampa?"

He took the oatmeal from the burner and set it on the stove where it rested for the night to be eaten in the morning. Then he sat down again. Eric's eyes followed the steam drifting faintly from the pan and disappearing into the air. He wondered where it went and if it took oatmeal with it somehow. Where did the smell of oatmeal go after it left your nose?

"The Germans were too pushy, Eric," his voice jolted his grandson's daydream. "They wouldn't leave well enough alone. And the French and the Brits couldn't handle 'em. Not surprisin' in the case of the British, for they had the Irish troubles. Did they larn ya *that* about the war?" His voice sharpened and his eyes turned away with a suddenness that pierced the contented old lines of his face. "The Irish troubles," he repeatedly distantly.

Slowly Grampa's gaze took in Eric again, and as the boy drew strength to dare a question about the Irish troubles, a crack from the back stairs startled him up and halfway to bed before Grampa asked, "Is it your mother?"

"I think so," Eric whispered. Grampa looked past Eric to the closed door at the top of the stairs and listened.

"I don't know. Do you hear anything now?"

"No."

"Then maybe it's all right," he said with a diplomatic smile.

Eric walked carefully back to the table and sat down, still facing his bedroom door. He squirmed a little in his pajamas and jiggled his feet against the crossbar of the empty kitchen chair.

"Oatmeal's good for ya, ya know," Grampa suddenly proclaimed. "Best food there is. I've had it all my life, every mornin'. Ya sure ya wouldn't have a taste now?"

He lifted the cover and beckoned Eric to the stove. The boy stepped cautiously across the floor and took a whiff.

"Phew. I still don't think I like it, Grampa."

"All right," he said and covered it over. "Maybe when you're older."

"Maybe."

Grampa's hand combed back the long white hair that still grew to the edge of his forehead. Eric thought of that old picture Mom had on the piano: the dark, handsome man in the old-fashioned high collar with a serious look. *When I grow old*, Eric thought, *I won't get fat and bald. I'll keep my hair until it's long and white, and I'll live to be eighty-four.* When Grampa finished stirring the oatmeal, they both sat at the kitchen table.

"How old are you, Grampa?" Eric surprised himself by asking.

"As old as Jack Benny," Grampa said obscurely.

"How old is Jack Benny?" Eric countered. He had seen Jack Benny sometimes on TV, but his age was a mystery. Besides, he didn't have Grampa's white hair, but how much did hair tell you anyway? Dad had hardly any hair and was much younger than Grampa.

"It ends in a nine," Grampa said finally and waited. Eric's thoughts wavered between politeness and a sense of the game. What should he guess? He decided to be careful.

"Sixty-nine," he said quietly. Grampa seemed to frown but said nothing. Should Eric go higher? How could it be lower? Seventy-nine sounded very old, but what about all that white hair? He would guess younger.

"Fifty-nine," he said doubtfully. Grampa smiled slightly and rubbed his hands together in silence.

"But, Grampa," Eric grew bolder, "Mom is . . . forty . . . or so. How can you be fifty-nine?"

Grampa's eyes twinkled as he looked at Eric straight on. "Are ya sure about your mother, now? Are ya sure?"

Eric thought for a moment and leaned on the table. "Well, I think so," he said at last, "but Mom never talks about that."

Grampa sat back in his chair and waited for Eric's deliberations. But the question, like the smell of oatmeal, seemed to evaporate into the air. At last, Grampa walked slowly across the kitchen and into the pantry where Eric heard a cupboard door open and close and some water run. Then Grampa came back into the kitchen and leaned his elbows on the set-tubs by the wall opposite the table. He glanced at his grandson quickly; then his eyes drifted beyond the window toward the full moon that cast tree shadows on the lawn.

"Grampa," Eric finally decided to ask, "did ya know any other presidents?"

The new subject lit up the old man's face as he started in. "Well, I remember Teddy Ruze-vult. Best pres'dent we ever had. What a talker. He could tell 'em. Got after the rich folks and let 'em know the gov'ment was boss. He was all right."

"How did his teeth look, Grampa?"

"Oh, he was a funny lookin' one. Rugged, though. Very strong. He could ride a horse like a son-of-a-bitch." The phrase galloped around the kitchen before Grampa or Teddy Roosevelt could hold it down. Grampa didn't look at Eric right away but gave both their faces time to fade. "He was quite a rider," he added softly and cleared his throat.

Slowly Eric thought about horses again. The president rode horses. Eric recalled the round, soft face of President Eisenhower on TV as he stepped carefully down a wide stone staircase and into a large black car. *Could Ike ride horses, too?* Eric wondered. But somehow it didn't seem like a question for Grampa, so he let it go. Grampa opened the window for some night air and Eric felt a chill. Just then, two unmistakable creaks from the third and fourth stairs before the landing signaled an abrupt goodnight, and Eric said, "Have a good sleep, Grampa," and was already in his room when his grandfather answered, "Good night, lad."

Mom opened the staircase door and asked precisely, "Has Eric been bothering you?"

"Oh, no, he's in bed now."

"It's ten o'clock, you know," she added in a tone between deference and chastisement.

"Ten bells, is it? Well, I guess it's time for bed at that. Good night, Marian."

"Good night, Daddy," she answered and then creaked her way back down those valuable stairs.

Eric lay quiet for a safe moment and then slipped out of his big double bed and onto his knees and began: "God bless Mommy and Daddy and Betty and Marsha and Grampa Malone and Grampa Harrigan . . ." and soon he was too drowsy to think of more relatives but only of Teddy Roosevelt riding like a son-of-a-bitch over a hill and into the evening clouds that looked too much like his pillow to tell the difference.

IV

Back in school after the holiday weekend, the guys didn't meet again till the following Saturday when they decided to play stick hockey on the Jefferson School pavement. Eli Farrell wasn't interested. He wanted to read instead, so Jason, Simon, Jack, Ricky, and Eric took hockey sticks and a tennis ball to the school yard. Five guys couldn't make even sides, but when Jack volunteered to play goalie, Eric and Ricky and Jason and Simon formed two comfortable teams. They would clear the puck after each shot and play toward the one goal, marked by stones. With Jack leaping left and right to make saves with his stick, the game stayed scoreless for several minutes until the boys heard an unmistakable yell from beyond the school yard wall and across the street where Gilly Dennis lived.

"Hey, Malone, how's your neck?" Gilly shouted and his guys laughed. Three or four kids were with him, Eric guessed. The game stopped, and Ricky silently grabbed all the sticks and the tennis ball and ran them beyond the pavement to the gravel slope nearest the boys' way home.

"Better than your leg," Eric called back, but this time no one laughed. Quickly Eric and his guys took cover behind the corner of the building and along the school yard wall close to the stairs by the nearest entrance.

"The school yard's ours," Gilly announced.

"Where does it say that?" Eric wondered aloud. Gilly had always avoided these fights when Tom was around, but now he was bolder, as if Eric should be challenged. Everyone pried stones from the dirt or picked them up from the pavement. No shortage of weapons. Some stones would fly back and forth four or five times in a longer fight. No one ever quite won, but each gang tried to quit when it had made its point, whatever that was. Insults could be as appealing as well-thrown stones, though a direct hit showed power and skill. Everyone remembered a battle wound, giving it or getting it.

A few guys on each side moved quickly from their first cover to get more stones or find a better angle for a shot. A long silence followed the boys' opening taunts. Then Gilly jumped up quickly from behind a brick wall and fired between the iron bars of the permanent fence.

"That one's for you, Malone," and a stone whizzed by Eric's face, missing by inches. Gilly ducked out of range as soon as he fired, but Eric saw Randy Garabedian looking toward Jason and Simon, so he answered Gilly by hitting Randy in the lower left side of his back.

"Aghh!" Randy yelled as he fell to a sitting position and then scrambled for cover. Stones flew now from both sides. Simon got hit, but his brother Jason caught two of Gilly's guys in the shoulder from where they couldn't see him. Gilly shouted "Bastard!" and fired three quick shots at Jason, but that took his eyes off Eric long enough for him to step into the open and whip a direct hit into Gilly's right arm near the shoulder.

"You son of a bitch!" Gilly screamed as he grabbed his arm and ran across the street toward his house. Mrs. Dennis heard her son come crying into the living room, and she barreled out of her kitchen door toward the boys.

"Get outta heah, ya brats," she shouted. "I'll callah cops on ya. I'm gonna callah cops."

By then everyone was running. Eric's guys scrambled across the school yard, grabbed their hockey sticks and tennis ball, and ran past McDermott's little grocery store and around the corner, then up Medford Street and, slowing to a casual walk, moved quietly into Eric's yard and around the garage to the small pear tree behind it. There they sat and talked in low voices about the fight. No parents would know, of course. Eric was sure Mrs. Dennis would not call the cops because she didn't know any of their names. Besides, Gilly was the wildest kid in the neighborhood and the cause of most fights. Gilly, of course, knew who Eric was, but he wanted no adult help. He'd rather get Eric himself, and Eric was determined that he wouldn't. Not a second time.

After a suitable delay and a little daubing of Simon's cut, everyone went silently home. They'd play street hockey somewhere else for a while and leave the Jefferson School yard uncontested. Mostly, Eric's guys would head west toward Parker's Pasture, while Gilly's kids stayed on the streets from the Jefferson School east toward Chelmsford Street and beyond it to Hale's Brook. They all seemed to know when to keep to their own turf, though Eric would never give up the Jefferson School yard completely to Gilly. Why should he? He had gone to kindergarten there, hadn't he? Who knew, or cared, where Gilly went to school? He probably wouldn't finish high school anyway. They'd be reading about Gilly stealing cars or robbing banks when he got old enough. At least Eric had given Gilly a few shots to remember, and taken a good one in the neck himself.

V

A winter of family holidays, three big snowstorms, and cautious gang avoidance followed. Sometimes Eric talked with Ricky and the twins about giving Gilly some final message, whatever that could be.

"I think you did already, right in his throwing arm," Ricky said, and the others nodded and laughed.

"Yeah, he'll feel that every time he throws," Simon agreed. No one really wanted more rock fights, but they didn't know how to end them. They couldn't stop Gilly, but they wouldn't back away from him either. And Gilly would keep looking for another chance to surprise Eric. Eric always had to watch behind him, especially near the Jefferson School.

The spring came slowly with many false starts of warm days cut short by cold nights. An early April snowstorm delayed baseball pickup games at Highland Park. Grounders on the hard turf were horrible to field and might hit like a rock on the shins. So the guys waited and kept their Parker's Pasture hikes to drier trails and open meadows warmed by the sun. By May, they had played baseball a few times despite hard infields and clumpy outfields. Dad had even gone with them one Saturday to hit flies and grounders when they couldn't find enough guys for a game.

Then one supper time in mid-May, Dad came to the table with an unusual look on his face. He urged everyone to have all they wanted to eat, which Eric thought was strange because they always did that, at home anyway, and he said that when supper was done he had something to tell them. Betty and Marsha both wanted to know right then, but Dad wouldn't budge. Mom just smiled and said to obey their father. The dinner seemed longer than usual, though eating always took the edge off any worry for Eric. In the middle of pot roast, potatoes, and corn, and with ice cream and strawberries for dessert, how bad could any news be? At last the dishes were cleared and Dad brought everyone into the living room. Betty and Marsha sat on the sofa with Mom. Eric took one easy chair and Dad had the other.

"Well," Dad started, "you know that sometimes you have an opportunity that will make life better, but it may be uncomfortable just making a change. I have the chance to give you kids all your own rooms and to make going to work a lot easier for me. You kids will also have the chance to make some new friends."

"But what's wrong with our old friends, Daddy?" Betty asked.

"Well, nothing. You can still see them sometimes if you want."

Eric shifted in his chair and looked carefully at his father, who took Mom's hand and smiled a bit self-consciously as he said, "We're going to have a new home."

"You mean we're moving," Eric said.

"Yes, we're going to move to Belvidere. I can buy a larger house . . . at a good price . . . and we'll have more room. It has a nice side yard for playing, and we'll have both upstairs and down."

"How many stairs does it have?" Marsha wondered. At six that still mattered, Eric supposed.

"Well, I didn't count them exactly, but I'm sure you'll handle them just fine," Dad answered.

Eric's mind raced through the meanings of this news. A new school, new friends (and no friends at first). The end of Parker's Pasture and Cowboy Rock and rock fights with Gilly Dennis.

"You kids will go to the Assumption School," Mom explained. "It's a very good school with nice nuns and lots of new kids to meet. Daddy will be closer to the office and we can visit Aunt Emma more often." Mom and Dad looked around and waited. Eric and his sisters seemed deep in thought, not upset, but just thinking about all the changes and what might be good or bad.

"And Eric," Dad added at last, "Assumption has a baseball team for sixth to eighth graders, and I've decided to help coach them." Eric smiled broadly at that, and Dad relaxed into his chair. After some more talk and a few anxious thoughts from Betty and Marsha over lost friends, Eric nodded and finally asked, "When can we see the new house?"

"Ahhh—I think we can do that next Tuesday after school. The Daltons, who live there now, want us to have a look so that everyone will feel comfortable with it."

"OK," Eric said, as if summing up his many calculations. "I think this will be OK."

"Good," Dad smiled and turned to Mom.

"I think you are all going to like this very much," she added as conclusively as possible.

"But what about Grampa Harrigan?" Eric suddenly asked. "Is he going to live here alone?"

"Oh, no," Dad answered quickly and looked at each of his kids. "Grampa will have his own room upstairs and even a large sun porch next to it. And you know what? He's even going to have a friend next door." Eric looked puzzled.

"The three Flynn sisters live there with their father. He's about Grampa's age and he once worked for the same railroad that Grampa did. They knew each other a long time ago." The girls exchanged glances of amazement.

"That will be nice for him," Eric said, though Grampa Harrigan's opinions of American presidents still impressed Eric more than some old man living next door to their new house.

"Yes, it will," Mom agreed, and she patted Eric on the shoulder for being so considerate.

That night in bed after another oatmeal evening with Grampa Harrigan, Eric thought again about the move. No more Gilly Dennis to worry about. New turf to explore near the banks of the Merrimack River. No more sitting on the Rock with the guys. New nuns and new kids and baseball with Dad as a coach. Maybe he could visit Ricky or have him over for a day. Dad had said that would be all right if Ricky's parents agreed. The girls could have visits with friends, too, if they wanted. Eric got up from bed and looked out at the night sky. Clouds obscured most of the stars, but the moon was bright near the horizon. He saw the old Tull estate dimly through the trees. Plum Island and Cobbetts Pond. The Highlands and now Belvidere, whatever that odd name meant. Back in bed, Eric closed his eyes, breathed deeply a couple of times, and wondered what dream he would have tonight and if he'd be able to figure out "forever" any better in Belvidere than he had in the Highlands. Or were some mysteries the same everywhere?

BELVIDERE

I

The Malones' new house in Belvidere nearly doubled their flat in the Highlands. Eric's upstairs bedroom was across the landing from Grampa Harrigan's room, and the sun porch beyond it. Eric slid his left hand along the wooden banister as he circled by his parents' room, past the den with its second TV and upstairs phone, by the girls' bedroom, and finally to the bath at the end of the hall. Grampa had less space now and no kitchen, but he didn't need one because he ate with everyone else. His nightly oatmeal ritual was over. Eric now called him to supper in a clear voice at his door. His hearing was slipping lately.

Downstairs the girls often listened to music at the back end of the living room near the piano that Mom sometimes played. After school, they turned on the hi-fi, and later the stereo, for Broadway show albums more than popular rock. Eric got used to *Oklahoma*, *Annie*, and *South Pacific* as the soundtrack of Berenger Street. Beyond the living room was a screened porch (under Grampa's sunroom) where they sometimes sat or ate on warm days. To the right of the front door and its small entrance hall was the dining room (mostly for holiday dinners) and behind it the kitchen with a downstairs bathroom by the back door.

Outside, the Malones had a two-car garage and two ample yards, the upper one and the lower side lot. Dad expected Eric to handle most of the yard work, and he quickly learned to do it in stages: the upper lawn around the house all at once, the lower side lot another time, and the grassy banks later. Those were especially tricky. The gas mower could do some of them, but Eric used the lighter push mower on steeper parts. In the worst spots, a sickle was easiest, even if the results were a little shaggy.

Between mowings, the side lot often hosted imaginary baseball games. Eric batted pebbles or wood chips with a wiffle bat (he didn't like the airy wiffle ball) and announced the hits, outs, and homers. The side lot bank was the right field wall, like the short porch at Ebbets Field, the reverse of the Fenway Green Monster. When he tired of hitting wood chips for homers, Eric sometimes took a screwdriver and invented new competitions. He'd spin the tool end-over-end several feet in the air and "score" with upright stabs into the grass or fail with blunt-handle flops. How long these imaginary contests might last on a Saturday morning or a weekday afternoon, Eric never really knew. Sometimes, though, he'd notice one of the middle-aged Flynn sisters looking out her window. She was watching the new neighbor boy toss a screwdriver endlessly into the air and gesture in silent commentary about the results.

11

At school, Eric had a lay teacher rather than a nun for the first time since kindergarten. Mrs. Agatha Degnan, the only non-nun at Assumption, taught her twenty-four seventh graders in all subjects with unvarying precision. Somewhere between a nun and a mother, she had a plan for everything, including spontaneity. Eric liked her and did well right away. Mrs. Degnan had a clipped sense of humor and was more outspoken than any nun he recalled from the Mary Magdalene School. Catholic but never pious, she applied a no-nonsense practicality to everything and kept students alert.

"Loretta, show me your math folder." Loretta did.

"You need to get organized, young lady. No wonder you couldn't find yesterday's homework. Put the date on the top right corner of each paper and then arrange them in chronological order. Do you understand what I mean by 'chronological'?"

"Yes, Mrs. Degnan."

"Then do it. You have three minutes, and then I want to see all those papers arranged sensibly."

Loretta got to work while Mrs. Degnan put the outline of today's science lesson on the blackboard and turned to the class.

"Everyone put your science book and folder on your desk, please." She then checked Loretta's math folder. "Much better. Now keep it that way." As Mrs. Degnan moved into a science lesson on gravity and the ocean tides, Eric thought back to all those nuns he'd had. He couldn't blame them now for their occasional bursts of temper. Poor Sister Andrew Veronica, for instance, had faced sixty first graders every day all alone. No wonder she always insisted that everyone's paper, left-handers included, be aligned the same way on their desks. She could then see at a glance that all students were working. So what if that meant that Eric had to drag his left hand across the writing as he wrote? And once, when Eric was talking in the lunch line, she had told him to stand by the hallway wall outside her room until she came back to talk to him. Then, with so much on her mind, she forgot about him. An hour later, when Mom came to take him home, sister suddenly remembered where he was. He was not always so obedient, he recalled, as Mrs. Degnan went on about the moon's gravity. In the third grade once, Sister Augustina had told four boys who wouldn't stop talking to stand on their desks until the bell rang to end the school day. For about twenty minutes, Eric and his three friends got to look over everyone's work from this unusual point of view. Not much of a punishment, really, but he supposed that sister had run out of ideas.

"Mr. Malone, are you with me?" he suddenly heard Mrs. Degnan say.

"Yes, Mrs. Degnan."

"Very well, then. Explain why we do not feel the moon's gravitational pull, even though the oceans do."

"Well, compared with the earth's gravity, the moon's is so slight that we cannot feel it, but a liquid like ocean water is much more susceptible to that force, even though the earth's gravity still keeps the seas in place."

Mrs. Degnan cleared her throat. "All right," she said and turned again to the blackboard. Eric had escaped once more. When had he really become a serious student? He had to say it began in grade five with Sister Mary Fatima, who gave points for homework done each day. He never missed a point all year and found the classes more interesting when he knew the material. Then by grade six he had started to like reading, especially history lessons and stories in literature. Sister Ignatius Angelica provided vocabulary words with each reading, and those vocabulary points were easy for Eric to get on her tests. So when he switched to the Assumption School, he felt confident that he would do well, and he was.

"Eric, you seem to have a glazed look again. Would you tell us, please, why the earth's gravity doesn't pull the moon downward?"

"The momentum of the moon's forward motion and the gravitational pull of the much larger earth have reached a sort of balance—ah, equilibrium, I think it's called—so that the moon is in a permanent circular orbit around the earth."

"Yes . . . good," Mrs. Degnan said with a trace of irritation. "All right, everyone. Put your books away and get ready for the lunch bell."

I I I

At school, Eric met many new classmates and one that he already knew. She had lived across Stimson Street from him until the fourth grade when her family moved to Belvidere. Lily Mullane was also one of the top students in Eric's new seventh grade. Several girls were very smart in his class, and a few of them, including Lily, became unspoken competitors with him. And whether they were top students or not, the girls this year seemed suddenly more confident and somehow smarter than the boys about people, if not always about books. They were prettier now, too, even in school uniforms that didn't allow for much individuality. Lily seemed friendly to him at first—a familiar face in the hallway—and then more reserved when their competition became clearer. Not sure what to say to her, Eric said less and soon not much more than "Hi."

Another girl he noticed was Deidre Hollander, who sat beside him in the next row. Sometimes she would ask to borrow a pencil or complain about a math problem she couldn't get. Her curly black hair was thick on either side of her narrow face and gave her head a more rounded look. She didn't talk so much with other girls and liked to read, especially poems. During one of Mrs. Degnan's English lessons, Deidre's fingers had flipped away from today's pages and over to some poem about flowers around a lake. She caught Eric's eye and slid her finger along a line that she liked. Eric nodded that he liked it too, but he was nervous about catching Mrs. Degnan's attention. Deidre read the next few lines of the poem in a low whisper that Eric managed to hear.

"What does it mean that the flowers 'outdid the sparkling waves in glee'?" she asked as quietly as possible.

Eric whispered back, "The breeze blows the daffodils more than the water."

"Oh, of course," Deidre said with a faint laugh. "That's beautiful. But why does the speaker say he didn't really appreciate it?"

"He does later, when he's in his study."

"Ah, he's a student of flowers," Deidre added under her hand that she had lifted to cover her mouth.

"Well, sort of," Eric said with a side glance. And then he was aware of Mrs. Degnan's eyes on them both from the front of the room. She waited a moment and then said in a firm voice, "That's enough from you two love birds." A few of the girls giggled as Deidre and Eric blushed and turned obediently toward the front of the room. Johnny Tessier, who sometimes played baseball with Eric after school, winked quickly at him and rolled his shoulders knowingly. When Mrs. Degnan turned again to the blackboard and resumed her comments on a Poe short story, Eric thought how clever she was. In one sentence, she had ended Eric's whispering with Deidre—and for good. She'd embarrassed them both just enough so that they'd never risk such a moment again. She knew that they weren't any kind of "love birds," but the phrase had given her complete control again.

IV

That afternoon as Eric walked home along East Merrimack Street, Mel Barnett's dad pulled his car along the curb beside him.

"Want a ride, Eric?" he offered.

Eric thanked him and sat in front. Mel Barnett and Barney Stobbs were in the backseat. They both lived near Eric, and the two seemed inseparable. Barney was chubby and never quite got all of his shirt tucked in. His grey skin looked vaguely unwashed, and Eric guessed that his hair enjoyed complete freedom from combs. Mel was much thinner, even a bit frail-looking from some childhood illness that Eric did not quite understand. Anyway, Mel almost always rode home from school, and Barney, too lazy to walk, often benefitted.

"So, how's Deidre doing?" Barney couldn't wait to ask.

"Who is this Deidre?" Mr. Barnett wanted to know with a big grin. Eric played along.

"Oh, just a fan of mine."

"Ahhhah," Mel jeered from the back seat. "Old Eric's making a move."

The laughter died down pretty quickly as they approached Berenger Street because everyone knew that Eric had no moves. Guys just said these things to impress each other. *Who knew how to "make a move,"* Eric thought.

"Ya comin' ta Kelleher's?" Barney asked as Eric got out at his house.

"Yeah. I'll be there in a while," Eric agreed.

Kelleher's was a vacant lot across the street from Cliff Kelleher's house and a quick walk from Eric's. Cliff was in his first year at Lowell High now, and he liked the fact that some seventh and eighth graders still played pick-up games on his dad's extra lot. Some trees and a row of mulberry bushes formed a wall from right to center field, while Bultmann Road was the left field barrier, a short poke like the Fenway wall, though no "monster" rose up from the curb. The guys argued about whether such a short left field should be a double at the street and only a homer if the ball landed beyond the opposite curb. Sometimes a high bouncer from the street did land in an old lady's open porch on the other side. Once, a ball had bounced from the street directly into her front window and smashed the lower half of the glass all over the porch floor. Several guys, including the batter, ran behind the barn near the third base line. Eric and the other outfielders just waited as a frail but loud old lady opened the front door, stood angrily on her front steps, and shouted, "Why don't you boys hit your balls in the other direction?" Eric heard laughter from behind the barn at the old woman's unconscious sexual humor. Mel Barnett, who'd been coaching at third, walked toward the lady. He said the players were sorry about the window and promised that they would pay for it. That calmed her down, especially when Mel actually went inside with her and wrote down his name, address, and phone number. A week later, Mel had collected a few dollars from most of the Kelleher regulars and brought the money to old Mrs. Fargo, whom a few guys called "Dakota." From then on, the right-handed hitters tried to aim toward right center and to avoid long drives straight at Dakota's porch. A fence along the nearer curb would have helped (and given Kelleher's field an even more "Fenway" feeling), but Mr. Kelleher never provided a "monster" to contain the young sluggers.

As a lefty, of course, Eric seldom hit that way. The trees and bushes in right and center were his more likely targets. They looked reachable but were harder to hit than he thought. Eric annoyed himself too often with groundouts to second from taking bigger cuts than he should have at pitches beyond his strike zone. He liked to stand and move at the plate like Ted Williams, but the results were not consistent. Now and then he'd catch one, though, and his home run dreams lingered.

From June to Labor Day, the Malones still spent the summers at Cobbetts Pond, but in May and September and maybe into October, Kelleher's field kept drawing Eric back until supper and homework ended the pick-up games. Barney Stobbs was slow-footed but a powerful hitter. He reminded Eric of an old picture he had of Rudy York. Mel's weak frame made him a singles hitter. Sometimes he'd play a few innings until he tired and then he'd coach everyone else from behind third base. Eric played the outfield mostly, though several times he agreed to pitch to see if his leg kick resembled Warren Spahn's. It did, but his pitches didn't.

V

Through the winter and into the seventh grade spring, Eric settled into a study schedule and got high grades. He read and reread his texts and sometimes recopied class notes that seemed sloppy or incomplete. At the end of the year, he won the award as the top-ranking seventh grader, just beating out Lily Mullane. He was proud of that but he said little, and Lily said little to him beyond "congratulations" after the awards assembly. A year later, a transfer student named Eddie Alston pushed Eric into second place. Anyway, they liked each other and talked much more easily than he and Lily. Eddie even went bowling on a few Fridays with Eric, Mel, and Barney. When they decided to change from duck pins to ten pins and the larger bowling balls, Eric's height, already six feet, gave him an advantage and he usually led the group, except when Alston bowled "over his head."

On school vacations and during the summer, Eric did more reading on his own. He liked biographies of historical figures like Sam Houston, Winston Churchill, and FDR—men of action who could also speak well appealed to him. He learned some of their famous phrases and delivered them in his room with his door closed. "Where are your Washingtons, your Jeffersons?" Sam Houston had challenged Confederate leaders. FDR's "the only thing we have to fear" and "rendezvous with destiny" sounded so good, and Churchill was eloquent about Britain's "finest hour." Eric did variations on these speeches with a fountain pen in hand like a conductor's baton. The crowds roared in his mind when he made dramatic points about how enemies would fall and victory and prosperity would come. Then one day as Mom had finished reorganizing his closet—and discovered two lost pairs of winter gloves—she looked around his room at the wallpaper. She walked up close and looked again.

"Eric, what are all these dark spots on the wallpaper? They look like ink."

"I don't know," Eric answered with a puzzled expression.

"Have you been waving a pen around?" she asked. Eric didn't recall that.

"Well, I don't think they got there by themselves," Mom concluded and exited his room, leaving Eric to have a closer look at the ink spots.

VI

As he had promised, Dad joined the coaching staff of the Assumption Church baseball team for sixth to eighth graders. Eric had played briefly for the Mary Magdalene team in the sixth grade, but having Dad actually hitting infield grounders and outfield flies to him at practice was a new and very good feeling. Vic had no intention of going easy on Eric, and sometimes his son felt added pressure. Mostly, though, he liked his dad's interest and his frequent smile. He was even impressed by Dad's very smooth swing. At BC, Dad had captained the tennis team more than twenty years before. Were those two kinds of swings related?

The Assumption team played a ten-game schedule against other parish teams during May and June. Eric began in left or centerfield, but as the '57 season developed, his height made first base a logical choice, especially when no one was playing well there. Eric stretched wide for throws and gave infielders a bigger target, but he never mastered the throws in the dirt. Sometimes they got by him or hit him in the foot or shin. Bad throws annoyed him, but with Dad nearby, he had one more reason to control his temper. Kelleher field pick-up games were one thing; an organized team with uniforms was another.

Dad coached for manager Ralph Mulligan, an old high school pitcher and then college player at Tufts University in the '40s. Mulligan knew more about pitching than Dad, and together they agreed that a tall left-hander would be an asset. So Eric came to the mound occasionally. He lowered that Spahnian leg kick and made his delivery more efficient. He learned to throw a noticeable curve ball, but mixing fastballs and changeups got the best results. Control was sometimes a problem.

In one game against his old Magdalene team, Eric had struck out five in four innings until he got careless with a changeup after a couple of walks and gave up a three-run homer just over Tessier's glove in right. After another walk, Mulligan moved Eric to first and brought in a stocky right-hander named Billy Foster to finish the game.

"OK, Eric," Dad said from the bench. "Let's get those runs back next inning."

Eric did get a single in the top of the sixth and scored on a double by third baseman Sharkey, but Assumption lost 7–2 with Eric as the losing pitcher.

"You did OK through the fourth, Eric," Dad said after game, "but then you started missing outside. Maybe you were overthrowing a little."

"I guess so." Baseball was a complicated game, especially for kids with uneven skills. Hitters sometimes overwhelmed the defense with liners and hard grounders. *Too many errors, physical and mental,* Eric thought. Then a big pitcher with speed could shut down the same hitters, who suddenly felt helpless.

Eric knew the feeling—against one hurler especially, St. William's Archie Malden. At six foot two and maybe two hundred pounds, Malden was scary. In one game he struck out Eric three times. A loud foul was all he could manage. Then he faced Malden again at Shedd Park on a hot Saturday afternoon. Assumption had managed a run off Malden in the second on a walk, a wild pitch, and Sharkey's bloop single, but by the fifth inning, St. William's led 6–1 as Eric led off. He had fanned in the first and grounded back to the pitcher in the third. *You've got to be quicker,* he told himself. *Start swinging early and then hold up if it's a ball.* Easy to say, hard to do. He swung late through the first pitch and felt overmatched again. Then as Malden whirled to deliver another fastball, Eric estimated his release point and started to swing. A second later he saw a hard bouncing ball jump down the third base line just fair. Eric took off as the ball rolled well into foul territory. The amazed left fielder reacted slowly, then ran hard to the ball as Eric turned at second base and headed for third. The throw was a good one but a few feet to the shortstop side of the bag. Eric pulled into third with a stand-up triple. A quick smile to a couple of guys on the bench let them know how lucky he felt.

As Tessier got ready to hit, Eric framed a silent sentence in his head: "I just hit a triple off Archie Malden." Pay attention, he quickly told himself, despite the shivers that ran through him. Peeved at Eric's lucky hit, Malden fanned the next two and got Sharkey on a foul pop near first. Eric had no chance to score. But he would remember his triple off Archie Malden. Maybe he could still become a better—and smarter—player. But as guys caught up to Eric's height advantage and put on more muscle, the competition seemed better by the month. Either he needed to give playing baseball as much time as he did to thinking about the game, or he wouldn't be a player much longer. Anyway, he loved learning about major league history and following the last few seasons of the best hitter of all, Ted Williams.

VII

"What does Belvidere mean?" he asked Dad one day.

"It comes from two Latin words meaning 'beautiful to see.' I guess the people who first settled this part of Lowell thought of it that way."

Like most kids who took their neighborhood for granted, Eric didn't know if Belvidere was so beautiful, but one thing he did know: Ted Williams was belvidere. No one else looked anything like Williams at the plate. He twitched and swiveled with electricity in the batter's box until he coiled the bat close to his body and rippled into a swing that always ended with a classic follow-through, like a Greek statue of a baseball player. He pulled line drives so hard that not even the "Williams Shift" of three infielders to the right of second base could stop them. Eric remembered seeing Ted once on television hit a towering drive to right just a few feet foul and deep into the upper deck. The very next pitch he hit almost in the same spot—but three feet fair for a homer. Had he made some minute adjustment in his swing? One could imagine Williams, and no one else, being that exact. Watching anyone else play baseball left Eric wanting to play. Watching Williams was different. He just wanted to watch Williams some more.

Eric also liked to hear what pitchers said about trying to handle Ted. One smiled to a reporter and explained that he planned to pitch "low—and *behind* him." But Early Wynn, a great Indians' pitcher, had said it best: "Pitching to Williams is never quite fair. He belongs by himself in some higher league." Eric imagined all-time all-stars like Cobb, Ruth, and Gehrig facing Matty, Johnson, and Alexander. That was the "higher league" where Williams belonged.

When the Malones arrived in Belvidere in the summer of '57, Williams was even outdoing himself. Through much of that summer his average hovered in the .380s and .390s. Even Mickey Mantle, the triple crown winner in '56, trailed Ted badly now. On one August day Ted lifted his average to .393. When a reporter asked if he could hit .400 again, Ted said, "The odds are against it, but no one will try harder than I will." Slow-footed now and late in his career, Ted couldn't leg out the infield hits that might have made the difference. But still, what a show it was. Eric listened to most games on the radio and checked the daily box scores. He daydreamed the improbable. Ted slumped a little from .393 to the .370s, then surged near the end. In his final game he went two-for-three to finish at .388, easily the best major league mark since his own .406 in 1941. Young Mickey Mantle had his best average yet that year at .365, but he trailed a thirty-nine-year-old by twenty-three points! Eric knew what "belvidere" meant. Come to think of it, maybe now he knew what "forever" meant, too. Eric smiled to think how seriously he'd taken that mysterious word at Cowboy Rock. Williams' fame as a hitter would last forever. What more did a fan (or a philosopher) need to know?

Ted won another batting title (his sixth) in '58 with a more earthly .328. He beat out teammate Pete Runnels by six points. There had never been a forty-year-old batting champion. There was now. Some people thought Eric was a bit obsessed about Williams. What was it that they didn't get? Had *they* ever seen such a hitter?

VIII

Late in the eighth grade, Eric took the admissions test for BC High, a Jesuit school near Boston. He was admitted. So where would he go, BC High or the local Xaverian Brothers school for boys, Kenton Academy? Both were very good, his parents thought. Maybe the commute was the biggest difference. He'd have to spend a lot of time traveling to the Jesuit school. Extracurriculars would be almost impossible. Kenton Academy was close by, even a nice walk home in good weather. So Eric chose Kenton.

After graduation, Eric went with his parents for a New York weekend and saw his first Broadway musical, *The Music Man* with Robert Preston. What a spectacle musicals were, even if breaking into song seemed ridiculous sometimes. Well, you could just accept that, he decided, and then enjoy all the dancing and singing. It was good, but not quite *belvidere*. Only Ted Williams deserved that word.

KENTON RHYTHMS

I

Walking home from Kenton Academy on most afternoons gave Eric forty minutes to relive each day and then to forget about all of it along the mansion row of Andover Street. He cut across the South Common behind St. Peter's Cathedral and soon walked by the tenements and little ethnic markets and shops on Appleton and Church Streets. Then climbing the two-tiered hill beyond the Concord River led him past Dad's office at High Street and up again to the hilltop estates of Belvidere, so different from the middle-class Highlands and from the gritty life near the confluence of the mill city rivers. Dad's "good deal" on Berenger Street was surely that. The Malones had an ample new house with plenty of grass for Eric, now fourteen, to mow, yet it was far from the richest or poorest home along his two-mile walk from school. Only bad weather or late after-school meetings could justify calling for a ride. Today did not qualify, though Eric was hurrying home to catch some of the Series game between the White Sox and the Dodgers. Strange to see Podres, Snider, and Hodges in LA uniforms after all their great Brooklyn years. And Bubba Phillips and Sherm Lollar had made it to the Series at last. Dutch Saulnier's "Bubba Lollah" had arrived.

The pace of classes at Kenton had picked up quickly from the easy opening days to the demands of early October. After the first school assembly with its blur of announcements and directions, the freshmen had filed off to homerooms 1A, 1B, and 1C, supposedly ranked by academic ability. How the Xaverian Brothers judged such things from grammar school records and admissions tests Eric did not know, nor much cared. He had been near the top of his seventh- and eighth-grade classes at Assumption School, so 1A made sense for him, but it also brought an immediate feeling of competition.

When the 1A guys had all found their homeroom and sat down in random order, Brother Philip, their new religion teacher, read their names alphabetically and reseated them that way *for the year.* Thus Eric found himself just past the middle of the middle row—permanently. Two Assumption kids had come to Kenton with him. Barney Stobbs was in 1B, but Mel Barnett sat in the first row of 1A, behind a smiling blond guy that Eric had heard of before—John Nelson Abbot, whose dad owned the *Lowell Star.* Eric tapped his fingers lightly on the desk and looked around as a few guys whispered to each other under Brother Philip's declarations. Lots of Irish and French names and some Polish, Greek, and Italian kids filled out most of the class roster. Thirty-two of them had made it to 1A, mostly from the parochial schools around Lowell, with a few guys from the public grammar schools or from Chelmsford and other nearby towns.

"Gentlemen," Brother Philip intoned, "let's look over your class schedules so I can tell you where various rooms are and answer any questions." As Brother went on, guys kept taking quick looks around and behind them to see if they knew someone else, or might want to. One big-shouldered kid named Archie Robideau already looked like a varsity football lineman. Eric heard Abbot whisper to a crew-cut kid named Roger Hallihan that his dad was in Paris this week and then would fly to Naples. He was meeting European newspaper owners to get ideas for the *Lowell Star* and was also writing some travel articles that he'd sent home to Jack, who said that he wanted to be a writer and had learned a lot from his dad.

When Brother Philip paused to find a sheet of school policy statements among his pile of papers, Abbot whispered across to Robideau that his father preferred the European soccer games he'd seen over football, but Archie turned thumbs-down and gave a "don't be stupid" look. Behind Eric's right shoulder at the back of the first row, a kid named Hubert Gellhorn busily picked his nose with a squeezing and turning motion that Eric had used himself, but more privately. No hurry to meet Gellhorn. And near the front of the same row, two seats behind Mel, sat a dark-haired guy with a slightly olive complexion. He was Roland Belisle, who caught Eric's eye once and nodded with a tentative smile.

* * *

By November, Eric was getting used to the new reality of all-male teachers after so many years of nuns. The Xaverian Brothers were louder, blunter, and far more physical. A direct answer was a better strategy than just being polite because many of the brothers had little patience with anything wimpy or hesitant.

"Spit it out, Mr. Patterson," one might shout at a slow responder.

"The ice caps are melting, Santoris. Let's take a shot at it, shall we?"

"Oh, sure, Riley. You get one right and you want the Medal of Honor. Miss any more and you'll get the Purple Heart."

Eric liked these creative insults as long as someone else was the target. He brought the best of them home to get a laugh at supper time. Dad especially liked the sharper putdowns that reminded him of Boston College Jesuits a few decades earlier. Betty and Marsha were amazed that teachers were so blunt, not like their quieter nuns, who were seldom tough with anyone but the rowdiest boys.

One day in Eric's English class, the teacher had even reseated the biggest guys in the room (Eric's height and Robideau's bulk had doomed them both) in the end row of seats. Then, raising the knuckle of his right middle finger and bracing it at the fingernail with his thumb, he jogged down the row and hit each guy hard on his left arm just below the shoulder. No flinching allowed.

"I always wanted to do that to the biggest guys in the class," he announced with a bizarre grin as he waved his victims back to their normal seats. Students glanced at each other with amused bewilderment. Anything might happen in this boys' academy housed in a converted nineteenth-century prison. Ro gave Eric a quick grin at having escaped the gratuitous blows, and Eric rubbed his arm as if hurt. Sometimes, Eric thought, a teacher's comments did get too personal or were more about the instructor's frustration than anything else. But they were often right, he admitted, given the way *certain* guys behaved. The worst ones would say things that he'd never imagine saying to adults. He might *think* them but never speak them, which meant keeping things inside until he'd get irritated at some trivial thing and snap at Stobbs or Barnett, not the offenders. His temper bothered him sometimes, and he thought about how to get beyond it; but he couldn't see a way when "respect" for teachers, especially religious ones, ruled out any back talk. Yet petty irritations did not linger as homework, deadlines, and extracurriculars kept most of his classmates too busy to dwell on nameless feelings that they seldom dared to share. All the guys quickly understood the good and the bad of Xaverian discipline and helped each other cope with it, sometimes by private ridicule of the disciplinarians.

I I

As weeks passed and quizzes, tests, and papers came back with good grades, Eric gained confidence. Like his feelings, though, he kept his grades mostly to himself. Roland Belisle, however, had none of Eric's reserve. Once he knew that Eric was among his best competitors, he'd turn to him after a test and ask how he'd done. Eric decided to answer and came to find Ro's questions almost appealing. And Ro would always follow Eric's answer by sharing his own grade and adding some self-deprecating comment: "I didn't think I'd done that well" or "I just guessed on those three and got two of them right." Rarely, if everyone had done badly, Ro might whisper "Eee, gads!" and hope for a curve. Ro obviously wanted to rank first, but he flashed that "we're all in this together" smile too often to breed resentment. Ro's engaging candor and humor complemented Eric's shyness, and Eric accepted Ro's questions as a recognition of his own success. So they were rivals, Eric thought, sort of like Gilly Dennis without the rocks, but their friendship grew as their competition continued.

Friday nights were a welcome escape from the Kenton pressures. There, too, Eric felt at home in a more passive role because Stobbs was still the relentless social organizer and irritant he had been since the seventh grade at Assumption, when Eric had first met him and his best friend, Mel Barnett.

The phone rang and Eric picked it up, knowing the routine. "Hello."

"Hey, Eric, doin' anythin' tonight?" Stobbs began almost in mid-idea.

"I don't know. I thought I'd probably just watch TV or read."

"Aw, c'mon, what good's that shit? Let's do somethin'. Ya wanna do somethin'? Ya know ya want to, Eric."

"Actually, I don't know that."

"Aw, c'mon, Eric."

"Well, what should we do?"

"I dunno. Whadda *you* wanna do?"

"Barney, you called me, so don't you have any ideas?"

"Not really. Tell ya what, I'll call Mel and maybe Billy McKenna—you know him, from Lowell High—and see what *they* wanna do. Call ya back." Click.

Eric imagined the same conversation repeated with Mel and Billy until, worn down by Stobbsie's relentless blather and perpetual lack of plans, Mel might finally decree, "OK. We're going bowling! Tell Eric to meet us at the Wannalancit Lanes at seven thirty." Bang. So they'd arrange their rides and bowl. Maybe Stobbs would even drag McKenna or some other reluctant friend along. Bowling, a movie (maybe a drive-in on a late spring or summer night), or just pizza and cokes pretty much marked the range of their social lives for several years in Lowell, almost always at Stobbs's insistence. *Can't this guy ever be alone?* Eric wondered. Well, they usually had a good time once Stobbs had steamrolled over their inertia, so maybe the odd chemistry worked in its way. Just ending Stobbs's phone calls was pleasure enough on some Friday nights.

As Eric's friendship with Ro ripened, they might also get together on a weeknight or weekend. Ro liked to study with Eric before a tough test or on a subject where Eric seemed a bit sharper. They'd quiz each other and compare class notes. On a weekend, with more time, they might just talk, or Ro would play the piano and tell

Eric about the Chopin or Mozart piece he was learning. Some book they had read during Kenton's free reading time might also come up. Eric's meticulous knowledge of baseball amused and intrigued Ro as both "working class" and impressively exact, like a statistical obsession to fascinate a less mathematical mind. If Ro knew Chopin and Mozart, Eric had mastered Ted Williams and Warren Spahn.

"Do you actually memorize all those numbers?" Ro would tease.

"No need to," Eric took the bait. "Every time I see a clock or a calendar, almost any number will have some baseball meaning."

"Like what?"

"Well," Eric pointed to the wall clock in Ro's living room, "it's 4:24 p.m. right now. That was Rogers Hornsby's batting average in 19 . . . 24! Highest National League average in this century. Or it's January 30th, and no major league pitcher has won thirty games in a season since Dizzy Dean for the St. Louis Cardinals in 1934."

"Dizzy?"

"Yeah." Eric smiled. "Dean was pretty eccentric. In fact, they called his brother Daffy." Ro laughed out loud. "And once, when Dean had a head X-ray after an injury, the newspaper headline read 'Dean's X-ray Shows Nothing.' Even Dean liked the joke."

Ro just shook his head at Eric's endless stock of baseball trivia. "So how did this guy win thirty games if he was so dumb?"

"Well, Ro," Eric grew pontifical, "there *are* different kinds of intelligence, you know."

They both laughed, and Ro conceded that some of his favorite composers also led pretty eccentric lives—lovers, phobias, exotic pets—so maybe athletes named Dizzy and Daffy weren't so weird after all.

Eric's friendship with Ro seemed a bit too high-toned for Stobbs and Barnett, and that tension annoyed Eric sometimes, as when Stobbs would make some crack about "Belisle and the beautiful people." Mel was not as explicit, but as a baseball nut like Eric he also found Ro's "culture" a bit much sometimes. Eric decided early on at Kenton that the chemistry among his very different friends would never quite work, so he kept his separate loyalties and made excuses on the rare Friday nights when *both* friends might want to see him. Ro got the point almost immediately and settled for a nodding politeness with Stobbs and Barnett. He knew that Eric, Mel, and Barney were all Irish kids from Assumption and not likely to care much about Ro's French culture and bilingual ability—or his classical musical training—though Eric's curiosity about these new realms was a nice surprise to Ro. And then there was Ro's ease with girls. *That* intimidated pretty much everyone in Eric's circle of friends. Here was a high school guy—their age!—who seemed to understand worlds that Eric knew nothing about and had therefore carefully avoided. With girls, Ro looked about ten years older than them all. Eric smiled to think that he and Ro were academic rivals, for once he looked beyond the little world of courses and class assignments, Ro had a sophistication that Eric could not approach. Still, Ro seemed curiously interested in Eric and impressed by his abilities and even by his boyish baseball mania, as if Ro might find something of value there, too. Or was Ro just looking for ways to make this quiet guy his friend? If so, Eric liked him all the more for it. So in '60 Eric fed Ro the details of Ted Williams's final milestones and got lyrical on Mazeroski's Yankee-killing homer. In '61 they talked about Maris and Mantle and their race toward sixty home runs.

"He's getting hideously close, isn't he?" Ro said one September day after Maris had slammed #57.

"Yeah," Eric agreed, "but this year the American League is playing eight more games than Ruth did in 1927."

"I hadn't noticed," Ro answered dryly.

"Not only that," Eric charged ahead with a smile, "but Maris already has more at bats than Ruth did in '27. That year Ruth walked 137 times and hit sixty homers in 540 at bats. That's exactly one homer in every nine chances. But Maris will probably have close to six hundred at bats and probably won't walk even a hundred times."

"No kidding, Eric," Ro yawned. "So why don't they walk Maris as often as they did Ruth?"

"Ro," Eric feigned exasperation at such an elementary question, "Mantle's been hitting behind Maris for most of the season. You don't walk Maris to face Mantle because he homers even more often—percentage-wise—and has a much higher batting average than Maris."

"Of course, how stupid of me," Ro conceded.

"That's OK. It happens." They both laughed.

"Now, as you know," Eric went on, sure that Ro did not know, "Gehrig hit behind Ruth, but he didn't homer at Ruth's *rate*, so naturally pitchers might prefer to take their chances with *him* sometimes." By now Ro had slumped back in his lunchroom chair as if overwhelmed by Eric's scholarship.

"Have you got all that?" Eric asked.

"I think so," Ro said with concern, "but can we go over it again before the test?"

"I'm always available," Eric assured him with upturned hands.

When Eric wasn't scanning his baseball encyclopedia or studying with or without Ro, he took to writing thoughts in a private notebook. Words just came to him sometimes, or random phrases whose sounds he fashioned into private meanings, like those word games on drives to Plum Island. "Slight blight of white flight . . . penned in and pinned down . . . elucidating elocution . . . Stobbs's blobs . . . weird cries of winged warblers." Or he would jot down little scenes from his days and play with the best titles for them. "Malone Spends Time Alone" became simply "Malone Alone," or "Phony Maloney, Full of Baloney." He'd cross out and revise endlessly and save these absurdities that rolled around in his mind searching for meanings. And sometimes a carefully revised image or phrase would find its way into an English essay assignment for Kenton, as if it had never had a secret prior life in his notebook.

III

All of Eric's years had been filled with Catholic ceremonies and sacramental rituals and with the poetry of holy imagery repeated until monotony made him wonder what an exciting new heresy might feel like. Or at least why God's love seemed so abstract and otherworldly. When aged Pope John XXIII, seemingly out of nowhere, called the Second Vatican Council to order in Rome, Eric had thoughts of changes that might make the church feel more like the early days of

Christianity as he imagined them. Catholics and Protestants might start talking to each other about something other than the cost of living. This Pope even seemed open to dialogue with non-Christians and with Communists also. Maybe priests could marry, and Catholic ornateness might be trimmed a little, as if the church could change without losing its identity. Talk was that the all-Latin liturgy might be replaced with modern languages so that people everywhere could understand what was going on at mass. The Brothers cautioned against expecting too much, but they also hoped for some updating of their ancient church.

One day in sophomore religion class, Brother Stanley decided to have an open forum about Vatican II. The normally structured syllabus about Catholic doctrine and church history would pause so that students could voice their thoughts about the historic ecumenical council in Rome. They'd been assigned to watch any news report on the council and to read an explanatory article by a leading church historian, a Jesuit theologian named Ralstenburger who taught at Notre Dame University and was now on the scene at the Vatican. "All right, gentlemen. Before I open this class to your questions and comments," Brother Stanley began, "let's set up a few ground rules. We want to respect everyone's opinion and to listen to all comments, even if we disagree. As far as possible, let's also try to keep Catholic teaching in mind as we talk about possible changes in the church. Remember Ralstenburger's article. And gentlemen, no long speeches, please. Keep questions brief and comments, I'd say, within a couple of minutes, so we can hear from as many of you as possible."

Eric glanced around the room at his classmates. The guys were attentive because such a free discussion was hardly typical, especially in religion class. What would certain guys say? How candid would Brother let the conversation get? Of course, not everyone cared very much about a meeting of bishops in Rome. Jim Stankowski was already hoping to get some homework done by screening himself behind Marshall Reardon. Eddie Shanahan had made clear in some hallway comments that he thought practically everything in the church needed changing. "All this mind control is a bunch of crap," he had said to Eric and Ro after religion class a week earlier.

"Well, maybe some of it is overdone," Ro had cautiously agreed.

Just then, Gellhorn marched by solemnly with hands folded as if in a papal procession, and laughter followed him down the hallway until he ceremoniously disappeared into the men's room while loudly intoning "Kyrie eleison."

"There's another comment," Eric joked to Ro.

"Yeah. Gellhorn has a theology all his own."

So what would the guys say in class?

"All right," Brother Stanley scanned the room, "who has the first comment or question?" After perhaps ten seconds of silence, Thomas Wilson raised his hand. "Yes, Mr. Wilson."

"Well, I'm still trying to figure out why the Pope called this council. The church seemed all right to me without raising all these questions." Brother Stanley shushed some background chatter and a couple of skeptical groans at Wilson's conservatism.

"Who can answer Thomas?" Shanahan and Stan Jenson raised their hands together, and Brother decided on Jenson. *No wonder,* Eric thought.

"The church hasn't had a council in about ninety years, so it's a good idea to examine itself. Besides, times have changed with Communism and new technology and all. The bishops need to decide how to handle these things." Shanahan raised his hand again.

"Yes, Mr. Shanahan," Brother Stanley said slowly.

"I think there's so much wrong *inside* the church that the Pope needs to get on with reforming that rather than worrying too much about the rest of the world. If the church doesn't change, I don't see how it can get governments and countries to take it seriously."

"Mr. Shanahan, those are pretty broad statements," Brother Stanley responded. "You should name a few specific changes you think the church needs, and then we'll let others comment."

"Yes. I think the church should let priests marry so that priests and bishops can understand how family life is for most people. I also think that the Vatican has too much power. Church policies should come more from members instead of from Rome."

"A more democratic system?" Brother Stanley suggested.

"Yes."

"Who wants to comment on Mr. Shanahan's ideas?"

Several hands went up. "Mr. Mailer."

"I agree about priests marrying, but the church won't do it because Jesus and the apostles weren't married. The church believes that celibacy is morally better and that it lets the clergy focus on the needs of all their people rather than on their own families. I can see that, but I also think it stops them from understanding family problems." Several guys mumbled their approval as Brother Stanley looked for another hand. "John Harrison."

"The Vatican has power because the Pope succeeds St. Peter. Jesus gave Peter the keys to the kingdom of heaven, one of the gospels says, so the Pope is supposed to have authority. It's not like a democracy because divine truth is involved. You don't take votes on that. So the council should let many voices be heard, but final authority has to stay in Rome." Shanahan swayed his hand energetically, but Brother Stanley waved him off for now to hear from others. "Mr. Buhl."

"One way for the church to get updated would be to put away all those robes and vestments and just wear something normal so they don't look so medieval." Brother Stanley made an offended face. "Oh, not you, Brother. You look great." Buhl smiled and the class laughed.

"Thank you," Brother said with restored dignity. "So what about Peter's point? Do the clothes really matter? Is the council about a new dress code?" Several guys laughed, but Brother held to the question. Then Eric raised his hand.

"Mr. Malone."

"I realize that the church vestments are all symbolic of church authority, and some people really like all that ceremony, but many just think it's confusing and archaic. When you combine that with the Latin mass that most people don't understand, the church can seem pretty remote. I'd like to hear the mass in English and have simpler vestments that people could relate to better."

"What about that, anybody?" Brother Stanley prompted. Montgomery raised his hand. "Richard."

"I agree mostly with Eric, but I think it's hard for the church to let go of all that tradition. Besides, it means a lot more in Europe and other places than it does here. Maybe the bishops could have choices for different parts of the world so that the mass would have the same content but be more in touch with different regions." Several heads nodded. When no more hands went up, Brother Stanley asked another question: "Do you think some of these changes will happen?" Shanahan's hand shot up again, so this time Brother called on him.

"A few things may change. I mean, the Pope called the council, so he must be thinking about some church reforms, but another Pope might not like certain changes and then the church is back to square one. More authority for the bishops and even for lay people would be a real change. Otherwise, Rome just goes back to being Rome." Brother cleared his throat uncomfortably while several guys smiled at Shanahan's boldness.

"Well," Brother said at last, seeing that the bell was about to ring, "I wouldn't expect Rome to stop being Rome, and sometimes we certainly benefit from Rome standing firm, but these have been very interesting thoughts. Let's continue this discussion tomorrow. Everyone should be thinking about a paper topic related to the Vatican Council. Have a good lunch," and he waved his hand to dismiss the class as the bell rang. While guys filed into the hallway and toward the lunch room, Ro pulled up beside Eric.

"Pretty interesting class," he said.

"Yeah. It's nice to get away from the syllabus once in a while."

"What do you *really* think about this council anyway?"

"It could be exciting if real changes happen. I wonder what we'll think of it twenty years from now. Will it be a new beginning or just a big letdown?"

"Good question," Ro answered in his best Stanley monotone.

"Are you mocking me, Belisle?" Eric said stiffly, and they both broke into laughter.

IV

In October of Eric's sophomore year, Brother Daniel announced a meeting to restart the Kenton Academy Debating Team. A few meetings the year before had come to nothing. Eric and Ro attended the meeting, along with several freshmen and a couple of juniors and seniors. Eric knew little about organized debating, but he thought that the challenge of speaking and thinking on his feet would be good, and he had been disappointed in last year's false start. Brother Daniel explained the format of debates and mentioned some tournaments, Catholic and public, in the area. High schools all over the country would debate one national topic for the whole school year, and debaters would need to keep researching that topic to come up with fresh information. Sort of like an ongoing research paper, Eric thought, where they would really become expert on a subject. If the topic was boring, that could be deadly, but if they kept uncovering new ideas and information about it, they could stay interested.

A few meetings later, Ro had decided to give more time to *The Bulletin,* the school's newspaper, but Eric continued. Soon he met senior Jack Webber and they became Affirmative team partners. Two sharp freshmen emerged as the leading Negative speakers, Barry DeSoto and Daniel O'Doul. One nice thing about a new or reviving club was that no one stood in their way. No waiting in line. The downside, Eric realized, was that none of them knew what they were doing at first. Brother Daniel helped them to decide how to use the research they began to accumulate and how to structure arguments, and by late in the first semester after many practice debates, they had attended three small tournaments and done pretty well.

Eric discovered that he could analyze ideas quickly and even eloquently at times. Delivering the prepared First Affirmative speech to start debates also allowed him to work on phrasing, timing, and eye contact with the audience. Starting with complete speech texts, Eric quickly progressed to speaking from an outline so that his phrasing could be more varied while staying close to his subject. Jack Webber, a senior who thought that even one year of debating would be worth it, anchored the team as the Second Affirmative speaker. During debates, he whispered suggestions to Eric about cross-examination questions to ask and quotations to cite. They built a file card collection of quotations and soon knew many of them by memory. Brother Daniel had his four debaters practice specific arguments with each other, and he gave them closely reasoned critiques.

Having just four "varsity" debaters right away meant that everyone got all of Brother's attention and also had plenty of time to help each other. Their progress was rapid. By the spring they had won their first debate tournament and received a couple of speaker awards. "He who asserts must prove" became Danny O'Doul's catch phrase for the Negative team. "Is that logical?" or "Does that apply to our plan?" Jack Webber would often ask Negative teams. Such tactics were good as long as they had specific references in each debate and did not become mere slogans too easily ridiculed.

Coaches from all the teams in a tournament served as judges, and as months passed, the same judge would hear some debaters several times. Eric quickly realized, especially with the prepared First Affirmative speech, that a judge should never hear *exactly* what he had heard before. The Affirmative plan must "evolve" and the evidence to support it must get subtler and, if possible, more and more current. The pressure was on before each new tournament to mix the familiar with the new in creative ways and to think quickly in responding to opponents' arguments.

Eric also discovered that simply *sounding good*—as if you always understood exactly what you meant even when you didn't quite— scored points with judges. He came to like articulate delivery and original refutations better than the research grind. O'Doul, on the other hand, became a voluminous researcher with a less polished, more scrappy delivery, an irrepressible arguer. And what the Negative team found in books and articles, the Affirmative team might find a way to use, and vice versa. These four debaters and their nurturing, candid coach soon became good friends based on their skills and teamwork. And month by month, as successes multiplied, Kenton Academy began to notice its first debaters.

Writing for *The Bulletin*, Ro sometimes covered debate tournament results, but he also wrote book and film reviews and reported on Kenton's weekly Saturday night dances. Sometimes he would do a feature on Kenton Hall, the guys' sister school with many girls they'd known from grammar school. Stobbs and Barnett still called Eric on some Friday nights, but Ro seemed more interested now in other friends and in the dances and dating that all these Catholic parents gradually permitted their teenagers. Eric's mental world and Ro's social one diverged more and more, and in the classroom Eric was usually a close second to Ro. A few classes were not even close, such as French, where Ro excelled. In English, both did well, but Eric's writing was more analytical and essay oriented, while Ro had a creative flare and got wider visibility in *The Bulletin*. Math and science might go either way, though Eric's analytical abilities sometimes gave him an edge in these subjects. And Eric loved history as well, especially if it featured world leaders—and great speech makers—like Churchill and FDR. Ro knew more about French and other European history and enjoyed laughing at the pageantry of upper-class life and at the absurd excesses of the various kings of France, not to mention the ego of Napoleon.

Eric and Ro still talked at school but saw less of each other outside. Debate tournaments on Saturdays sometimes took Eric's time. And then, when Ro did suggest that maybe they could study before the next science or history test, nothing might come of it. On those days, Eric withdrew into himself and let the demands of his schoolwork rule him. He slowly understood that sometimes an offer from Ro was more an expression of good feelings than a promise. Gregarious Ro seemed quickly caught up in each new school event. Or maybe Eric was just too literal about what friends said and meant and too reluctant to reach out himself. His own emotions confused him sometimes. Slowly he learned to put Ro's suggestions in a special category at the opposite extreme from Stobbs's Friday night lobbying to "do somethin'."

V

In his freestyle notebook, Eric often wrote imaginary conversations to resolve unspoken issues with friends or to make relationships clearer. Venting some anger in a strident verse also eased his darker moods. A day later, it often seemed ridiculous and eventually he'd throw most of it away. Occasionally he'd touch on the safer edges of these subjects with Dad, who liked to call Eric down from his room for a study break and a sandwich to watch the evening news.

"Eric, your sandwich is ready."

"OK, Dad." Eric put out the light at his desk and tapped the stairway railing on his way down.

"What's on the news?" Eric glanced at the TV.

"More trouble in the Middle East, and the police in Alabama have been using fire hoses and dogs on some Negro demonstrators."

"Why?"

"Crowd control, they say, but those people are not armed. All they want to do is vote and end the segregation in hotels and restaurants. Kennedy and some advisors are discussing whether to send in federal troops to quiet the trouble."

"I suppose the local police don't want that."

"No, and neither does the governor. He seems to think segregation can go on forever. I guess the whites down there support him. Some of those people are still fighting the Civil War." Eric ate his sandwich and sipped a glass of milk. Dad had put several cherries on his plate, which Eric savored. They watched a few more news reports and a bunch of commercials.

"So how are things going in French? You were worried about that test last week, right?"

"The test actually turned out OK. I think maybe I'll get a B. We haven't gotten it back yet. The trouble is that Brother Victor doesn't like repeating explanations of grammatical points once he's taught them."

"With a name like that, I don't see how he can be so inconsiderate," Dad joked.

"I know it's hard to believe, Dad, but it's true. Of course, sometimes Ro will ask a complicated grammar question, and Brother will fill the blackboard explaining some points that no one cares about except Ro."

"But that doesn't help the rest of you understand what you need for the test, does it?"

"No," Eric smiled, "but it keeps Brother Victor interested and gets us through quite a bit of class time." Dad shook his head and looked back at the news. After a minute, he asked, "How are things with Stobbs and Barnett?"

"Oh, the usual. Except that Mel says he's trying to write a novel but won't let anyone see it."

"Well, a novel! That's pretty ambitious. Any idea what it's about?"

"Probably about dealing with Stobbs." They both laughed.

"Do you write any creative assignments for class?"

"Very seldom. Mostly we do essays. Once in a while we have to write a poem in response to a poem or maybe some dialogue as an extension of a scene in a play that we're reading. But essays are the main thing."

"Well, that makes sense. A good essay is what you'll need to write later on."

"Yeah, but creative writing is fun sometimes. It's actually a lot harder to do than it seems, at least to do anything good." They both thought about that for a while and watched more news.

"How are those dances going on Saturday nights?" Dad finally asked in a neutral tone.

"Oh, OK."

"Do many Kenton Hall girls show up?"

"I guess so. I spend most of my time with the other coat checkers upstairs, so I don't see much of the dancing."

After a pause Dad said, "Well, that doesn't sound like much fun. You might enjoy it more on the dance floor, don't you think?"

"Oh, I like just talking with different guys instead."

Dad didn't answer. "How's the sandwich?"

"It's good. What kind of cheese is this?"

"Mozzarella. A little different, isn't it?"

"Yeah. I like it." Eric finished his sandwich and ate the five cherries slowly, one by one. He swallowed the fruit and rolled each cherry pit around on his teeth. He remembered Tom Barnes in the cherry tree spitting pits at him so fast that he sometimes had to block them with one hand and hold onto a branch with another. What would happen now if he fired a pit across the room at Dad? He decided not to find out.

"Great cherries," he said when the last one was gone.

"Yes, I like them, especially cold," Dad answered. He clicked off the news and looked some more at the *Star*. An article caught his eye and he scanned through it quickly.

"Quite an event going on in Rome, isn't it?" he asked Eric.

"Yes. I hope they consider lots of changes for the church. You don't often hear from all the bishops at one time like this."

"That's true," Dad agreed. "Of course, some church policies could be revised, but nothing essential can change." Eric looked at his father for a moment as Dad kept reading over the Vatican article. He thought about how to answer.

"I suppose deciding what's essential is a key point in making any changes. Maybe different bishops have different ideas about that."

"Well, I doubt that, Eric. They all know what the fundamental doctrines are, so they are likely to reinforce those."

"I suppose so," Eric said neutrally. This wasn't a subject to pursue. "Well, I guess I'll get back upstairs. Still have some reading to do. Thanks for the sandwich."

"Sure. Now don't stay up too late studying. You want to be wide awake in the morning."

"OK," Eric answered as he climbed back up to his room. He closed the door and turned on the reading light by his bed, then stacked *Great Expectations*, his history text, and the Latin book on the blanket beside him. Sometimes after a sandwich with Dad, he'd get a second wind and read until one a.m. or later. Whenever Mom knocked on his door and told him to sleep now and leave any more homework until tomorrow, he always obeyed, though stopping a late-night rush of energy was hard to do. Studying came in waves for Eric, and he liked to let each wave break when it wanted. Most Friday nights he was ready to stop, but even then a good non-school novel or biography might be more interesting than another bowling and pizza night with Stobbs and company. Eric didn't really like pizza anyway, though he was learning more about different kinds of cheeses and liked trying new ones. Some were just bland while others smelled unbelievably bad. He leaned on his left side toward the reading lamp and got through two more chapters of Dickens before sleep finally became too tempting. He put the novel back onto his stack and then lowered all the books slowly to the floor with a stiff left wrist. Pulling the blanket up under his chin, he let his head sink slowly into the pillow.

V I

By early in his junior year, Eric knew the rhythms of Kenton life well. On one October morning, Dad left him off at the Kenton front sidewalk. Usually Eric walked through the ground floor door and up the stairs to his homeroom. Today he moved slowly up the imposing stone steps—all twenty-one of them—that led to the second-floor entrance. At the top he looked down to Thorndike Street and across the South Common. To the left, the old brick church thrust itself toward the sky from the hill where John Eliot had built the first chapel for Indians and established the Christian Indian village of Wamesit over four hundred years before. Jack Webber had pointed out the historic marker to him and said that Eric would read more about Eliot in *The Scarlet Letter* in junior English. Eric scanned the Common and the rear facade of St. Peter's Cathedral, a monumental Catholic church there for eighty years or more. Kenton's own fortress of grey stone had housed prisoners for decades before the Academy took over. So much history lingered in one little patch of Lowell real estate. Mostly the pressures and pleasures of high school life caused everyone to ignore all these old ghosts on the land, if they had even heard of them.

Today, Eric felt oddly aware of them all, as if he should now walk into Kenton and make some history of his own. Most guys would think him weird or arrogant to spin such thoughts. It's only high school, they'd tell him. Teenage identities seemed eternal until they were suddenly gone. Then some of the biggest jerks would probably end up the most successful. "Gellhorn for Governor"—Eric could see it now. The class clown would rise to the top, and where would Eric be? Teaching somewhere and hoping that the comedian governor believed in state aid for schools and universities. Eric *could* imagine himself as governor or even, in his best fantasies, as president, but shaking all those hands and raising all that money to get elected? No. Gellhorn would do all that much better than Eric could. He'd be a better advisor than an office holder. Maybe Secretary of State like Dean Rusk, or even better, Ted Sorenson, speech writer for the president. Let someone else be Kennedy. Ro would be perfect. Yes, Eric could be Ro's idea man. Let his friend do all that social stuff while Eric crafted policies and eloquent speeches. Maybe Ro would appoint him ambassador to the UN. He could be Ro's Adlai Stevenson, telling off the Russians in the best English the Security Council had ever heard. But much would be lost in translation.

He heard a bell ring inside and turned quickly past the wrought-iron pillars toward the front door. Down the hallway to the left he hurried among students heading in all directions at once. The black and white stone designs along the floors of each hall looked like an abstract mosaic. Three doors down on the right he slipped into his homeroom and found his usual "center of the room" seat. He could never hide at the edges of a Kenton classroom, though no one ever hid anywhere at Kenton for long. Perhaps that was why the dungeon legend endured.

Deep in the bowels of the old prison, there had to be some undiscovered place to hide. Or were those mysterious caverns reserved for eternal detentions? JUG was the school's word for it, or "Justice Under God."

Meanwhile, back above ground, Eric would have moody old Brother Victor for both French and religion as a junior. He'd also have Brother Robertus for a third straight year of Latin. Each year, Brother's cigarette cough sounded a little worse. He looked almost feeble on some days. Yet just when guys were thinking that Robertus had lost his edge, he'd fire off one of those gems that let everyone know he was still in charge.

"Moran, are you sure you don't spell your name with two o's? We've been over that declension enough times to raise Cicero from the dead."

"Great Caesar's ghost, Donovan! Have you learned anything this semester?"

Everyone liked Robertus, and a guy felt overlooked if he hadn't been insulted by him a few times. With his better students, Robertus had to get a little more creative. When Eric botched a translation one Monday morning after winning a debate trophy on Saturday, Robertus smiled. "Looks like a case of debater's hangover, Malone. Take two rebuttals and call me in the morning." Eric smiled, and everyone laughed at the novelty of Eric's lapse and Robertus's backhanded compliment.

Driver Training was another sure place for putdowns. After one frustrating road session with Eric, Stobbs, and Gellhorn, Mr. Charles Lavallette, a history teacher who doubled as the driving instructor, finally had Eric pull over to the curb. Lavallette took several deep breaths in silence. "They don't pay me enough to do this," he finally observed while his students exchanged quick smiles but dared not laugh. Then he looked at Eric and said almost philosophically, "Malone, in this country we drive on the *righthand* side of the road." Now everyone laughed a little, and the tension passed.

During the last part of each lunch period, about twenty smokers headed to the school yard behind the small chem lab building and lit up. Kenton didn't want students to smoke, but since maybe a third of the faculty did, even to the point of yellow stains on the fingers of Brother Robertus, they could hardly ban it completely. Soon a little pillar of smoke rose behind the lab, as if from a failed chemistry experiment, and it lingered until the wind blew it away and the smokers, reeking of nicotine, rejoined their classes.

By mid-October of '61, the Yankees had crushed the Reds in the Series, as if to avenge the Pirates' "stolen" championship of the year before, and Red Sox fans faced the usual winter of vague yearnings for that "next year" that had finally come to Brooklyn in 1955. Two years later the Dodgers were off to LA. Would the Sox move to Bolivia or Timbuktu if they ever actually won the World Series, or would the world just quietly end because it had seen everything?

In the same month, Eric and Danny were chosen captain and assistant captain of the debate team, and several new sophomores and freshmen had come to the opening meeting. Success was starting to draw a crowd. Brother Daniel promised that they'd enter more tournaments this year and even have a junior varsity team if students showed enough interest. The next week, Ro became associate editor of *The Bulletin*. He'd be editor-in-chief as a senior, and Will Blanchford, now the starting quarterback, looked like he'd fill the next two football seasons with his heroics and put his square-jawed face and classic passing form all over the paper's sports pages. Nor could Eric wait for the debate season to see how good they could be. He'd seen Jack handle evidence and cut to the core of opponents' arguments last year, and he felt ready to do that himself now. The class of '63 was already feeling its power in the fall of '61. They were primed to make their two-year run toward colleges and universities where they would have to start all over again. Even Stobbs with the golf team and Gellhorn, who had started attending student government meetings for no apparent reason, seemed ready to cut their little slices of school history.

In a practice debate against DeSoto and O'Doul on the Thursday before the season's first tournament, Eric and his new sophomore partner, Jon Lewellyn, had found their groove. Not even O'Doul's rapid-fire quotations and DeSoto's precise little questions could overwhelm the clarity of their connections. As the anchors of the Affirmative and Negative teams, Eric and Danny followed their spirited cross-examinations of each other with final rebuttals that left Jon and Barry smiling in amazement. Even Brother Daniel, busily writing notes through most of the debate, finally rested his pen and just listened.

When Eric wove a final overview of the whole debate into the last ninety seconds of his rebuttal to end the contest, Brother Daniel leaned forward and took it all in. At the end he looked at all four debaters and shook his head slightly.

"Gentlemen, you were all excellent, and Danny and Eric, you have never been better. Think like that on Saturday and no one will be able to stay with either of you." Danny and Eric, who always felt a slight tension between them as teammates and competitors, traded smiles and a quick handshake. What a season this would be!

It was quarter to five when they'd finished, and Eric would normally call Dad for a ride home. This time he called to say he would walk.

"Are you sure?" Dad asked, a bit surprised. "I can be there in fifteen minutes."

"No, I just had my best debate ever and I'd like to think about it on the way home."

"Well, congratulations! I understand. See you at supper, kid."

Eric walked alone down the Kenton stairway and looked all around. From a clear sky, the descending sun struck the Eliot Presbyterian Church and the row of homes along Summer Street, giving off a reddish glow that Eric had not noticed before. The light shifted slowly as he crossed the South Common and heard children shouting in the tenement yards. Among the little markets of Appleton and Church Streets, the rushing traffic cut and beeped suddenly, keeping pedestrians alert. And then, beyond the Concord River, he could feel the sun at his back as he passed Dad's closed-up office and climbed to Andover Street beyond Nesmith Street and the Christian Science Church. The mansion row looked strangely inviting today, like some wild future that rushed his heels along the sidewalk and finally down Berenger Street to the house that *was* his dad's future, Eric suddenly realized. He bounded up the front brick steps and through the unlocked door toward the savory aroma of a sliced ham and raisin sauce supper that waited for him.

WIDER THAN A MILE

I

From Highland Street at the far edge of the South Common left of St. Peter's Cathedral, Eric looked back at the whole face of Kenton Academy. Twin towers of dark granite stood guard on either side of the central staircase that led past the first landing and up to the top porch. There, a wrought-iron canopy of four columns framed the front entrance. Directly above, atop the central eave, a granite cross projected a monumental Christianity impervious to weather and time. On either side, the adjacent buildings of cream-colored stone, with granite inlays at each corner, softened the darker central fortress. The left building housed the Xaverian community of celibate men, and the right contained many of Kenton's classrooms. Eric thought of all the effort behind those lighter stones to emulate the heavy symbol above them. Fallible teachers and insecure students worked under the weighty towers, two stone sentinels guarding the immutable mounted cross. Sometimes the backlight of an approaching sunset thrust the granite fortress into bolder relief, and the whole seemed to Eric like an altar of endless striving. Who could live up to it? Who was not stronger for trying?

Beyond the Kenton facade was the busy network of classrooms and offices and the stunted basketball court pressed against the stage in a hybrid gym-theater-assembly hall. The rear exits of all three buildings opened to a paved courtyard between the chem lab and the chapel, two stone boxes like architectural afterthoughts. At lunch and for sports practices, the Kenton guys spread across the old prison yard that sloped downward and finally rose again toward the far brick wall adjacent to the Lowell-Boston railroad tracks.

Old jailhouse, present school, and virtual church, Kenton never rested, nor gave its charges rest. On Monday morning it would all start again, but on this Friday with no debate tournament tomorrow, Eric gladly turned away and walked home.

11

Beyond impressions of individual Xaverian Brothers, Kenton guys slowly gained an awareness of this whole group of Catholic taskmasters who demanded much, conceded nothing, and gave everything. They could impress, frustrate, anger, and inspire, sometimes all in an hour. On the home turf of their academic subjects, they were very good, Eric thought, and occasionally brilliant. Not creative especially, they were relentless and unavoidably *there*. Some were scholars more than teachers, but most were both. More than a few were also exuberant cheerleaders, who joked, shouted, and mimed their way to results. They knew all the Kenton boys too well and set expectations accordingly. Yet beneath their common black robes and shared theology, their individuality was refreshing, if occasionally unnerving. Eccentricities had not been educated or spiritualized away, just set in a deeper context, like the bedrock beneath a free-flowing river. And like all teachers on the daily firing line, they were objects of respect, curiosity, and caricature. Brother Randall James, for example ("Randy Jim" to the *cognoscenti*), wore thick glasses and a hearing aid and seemed to be communicating geometry theorems by remote control. "Please again" was his calling card for all the questions he could not hear. "Please again" the guys would say to each other at lunch after some shouted insult.

"You're an idiot, Gellhorn."

"Please again," Gellhorn pleaded softly, blinking and cupping his ear.

Eric liked Randy Jim's geometry and also the orderliness of algebra with its Kenton master, Brother Phineas. "Brother Pythagoras,"

Eric called him, but the nickname never caught on. During one Algebra II class, as Phineas was pursuing the logic of some formula in his low-pitched monotone and jotting down blackboard equations, the tall, round-shouldered principal, Brother James Gerald, came to the door and asked to speak to the class. Phineas nodded, stopped in mid-sentence, left a blackboard equation incomplete, and stepped into the hallway. Three minutes later, after the principal had finished his explanation of some upcoming Kenton event, Phineas returned and continued exactly in mid-sentence and mid-equation, as if a "play" button had ended a "pause" command. Only with the trace of a smile at the end of the class did he ever acknowledge the joke. Eric thrived in Algebra II with Kenton's Pythagoras, whose whole existence seemed to embody mathematical order.

In junior year physics, and again in senior trig and advanced algebra, unflappable Brother Willard ruled. More animated than Phineas, he regarded no concept as difficult. "Well obviously, gentlemen, we have here an example of the Second Law of Thermodynamics."

"Ob-vi-ous-ly," Ro mouthed across the room to Eric, who shrugged self-evident shoulders.

Willard was perplexed that ideas in his physics or trig classes could ever confuse anyone, and he granted answers to questions only as perfunctory little reviews of what everyone knew, not as explanations of complex abstractions. When several hands went up one day seeking help with a test question that nearly everyone had missed, Willard scanned the class in amazement.

"Gentlemen, if you don't understand *that*, you don't understand physics. Let's move on, shall we?" And Willard moved on, his befuddled students in tow. By contrast, Brother Leonard's elegant clarity marked his class discussions of poets and novelists, and Brother Robertus's Latin class insults left no trace of ambiguity.

A few of the Xaverians were outright performers, so odd and theatrical that guys wondered how they had ended up in a religious order, and whether they would stay there. Brother Petrarch, for instance, was the absentminded, fun-loving chemistry teacher. He improvised experiments to illustrate concepts that no one had quite understood from his circular explanations. His quick, out-of-context laughs over unplanned lab results made Eric wonder why Petrarch was not teaching theater or gym instead of chemistry. After one particularly foul-smelling lab product, Petrarch had carefully removed the offending container from the chem lab and into the fresh air of the courtyard. An hour later, eleven pigeons lay dead on the ground near the sulfurous concoction. No explanation was ever given, and the deceased were quickly disposed of before the next morning's classes.

The most remarkable Xaverian, however, was Brother Orlando, the "Jackie Gleason" of the faculty. Loud, physical, and nimble despite his girth, Orlando might surprise students from behind with a booming, "Howdy, partners." Or he could burst into his classroom singing some popular song with his own special lyrics. "Because I'm mine, I walk the line" or "I don't know why I love me like I do. I don't know why, I just do" were sure to get students' attention. Orlando could be "in your face" as well, like Gloria Swanson in *Sunset Boulevard* ready for her close-up. Brother Orlando found a perfect outlet for his bursts of choreography in the annual Kenton Academy Vaudeville Revue, a fund-raiser designed to make students, and especially the graduating seniors, look as ridiculous as possible while showcasing the legitimate singers and musicians and letting the class clowns loose as vaudevillian end men in blackface. The show took place each February at the Lowell Memorial Auditorium and drew an audience of hundreds, yet Orlando seemed to be in perpetual rehearsal. His English classes often resounded with the teacher as Walt Whitman or Lady Macbeth. For some students, Orlando's antics could be intimidating, especially when his mood was more angry than festive. How Orlando had chosen the disciplined order of Xaverian Brothers—and stayed with them—was a mystery; yet Eric supposed that it took all kinds, even in the deep core of Catholicism, and that Orlando too must have his subtler side, though students had never seen it.

Within the order and oddities of the Xaverian regimen, Eric competed and grew and struggled occasionally; he succeeded mostly but always felt the pressure. For Ro, success looked easier, even if it really wasn't. His self-confidence and broad humor lit up whatever he did, and he did nearly everything at Kenton Academy except play sports and debate. Even those events he covered for *The Bulletin*, where he became the leading reporter with a graceful, humorous style. In class, Eric excelled in physics and the math courses and was good in English, though still more plodding as a writer than Ro. Eric also liked thinking about the issues of history and religion classes. The tensions between Christian ideals and church politics, past and present, intrigued him. Why was ornate Catholicism so different from the earthy simplicity of the Gospels? How did all those nefarious Renaissance popes live with themselves? And what would this new Pope Paul VI do about the Vatican Council now that John XXIII was gone? Latin and French got gradually harder for Eric, while Ro took easily to foreign languages. They still talked about courses and occasionally studied together, but as their different talents became clearer and Ro's slight but steady superiority emerged, Eric thought less about competing with Ro and more about the strange little world of high school debating, where his skills surprised even himself.

III

The debate tournaments rolled by like a Saturday football schedule (minus the cheering thousands), and the Kenton four quickly dominated the Greater Lowell Debate League and tied for the seasonal title among Boston Archdiocesan teams. Eric and Danny were often best Affirmative and Negative speakers, respectively. Soon a reporter for the *Star* came to Kenton to interview the boys and to photograph their shelf full of trophies. Analysis, evidence, logic, and summation skills came to Eric faster than ever. And while his English writing was capable but less than lyrical, on his feet about the debate topics of federal aid to private education and a stronger world role for the UN, he explicated, synthesized, and advocated until coaches and competitors alike came to know who he was and what they faced against him. He worked with Jon, as Jack had done with him. Together they picked up each other's missed details and anticipated the other's rebuttals, where debates had to be won. For Danny and Barry, the chemistry was just as good, but of a slightly different kind. Danny was the encyclopedic evidence master, and Barry tied the details together and helped the judges to see exactly how devastating Danny had just been. "Danny won the debate," Brother Daniel joked, "and Barry helped the judge to fill out the ballot."

Sensing the greater potential of his foursome, Brother Daniel sought more competitive college events and contact with the New York–area teams. How would Kenton do beyond the Greater Lowell and Boston Catholic circuits? What would those high-powered New York teams be like? And could his debaters handle two-person, switch-side debating beyond their four-person comfort zone, as they would have to at the NCFL Finals in Miami Beach? Eric liked these challenges, but he also realized that their school, with its brief debating tradition of less than two years, had an uphill climb against debating powerhouses with decades of success behind them.

"Never mind," Brother Daniel said. "Let's try it."

So in Eric's junior year they ventured out, held their own, and had some moments of glory. At the Xaverian Brothers Provincial Tournament ("for schools in New England and New York, except Brooklyn," a flyer announced precisely), they rolled to a 7–1 record and the tournament title. Danny was the Best Negative, and Eric won Second Best Affirmative behind a very affable senior from St. Joseph's High School in Shrewsbury, named Roger Preston. *Roger is more like Danny than I am,* Eric thought, *shaking hands with everybody and full of tournament trivia, but without Danny's edgy competitiveness.* Sometimes at tournaments Eric met rivals who would be good company far from debates, for a day at the beach or on one of Stobbs's bowling Fridays. Preston was one.

At two college tournaments, St. James and Thoreau, Eric had a different feeling from anywhere else. Here were two possible futures. Best speakers even won small scholarships to the host school, which raised at least the passing thought of applying there. Did Eric want a school with debating strengths? Would a debate award tip the scales? And where did he want to go to college anyway? Probably closer to home than on some adventure to a faraway state.

The St. James College Tournament in Worcester came first, and the four were hopeful. Barry and Danny did well with a 4–1 mark, but Jon and Eric struggled to 2–3 result. Eric felt that he could think with kids from these "powerhouse" schools, but their research was often more advanced. Some schools had twenty or more debaters with many researchers working for the varsity lineup. Kenton, with just the beginnings of a novice team, was far from that. But St. James College itself appealed with its tree-lined entrance and multi-level campus in the virtual center of New England. Here was a possibility.

About a month later, on their way to the Thoreau College Tournament in downtown Boston, Brother Daniel was his fidgety self at the wheel. He drove with the left hand only and endlessly changed radio stations with the other. For a religious brother and a highly analytical debate coach, Daniel had an almost teenage obsession with popular radio songs. His tension-reliever, Eric supposed, for hyper-rational debating.

"Oh, let's skip that one," he'd say with his short little laugh and work the nob again. And then he'd strike gold: "I heard this group last week and can't get enough of them." The debaters smiled to each other.

"Brother," Eric finally asked, "how come you care so much about popular songs? It's sort of . . . unusual."

"I know, ha," Daniel smiled. "I guess we're not all what we seem." When Brother finally settled for a few minutes on one radio station, Danny asked him about Thoreau College.

"Well, it's not much to look at, but a good place for media and speech studies. It's small, but excellent in communications fields."

"What about for graduate school later?" Barry asked.

"Thoreau doesn't have the large selection of liberal arts courses of a bigger school, but the recommendations you could get there would be very specific about communications skills. They also do some internships and job placement with radio and TV stations around Boston, so you might have some good job experience before going to graduate school."

Eric thought about the idea of a small speech school in Boston. Was speech really *that* important to him? Could he be a broadcaster, a reporter, a radio or TV "personality"? Not likely. Did he want to live in Boston? Maybe, though the cost and the pace of the city were far beyond his Lowell life. A tiny school building—with no campus at all—crammed between row houses was not his "postcard" of a college. More land to wander around alone at night seemed better than the honking, smoky city, except maybe on weekends when Boston offered everything. Who knew? Such choices came faster than the experience to make them.

At the tournament itself, the boys debated in old buildings with shabby-looking classrooms and dingy restrooms, but the ambiance hardly mattered. Danny and Barry went 2–1 while Eric and Jon won all three of their contests. In a final championship debate, Eric and Jon unanimously defeated the Negative team from St. Robert's High in Somerville. And then came the awards ceremony. Beyond the tournament victory, Eric and Jon were the Best Affirmative Team in the tournament, and Eric was both the Best Affirmative Speaker and the Best Debater, winning a $550 scholarship to Thoreau. The announcer added that in the three regulation debates, Eric had scored 71 of a possible 75 points. If he had ever *been* better, the *results* had not. And now a college officially wanted him. All those thoughts about this little speech school in the big city ran around his mind again.

Despite the hours of preparation, Eric still felt a little embarrassed and even mystified by his success. Where did his sudden poise come from in this specialized little realm? And why was he still oddly shy without a podium in front of him? Danny was far more gregarious and loved to argue about anything anytime. At tournaments, he quickly knew everyone. Not Eric. He debated, took whatever success came his way, and went home. His Kenton celebrity felt oddly uncomfortable. Nice, of course, but somehow too much. Since he didn't really understand his own talent, he felt strange taking credit for it. But the credit still came at school assemblies where he'd quickly nod or wave a hand to frequent announcements and applause. If debating was nerdy, he found himself king of the Kenton nerds, which was something. Even Stobbs and Gellhorn, if they teased him, shook his hand when they did. And Ro was as generous as always.

Here was Eric's domain, and Ro made sure it got plenty of press in *The Bulletin.* Ro's younger brother Pierre even joined the novice debaters and helped to carry on this new school tradition.

At the season's end in early May, Brother Daniel and his foursome flew off to the national tournament in Miami. Eric had flown just once before on that eighth-grade *Music Man* trip with his parents. He and Barry traded the window seat several times to get a view of the New York City skyline and the delicate ribbon of earth called Cape Hatteras. In the setting sun, the hotel lights of Miami Beach were the proverbial string of pearls, more glittering almost by the minute until in near darkness they lit the long beach and the lapping waves with a spectral light.

"Amazing," Barry said quietly to Eric as they took in the exotic vision together. Eric noticed the changing perspectives and hues brought on by the circular path of their plane in its slow descent.

That night on the beach by the Green Parrot Hotel where they were staying, Eric saw the weird glitter of the hotel row for miles north and south and felt the wonder of all the opulence before him. A rich few probably spent half their lives and much of their fortunes here, he imagined, while for most others it was a theme park for adults, the setting for weekend escapes or vacation fantasies to talk about years later in the tedium of their working lives. The next afternoon by the hotel pool, an absurd little episode broke the "gold coast" spell. One dogged hotel social director kept badgering patrons into a swimming race across the pool. Here was Mrs. Sanderson reincarnated and the Cobbetts Pond racing anxiety again, but now Eric could happily refuse (again and again) and no one could force him. Did they actually pay someone to harass people into "having fun," or was this just one strange character's vision of his job? A mindless employment, Eric thought, and maybe the guy would agree after hours with a drink in his hand.

The tournament debates occurred in the most elegant suites and conference rooms he could remember, but the results were anti-climactic for Kenton. Eric and Danny teamed up as the two-person entry, while Barry and Jon looked on with Brother Daniel. The format was still new for the two competitors and demanded too much shifting of gears. Besides, each was better with his own complimentary partner than with each other; their chemistry and strategic timing had not yet evolved. They went 1–2 and exited early, and Eric saw how far the four of them had come and how much they still had to do if they wanted to be a national rather than a regional power. More "endless striving" awaited if they chose it. Yet what a season it had been.

IV

When debating was finally done and before it started again, Eric had some Saturday time, and he often volunteered to check coats with some of his friends at the weekly Kenton dances. For some reason he wanted to be there, but he shied away from looking clumsy on the dance floor. No amount of debating fame had done much for him in that other world of teenage girls. A "debater" wasn't what they were looking for.

"Come on down, Eric," Stobbs called from the edge of the dance floor to the little balcony from which Eric took a quick look at the action.

"As soon as I get my footwork right," Eric smiled back. Stobbs and Barnett both waved him off with hopeless shrugs and took their partners into the next dance.

Tonight Russ Bergeron hung out with Eric in the classroom used as a coatroom along the second-floor hallway. He'd just broken up with Dana Hathaway, one of the most beautiful Kenton Hall girls Eric or Russ had ever seen, and Russ knew she was down there somewhere with a new guy, or several of them.

"Can't deal with that now," Russ admitted, looking up from the book he was barely reading.

"What happened?" Eric asked too quickly. "Never mind. None of my business," he corrected himself.

"No, that's OK. I don't mind." Eric caught the suggestion that since he was not a social "player" and no rival for Russ, he could be trusted with a romantic confidence. A deflated feeling passed quickly through him and away as he prepared to listen.

"What happened?" Russ repeated the question. "I guess I'm still trying to figure that out. She's so damn moody. I'm a little late picking her up or I don't hold her hand sometimes, and bam, I'm *insensitive*," he mimicked Dana's high-pitched whine, and Eric smiled.

"Sorry," Russ responded. "You don't need the sound effects. Anyway, the least little things are all of a sudden 'problems.' I mean, with guys you just say what's on your mind and that's that, but women . . ." He hesitated. "Women don't say what they mean, and they hear messages you aren't sending. Now she's probably down there dancing with six or eight guys just to convince herself how brutal I am."

"Shall I take a look?" Eric offered with a grin and pretended to head for the balcony.

"No," Russ almost shouted and grabbed his arm, then relented at the joke.

"So that's why you're up here, Malone, to check out the social scene from the safety of the balcony?" Eric laughed and leaned back against the classroom wall. Why was *he* here? Another good question.

"I guess I like being on the edge of it all without getting involved," he said at last.

"Yeah," Russ agreed. "Tonight I'm with you, but I'll be down there again soon enough."

"Does Dana know you're here?"

"You better believe she does," Russ insisted. "She wants me to see just how good a time she's having without me."

"And you?"

"I guess I want to *know* what I'm missing so I can torture myself a little more and give Dana exactly what she wants."

"Man, you're way over my head." Eric shrugged. "Wouldn't you rather just go bowling with Stobbs? He could start a Saturday night group." They both laughed hard at that choice: Dana Hathaway vs. Barney Stobbs.

"I guess not," Russ said quietly at last, and they laughed again.

"So what about you, Eric? I'm sure they're a lot of girls down there who'd like to be dancing with you if you'd let them."

"They'd be risking injury," Eric joked. "Do you see these feet? Size twelve. Already bigger than my dad's."

"Eric, this isn't really about shoe size, is it?"

"No," Eric acknowledged and looked at Russ for a long moment. "It's all just . . . well, what you're saying . . . so complicated. All this reading of signs and the up and down of emotions. Life's hard enough without adding all that mystery to it." Russ nodded agreement and absently fingered the pages of his book. Eric peeked at the cover.

"*Walden?*" Eric said in surprise. "Shouldn't I be reading *Walden* and you *The Count of Monte Cristo* or *Lady Chatterley's Lover?*" Russ leaned his head back against the classroom wall and laughed slowly and long at the joke.

"Very good," he said at last. "You and Thoreau avoiding women."

"Not bad company, you have to admit," Eric mocked himself. Russ laughed again. After a few quiet moments he asked an unexpected question.

"Who's your best friend at Kenton?"

"Ro," Eric gave the obvious answer, knowing that Russ already knew.

"And who's the suavest ladies' man at Kenton, Eric?"

"Ro," Eric nodded with a smile, knowing where Russ was going.

"Well, Eric, wouldn't old RoBel"—he used the elegant nickname that Ro himself liked—"be willing to set you up with someone? Talk about learning from the master."

Eric laughed at the truth of the joke. "Yeah, he'd be willing if I'd let him. When the topic comes up, I say something pompous like, 'Women are out of my realm,' and he says, 'They're only out of your realm because you keep them there.'" Russ started to answer with the obvious advice, then stopped. He looked at Eric with a mix of understanding and regret.

"I guess every guy has to figure that out for himself," he said carefully at last. "I just think some girl would be damn lucky to have you."

"Thanks," Eric said, looking away from Russ and out at the night sky.

"Just keep your grubby hands off Dana," Russ added coldly, and they both laughed again.

"Man, I'm the least of your worries," Eric assured him. A half hour later, another Saturday night dance was over.

V

As senior year debating began, Eric came to it with mixed feelings. They now had perfected their skills and ought to be better than ever, he thought, yet could they really do that well again, and if they didn't, wouldn't people think it had all been a fluke, a "one-year wonder" as poorly informed baseball fans liked to call Roger Maris?

"He's at least a two-year wonder," Eric would explain pedantically. "Maybe three." And Eric hoped that he could be the same as a senior debater.

The new debate topic about a greater world role for the UN raised interesting questions of pursuing world peace in the Cold War while preserving national sovereignty. Eric liked learning more about foreign governments, global trouble spots, and international politics. Information poured from daily headlines and the evening news, and various foreign affairs journals offered deeper analysis. Kennedy and Khrushchev epitomized perfectly the different world views of their nations, from the urbane Democrat to the crude, aggressive Communist. After the Cuban Missile Crisis of October 1962, Kennedy's confidence, and voter confidence in him, seemed to grow stronger by the month. By mid-'63 he had negotiated the first nuclear test ban treaty with the same Soviet Union that had been so threatening in Cuba and Berlin not long before. Here was a debate topic that mattered at the time when it seemed most relevant. What could and should the UN do to expand superpower cooperation and to prevent small problems from becoming threats to world peace? Eric liked these issues that forced high school debaters to think like world leaders, and the foursome soon felt ready to roll.

On the familiar turf of the Greater Lowell Debate League and the Boston Archdiocesan League, Kenton won thirty-nine of their forty-two debates in seven tournaments. They won all three Lowell events with Danny (three times) and Eric (twice) taking five of the six best speaker trophies. On the Boston circuit, they had two firsts and two seconds in four tournaments and beat their previous year's co-champions, Catholic Prep, for the title. Danny won a Best Negative award, and Eric took two Best Affirmative trophies in the four tournaments. The core of their season was secure, and once again they would go to the NCFL Finals in May, this time in Pittsburgh, to try switch-side debating again. As if to underline their dominance, the boys even won Catholic Prep's own tournament with a 6–0 record and Eric as the Best Affirmative Speaker. At the trophy presentation, Paul Swift, CP's best debater, shook hands with all four of the Kenton speakers. When he came at last to Eric, he said quietly, "You're awesome." No one had ever said that to him before, and he felt a catch in his throat before he managed a quick "Thanks." Sort of like Musial congratulating Williams, Eric imagined. Maybe this was as close as he would get to feeling like Ted Williams. High school vanity was always a risk, but at least Eric knew how to keep his mouth shut once the debates were over. Besides, even debating humbled him sometimes.

Since Kenton had finished second and first in the last two Thoreau College tournaments, Brother Daniel decided to send a strong novice team of sophomores there instead. Against varsity competitors they were a solid 3–3. Then a few weeks later at the University of New Hampshire Novice Tournament, this new foursome went 6–0 and finished a close second on points. The tradition Eric had helped to start would soon pass into very good hands. More than ever, Eric realized how effective Brother Daniel was, now that he could see it in a new group of debaters. "It's wonderful training," Dad liked to say until Eric tired of the phrase, but he had to agree. A high school kid wasn't the same after a year or so of debating, and if he *won* most of those debates, a quiet strength welled up inside.

Meanwhile, the varsity team had three tournaments left before another shot at the Nationals. They went again to the Xaverian Brothers Provincial Tournament and won it with a 7–1 record. Eric and Jon did lose the one debate, but with rival Roger Preston now graduated, Eric won the Best Affirmative award. At least in the four-person format, they had beaten some of the most notable New York teams. Maybe the Nationals would be different *this* year, though their schedule had not included any switch-side tournaments so far. Eric wondered why, but he soon figured out that those events were most often at universities with higher entry fees and more travel time for Kenton. Besides, turning their foursome into two twosomes meant changing the dynamics of each partnership and probably, for a while at least, losing more debates. Brother Daniel never said much about it, but Eric figured that tampering with their success in the time they had left wasn't worth it. They'd need to start switch-side debating in October or November and do it several times to get good, and that would take them out of many four-person tournaments that they were often winning. Roger Preston's coach, the heavyset and red-faced Brother Samuel of St. Joseph's in Shrewsbury, talked of "big ducks on small ponds."

"Son," he'd say with wide eyes and a grin, "that's more fun than being a small duck on a big pond." Eric smiled at such a bare-faced retreat from the pursuit of excellence. Maybe in the future the eastern Massachusetts debate leagues would switch to the more demanding format, like changing from slow-pitch to fast-pitch softball, but that would probably leave too many teams out of the competition. In Eric's years, anyway, switch-side debating would remain the "next level" that Kenton never quite reached. But Brother Sam's "small pond" was still a nice place to rule.

They would get at least one chance, however, at the harder format before the Nationals—the St. James College Tournament again. Rather than pairing Eric and Danny, as he had in Miami, Brother Daniel decided to leave the Jon-Eric and Barry-Danny teams in place and let each of them debate both sides. Since the tournament had five rounds of debates, not four or six, each team by the luck of the draw would take one side three times and the other twice.

Eric liked being back at this "college on the hill" again, especially since it now *was* his future. He had applied for an early decision the previous summer and been accepted by early fall. What could be easier than taking the offer and ending all the doubts of seniors in search of a college? So now he saw the elegant campus with different eyes, but still the old "switch-side anxiety" intruded. When he learned that he and Jon would be Affirmative three times, that eased the tension a little. Barry and Danny got worse news *for them:* they'd also be Affirmative three times. Now Danny's favorite dictum had been turned against him. He must assert and prove, not just criticize and reject. Eric wondered if certain personalities were more natural as Affirmative or Negative debaters. The best, of course, could do both, but advocating solutions suited some competitors (like himself) better than tearing them down. By default sometimes, a Negative team could find themselves defending the status quo, or a skillful Affirmative team could maneuver them into it, but Danny was a brilliant Negative speaker because he never tolerated the "status quo trap."

"It is not our task to prove that the way things are is good," he would insist, "but only to show that the Affirmative proposals won't make them better, and might even make them worse." Here was the hardcore mentality of a Negative debater, a born dismantler who rejected any "problem-solving" burdens. Yes, the best could do both, but almost everyone preferred one role over the other. Switch-side debating seemed to Eric like telling left- or right-handed hitters that they had to switch sides of the plate in every other at bat. That would have changed some careers. And should the pitchers have to alternate arms with each pitch as well? The whole game would break down, he supposed, but there the analogy with debating failed, for the mind was more nimble than the "handedness" of the body. The brain *could* learn to propose and reject on command, like a lawyer who makes a case for whichever client pays him.

At the St. James tournament, however, "nature" prevailed over "nurture" for Kenton. Jon and Eric compiled a 4–1 record with three Affirmative wins, and Barry and Danny went 1–4 with three Affirmative losses. Being "out of one's element" had made virtually all of the difference. Barry and Danny had never lost four debates in a semester, let alone in one tournament. This bigger pond had rough surf. For Eric, it was the best he had ever done in high school switch-side competition. He was Third Best Debater for the tournament, and he began to feel that eventually, with more practice, he *could* take this next step up.

* * *

By spring of his senior year, the debating season had lingered long, and Eric wanted it to end. They all needed a break and some prep time before the May Nationals. However, Brother Daniel had committed them to one more event at the Queen of Heaven School in Fitchburg. A final tune-up couldn't hurt, he said.

The ride there on an April Saturday morning took them through the budding woods and fields of early spring. Surprisingly, Brother Daniel's tuning hand had quickly found a station it liked, and Eric watched the scenery to the sounds of Chuck Berry's "Nadine" and "Johnny Be Good." Rockin' Brother Daniel!

As he and Jon set up their files and notebooks for the first debate at the front of a science classroom, Eric thumbed through a short stack of paper-clipped magazine articles on recent UN peacekeeping efforts in Africa and the Middle East. He could not find a particularly good piece that he was hoping to use. Jon didn't have it either. They must have left it at home or in one of their school lockers. No matter. He knew it well enough to refer to it if needed without quoting directly. So they shook hands with their opponents from Mount Hillsdale Academy, two girls wearing what looked like school uniform blouses and slacks. A few times they'd debated girl and boy pairs from coed high schools, but never two girls that he could remember. The judge at the back center of the room was ready, the timekeeper nodded, and Jon stepped to the podium to deliver his First Affirmative speech. About three minutes into it, Jon stopped for several seconds. Eric looked up quickly from some file cards he was scanning and realized that Jon had left one of his speech outline cards on his desk. He pointed to it and Jon quickly retrieved it, apologized to the judge, and continued. The whole debate seemed to follow from that misplaced card. Little forgotten details, surprisingly strong cross-examinations from both opponents, and a couple of verbose explanations in their rebuttals left Eric dissatisfied. They might still have won, he figured, since they'd made many familiar and effective points, but these opponents were sharp, thorough, and well organized despite their small file boxes that suggested limited research.

Three more debates followed. In them, he and Jon corrected some of their earlier flaws, though their energy level was still oddly flat. Had they been saying too many of the same things for too many months and no longer sounded convincing?

"Well, we weren't great, but I think we won the first two debates and maybe the last one. The third round I'll concede to Catholic Prep," Jon assessed.

"Yeah, I guess they got some payback today for how we handled them in the Boston tournaments."

In mid-afternoon, the debaters all gathered in the school auditorium for the tournament results. This event would be scored on points with no championship debate. Maybe Barry and Danny had been their usual selves, Eric hoped, and if he and Jon could get lucky at 3–1, the team still had some kind of a chance at 7–1 or possibly even with a 6–2 mark. But as the top three speakers on each side were named, neither he nor Danny was among them. And then Kenton was absent from the top three trophy-winning teams. Brother Daniel just shrugged and smiled. "It doesn't happen every time," he said generously.

This tournament belonged to others. Catholic Prep was 7–1 but was second on points to a BU Prep team—not even their best, Eric assumed—that had come west to this Fitchburg event for the first time. And in third place were the two girls and their girl-and-boy teammates from Mount Hillsdale Academy.

"So much for that first debate," Jon whispered to Eric, who just smiled back.

With the ceremonies done, each team picked up its debate ballots in a sealed envelope. Jon passed theirs unopened to Eric, who passed it back. Brother Daniel laughed, took the envelope himself, and opened it. Meanwhile, Danny and Barry scanned their results, 3–1 overall. They had lost to BU Prep. As Brother Daniel scanned the Affirmative team ballots, he passed them one by one to Jon, who then handed each one to Eric. The pair had lost all four of their debates.

"How did you do?" Danny asked to break the prolonged silence.

"0-and-4," Eric said with a shrug of embarrassment. Everyone looked at each other with bewildered faces.

"What do you think happened, Eric?" Brother Daniel asked at last.

"I don't know. We never quite felt right today, but I thought we had won two debates and maybe a third." Jon nodded agreement but said nothing. Barry and Danny both gave Eric a quick pat on the shoulder, knowing that as a senior he must have wanted a strong final tournament.

"Well," Brother Daniel said in an upbeat tone, "it's been a great year and we still have the Nationals in Pittsburgh. Let's just let this one go." They all nodded and gathered up their materials. On the ride home, Brother Daniel was back to the tuner with a vengeance. He must have changed the station thirty times, but Eric didn't hear any of the songs. He kept reliving key moments from the four debates. Was he *that* unconvincing? He and Jon had lost just four debates all season that he could recall. Now they had done it in one day. He knew how Barry and Danny must have felt on their "bad day" a few weeks earlier, but this time he had no switch-side excuses. He'd never quite understood his own success, and today his failure confused him, too. The sheer difficulty of debating well weighed on him, like an 0-for-4 day that Williams might have at the end of a .350 season. Success was easy to take for granted, but a failure now and then gave the success more meaning. Yeah, right, he sighed, with disgust. Never again start a tournament by debating two women in the opening round, he teased himself back into a better mood. They could probably dance circles around him, too, he imagined with a grin. Maybe that's what they all should have done instead of having a debate.

"What?" Jon said suddenly as he noticed Eric's purposeless smile.

"Oh, nothing. Just thinking of a dumb joke." Neither one wanted to pursue it.

With senior events building toward graduation, the Nationals were Eric's last piece of debating business at Kenton. Would the tournament be more fruitful than a year ago? For no particular reason except to try something different, Brother Daniel decided to enter Barry and Eric this time as the Kenton switch-side team.

Pittsburgh was hardly as exotic as Miami Beach, though Eric liked the setting of the city at the confluence of rivers. The place had a much more real-life feeling than Miami's gaudy hotels. "Steel City" looked like a magnification of "mill town" Lowell, another of those past-their-prime Northeastern cities that took some pride in their history while hoping to avoid museum status for industrial glory days. Eric remembered a more recent day of Pittsburgh glory, when Mazeroski's homer had sent the almighty Yankees home empty, but with the tournament schedule and the flight times so tight, no side trip to Forbes Field would be possible. As it turned out, though, Barry and Eric would have more free time than they wanted. Despite working as well as they could together, they repeated the 1–2 record of the year before. Kenton was still not a competitive switch-side school at the Nationals. The new Kenton debaters would have to take that next step forward, if they wanted it badly enough.

Eric felt both relieved and a little sad that high school debating was over, and amazed at the titles and trophies the Kenton foursome had won. A few years earlier, who could have imagined it? Brother Daniel apparently had. What could they say about all that this man had done with the lightest of touches and the steadiest of hands, except, of course, with a car radio in reach?

VI

The senior year, as everyone predicted, seemed to roll by. Or maybe the months sped along while some of the days and hours never ended. The compulsion to be done pervaded everything.

French and Latin were either getting harder, or just harder to care about now. Once, in a tense class moment, Brother Victor lashed out at the mediocre recent French work of nearly everyone and then suggested that Eric was more motivated by grades than by the language. Eric held his tongue, as one did with angry Xaverians. The guys knew what was fair and what wasn't, and their silent support meant more than Victor's approval or criticism. Then early in February when he'd messed up a couple of oral Latin translations in class, Brother Robertus said aloud that his 75% for the latest marking period was probably the worst grade that Eric had ever taken home. It was. But these were the lowest points. He still did well, though he knew that second in the class was the best he could hope for, and even that could change. Yet the debating awards were still there. The whole picture was good, very good.

Rehearsals for the Kenton Vaudeville Revue were more frequent in January and early February as the show date of February 15 approached. Ro in his all-white suit and top hat was the Interlocutor with many introductions and transition lines to learn, as well as a vocal solo of "Younger Than Springtime." Brothers Orlando, Petrarch, and Justin did most of the casting for the solos and group numbers, and Eric found himself in a silent skit called "Children at Play" and "The Spanish Dance" routine, to accordion accompaniment. No real acting or dancing was involved, so he'd just do it all for laughs. Anyway, he had at least avoided "The Charleston" and "The Can-Can." The night came, a huge crowd filled the auditorium, and so much of the talent was so good that Eric was happy just to have a low-key part in it all. Quarterback Will Blanchford and class comic Roger Pleschette gave each other some unrehearsed twirls in "The Spanish Dance" and loosened up everyone else. Ro laughed at Eric and the others from stage right and teased after the show that he should have joined in.

"That's all right, Ro. You've done enough already." Eric waved him off with a laugh.

"Never. I should have spun you around a few times."

"Well, you can't think of everything, thankfully," Eric said in mock weariness, and Ro laughed at his missed opportunity.

For Eric, the resounding final chorus of "Moon River" from the whole cast across the stage filled the hall and gave that night a touch of wonder. The possibilities seemed palpable then, and the future, like the river of the song, stretched "wider than a mile" before them.

VII

"So how are you feeling about attending St. James?" Dad asked Eric one night in April as they watched the news together.

"Good. I think I'll like it."

"Do you still feel OK about not applying to other schools?" he asked cautiously. Dad had thought that one early decision application limited Eric's options, but when Eric got word of his acceptance in September, he liked the idea of not having to do more paperwork for schools that didn't interest him anyway. St. James seemed just what he wanted, and debating there twice had surely helped persuade him. Besides, Ro had won a scholarship to St. James in an essay contest, and what could be better than high school best friends in college together? Dad surely felt disappointed that Eric had not even applied to Boston College, but Jesuits were still Jesuits, he reasoned, and he could always enjoy calling Eric his "prodigal son in Worcester."

From Xaverians to Jesuits. How would they compare? More celibate Catholicity from sisters to brothers to priests. And what would he do at St. James beyond the classroom? Debating again? Probably. The Sodality, a religious club he'd been part of at Kenton while feeling more dutiful and moral about it than inspired? He didn't know. Dad's expectations were clearer for him. "I'm sure some requirements have changed," he conceded, "but Latin, Greek, theology, and philosophy courses will still be a big part of any Jesuit education. You'll probably read a good deal of Thomas Aquinas's *Summa Theologica.*"

"In English, I hope," Eric joked.

"Yes, I'm sure, in English," Dad smiled back, "though a little of the Latin wouldn't do you any harm." He paused for effect. "Anyway, it will stand you in good stead. You should learn Thomas well so that you can see the errors in all those other philosophers." Eric didn't like such a sweeping pre-judgment of people he hadn't even read yet, but he just nodded. He would not debate his father. He would just have to see how Dad's BC of the '30s compared with St. James of the '60s.

VIII

In May when the graduation edition of *The Kenton Bulletin* arrived from the printers, seniors snapped up the first copies. Ro's last issue of the paper included the senior survey, class will, and articles on the official student awards by the faculty. Here was the class of '63 set in permanent relief. Best this, Most Likely that, Outstanding something else. At the back corner desk of his senior homeroom, Eric sat alone and scanned the lists.

Archie Robideau was voted Best Athlete, though Will Blanchford as quarterback and leading offensive star had credentials. Billy Harold, to no one's surprise, was the top golfer, but he also edged out Eric for second place behind Ro in the academic medals. He had worked his way from 1C to 2B to 3A and 4A in the classroom and had surely finished stronger than Eric. Those slipping French and Latin grades had probably made the difference. Ro was not only valedictorian, but also the Xaverian Award winner as the most accomplished Kenton senior. No one doubted that either. Eric was at first a bit amused to win the Debating Award. As the only senior debater, he was a cinch. He thought maybe the award had been newly created with the rise of Kenton debating, but anyway it was a generous recognition. In the future, there would be some real competition for it. The Class Prophecy, most likely compiled by editor-in-chief Ro, had Eric leaving "his eighteen-letter words" to Danny O'Doul, who knew all those words already.

Most interesting to Eric was the senior survey, both serious and comic. What did all of his classmates have to say about each other? The Most Carefree (and Best Author) was John Nelson Abbot, who had seemed destined for those honors since his first day at Kenton when he'd talked about his father's European travel articles for the *Star*. Archie Robideau was Best All Around, and the top class politicians, Brian Crockett and Marshall Reardon, ruled the Most Popular and Did the Most for the Class categories. Ro was Best Student and Eric Best Orator, and it occurred to him that Best Friends could have been added for them both. They also shared the Most Likely to Succeed label, always a strange idea to Eric to guess about the rest of people's lives while leaving "success" conveniently undefined. One award surprised Eric, and the other probably meant the most to him. First, he shared the Best Conversationalist honor with Jason Wilson, who was also named Wittiest. Depends on what kind of conversation you want, Eric thought with a smile. And then there he was all alone under Did the Most for Kenton. The king of the nerds had found a wider audience after all. Hardly a classmate had even heard him debate, yet they sensed how much acclaim these specialized Saturday rituals had brought to their school.

Eric folded the paper under his arm and walked slowly past a few departing seniors and toward the second floor exit. When he was an old man, if he should ever be, here was a document to rekindle the distant '60s. He would tuck away this issue of *The Kenton Bulletin* for such a time when his high school years would glow like the remnants of some half-remembered fire.

A HIGHER LEAGUE

I

Their ride to Worcester was quiet. From the backseat, Eric watched the morning traffic edging eastward toward Boston. He leaned an elbow on his canvas bag of paperbacks and binders that took up the other seat. From the front passenger side, Mom glanced back at him a few times, asked once if he was comfortable, and then looked out at this clear morning just after Labor Day. Dad checked the rearview more often than usual. He smiled twice when he caught Eric's eye and seemed about to say something, but he waited. Eric didn't want to talk yet. Instead, he tasted the anticipation. So here it was. A new life at St. James College, where debating had lured him but where so much else was waiting. Dorm life! God, what would that be like? Who was his unknown roommate, a Leonard Jepson from Greenville, North Carolina? The name was all the school mailing had provided. And what did the Jesuits intend—if it was their idea—for the freshmen with these three disparate summer readings—*Lord of the Flies, The Lonely Crowd,* and *The Late George Apley*? Two studies in alienation and one charmingly outdated portrait of Yankee New England. Not quite what he had expected, whatever that was. But he had liked them all. Reisman's writing was dry sociology compared with the novels of Golding and Marquand, yet his thesis rang true enough: affluent American loneliness caught in a pervasive materialism that could slip into Golding's nightmare or prompt Marquand's quaint escape into the past.

At last, Dad could hold back no longer. As they turned onto 290 and passed through the Worcester hills, tiers of brick buildings climbed the steep slope straight ahead. Dad cleared his throat and suddenly intoned, "Oh, St. James, oh dear St. James. My son's new life. I'm not to blame." Mom laughed with a dismissing flick of her hand, and Eric smiled broadly at his playful father.

"It'll be OK, Dad," he offered mock reassurance.

"I know, Eric," Dad's voice quivered, as if trying to calm itself. "Besides, you're not too far from BC. Just down the pike."

"I'll visit there every chance I get, Dad."

His father laughed as he took the college exit and drove up the hill through the St. James gate and onto what the school brochure called Linden Lane. Didn't BC also have a Linden Lane? Another of their thousand similarities to counter who knew how many differences. Dad knew, Eric was sure. Cars lined each side of the road already, so Dad circled in front of Fenton Hall and back down the road until he found a couple of spots. They all got out, and Eric lifted his suitcase from the trunk.

He laid his bag of books on top of it and looked around for signs telling freshmen where to go. Several upperclassmen were directing new arrivals this way and that, but mostly toward the two freshman dorms. As he started that way with his parents and the luggage, he saw Ro Belisle and his mother unloading their car a few hundred feet away. He waved and caught their eyes, and they returned the greeting. For a moment he was tempted to run over and share the moment of their college arrival together, but he didn't. Each of them should have this time with parents, he supposed. Besides, their friendship might not be the same here, with a few thousand new guys from everywhere competing for attention. He'd let Ro decide how much contact he wanted. No sign yet of his other Kenton classmate, Rod Zachary, but he and Zack had never been especially close. Maybe now the two quieter Kenton guys would get to know each other better while gregarious Ro made new connections.

At the dorm, Eric's unseen roommate had already set himself up on one side of their narrow quarters. Eric and his parents set his bags by the opposite bed and walked down among the freshmen families and across the lower quad to the cafeteria below the dining hall for some lunch.

"So what do you have today?" Dad asked.

"A meeting for all the freshmen at one thirty. Then there's mass at two thirty or so. I think that's it for today."

Dad nodded. "Here's some more cash," he said, pulling two twenties from his wallet.

Eric looked surprised.

"No, no," Dad preempted any questions, "you'll need it sooner or later. Just spread your spending out, as I know you will." Eric smiled and tucked the folded bills into his wallet.

"Well, this lunch was pretty good. Maybe the food will be all right here," Dad concluded.

"Not like home, of course," Eric added, and Dad brought his hand down firmly on the table to punctuate the excellent point. Mom just laughed at them both.

Dad hesitated. "Eric, I wish you a great start and lots of success here," he said almost formally. "Call us if you have any problems, ah, that we can help with."

"OK," Eric answered. "And thanks," he said quickly. He hugged Mom and shook hands with Dad. They walked together back up to Linden Lane and found their car. Mom waved through the back window to Eric, and Dad quickly rolled down his window as he started to pull away.

"Oh, St. James, oh dear St. James," Eric heard him sing out with a backward wave of his left hand. Eric stared at their white Ford Falcon as it descended toward the college gate and disappeared behind the curve of the hill.

II

The first weeks went well enough as Eric's schedule of classes soon ruled the days, and homework filled most of the evenings. The anticipated Jesuit wit cut across young egos and social pretensions with sudden thrusts. At one orientation meeting, the Dean of Men, the monotone and stocky Fr. Hunt, made some benevolent announcement about a grace period before detentions would apply and concluded dryly, "That is the last positive thing we will do for you." A few seconds passed before the auditorium full of freshmen understood to laugh.

In class, the put-downs were bolder, and everyone expected to be a target before too long. You *belonged* once a black robe had looked with disdain over the hieroglyphics of your class notes or wondered out loud if you had actually seen a copy of the novel they were now half-done discussing. "Lovely cover," Fr. Michaelson offered, holding the book at bifocal length, "You should have a look, Malone." Michaelson in particular thrived on the artful insults that punctuated the high seriousness of his literary lectures and digressions. Endorsing Emerson's disdain for the "jingle-man" poetry of Edgar Allan Poe, for example, Michaelson glanced across the class with an air of sad realization and concluded of Poe, "His place in literature is only slightly higher—*than yours.*" With everyone chuckling at Michaelson's appalled expression, the literate one permitted himself a fleeting smile and moved quickly on to better writers.

Students soon acquired the prevailing sensibility and crafted (or inherited) lively nicknames for some of their mentors. One theology teacher was "Smiling Jack, knife in the back" for the contrast between his demeanor and his grades. A lay professor of history fond of three-piece suits and continental manners was dubbed Lord Killian. And a Jesuit who seemed to bounce as he wrote across a blackboard and to lunge toward the front row with finger-pointing emphasis was "the Dancing Bear." The luckless Fr. Budrock of the Biology Department was simply "Buttocks" or "Buttrocks," depending on a student's mood or his biology grade. Wilder guys from New York or New Jersey took the lead in the creative underground, while polite Southerners and inhibited New Englanders laughed cautiously or pretended not to hear the grosser allusions. Of course, satire was its own kind of tribute, as well as a quick release from relentless expectations.

* * *

135

Eric's roommate turned out to be an interesting kind of Southerner. Lennie Jepson had a wide smile, a ready handshake, and a twangy profanity that Eric came to like but decided not to imitate. Anything remarkable to Lennie was a "genuine pisser," nerds were "numb nuts," and Lennie's random humming of a familiar hymn might suddenly flower into "What a friend we have in Jesus, Christ almighty, what a pal!" Eric soon realized that Lennie was not ridiculing the old hymn, just paying it an updated tribute. For Eric, Lennie had a knowing tolerance seasoned with occasional teasing for his bookish roommate. And Eric came to think of Lennie as some sort of Southern Baptist Country Catholic with an earthy flavor. Not an easy concept, he admitted, but OK once you knew the territory. Like most odd couples, Eric and Lennie got along well enough as long as they had plenty of time apart.

New territory faced Eric everywhere in this higher league of St. James College. Priests and professors set an academic pace much faster than Kenton Academy had and expected new arrivals to find their rhythm and keep up. Clothes quickly got more casual, and last-minute arrivals to morning classes became an art form with many practitioners but few masters. Tests and papers were due quickly with few reminders, and they often came back with blunt comments. Grades seemed more revealing of the mind of the grader than of the nature of the material. "What he expects" meant more than any "requirements of the assignment" that might (or might not) have appeared in print. So everyone learned practical psychology, no matter what his courses.

Eric did well enough in the early weeks, but the foreign language threesome of French, Latin, and Greek weighed more on him than he thought they would. The Latin-and-Greek curriculum led to the humanities majors (English was most likely his) while the Latin-and-math sequence fed into higher math and the sciences, where he would not be. The curriculum Dad had remembered from BC in the '30s was mostly intact at St. James in the '60s. To Eric, it seemed strong on reading and writing skills and ancient wisdom but short on imagination and contemporary content, at least in his humanities courses. Lasting values and enduring knowledge meant more here than whatever the latest crop of teens thought was "relevant." Eric made an uneasy peace with that, while yearning at times for something else that he could barely describe. Meanwhile, the pace quickened and the stimulating newness became pervasive pressure.

One way to smooth the transition between high school and college, Eric thought, was to join the same extracurriculars. Not very daring, he admitted, but reassuring in all the uncertainty. That meant Sodality and debating. At Kenton, the Sodality had fostered a familiar Catholic spirituality while planning various "community service" projects, only some of which ever happened. At early meetings of the St. James Sodality, however, Eric slowly realized that a Jesuit spirituality build around Ignatius Loyola's *Spiritual Exercises* sometimes seemed dissonant from a church-in-the-world agenda shaped by the Second Vatican Council, though in theory the two supported each other. He met some impressive Sodality guys there, upperclassmen and freshmen, eager for an applied Christianity and a reformed Catholicism. Some even speculated about women and married priests, interdenominational religious cooperation, and a church politics of peace in a world too well symbolized by the Berlin Wall and hearing more each day about a little country called Vietnam.

Craig Bettinger from Baltimore—a future doctor, he hoped—wanted more Catholic clarity and "realism" about medical ethics issues. Why shouldn't Catholicism be comfortable with science, and much more sophisticated about it? Likely psychology and sociology majors Todd Eslin and Ben Sandusky hoped for more social service projects in Worcester and perhaps even cooperative work with other Worcester colleges. Eric liked all these ideas, but he measured the time they would demand and the ways they would challenge him. Academic doubts held back his extracurricular commitments and tempered the enthusiasm he shared with sodalists who wanted to remake this Catholic club with a stodgy old name and a "holy boy" image.

The faculty sponsor of the group was a wide-faced, gregarious Jesuit of long-winded warmth, Fr. Latourelle. Phrases rolled from Latourelle with a cadence of exaggerated emphasis on selected syllables that was soon affectionately mimicked.

"We want to be MEHN of deep spirituALity and Christian CHARacter, who live ALLways for the SERice of OTHers." He almost pleaded with wide eyes and active hands.

Latourelle had spent his early missionary years in Iraq and talked often of his memories of wonderful friends in "BaghDAD" and of the great humanity of Arab and Islamic peoples. He shared what he called a progressive social agenda with his young sodalists, but on strictly theological matters he cautioned against radical expectations from the council in Rome. Renewal was its purpose more than reform or revolution, and a deeper spirituality, meaning more Ignatius for the Jesuits, was always at the center of his urging. "You cannot GIVE what you have not GOT," he often warned young reformers whose prayer lives were suspect and who knew too little of the "MYStical Body of CHRIST" hovering all around them, just out of sight but never out of spiritual reach. "Only as MEHN of PRAYer do we have ANYthing of VALue to give the WORLD," he concluded with a passion that reverberated in the mind and troubled the conscience.

So the Sodality met weekly and discussed news from the Vatican and prospects for on- and off-campus projects. An annual Ignatian Retreat at some Jesuit house was expected of each sodalist for a three or four-day span, and Eric looked forward to them as a respite from college pressures and a chance to face again, if not ever resolve, his own spiritual ambiguities. Meditations on the *Spiritual Exercises* focused mostly on the "discernment of spirits" that Ignatius, a soldier-turned-spiritual-warrior, had made the hallmark of his religious regimen, all within a fully orthodox heaven-and-hell theology. How could the soul tell good promptings from the seductive evil voices within? To Ignatius's preoccupation, Eric added questions of his own. Where did rationalism and science cross the line into intellectual pride? What about the creative wisdom of writers and artists who strayed beyond orthodox theology to ask dangerous questions and seek their own "revelations"? How, if at all, could a "healthy sexuality" coexist with a world view that proclaimed, "The flesh kills, but the spirit gives life"? Moral growth could happen, but being perfect—"even as your heavenly father is perfect"—only meant perpetual striving and constant failure. Here was another layer of spiritual pressure in a life already calibrated in waves of rising expectations from the classroom to the playing field. Guys who cared acknowledged the ideal and then went about the business of being very imperfect. Others were likable characters with more worldly standards. Forgiveness and sacramental renewal were at best pit stops in the unending race. Even the consolations felt demanding.

Eric tried to keep his own life as simple as he could in the whirl around him. Between piety and skepticism, he sometimes chose no talk at all. The best times were the solitary evening walks to the top of the hill where, on clear nights, he could see the two semicircles of lights (the college and the city) under the starry canopy, as if inviting him to heaven and earth at once. He recalled the sign-off lines of Dave Garroway from the first years of the *Today Show*: "The world stands out on either side, no wider than the heart is wide. Above the earth is stretched the sky, no higher than the soul is high." Garroway always added "Peace," as if to say that we could measure any tasks we faced against the wide resources of the mind and heart and have nothing to fear. For a half hour or so, Eric could believe that, until it was time to step back down the hill into his dorm and everything that awaited him there.

III

Sometime in mid-October of '63, Eric attended his first meeting of the college's debating team. Why not continue what had given him distinction at Kenton? But very little was the same. Two faces were, however, which was both reassuring and surprising, for he had not noticed their names on the various lists of his '67 classmates. He nodded to Leonard Alvarez, a debating opponent from Archbishop Hillian outside of New York City. Eric remembered that Alvarez had finished just ahead of him (second best debater to third) at last year's St. James tournament. They had faced each other once, and Alvarez and his partner had won a close debate in the rebuttals. Good to have Alvarez on *his* side now. Then, at the back door of the classroom, a latecomer slipped in and took a quick seat. A moment later he noticed Eric and moved up three rows to sit beside him. It was Roger Preston, who had beaten out Eric for the Best Affirmative Speaker award at the Xaverian Tournament when Eric was a junior. Eric thought for a moment that Roger must be a sophomore now, but the sign-up sheet for all new debaters quickly showed he was a freshman. All the better, Eric thought, for they might be together for four years.

"I knew you'd be here," Roger whispered and smiled.

"Well, I didn't expect to see you. I wonder what this will be like."

"Most of these guys look as green as we are. Freshmen will probably get to do some varsity debating quickly."

The team, officially the Fenton Debate Society after the college's founder, had a pleasantly rotund Jesuit sponsor, Fr. Leo O'Leary, who welcomed everyone with a few words about the school's great debating tradition and then turned the meeting over to the actual coach, a Harvard Law School student and long-time debater named Harry Snelling.

"Call me Harry," Snelling began. "We won't stand on formality." Snelling said a little about this year's topic and how the debaters would break into research teams to gather data on it. Even freshmen could expect to enter a mix of novice and varsity tournaments early on, so all needed to be ready quickly.

"We believe that throwing you to the wolves early is the most encouraging approach," Snelling joked with a tight, quick smile and a side glance. He was a thin, angular man with prominent eyes and cheekbones and slightly rounded shoulders. Not exactly emaciated, Eric thought, but cerebral and even a bit jaded somehow, if that wasn't too judgmental too quickly. Verbal dexterity was Snelling's forte, and *theirs* very soon, the coach obviously intended. Eric and Roger volunteered to be research partners and took away a common assignment about federal educational policies and funding in recent years. Then they walked to the caf beneath the dining hall for a snack.

"So you're a freshman?" Eric asked and instantly regretted it.

"Yes," Roger nodded. "Some family complications last year changed my plans."

"What do you think of St. James so far?" Eric quickly changed the subject.

"It's fine. Of course, growing up literally in the shadow of this place has given me all sorts of impressions before I actually arrived here. I'll just have to see what's true and what isn't. Being a day student is also different; you're here but not totally here, you know."

"Yeah. I guess that is different." Eric paused. "The Day Room's in Bevington Hall, right, on the bottom floor?"

"Right. I do homework there sometimes until I want to escape the locals," Roger smiled, "and then I go up to the main library."

They talked awhile longer and then departed, each taking a share of their research assignment. Debate meetings quickly followed, research made its way onto file cards for a master set that everyone could share, and practice debates or parts of debates happened as soon as provisional teams were ready. It began to feel like another course to Eric, but now he lacked the classroom confidence he'd had at Kenton. Everything demanded so much time, and no one seemed concerned about any other agendas. "Get it all done or don't commit to so much" was the unspoken message.

The clipped rationality of debate meetings often clashed with the idealism of Eric's Sodality discussions and with the candor of occasional dorm talks among the resident free thinkers. George Delaney was one of these. He and Eric spent snatches of time talking about favorite writers or about the crazy extremes of dorm life that both tried to avoid. Eric enjoyed Lenny Jepson's irreverence, but a randomly assigned roommate was rarely as compatible as a deliberately chosen friend.

Several college "lives" seemed to be unfolding for Eric, and sometimes they collided. He wondered if he shouldn't let something go, but changing came hard, and people's expectations grew as long as he showed up at this meeting or that. Each activity was self-perpetuating unless he stopped it in its tracks. Each small success kept him coming back and ruled out decisive changes. A good day in class, a strong paper finished on time, or the occasional flashes of his old debating success or Sodality idealism renewed his ambitions in each arena. But the conflicts could be acute, and they gave him little rest. His own indecision prolonged the stress.

At one debate meeting, for example, Snelling walked slowly into the classroom wearing sunglasses, flashed his Cheshire cat smile, and moved directly into debating talk. A long night and bloodshot eyes, Eric guessed. What was law school life in the heart of Cambridge really like? He didn't think he wanted to know. Then as Snelling, Alvarez, and two others were fine-tuning some awkward point, Snelling raised a limp hand and said, "Let's pursue truth for a moment." Eric smiled with everyone else, but he couldn't erase the phrase from his mind. For hours, they could "talk strategy" and "frame evidence in favorable contexts" designed to score points and win debates by ambushing opponents. A moment of pursuing truth was just to clear the air long enough to agree on some "actual facts" that more cleverness could then distort for competitive advantage. Knowing where "the truth" might be, they could artfully avoid it. Maybe that's what law school was like. Would college debating lead him there? Then why keep doing it? Shouldn't he get off a train that, for him at least, had changed course and was now headed where he didn't want to go? Not yet, apparently—not as long as the taste of victory still lingered, or could be imagined. What would Sodality friends think of that? He didn't bother to ask.

* * *

In his half-dozen tournaments as a freshman, Eric had some bad days, other promising ones, and a few flashes of high school glory. The most unlikely result came in early November at the Harvard Novice Tournament. He and Roger had usually been Affirmative speakers in high school, but now, to stretch them, Snelling had entered them as a Negative team in this four-person tournament. As usual, Roger had quickly picked up inside knowledge about other teams and their coaches. From round to round, he surmised how he and Eric might be doing from the strength of each new opponent or the supposed caliber of the assigned judge. He guessed that winners were being paired against winners with the more experienced judges assigned to these better debates. Eric felt good about their early efforts but doubted Roger's prognosticating. *Debate one round at a time*, he thought, *and just let the results happen.*

Eric smiled to think how he and Roger were unlikely partners with a strangely effective chemistry. Roger was brilliant with evidence and seemed to surround opponents' points with more counter-quotations and questions than they could answer. Then he might fly off into a lofty metaphor or—to Eric—a glorified cliché, like the time had accused their opponents of promising "pie in the sky, bye and bye." Eric had turned away from the podium (and the judge), but the dissonant moment could not be missed. After such verbal bouquets from Roger, Eric felt that his job was to find a straight line for the judge and walk it for a while—analyze, clarify, simplify. If Roger offered a quotation to rebut each piece of the opponents' evidence, Eric preferred to show logically how some evidence did not apply to the issue at hand. No need to counter it if he could just dismiss it. Less of a researcher than Roger, Eric played to his own strength. As a high school debater, he had seldom out-researched anyone but often out-reasoned them. Anyway, if Roger's predictions were right, their chemistry seemed to be working again in these old Harvard classrooms.

At the end of the five-round tournament, all the debaters assembled in an auditorium to hear the results. No playoff debates and title round were scheduled, so the winners would be chosen on record and points. The host, a Harvard upperclassman with clipped, precise diction, began with the Affirmative results. None of the announcements indicated that Roger and Eric had debated any leading Affirmative teams. Roger frowned, but Eric whispered that it probably meant nothing.

Then the Negative honors unfolded. In this novice tournament designed to encourage young debaters, the top ten speakers and teams from each side would receive certificates. But as the names were announced from tenth place upward, Eric and Roger both settled slowly back into their chairs, Roger in disappointment and Eric with resignation. All of Roger's guessing had amounted to nothing. They both had nearly stopped listening when the host said in an even tone, "The second place Negative speaker is Roger Preston of St. James College." Roger's eyes suddenly brightened and he stood up a bit too quickly for Eric to shake his hand. Maybe they'd done OK after all.

When Roger sat down, the announcer cleared his throat and continued, "And the first place Negative speaker, also from St. James College, is Eric Malone." Eric glanced at Roger with a stunned look until Roger gestured for him to get up and accept the award. Slowly Eric did. What were the odds against such a result? Never mind—it had happened! When all the ballots were released, the St. James team was 6–4 with Eric and Roger at 4–1. On points and with their one loss, they were oddly the second best Negative team despite their individual speaker awards. With a result like that barely a month into college debating, how could Eric think of quitting? He couldn't, and he didn't—at least not for many months after this Harvard surprise.

I V

Ro had not joined the Sodality or the debating team at St. James, and Eric noticed that they saw less of each other as months passed. Ro always waved and smiled whenever he caught Eric's eye, but they had no classes together and lived on different corridors. More than that, Eric sensed that Ro would rather make new friends than spend time with his old high school classmates, Eric and Zack. College was about new directions, wasn't it? So why did Eric cling to Sodality and debating while Ro ventured out? Confidence was the answer, Eric knew. Ro assumed that his smile and humor would win friends in anything he did. So he attended a couple of drama club meetings, learned a little about student government from the politicos of the class, and laughed at the stories of some campus renegades without getting too committed or too implicated anywhere. Sometimes Eric would see Ro walking across the lower quad or down the steep campus stairs toward a class and laughing loudly at some classmate's account of late-night escapades. Eric remembered their brief separations at Kenton, but he felt a more permanent distance now. Their high school chemistry was gone, probably forever, and Eric, unlike Ro, had yet to find his college groove, if there even was such a thing for him. Speculative readers and thinkers made him more comfortable than the drinkers or footloose dancers, but such guys were too free-thinking for Sodality theology or debate team calculations. So was Eric, at least in the moments of candor and skepticism that he shared with George Delaney, a future philosophy major from Chicago, and Jeff Sanderson, who thought psychology was the only subject compatible with the mysterious irrationality of human beings. George and Jeff together in their room—or even better, on an early-evening walk around the campus—could keep Eric away from homework about as long as he dared. But tonight they were avoiding work in the pair's "radical" dorm room.

"So these Jesuits create a clean, unambiguous celibacy for themselves—"

"Or choose that comfort zone that Catholicism has created for them," Jeff corrected George.

"OK, OK," George conceded, "either way, they remove the economic and glandular variables from their lives"—Eric and Jeff both laughed—"and then they make careers trying to tell young men lured by the wicked world how to live without greed or sex while having just enough of each to support the alumni fund and send sons to St. James."

"You oversimplify beautifully," Jeff said with a slight bow.

"No," George continued urbanely, "I see with great clarity and speak with eloquent precision."

"And keep us from studying very seductively," Eric added.

"Exactly, Malone. I give you what you need beyond your own understanding. I save you from your books." Just then, Ron Zachary walked by, stopped at the open room door, and invited himself in.

"Ah, Zack, another Kenton Academy gem," George exuded. Zack shrugged meekly as everyone laughed.

"You offer no objection, Mr. Zachary?" Jeff teased.

"We are pitiable creatures," Zack conceded, "and what's to become of us cannot be good."

"Is that what the Xaverians, not to mention the Jesuits, have taught us?" Eric wondered aloud and smiled to hear Zack's answer.

"Aye, lad," Zack took on a slight brogue, "and better than they know."

"You see, beloved classmates, young Christian gentlemen all, we are at the edge of the abyss where no doctrines can save us. No place for the faint of heart." George awaited contradiction.

"Speaking of the abyss," Jeff ventured, "what did you think of that sadistic French test? The 'bon mot' gave me the slip on that final translation."

"I was in trouble before that," Eric said with no humor. "These three languages at once are killing me."

"All those beautiful words and so little to say," George archly regretted.

"Sure, George. All we need is Marcus Aurelius, right?" Jeff countered.

"A man too fine to be emperor and too fine not to be," George sailed on. "The philosopher-king that Plato dreamed of."

"I guess it didn't rub off," Zack shot back.

"Well, you have a point there, Mr. Zachary," George assumed a Jesuitical condescension. "An obvious one, but a point nonetheless."

Eric smiled. "I'm going to leave you higher intellects for some French declensions. What a comedown it will be!"

Everyone smiled, and George waved them all from his room, even roommate Jeff. "I despair of your muddled minds," he called after them.

"Don't strain yourself," Zack hollered back, and the three headed out into the cold air. Jeff nodded good-bye as he veered toward the library, and Zack and Eric walked together back to their dorm. Eric liked Zack's sharp tongue and deadpan face. He'd say nothing, zap you with a verbal dart, and then retreat into coy silence. Eric also respected Zack's quiet studying and steady success. He wondered if maybe he and Zack might not make better roommates than he and Lennie. A year of Lennie's flamboyant opinions and "gen-u-ine pissers" was probably enough. He figured Lennie would politely agree.

V

On a sunny November Friday just after lunch, Eric wandered back to his dorm to do a little reviewing for a two o'clock theology class.

Lennie was out, and the neighboring rooms seemed oddly empty despite their wide open doors. As he reached the threshold of his room, Eric noticed a cluster of guys halfway down the hall and crowded at Bob Franzoni's door. He looked at their backs for a second and then, in their unusual silence, he heard a radio voice that had everyone's attention. He walked closer and began to make out the announcer's words. President Kennedy had been shot in a Dallas motorcade. He had been rushed to a nearby hospital. Police were searching for the shooter somewhere in the city. Governor Connolly of Texas had also been hit, but was not in danger.

"Why couldn't it be you, Lyndon?" Franzoni attempted a joke, but no one laughed.

The announcer filled a few more seconds with background information of Kennedy's schedule for this trip and of his hopes for easing tensions with Texas Democrats. Kennedy had been warmly welcomed at the airport and was riding through the city in an open car. The vice president was also in the motorcade but was apparently safe. Secret Service agents had ridden near the president's car, but they could do nothing against a sniper's bullet from a nearby building. Some witnesses even thought that one shot or more had come from another direction, but that was still unconfirmed speculation. The announcer paused. He had just been handed a late bulletin: "The Associated Press reports, and hospital authorities confirm, that the president has died of massive head wounds. The First Lady and others were with him. No word yet on when the vice president will be sworn in and how soon he will return to Washington. Again, President Kennedy, after less than three years in office, has died in Dallas from an assassin's bullet at the age of forty-six. Stay tuned for further information."

Students began to break away from the tight cluster around Franzoni's radio. Some headed for the TV lounge in the basement. All the networks would be full of coverage. Eric went back to his room and just sat on his bed. He didn't want any television pictures just yet. Instead, the newsreel of his memory reran all the familiar images of Kennedy's career—his Senate election, the vice presidential concession speech at the '56 convention, and dozens of scenes of JFK on the campaign trail with his clarion voice and movie star looks. Who had ever seemed more youthful and futuristic than Kennedy? His loss was beyond sad or tragic; it was simply impossible, unbelievable. Kennedy would be reelected president in '64 and serve for the full eight years. Then, as a young ex-president, he would be prominent in American politics for decades to come. JFK had just begun his work. Already he had drawn thousands of young people into politics. He would keep doing that far into the future. His impact would be durable and immeasurable. This Irish Catholic politician with the Harvard degree had given Eric and so many New England Irish a stunning shot of pride. One of them, even if he was hardly "one of them," had risen to the pinnacle of American politics. "An idealist without illusions," he had called himself in a phrase that Eric admired. JFK had grown so much in his short presidency and seemed ready to lead the world as no one had since FDR. All that could not suddenly be gone. Where would the country go now with a very different sort of leader? Where would Catholicism go, he thought, with a very different new Pope? Eric propped his pillow against the bed frame and leaned against it, eyes closed.

"Who can believe," Fr. Lionel asked in his sermon of Sunday, November 24, 1963, "that JFK is no more? How can we comprehend this wrenching act against our society, against the whole world? I don't know what to think today. I cannot tell you what to think. Faith tells us that this act, like every earthly event, has a place in God's plan. Rarely have we been asked to make a greater leap of faith than in this time, in the killing of our new young leader. We all pray for the strength to endure this loss and to do our small part to help our country move forward. Any larger understanding of such an event in divine terms must come much later, perhaps only at last when we join JFK in the presence of God."

Lionel stepped slowly down from the pulpit and continued the liturgy of the mass. Sometimes Eric thought that Catholic ritual could smother more personal feelings with endless formulaic ceremonies, but now he had a sense of its strength. When no one had anything left to say, any more wisdom to offer, the liturgy returned to ancient words that had taken Catholics and others through centuries of human history and countless traumas. What else could anyone do now but, once more, set cruel events in a higher context? "Let us pray" was really the only option. The doubter in everyone might mouth the empty words, and the believer in everyone would join the prayer, not knowing what else to say.

VI

The winter snow drifted high on the St. James hills and blew across the stairways and paths that became precarious routes to class and meals and home again to warm dorms. The snow yielded slowly through the false New England springs that made sense of T.S. Eliot's assertion: April *was* the cruelest month because March promised less and May gave much more.

For Eric, Christmas vacation had passed quickly, and relief at one semester's end slipped like a January thaw into the chill of the next. History and English sustained him, but a promising theology seminar on "ecumenism" degenerated into "ecclesiasticism" or "churchianity" and ended in a multi-denominational swamp choked by confusion.

"Well, I hope you can all pull this together for yourselves," the heavy-eyed Jesuit professor had actually said to the eight surviving students at the end of their last meeting. Eric nodded vaguely to him and exited with the rest.

"I wonder if he even wanted to teach this," a classmate thought aloud as they moved down the mahogany hallway toward the door.

"It looked good in the curriculum guide," Eric answered, "but I guess he never quite figured out where the course was going. We got lost in all those handouts and speculative articles."

"Will that be where Vatican II ends up?" a third voice added. They shrugged at the thought and went separate ways, no longer joined by false seminar hopes.

All that spring the three languages confronted Eric like an uneasy tripod about to collapse. An encouraging B here was soon deflated by a D there. Oddly, the very familiarity of Latin and French made them duller and harder instead of easier, and the new wilderness of Greek lacked even the freshness of a novelty. By June, Eric's GPA had slipped to something like a 2.8, C+ territory. The middle of the college pack was far from third in the class at Kenton. In high school, success had bred success. Winning a debate tournament on Saturday might back up into Sunday night's homework, but by Tuesday or Wednesday, Eric would be on top of everything again. A strong test or paper would reassure him that he could manage everything and create his special niche in the class. No one said much to him, nor needed to. Everyone knew more or less what he was doing on the "small pond" of Kenton Academy debating. But now, this "small college" felt vast to Eric. He was no world-beater in this league, and he knew it. Other guys might be sympathetic; many of them had also gone from high school stars to college also-rans. Yet everyone struggled with his own pressures and left Eric to his. Not that it should be otherwise, but still it was somehow deflating to see school catalog rhetoric run aground on the shoals of competing agendas and those unyielding smiles. The first year must be the hardest, he thought, as he rode home with his parents in June. He wondered what he could change in the fall and understood what he could not. He nodded uneasily at Dad's teasing assertion that there was nothing like a Jesuit education, even if it was *only* at St. James.

VII

The summer of '63 had been the Malones' last at Cobbetts Pond. As the kids all became teens and the teens kept getting older, Cobbetts seemed less exciting than the ocean beaches and boardwalks nearby, or the movies and music of Lowell or Nashua or, if one could ever get there, Boston. But the Malones didn't care to have Eric, Betty, or Marsha very far from home, so they had kept the family summers at Cobbetts Pond for as long as they could. When they stopped in '64, the Malones rented a cottage for two weeks at Dennis on the Cape and still visited several times to Aunt Emma's at Cobbetts. Eric saw Dutch again for a couple of afternoon hours in the water, and he played the last of those intense teenage male games of horseshoes and badminton with younger guys or with the older men, who sometimes beat him and sometimes didn't. On a few Sundays he returned to play in the softball game; he still hit pretty well but never quite learned to field in the clumpy grass of the unkempt outfield. He wasn't even the best *young* player anymore.

All his Ted Williams and Warren Spahn fantasies amused him now. The magic of his baseball youth was slipping away, just as Ted himself had and old Warren soon would. *Nothing worse than a great player who plays too long*, Eric thought. Ted had avoided that with a beautiful final season, but Spahnie's collapse in '64 was painful to see. So Eric mused on quiet walks in the woods near the lake. Whatever he might now do at Cobbetts, he had already done. Not even Dutch's perpetual chatter and finger-snapping antics were as funny anymore.

When they sold the camp, only Marsha made any sort of protest because at thirteen she still had a few more lake summers in her. Betty listened to music and went out with girlfriends and occasionally had a boy come by as a date or a potential date, and Eric read and kept his thoughts to himself and then read some more and started keeping a list of all his readings until he felt bound to finish every book he started so he could honestly include it on the list. History, fiction, and religious reading—poetry sometimes and politics more often—reading in search of what to believe and who to believe in. Biographies of FDR and Churchill and Lincoln fed his "giants of history" taste, though he knew more and more that no leader was flawless and that imagery had a lot to do with reputation. Robert Kennedy's *The Enemy Within* seemed like a good counterpoint to his brother's *Profiles in Courage*. And when Jimmy Hoffa had called Bobby a ruthless little bastard, Bobby had smiled and answered, "I'm not little." Politics produced a flawed greatness at best for those who could survive its endless verbal abuse. Eric imagined himself as a senator or as president signing great laws and giving inspiring speeches, like some memorable flourish at a debate tournament, but he never warmed up to the idea of *getting* elected, of shaking hands and raising money and smiling at people until his face hurt. No, he wasn't going to be Ted Williams or Jack Kennedy.

Or could he be a priest perhaps, like his uncle? There was a certain beauty in it and in the fellowship that priests felt with each other. His uncle had priest friends at churches and seminaries all over the East and Midwest. Eric had met some of them and liked how Fr. Eric was with them. And the Xaverians at Kenton and the Jesuits at St. James had bonds one could only imagine, and envy. They would never be without their brothers-in-the-cloth. But what of the bureaucracy they all either defended or silently submitted to, whatever their thoughts? And just when Vatican II seemed ready to open the ancient doors to a new Christianity in-the-world and on-the-move, the new Pope was hesitating. Some of the best professor-priests at the college sensed a new mood of caution. What would Eric be defending if he committed to all that? What about the liturgical monotony and the endless fund-raising appeals of priestly life? And the theology beyond which one could not go without scrutiny or church discipline? Could Teilhard de Chardin (or one of his disciples) ever clink glasses with Paul VI and chat about Christogenesis? Eric couldn't picture it. Celibacy, too, must be a lonely commitment, though just then Eric didn't think it would be the toughest challenge for him. He smiled. About women, he hardly had anything yet to give up. And was that a good state for choosing the priesthood or just a likely reason for leaving it later on? Hadn't too many priests and brothers committed to celibacy without knowing anything about sexuality? And how would Mom feel a few decades from now to have an *ex-priest* in the family?

No option before him seemed inviting that summer, and the limitless world of books was an irresistible escape. He loved the density of Shakespeare plays and the sparse clarity of Hemingway prose. School readings of Hawthorne and Melville got him into the best of nineteenth-century New England literature. Thoreau's earthy paradoxes and stunning boldness appealed more than Emerson's grand abstractions: "The spur of the moment is a thorn in my side," or "Only that day dawns to which we are awake." And getting lost in the "insular Tahiti" of *Moby Dick* was a wonderful abandonment. So he read, yet no one shared his reading or challenged his opinions or his tastes. That would have to wait for college classes when there was never quite time to unravel big ideas because something else was waiting in the syllabus. Working on those three infernal languages would have made plenty of academic sense in the summer of '64, but who could bear it when free reading seduced him every day? Would he pay a price later? Then he would pay it. The mind's eye had to catch a little light sometime.

In late June, Ro surprised him with an invitation to spend a weekend together on the Cape when both the Malones and the Belisles would be renting there. Eric did stay with Ro for a few days of swimming, beach talks, and salad-rich meals with Mrs. Belisle and Pierre. Yet for Eric the days had a shadow of finality about them. Ro hinted that he wasn't feeling so happy at St. James and might look at other schools with greater academic choices. Ro was ready to reach higher and wider, while Eric just worried about passing the three languages so he could finally get to the best literature, history, and philosophy that St. James could offer. Finish the requirements to begin savoring the electives! But Ro saw something else beyond Eric's vision. Or maybe he just didn't know what he wanted, and nothing would ever be good enough. Kenton had been a much more shared experience for them both, but each semester at St. James felt like a separate era with no precedents to point the way.

So his first college summer brought its beautiful relief and left all the hard questions still sitting on Eric's plate.

BREAKING POINTS

I

When their sophomore classes started at St. James, Eric and Ron Zackary moved in together, and the fit felt good right away. Zack's antisocial quips made just enough fun of the solitary tendencies they shared. And they each knew better than most guys when to leave a roommate alone.

Once on a quiet Thursday night as both were reading, Zack had the radio on for some news. Each half-listened to a story about some siblings reunited in Utica, NY, after decades apart. The announcer went on about all the near-misses in their search for each other after childhood tragedy had taken their parents and left the two sisters, unaccountably, in separate orphanages. Finally, an incredible accident had brought them into each other's arms back at their childhood tenement in Utica. Zack suddenly twisted the off knob so hard that the radio knocked against a metal bookend on his desk. Eric glanced from his reading chair in surprise, and Zack gave a little shrug.

"I'm so damn sick of these human interest stories," he explained with a world-weary look. When Eric leaned back in hard laughter, Zack allowed himself a brief smile and returned to his chemistry text. *Vintage Zack,* Eric thought. *ExZACKtitude!*

II

For Eric, the three predators—French, Latin, and Greek—continued to feed on his GPA, only this time he had unaccountably landed in a French course where NO English could be spoken, not by departmental mandate, but by teacher preference. Two Fs on early quizzes, a D+ on a test, and then another F on an in-class essay sounded warning bells that Eric had never heard before. "Up the Seine without a paddle" was all the weak humor he could generate for classmates, who wondered how their sometime-tutor in English and philosophy could be so lost in French. From marginal mediocrity, he now plunged into real trouble purely by the chance of a teacher assignment.

Knowing that official relief was impossible, he still summoned the nerve to knock on Fr. Duchenes' door. The Foreign Language Department chair, a fastidious French-teaching Jesuit with tightly combed black hair and elegant manners, offered him a seat, listened attentively, and then explained that Eric was mistaken, that all French 201 courses were of comparable difficulty, that Dr. Montreville was a wonderful teacher who would provide all necessary help, and that a transfer from one teacher to another in French 201 was not possible. When Duchenes offered his tight little handshake, Eric understood that the meeting was over and his destiny sealed. Barring some academic miracle or the regrettable assassination of Montreville, Eric was going to flunk the first course of his life. In September, he had felt it. In October he admitted it to himself to end all suspense. Montreville was ever-so-cordial about the prospect, but only (so far as Eric could judge) in flawless Parisian French.

Eric sought out a student tutor for a few sessions, but the pace of the course and the density of the readings did not yield, and Eric stepped slowly toward the inevitable. Dad liked to joke that in the two world wars the French army had lasted a total of forty-eight hours. Eric imagined that the gods hovering over Versailles were now exacting revenge upon the slow-witted son for the sins of the mocking father. He remembered Mom saying that if she had gone to college, she would have been a French major. Was there no way to enroll Mom in Montreville's "little Paris café" and let Eric try Swahili instead? Not at St. James College. And as consolation prizes, his Latin and Greek courses were as dismal as the underworld for Aeneas and Odysseus. Cs and Ds vied with each other for control of each course, and Eric treaded water in the River Styx, no doubt to Charon's amusement. Was Charon a Jesuit, too? Lord, they really were everywhere!

In the spring of his freshman year, Eric and sophomore Craig Mulrooney had managed a 4–0 affirmative record at the Thoreau College Varsity Tournament in Boston. Though Snelling called it a weaker varsity event, he congratulated Eric and Craig and predicted better things for them both. Thoreau College had been lucky before for Eric, and a 4–0 mark anywhere seemed like a good omen for sophomore debating, despite Eric's sinking GPA. So he dutifully attended the early debate meetings in the fall and prepared for another year of research and strategy sessions, this time on the role of the UN as a world peace-keeping force. At least he'd debated that topic before in high school, but that old research would need updating now. Once more, he was paired mostly with Roger Preston. Their first entry was in the varsity switch-side tournament at MIT in November. Eric took homework with him and got some brief help from Roger with French, but there was no time to get much done in the two-day, six-round tournament. They finished at 3–3, and Roger was named Seventh Best Speaker overall. Here was another "promising event" that made quitting debating seem as peculiar as Eric's bipolar grades with English and philosophy in a two-on-three against French, Latin, and Greek.

After one particularly obscure French class in late November, Eric summoned the courage (and rehearsed the vocabulary) for a meeting with Montreville. He would ask to do some sort of extra credit assignment to help his grade. Roger had urged him to inquire, so Eric proposed a comparison of French and English tragedy using Racine's *Britannicus* and Shakespeare's *Macbeth*.

"C'est possible," Montreville responded, with a slow nod of the head, "mais vos notes sont plus importantes."

"Oui, certainement," Eric agreed in his best accent. The professor decided that Eric could write an eight- to ten-page essay and submit it in French one week before the semester exams in January.

"Merci," Eric answered with a weak smile and departed with the first glimmer of hope he had felt since the opening week of Montreville's course.

I'll write the best damn paper I ever have in English, Eric thought, *and then translate it into French. I'll read* Britannicus *in both languages and get some good essays on the nature of tragedy. But how will I turn the English into decent, even subtle, French?*

Roger was too busy with courses and debating to help with Eric's translation, but he knew someone who might. A girl he'd met from Claraton University, a junior and a French major, would probably be willing to help. Eric even said he would pay her, but Roger doubted that would be necessary.

"Besides, Eric, she's a stunner, and that's what you need right now." They both laughed.

"And you'd make her available to me, Roger?"

"For a price, Ugarte, for a price," Roger answered in his best Bogart.

"No one ever loved me that much," Eric shot back, and they both shook their heads at the endless uses of *Casablanca*. A week later Roger introduced Eric to Michelle Forrester, and Eric's attempt to create a Maginot Line for his French grade began. All of this Eric kept from his parents for now. What could they do about it, anyway? And their amazement that Eric might actually fail a class was more than he wanted to navigate. When it happened, they would know. If it didn't, they would never have to worry about it. For the first time, Eric felt a twinge of sympathy for those Kenton classmates who had often faced failure. So this was the feeling of doom behind their self-mocking jokes. Some of them carried it off pretty well, he remembered, but Eric had never played this part before and wondered if he could.

I I I

Early in December, Roger and Eric were paired again for a tournament, a varsity switch-side at Tufts University. Their new debate coach had arranged for a dorm room at BC because all the available Tufts rooms were taken. The trip to Tufts on Saturday morning would be on the T, green line to red. After round one on Friday night, Eric and Roger returned to BC on a cold, grey evening with sleet falling already and snow forecast for the morning. Their dorm room had only a radio for weather reports and news, so Roger had bought the *Globe* to see what was happening in the city and for the weather as well.

"God, what an awful night," Eric said, looking out at the chilly streets and the descending fog.

"Yeah, too bad," answered Roger. "We might have tried to catch a movie or some music nearby."

Eric had brought the Racine and Shakespeare plays and some of the critical essays to read. He laid them out on the desk by his bed as Roger watched. Then Eric propped himself up on a pillow against the dorm wall and slouched along the bed. The Beatles' "Yesterday" sounded dimly from a nearby room, but otherwise the building seemed empty on a dreary Friday. Eric glanced around at a few film posters on the walls—*The Searchers* and *The Manchurian Candidate* dwarfed a few smaller ones—and he sipped steaming Earl Grey tea that Roger had heated on a portable electric burner.

"Nice flavor," Roger noted.

"Especially on a night like this," agreed Eric. "I guess we'll just have to see how things are in the morning."

"Yeah. The subway stop isn't far, but I wouldn't want to walk there in this stuff. Could be worse by tomorrow, they're saying."

"Do you think we'll be able to get to Tufts?" Eric wondered.

"I don't know. Kruger wouldn't like that, I guess, but we don't want to get stuck somewhere between here and there." Lloyd Kruger, a law student at Harvard, had replaced Harry Snelling that fall as debate coach. Kruger was square-jawed, soft-spoken, and well-organized. A very different sort from Snelling, at once more reliable and less adaptable to sudden innovations in debate strategy. Snelling liked playing intellectual roulette, but Kruger laid out plans and followed them. Only lost debates were reasons for changes. Barring a power outage or a shutdown of city transportation, Kruger, who was staying at Tufts, would be at his assigned room in the morning, and he'd expect Eric and Roger at theirs. Since the three other St. James teams had all been given rooms at Tufts, they'd be debating if anyone was. Only Roger and Eric had the trip from Chestnut Hill to downtown Boston facing them.

"So how's that ever-lovin' French paper?" Roger asked.

"It's OK. I like doing the reading, but working these essays into the paper won't be easy. They talk about the plays in different ways. And expressing all that in French . . . mon Dieu!"

"Well," Roger smiled, "that's where Michelle comes in."

"Yes. Thanks for getting me in touch with her."

"She's very good in French . . . and very good-looking in any language, don't you think?"

"She is that," Eric agreed. "Too bad we have to be preoccupied with Racine and Shakespeare."

"Ah, that's up to you frankophiles, n'est-ce pas?"

"Roger the matchmaker!"

"I try in my feeble way," Roger shrugged. "So what do you think?"

"I think it's time for bed," Eric evaded. Roger just snickered as they put on flannel pajamas and slipped into their dorm beds.

"Here's snoring at you, kid," Roger said among the ruffle of sheets. Eric let out a long groan until Roger laughed.

"Adieu, Casablanca," Roger answered at last, and they both went to sleep under collections of blankets and quilts.

* * *

Eric awoke first, focused slowly on five forty-seven a.m., and rolled over again to wait for the alarm to ring at six twenty. When it did, Roger turned it off and reached for the radio to get the latest weather. One look outside was pretty convincing. The sleet pattered down on the pavement and the dorm windows, and the fog hovered in a grey-white mass.

"I see a few people out there," Eric noted.

"Better them than us," Roger answered.

After some commercials, the newscaster turned to the weather. "Sleet changing over to snow until about noon. Six to eight inches of snow expected. Gradual clearing in the afternoon. Visibility is severely limited, and drivers are urged to stay off the roads if possible. An accident at Mass. and Com. Aves. has slowed traffic in the area as eight cars have piled up following the initial collision of a pickup truck with a taxi. T service continues, but above-ground stations will not be cleared of snow and ice for several hours at least. Footing at station stairwells may also be hazardous. Again, all who can remain indoors are best advised to do so until the afternoon at least." Roger turned off the report.

"What do you think?" he asked.

"The first debate is at eight a.m., right?"

"Yeah."

"We might get there and we might not."

"Can't go wrong there," Roger teased, but Eric pressed on. "I'll get dressed and see how the walking is. If we catch the T and it's not delayed, we might get to Tufts OK—if the tournament is still on."

"Or we could do all that for nothing. We should try their switchboard before we go anywhere."

"True. Let me see how it is." Eric dressed slowly, wrapped his parka around him, and put on a stocking hat and gloves. Roger started some more hot water for tea and waited. He turned the radio back on. Now an accident on the Mass. Pike had blocked one eastbound lane in Newton. Trucks had started plowing and some sanders had been out most of the night, but the snow estimate, with a sleet undercoating, was now likely to rise as low pressure had stalled over eastern Massachusetts and offshore. Eric returned.

"How is it?"

"As bad as they say. The sidewalks are terrible and cars are barely creeping along. I didn't see anyone at the subway entrance, though the fog makes it hard to see anything. I didn't walk all the way there." Eric shook off some ice pellets and snow from his shoulders into the nearby sink and wiped his face with a towel. He hung his coat on a chair back. Roger looked over the entertainment pages of the paper again.

"Ah, look what's here, my dear Eric! *My Fair Lady*'s playing at Newton Center Cinema today." Eric laughed.

"No, really. It's the new musical with Rex Harrison and Audrey Hepburn. Matinee's at two. That theater isn't far from here and it's out of the way of most traffic. By then, the storm will probably have cleared."

"Yeah, but—" Roger put down the paper and stared at Eric, whose wrinkled brow softened when he detected the slight smile on Roger's face.

"So what are you telling me, Preston?" Roger arose from the bed as if before a podium and cleared his throat.

"My esteemed colleague, the debate gods clearly do not want us to honor them today, else why isolate us here in a BC dungeon while the wind howls and the snows pile high?" Roger gathered momentum, and when Eric started to interrupt, the speaker raised a forbidding finger and continued.

"Now our opponents would have you believe that attending the Tufts Tournament today is both feasible and necessary, even some sort of bizarre duty." Roger stared down Eric like a debate judge ripe for the taking and then glanced left and right to the imaginary sprinkling of spectators and possible spies for other teams. "But consider these points. One, traveling in this weather risks our health and well-being. Two, Herr Kruger already has three debate teams on sight to win this tournament, IF they are up to it."

Eric laughed out loud but quickly regained his debate judge's composure.

"Three"—Roger now raised three helpful fingers—"man does not live by rebuttals and devastating logic alone, but by every piece of cinematic trash brought forth from the tawdry wasteland of Hollywood. Four, Eric and Roger, and the dour, French-oppressed Eric especially, are in need of spiritual uplift and aesthetic sublimity."

Eric feigned to puke, but recovered himself.

"And five, my dear judge, five"—a handful of fingers now spread before Eric's face—"when this debate tournament has joined all those tournaments of yore in the dung heap of oratorical obscurity, what will history say of this erstwhile pair of forensic fanatics? Did they slosh to their doom through the white drifts of Boston? Did they defy common sense and their souls' inspiration to do Marshal Kruger's bidding? Or did they, at last, think anew and act anew, asking NOT what the hell they could do for their nerdy debating team, but what they could do on a dismal Saturday in Beantown to have, dare I say it, some FUN, to dance with the beckoning fair lady, and to proclaim with Dr. King that they were free at last, free at last, thank God almighty, we are free at last?" Roger collapsed back onto his bed in oratorical exhaustion as Eric stood in applause and bent over in laughter.

"Roger Preston, you have never been better! You have just won the Tufts Tournament by refusing to attend it, and if that's not persuasion, I don't know what is." When their laughter ended, they stared across the little dorm room at each other. Roger finally broke the spell.

"So what do you think, mon ami?"

Eric looked out into the weather once more. "Debating is about the last thing I want to do today, especially if I have to struggle even to get there."

"Indisputable," Roger assured him.

"In fact," Eric added in a different tone that caught Roger off guard, "maybe a guy struggling in three college courses and likely to flunk one of them—" Roger hastened to object, but this time Eric held the floor "—I'm not finished. Maybe that guy must come to his senses and finally make some choices." Here Eric shifted pronouns and looked directly at Roger. "I ought to be back at school trying to get this Racine-Shakespeare monster under control, and instead I'm here in someone's boring dorm room trying to figure out how to get across a city of sleet and snow in time for debates I don't care about and am more likely to lose than to win because I can't decide NOT to debate at all anymore!" Roger made no move toward a rebuttal but just looked steadily at Eric and nodded.

"Yes," he said at last, "maybe that IS what you need to do."

And so it was settled. Roger made his way to a pay phone and left a message at the Tufts switchboard for Coach Kruger of St. James College. Roger and Eric were snowed in, would not be able to make the scheduled debates this morning, would attend a movie this afternoon, weather permitting, and would take a bus back to St. James and talk to him next week. Good luck if you are able to debate. Some messages were much easier to leave than to deliver in person. This was one of them. Roger thought that if Kruger didn't kick him off the team, he would debate again. Eric knew he would not and felt as fresh as the afternoon air once the storm had cleared and Roger and he had bought their tickets for *My Fair Lady*.

IV

The odd feeling of post-debate freedom soon merged for Eric into the odder prospect of failing college French. As December passed into January, he met with Michelle and they moved the great opus forward. She would read his English, ask a few questions to be sure of his meaning or to identify more exactly the tone he wanted, and then propose a French version of it, a few sentences at a time. He would either agree or ask why she had used a certain French phrase or this verb instead of that one. Sometimes he would opt for a simpler version over her more complex one as more credible coming from him. As he gained confidence, he tried translating his English text himself first and then letting Michelle review and revise. Page by page, the paper took bilingual form.

When they took breaks from the tedious work, they talked about Eric's difficulties with French. Despite her fluency, Michelle understood the overwhelmed feeling anyone could have when a subject was elusive. Certain math courses—"most math courses," she amended—did that to her. And what would she do with her French major and he with his eventual English degree? And how did they like their schools? She was particularly curious about the all-male Jesuit world of St. James, a different cosmos from secular, coed Claraton University? And their answers just led to more questions and to all the uncertainties of humanities' undergraduates studying what they wanted with only vague notions of practical prospects. They both agreed that Roger was a great friend and a talented, funny, sociable guy, more at ease with people than either of them. So Michelle said, though Eric wondered how that could be true for a beauty like her with all those Claraton men at her doorstep. But her looks could draw the wrong guys, he guessed, and even push potential girlfriends away.

Mostly, he and Michelle just edged around these personal sub-jects and stayed on topic, partly to meet Eric's mid-January deadline and partly because an academic project was safer turf than emotional revelations. He noticed her looks, of course, and sensed that she knew that he noticed, but that must be familiar territory for her. What guy would not find her shape and her face and her auburn hair attractive? She dressed with style but never revealingly, as if she need not flaunt the obvious or give guys the wrong idea. He didn't know if she had a boyfriend and never dreamed of asking. She treated him with interest and concern, with sympathy for his troubles in French, and sometimes with a supportive note of resentment at the rigid standards of Dr. Montreville.

"Will this paper let you pass the course?" she asked.

"Actually, I don't know. Montreville said I could do it but that course grades were still primary. So I don't know how he'll count it. If I ask, he might think I'm looking for some sort of guarantee, so I just need to do it and see what happens."

"That's pretty indefinite, isn't it?"

"Yes. Anyway, the topic itself is interesting and"—he paused—"with your help I am even learning a lot more French."

"Well, thanks. I'm glad." She sat back and brushed a strand of hair off her forehead. "A couple of more meetings and we'll be done," she said neutrally.

"I know," he agreed. "I still wish you'd let me pay you for this, like I would for any tutorial."

"No, no, I don't want that. I enjoy the work and am learning about these plays. Besides, I've never tried to do this sort of transla-tion before. It's interesting."

And so they met at the same Dinsmore Library table twice more until the translation was done and he shook her hand and thanked her. "It's been fun," she flashed a smile back at him, "and I hope you get the passing grade you deserve for all this extra effort."

"Me too. Thanks. Bye." They waved and left each other at the Dinsmore steps, and Eric finished his careful, tedious typing of the French version of the essay. Two days before the agreed deadline, he slipped it into a large yellow envelope with a brief cover note and left it in Montreville's mailbox, not knowing what he would hear back or when.

"It's done," he announced to Zack that night as they studied for exams in their room.

"Good. Talk about a lot of work for an uncertain reward! I'd have nailed down that old bastard about what this was going to be worth."

"I doubt that." Eric smiled at the idea. "He's keeping his options open and won't promise anything."

"So here you are," Zack intoned toward the ceiling, "a poor sinner in the hands of an angry Jesuit God."

Eric laughed. "Montreville's not a Jesuit."

"Not *in the cloth*, Malone, but in his diabolical heart, he cannot deny it."

"The Jebbies are OK," Eric said in weak rebuttal, and they both returned to their books.

* * *

When the exams were done, Eric waited a day before asking his parents to come get him. Time alone, or nearly so, on campus felt good, even in the January cold. He walked among the buildings and the tall trees and made a loose series of loops that slowly rose toward the top of the hill where, on warmer nights, he'd stared at the sky full of stars beyond the glare of campus and city lights. No night walk today in single digit temperatures. Instead, he looked down on the late afternoon stillness and on the snow of the distant Worcester hills, and he felt in that moment that anything could be endured, even a stupid French grade. If he weren't the scholar he imagined or the winning debater he had been, then he must be something else. All that mattered was to figure out what that was and how to pursue it.

The exams had gone well enough. Even French he might have marginally passed, so his course grade seemed to rest on how Montreville would handle the Racine and Shakespeare paper. He decided now to let his parents know in advance that a failing grade was possible. Once back in Lowell, he explained to them all that had happened. They were calm about it, more sympathetic than disappointed and not the least angry. From then on, Dad said no more about the classical curriculum he had long prized. "I'm sorry things have been difficult for you," he offered, "but one more semester and then you can major, right?"

"Yes, and won't it be fine!" Eric smiled back.

So when the F in French arrived with the other grades in the mail, it was simply the new status quo. Back at St. James, Eric made another appointment with Fr. Duchenes and asked if he *now* could switch to a different teacher. Duchenes nodded politely and signed the transfer form without comment. What had been impossible in mid-semester was now just a bureaucratic formality. Eric did not bother to ask why. The F was clearly his passport. To his relief, he quickly found that his new teacher, an older man named Dr. Brinkley, willingly explained French grammar in English. Eric's grades improved immediately, and soon he took aim at a B for the semester, and to his own amazement he hit that target.

With debate meetings and tournaments gone and having nowhere to go but up academically, Eric took to his reading with a new energy and a deeper curiosity.

"Best damn C+ intellectual egghead bookworm I ever saw," Zack teased him. Others who'd come to him for English and philosophy help were also glad his French trials were over. Only Latin and Greek held him back now, and however obscure they became, he would pass them—*he . . . would . . . pass . . . them . . .*—and he did.

Each week in the spring of '65 brought his English major closer, and meanwhile he had his own "consolation of philosophy," like his bookworm idol Boethius. The bearer of that consolation was surely the most extraordinary teacher of Eric's life so far, Professor J. Robert Lund. From Plato and Aquinas to Descartes, Kant, Nietzsche, and Cassirer, classmates agreed with Eric that whatever philosopher he taught, Lund *became* that philosopher. Who could tell what Lund himself believed? Like trying to figure out what Shakespeare *actually* thought! Lund's coy smile deflected all such direct questions as slightly obscene. "We are not what we seem," he conceded once when admitting a weakness for a certain daytime soap opera. Which one, he would not say. The magnificent balance of Aquinas and the boldness (was it craziness?) of Nietzsche he conveyed with equal persuasion. Soon his sophomore philosophers gave up trying to "uncover" him and just savored the presence of a superior mind. Here was a reason to be at St. James, the only reason finally to be in a classroom at all, Eric thought. Was Lund a Platonist, a Tomist, a Nietzschean, an Existentialist? Who could say? That spring the only philosophical certainty was that they were all Lundians.

"How God-damn good was *that*!" George Delaney had almost shouted to Eric on their way out of Lund's closing lecture on Jacques Maritain. "Makes me halfway Catholic, for Chrissakes!"

"Careful, pilgrim," Eric smiled, "your conversion would sent shock waves through your dorm. Imagine what Lund could do with Camus and Sartre. I'd like to read *The Stranger* with him."

"Yeah," George shot back, "I need a good dose of agnostic angst now to clear my theological sinuses. And what's that other one? *The Plague?* Sounds cheery."

"That's better, George," Eric patted him on the shoulder. "Take two Camus and you'll be OK in the morning. If that fails, read Marcus Aurelius for the thirty-fourth time."

As they exited Finnerty Hall, Jeff Sanderson caught their eyes simultaneously and shook his head in wonder at Lund's clarity and eloquence. They smiled back with nothing more to say.

V

Eric's paper on Racine and Shakespeare appeared in his mailbox on the first Monday in February in the same envelope he had left for Montreville. Eric was curious to see what his *former* French professor would say about it. He opened the flap and slid out the text. On the top center of the cover page by the title was a large check mark and "Excellent!" below it. Nothing more. No grade. By now, with the course behind him, Eric wanted some sense of how he had done. What did Montreville think of his thesis? How good was the French that he and Michelle had crafted? What about certain sentences they had struggled with? But as Eric paged through the paper, he found no further comments. None at all. Not even any marginal lines or marks. Montreville had nothing more to say about it. Had he even read it? Yes, Eric calmed himself, he had probably read it, but why no feedback? Was that Montreville's way of being noncommittal about counting such a paper for a course grade? Did he assume that Eric had gotten help and so did not want to open any "discussion" of the content or the translation? Eric could almost understand that. He *had* gotten help, but Montreville had never forbidden that. And if he knew in advance that he could not count the essay in the course grade, why had he agreed to let Eric write it? Why did he even specify a length?

College life was a strange mix of remoteness and engagement. Montreville was the epitome of rules, order, and detachment—of fidelity to his subject as if students hardly existed. Then Lund, with consummate dedication to *his* subject, could lift students out of their petty little minds into moments of wonder. If someone asked Eric what sort of school St. James was, the answer would waver between these extremes. Confusion reigned. Would Ro find an Ivy League school any different?

"Yes, I think I am going to transfer," Ro said to Eric the last time they had a moment together in the caf. "I just think I can find greater challenges elsewhere and more people to talk with about what I am studying."

"And what do you want to study?"

"Not sure. Maybe sociology or anthropology."

"Well, I hope it works out, whatever you decide," Eric said with as much enthusiasm as he could.

"Thanks. And good luck to you here, Eric. You've been through more than I think I could stand."

"Oh, no. We can stand plenty, I think. We just have to think of ourselves in new ways."

"Yeah." Ro paused as if thinking about that. "I guess I'm doing that, too." After another quiet moment, Ro moved to leave. "Got to go. Better be on time to my classes while I'm still here."

"So long, Ro."

In the rush of the semester's end, Eric and Ro never talked again apart from a quick "Hi" on the way to a class or an exam. Nor had Eric seen much of Roger since debating days had ended. Just before his English exam was to start, he saw old debate partner Craig Mulrooney in the hallway. Craig came over to him and said that Roger had been vague at the last debate meeting about committing himself to junior year debating. Craig wondered if Eric knew why.

"No," Eric answered. "I haven't actually talked with Roger in a few months."

Only later, at the start of school in September, did Eric realize that Roger was also gone from St. James. The following January, he received a belated Christmas card from some army base in the Midwest. Roger had enlisted in the army and could end up in Vietnam.

Undiscovered Wisdom

I

Ro had transferred to Yale. Roger was in the army and probably on his way to Vietnam. What would college be like without them, and without the pressures—and rewards—of debating? French, Latin, and Greek were also gone from Eric's curriculum and out of his system. He could study what he wanted at last, but not with two of the guys he wanted. College was beginning again, or had "high school" finally ended? Weightless at the top of the roller coaster, he braced for the plunge.

Classes suddenly came alive with Shakespeare, the Romantic poets, and modern British drama replacing declensions and conjugations. He soon knew more about particular writers and began to think about aesthetic truths alongside the rational and doctrinal ones. He talked about *Antony and Cleopatra, King Lear,* and Shaw's *Man and Superman* with classmates as galvanized as he was by professors who savored their subject. The best of Shelley and Keats emboldened him; the Irish theater of Yeats, O'Casey, and Synge made him feel Irish in new ways. Here was art ripe with life, and life at the intensity of art. Each week, new beauties illuminated and challenged old truths. This was literature's moveable feast.

Alongside the excitement of literature, philosophy was still intriguing, though no teacher would rival Dr. Lund. In his junior ethics course, Eric had Fr. Allen Flaherty, a fortyish Jesuit of military bearing. His central text was *Plato's Modern Enemies and the Theory of Natural Law* by a Harvard professor named John Wild. Any ethics course could raise moral and social issues and allow students to struggle with them, but unlike Lund, Flaherty tended to dominate his subject matter rather than disappear into it. For him, natural law ethics contained the answers to all moral dilemmas, and he never allowed discussion to wander far from his parameters. He even took to reading certain passages from Wild and directing students to underline specific sentences, as if "truth" had been captured in a sentence or phrase. Wild's book refuted modern philosophical criticisms of Plato as "misunderstandings" and described natural law as the essential tendencies in all things necessary for their fulfillment. Flaherty then added certain Catholic moral teachings as the Christian perfection of Plato's ideal forms, and the moral universe became a place of rigorous structure and order. Dad might have taken such a course thirty years before.

To find some thinking room, Eric decided to write about conscientious objection for his research paper. He read some of Thoreau, Tolstoy, Gandhi, and King on nonviolence, but their ideas about human perfectibility seemed too bold for natural law ethics or Catholic "just war" teachings. Flaherty was not much impressed with Eric's thinking or his use of sources. Fair enough. He could do better with these heady ideas. Yet with the news from Vietnam ever more complicated and American power in the Caribbean under challenge, not to mention the vast cost of the arms race, some fundamental questions were unavoidable and overdue. Where was the elusive peace that world leaders all said they wanted? Textbook ethics seemed impotent in the political world as '65 slipped away.

Then he thought of Roger in the army and probably on his way to the Mekong Delta or the Ho Chi Minh Trail. Why had they never talked about *that* instead of debate tournaments and the Red Sox's futile quest for another pennant? What had led Roger to such a radical change in his life, and how could he keep it all inside? Had he been guarding his own uncertainties or saving Eric from life-and-death choices? Maybe he was saving himself from a Vietnam debate in liberal academe. And how much did Roger's unexplained family life, another of their non-topics, influence his abrupt departure from college? Eric had a sense of what Ro was seeking, but about Roger he understood little anymore. Separate paths had cut in half his four college years with them. Nothing gold could stay.

II

Autumn blazed from the Worcester hills that October and climbed the campus tree by tree like a relentless fire until the whole college was canopied in color. On a Saturday in early November no longer claimed by debate tournaments, Eric at last got to a Knights football game, this one against Claraton University, their much larger local rival.

A dark ridge of clouds on the western horizon looked briefly ominous, then slowly receded until the sun and low-fifties temperatures ruled. A light breeze made jackets feel good, but fans toting blankets mostly sat on them. Eric found a place at the edge of the student section by himself. He liked seeing all his classmates without getting caught between shouters or sitting next to someone who had to second-guess every play.

The crowd had filled all but the highest few rows of seats above the end zones of Holden Field, a cozy oval stadium at the bottom of the St. James campus. Route 290 swung in a long loop around the park, and drivers who dared might see a play or two at fifty miles an hour until tailgaters forced them on. Today there wasn't much to see through the first quarter as the teams traded rushing yardage and long punts. Football had never gotten hold of Eric, so he watched the athleticism and cheered good plays without really caring where they led. Piles of bodies quickly smothering bursts of violent action seemed more about force than finesse to him. Only a great headlong catch of a soaring pass looked anything like Willie Mays in centerfield. And nothing in football resembled the intricate beauty of Ted Williams at bat. But what did, in any sport? His unfair examples fed a bias that would never pass. All the baseball drama of decades to come would fill his old age like a vintage newsreel of Cobb sliding or Ruth about to unload. Was he the only fan lost in baseball reveries at this college football game?

A sudden roar brought his eyes back into focus as classmate Jake Lawrence launched a forty-yard pass to sophomore wide receiver Eldridge at the Panthers ten-yard line. Two plays later, Lawrence took it in himself and the Knights led 7–0. But then the defenses resumed control, and Eric's eyes wandered all over the crowd. There was Zack about twenty rows below him and oddly with a group of sophomores. Quiet Larry Donovan loved to yell at football games (so Eric had heard), and there he was hollering about every mistake on the field. Eric looked closely across the stadium to the Claraton side at clusters of Panther black and yellow, like bees swarming in a vast hive of bleachers. At the two-minute warning before halftime, the cheerleaders and marching bands had crowded beyond each end zone and were ready to parade to midfield. He scanned the far corner of the Claraton side again, and somewhere near the twenty yard line he glimpsed Michelle Forrester with her arm hooked around the right elbow of a tall guy in a dark blue jacket. As he watched, the guy sipped a drink with his other hand and then passed it to Michelle, who drank deeply and turned the empty cup upside down in his waiting hand. She laughed and leaned into him. So there was her boyfriend, maybe. They looked good together. Minutes later Eric tried to spot them again, but either they had moved or he wasn't looking in the right place. He didn't see them again.

Halfway into the fourth quarter, Claraton finally scored to tie the game at seven. Two minutes later, the Panthers recovered a Knights fumble and set up a field goal attempt after their offense had stalled at the Knights thirty. A late afternoon breeze had stiffened into a wind helping the Knights, but the Claraton kicker leaned into the ball and drilled a hard liner through the air and just above the crossbar. It was 10–7 Panthers with less than four minutes to go.

Lawrence took control again on the Knights twelve and mixed runs and short passes to reach the Panthers forty-eight with 1:35 left. OK, Eric admitted, this was pretty good—like the bottom of the ninth down 4–3 with a runner on first and two out. Barring a homer, the home team needed at least two good plays, and maybe three, to win. An out, or a turnover, and the game ended. The Knights student section looked on tensely and shouted play options. Lawrence would probably try to get within field goal range, then throw for the TD (the home run swing) and finally call for the field goal to tie (like a liner in the gap after the runner had stolen second). But an end run by halfback Grabowski gained only four yards and took too much time as he fought the tackle. In baseball, of course, there was no time and no play had to be hurried. Lawrence took the next snap, evaded a defensive rush, and then threw a likely touchdown to Craig Nelson, wide open at the eight-yard line, but the toss was beyond his reach and Nelson's fingers deflected it high before he caught the rebound and fell forward, still inbounds. With just nine seconds left and no time-outs to call, Lawrence rushed everyone forward for a last play without a huddle, but his quick end zone pass to a well-defended receiver fell harmlessly away as the clock expired.

The game was over. A good one on a beautiful football day. Too bad, Eric thought, that the Knights didn't have other options. Suppose they could have called time, put a speedy pinch runner on first for the weak hitter who had just worked the pitcher for a crucial walk, and sent up a left-handed pinch hitter for their pitcher. Then, with two on and two gone, the batter would cross up the defense by stroking a liner over short into the gap to score the winning runs with a final, crashing slide at home. Oh, well. This was football, and the clock had run out.

Eric joined some disappointed classmates in the caf for a hot cup of tea (to their coffees and cokes mostly) and waited for the dining hall meal. A light brown "mystery meat" was often the weekend fare, but with all these football families and alums on campus, something better might be happening. And it was. Chicken with rice and mixed vegetables and an ice cream sundae dessert helped to soften the gloom of defeat.

I I I

The end of debating and of the three languages gave Eric time for more than just a football Saturday. Suddenly he discovered the weekly film festival of new and old movies. Dorm life got more interesting as he found time for evening "head sessions" with class politicians and dorm philosophers wandering beyond their majors. If Sodality guys wondered how Catholicism should (or would) change, the campus skeptics questioned why "the disciples" should be defending all that "patriarchal medievalism" anyway. And the politicos bemoaned where LBJ and McNamara were headed in Vietnam and how that escalating conflict would overrun the War on Poverty that Johnson had sententiously declared. And what was Bobby Kennedy really up to as a new senator from New York?

In church politics, how would Paul VI handle Vatican II initiatives now that the council had ended—prematurely? Would St. James ever consider going coed or admitting more than a handful of minority students? Wasn't it time to retire "in loco parentis" and let "young adult men" decide when visiting women should leave their rooms? If the right group came together, all this fur could fly and more. Even the Sodality types found this freestyle, unofficial curriculum too much fun to miss, though sometimes a somber conservative would leave abruptly and not show up again for a few weeks. And the radicals knew they were at St. James, not Columbia or Berkeley, so even they gave a nod to the official pieties. Some talk was just talk; everyone understood, no matter if a student government rep argued for a petition or a proposal.

"Let's form a committee," Jake Gordon urged about getting a coeducation discussion started.

"Ah, Senator Boredom," Delaney opined. "The bird shit has calcified on the coffin and the corpse is getting aromatic. By coeducation, the Jebbies mean for left- and right-handers, and woe unto the lefties who find themselves on the wrong side of the Just Judge."

Guys laughed at Delaney's endless flamboyance, which always made moderation sound like wisdom. Larry Donovan, the Sodality vice prefect who was slumming tonight with Delaney's coven, asked a little too earnestly, "Would we really be better off coed, I mean, for the integrity of the institution?"

"Well, Larry, you might not notice any improvement," Jeff Sanderson teased, "but normally equipped guys would." Even Donovan smiled and left the single-sex college cause to Eric, who took it up with uncertain convictions.

"Coeducation might cause some things that guys *wouldn't* like. Admitting women could mean that many guys wouldn't get in here. And suppose money for women's sports took away from men's teams. All the dorms, labs, and libraries would be shared. And wouldn't the curriculum have to change? Suppose we also had a lot of women faculty. That would probably mean some very different kinds of courses."

"Yes, yes, Malone. All of the above and mercifully so," Delaney countered. "What are we fearing? Is the *rigor mortis studiorum* so dear to us?"

"Yeah," added Jeff, "and wouldn't a woman theology professor have some points to make about women in the church, and maybe even one or two in the Trinity?" Donovan rolled his eyes at Eric, and Lenny Drexell, whom everyone figured for a future Jesuit, cleared his throat.

"I don't think we'll be changing the Trinity anytime soon. Being coed would not mean we'd stop being Catholic."

"Oh, that's right," Delaney sighed with feigned disappointment, as Drexell continued. "Women students and families who'd send them here would probably want some of the same things men want from a Catholic college. They might even reinforce some traditions that you heretics want to end." For once, Delaney's glibness failed him.

"Well, speaking for the heretics—and the heathens," Jeff gestured to Delaney who bowed, "I see your point, but I still think having women here would force us to ask some fundamental questions about the school."

"No doubt," agreed Eric, "but they won't really be *our* questions since none of this could happen till long after we're gone. Would you future alums give as much money to the school if it became coed?"

"I'd give more," Jeff answered quickly.

"I, on the other hand, would give exactly the same amount," Delaney interjected.

"Yeah," said Larry, "and we all know how much that would be."

"Nothin' from nothin' leaves nothin', right George?" Eric added.

"Ah, all you *cognoscenti* see right through me." George raised both hands in exasperation. "Well, gentlemen, given the geologic pace of change at dear old James, we can safely table these dangerous inquiries till, say, Thursday next, can't we?" Everyone agreed. "So off with you," George gave his typical dismissal, "and please ponder all that I have tried to teach you." Everyone smiled at Delaney's sweet condescension and shuffled off to bedtime or toward other voices in other rooms. A random guitar played gently at the far end of the corridor in solitary peacefulness as Eric walked back to his dorm and wondered where Zack was tonight. Their room was empty but only for another minute until Zack trudged in and laid a handful of books on his desk.

"Where have you been? We missed your wisdom at Delaney's tonight."

"Economics in a carrel at Dinsmore. You should have been there."

Eric laughed. "Couldn't make it. I was overthrowing the college with Delaney's cabal."

Zack smiled. "How far along is the conspiracy?"

"Dead at birth, I'd say." Zack waved an all-knowing hand and tossed his shirt and pants into the bottom of his closet and buttoned his maroon flannel pajamas for bed.

"We won't live to see the revolution, Malone."

"That's what I told George. Our only voice will be through the alumni fund." Zack chuckled a little into his pillow and Eric guessed that lights out was a good idea for him as well. He rolled into bed, briefly imagined the coed utopia, and fell quickly to sleep.

I V

Through that fall, winter, and spring Eliot Cahalane held forth on the comedies, histories, and tragedies of Shakespeare. His lectures wove textual analysis and allusions to critical essays with mini-performances of the crucial lines from a scene on which the meaning of the whole play might turn. Rosalind's insights and Romeo's exuberance reverberated against Richard III's diabolical wit and Lear's endless capacity for self-dramatizing anger and pain. It was all one vast, ineffable drama. Cahalane's contemporary analogies always sounded fresh, though Eric assumed that he had rehearsed them often and probably refined their delivery year after year. Of Julius Caesar's triumphant last entry into Rome, Cahalane said, "Imagine that kind of power. Suppose LBJ arrived at the Army–Navy game, raised his hand to the hushed masses, and declared, 'Mah fellah Americans, Army wins, 27–22. Drive home safelah.' And the stadium empties with never a play called. Gentlemen, *that* is power."

Cahalane saw Juliet's nurse as a profane old lady of embarrassing jests, which Lady Capulet could barely abide. Lady Macbeth, of course, was the evil seductress who mesmerized her husband into murder and then fell apart as he fought on hopelessly. And Cahalane never tired of finding little gems of Shakespearean imagery full of inexhaustible meaning. "When Antony is dying by his own sword," Cahalane reminded his packed lecture hall, "he says to Cleopatra, 'I am dying, Egypt.' Only then does he call her Egypt, as if Rome, or *his* Rome at least, is dying at Egypt's feet. You can't teach that kind of writing, gentlemen." Heads nodded, and all wondered why they hadn't caught that meaning before.

Delaney, Sanderson, and Esslin were in Cahalane's class with Eric. Sometimes they debated Cahalane's interpretations, which could sound too glib for the *whole* meaning, but which had a deftness that the bard himself would have liked.

Eric scribbled quick pages of Cahalane notes and rewrote them later to fill out sentences and add details that he hadn't been fast enough to write. Month by month, his binder of class notes filled, and his appreciation of Shakespeare—and of Cahalane—grew. Occasionally, Cahalane would slow down for a question, but most students found their own inquiries pedestrian after one of his expansive answers, with now and then a Shakespearean insult tossed in. "You dog, you knave, you slave, you cur!" Cahalane could roar at some obtuse questioner, but always with a theatrical smile that invited the victim to enjoy the battering. Eric often felt worn out after a Cahalane class, like an athlete who'd done everything to keep up with a brilliant coach's commands.

"Once in a while Will does err," Cahalane archly conceded one day, "but even then we should be attentive because the mistake is a step toward the transcendent genius to follow. A lifetime is no time at all to comprehend what he gave us. So, Acts II and III of *The Tempest* for Monday, you peasant slaves." He scooped up his notes for a quick exit but stopped when a student managed to impress him with a last-second question.

A mind like Cahalane's could be forgiven occasional impatience with the ignorant, the unimaginative, and the unread. The point was to keep up with him, not to expect that he'd slow down for you. Eventually the assignments outpaced Eric's ability to do them on time, and "behind in the reading" became a given, like being hungry or having a pulse. Everyone was "behind in the reading" and always would be, though some were behind on much more ambitious lists. They "failed" at what others never attempted. Yet what Eric *did* read kept him so stimulated that unread works just became "future pleasures"—unless they would be covered on the next test.

No one else in the junior year stirred Eric's mind like Cahalane, but the other English electives had their moments. A visiting British lecturer named Reginald Watson taught Modern British Drama and included in it works by Ibsen, Strindberg, Chekhov, and Pirandello, which made the course as much European as British. For Eric, Synge, Yeats, and O'Casey had the eerie charm of a vaguely familiar world just beyond his grandfathers' lives. And Dr. Alonzo Sousa took his nine seminar students through the high points of English Romanticism. Coleridge's "Frost at Midnight," Shelley's "Mont Blanc" and "Lines Written Among the Euganean Hills," and the half-dozen or so great odes of Keats lingered beyond all the others for Eric as the students presented their papers and critiqued each other's. Sousa's text-expounding discourses were conversational around the seminar table and yet mind-stretching in their reflections on words and levels of imagery and the interfused movements of sound and meaning within a poem. Here was the alluring work of making meaning that critics did consciously in essays, and poets did more intuitively in lines that seemed endlessly fertile and lush, as if they had always existed and could hardly bear a word change without collapsing entirely. For the most devoted, the greatest poems became secular scriptures, full of undiscovered wisdom. The Catholic conscience and Gospel images of Jesus vied with the aesthetic spell of free-thinking, free-feeling writers for the loyalty of Eric's mind and heart.

V

When spring finally came and the night winds relented, Eric took evening walks to the top of the hill to see the lights of the school and the city again and to savor the life that had finally opened to him at St. James. He always walked alone, but on the way down he might randomly see some friend from one tribe or another—Delaney's crew, the Sodality guys, old debate teammates, or gregarious jocks—and spend some time with them in a dorm room or at the caf all the way to the bottom of the stratified campus. On a few nights he stopped at the school chapel, more like a Gothic cathedral really, to compare one kind of inspiration with another: the stars and city lights to the ceiling lines faintly lit by a few votive candles far below. The warm night breezes and the austere church vault above the eternally motionless statues were like some mind-bending yoga that stretched him this way and that so the center could become more alive.

One April Saturday on his way back from the summit, he saw Lenny Drexell heading toward the junior dorms from Dinsmore, and fifty feet behind him were Albert Deleveaux and Randy O'Dell, an unlikely pair who had both left early from the Ave Maria College dance in the old gym. Deleveaux was a French major who loved all things European and got more Bs than As because he followed his impulses instead of the curriculum. O'Dell, slightly paunchy, had chased athletic dreams in football and basketball until his appetites overcame his abilities and his was cut from both teams. Tonight he had a drinker's breath and proclaimed himself hungrier than a horse in heat. The others laughed, and Eric blurted out a crazy idea. "Would you guys like to get some food at the caf and then come back to my room for a while? Zack's home this weekend, so we wouldn't be bothering anyone."

The four looked at each other and smiled at the oddity of the group. The weirdness of it appealed.

"OK," said Lenny first.

"Why not?" Albert agreed. Randy burped his approval, and the four ambled downhill to the caf below Durkin Dining Hall, bought food and drinks, and carried them all uphill to Hendrickson dorm. Eric cleared off his bureau for everyone's sandwiches and cups, then pulled the two desk chairs out into the room near the beds. O'Dell stretched out on Zack's bed with the pillow for a prop, and Eric sat on his mattress with his back on his pillow against the wall. Albert and Lenny took their hot coffees and sat in the desk chairs.

"So you're probably wondering why I've called this meeting," Albert suddenly announced with a smile.

"Shit, yeah," O'Dell answered. "Is this a Confirmation class or what?" He looked at Lenny, clearly the most devout of the group.

"Not tonight," Lenny countered, to Randy's noisy relief.

Everyone ate for a quiet moment till Eric looked at Albert and Randy and asked, "So how was the dance?"

"A pleasant array of incompatible fantasies," Albert quipped.

"The usual cattle call," Randy corrected him, and everyone enjoyed the jarring images.

"I didn't know cattle could have fantasies," Eric said, but Randy assured him that they could.

"Ya know," Randy continued between sips of Mountain Dew, "they bring in all those Ave Maria girls for us St. James guys, and everybody tries hard to pretend they don't care, and you can't even hear much talk over the sound system. So you holler at a few girls for a while and dance a little and get bored and go the men's room for a quick chug of vodka or Jim Beam and then pop a few mints to hide the smell and by the time you're back out there the one girl you half wanted to meet is with someone else or gone."

"Sounds exciting," Eric said. "What about you, Albert?"

"Oh, I was looking for a girl I met at Maria last fall. She called last week and said she'd see me there, but I didn't find her."

"Too bad," Lenny said.

"Yes and no. I like just watching everyone and seeing what the girls wear. I imagine too much and dance too little."

"Regular chick thief, that Deleveaux," O'Dell teased, and everyone laughed.

The guys ate silently again. O'Dell looked at some pictures and a small stack of books on Zack's desk and was careful to put everything back as it was. Lenny went down the hall to the men's room and returned.

"So what should we talk about?" Eric asked in the awkward silence.

"Well . . ." O'Dell hesitated, looking at Lenny.

"Well what, Randy?" Lenny said, shifting in his chair.

"How about a little . . . God talk?" Randy heard himself say.

"God talk?" Albert asked with surprise as the others stared at Randy.

"Yeah, I mean, hell, what do you guys really believe?"

"I thought you didn't want any theology tonight," Lenny looked back at him, confused.

"Right, I don't. I just mean, ya know, just . . . what we feel about it. No preaching. No judgments. Just how you guys deal with all that." Randy sat up on Zack's bed as if maybe he'd gotten too personal but didn't want to take it back.

"OK," Eric said after a long moment. "Let's just be honest. We spend so much time saying what we're supposed to say at a Jesuit school that maybe we're afraid to admit doubts or ask those *inappropriate questions.*"

"Yes," said Albert, "like why God must always be He and never She?"

"Or how prayers don't really seem to change anything," Lenny added.

Everyone looked at him with surprise.

"No, really. Yes, I pray and I believe in it for myself, but mostly to humble myself and just to sense God's presence. I don't actually expect answers to prayers."

"What's the Catholic teaching on that?" Eric wondered aloud. "God gives us what we need, not necessarily what we ask for."

"Isn't that pretty vague?" Randy countered. "And besides, people who starve to death or get killed in a war *didn't* get what they needed, did they?"

"Not in this world, anyway," Lenny added. "To believe in divine love or justice, you have to take eternal life seriously. Only there, in eternity, can God's promises be kept and wrongs made right. The Church speaks of the mystery of God's love. We can't know it or possess it or measure it. It's beyond our understanding, so faith is needed."

"That all sounds pretty abstract," Albert said. "Calling something a mystery is just another way of saying we're not sure what we're talking about. Besides, we are created in God's image, so we are told. I think that means that we can be creators of truth, just as God creates. I mean, say, through art a painter or poet envisions something beautiful or true and expresses it in a work that can become an inspiration for himself and others. That's not scriptural revelation or Church theology, but I think it is very spiritual. Like Keats's idea that beauty is truth and truth beauty."

"I've known some beauties and that's the truth," Randy chimed in, and everyone laughed.

"Art can be spiritual," Lenny pressed on past Randy's joke, "but Jesus wasn't just an artist."

"Well, art is fine, but what about sex?" Randy cut in again. Everyone smiled and waited. "Yeah, I know. Leave it me to drag sex in, but I'm serious. Is it only our minds that are made in God's image? What about our bodies? And if people are male and female—which I have noticed that they are—doesn't God have to include both sexes, too?"

"But God is a spirit, not a body," Lenny said.

"Yeah, but *we* are both! We are sexual!" Randy insisted with immense pride. "So where did that come from, and doesn't it relate somehow to the Creator? I mean, sometimes sexual, ah, intimacy"—Randy chose the word delicately, to everyone's amusement—"is about the only divine feeling a guy has. And how can any religion that discards or forbids that be the whole truth?"

Lenny was on the verge of speaking, so everyone waited. "I agree that our physical selves come from God, but the scriptures all suggest that we are to move from matter toward spirit. You know, 'the flesh kills, but the spirit gives life.'"

"A hard doctrine," Albert responded. "It leaves us dualistic, self-contradictory. Shouldn't the truth unify opposites and make wholeness possible? Doesn't truth *have* to do that?" Everyone thought for a moment.

"Are you all OK with this talk?" Randy asked suddenly. "I didn't mean to upset anyone. I just get tired of never really letting it all hang out."

"No, no, it's OK. It's good," Eric answered. Lenny and Albert nodded agreement. The silence resumed for several seconds as the four turned over the mystery of truth.

"Sometimes," Eric spoke at last, "I think there are different ways of knowing. Isn't that what we've been saying? Religious teachings claim to offer knowledge by means of faith. People believe that something supernatural has been revealed and that a certain religion or church—their own, of course—actually speaks for God. Others try to know truth by reason through philosophy or science. They think logically or conduct experiments and set aside anything illogical or unverifiable, like revelation and miracles. Then Albert was talking about art creating inspiration. That's a kind of knowing through imagination and creative energy. We don't limit ourselves to religious doctrines or scientific laws. In a sense, the artist 'creates' the truth. And then Randy mentioned sex, as we all hoped he would." A quick laugh broke the tension and Randy nodded solemnly, only too glad to have elevated the dialogue.

"But really, Randy's profound point"—Eric nodded to him and Randy smiled as if at a budding disciple—"is that sexual experience is another way of knowing truth and is not just hedonistic."

"At last you understand me, Malone," Randy shouted in mock joy as everyone laughed again.

"I mean," Eric continued, "if our bodies are also from God, don't they have a role to play in getting us back to God, to what the Church calls salvation? So we can know in these different ways, and we each decide which way to follow."

"Or don't we follow them all?" Albert asked. "Some are more theological, others more rational, aesthetic, or sensual, but we all experience life in all these ways. And don't we need to? Doesn't any real truth have to accommodate all these aspects of experience?"

"Yes," Lenny agreed, "but are they all equal ways of knowing? Can we equate divine revelation with artwork or science or sensuality? Are matter and spirit equally important?"

"Or," amended Eric, "equally true? If our bodies eventually die but our souls last forever, can we trust our souls to our bodily wisdom? Isn't spiritual wisdom more enduring?"

"I don't know," Randy answered. "Some of the so-called spiritual people are also the coldest and cruelest. They preach a love and joy that sound like the end of all joy and a goddamn abstraction of love. People in touch with their bodies are warmer and more alive."

"That's often true," Lenny admitted, "though I don't think it has to be."

"So do we each choose our own way to find truth?" Albert asked.

"Well yes, we can," Eric answered. "We have that freedom, but shouldn't we always be listening for the deeper voices within us and distinguishing them from every random thought or appetite?"

"I don't hear a lot of inner voices," Randy observed, and after a second he burped so loudly that he actually bounced on Zack's bed and set off loud laughter.

"A prophet lives among us." Albert pointed at Randy. "We have just heard his inner voice." A few bits of rolled-up food wrappings tossed at Randy signaled the end of the symposium.

"This has been good," Eric said at last, looking around at everyone. "We probably didn't solve anything, but I liked just saying whatever we wanted without worrying about being right or wrong."

"Yes," said Lenny. "Good topic, Randy."

"Hey, I'm always looking to elevate the discourse in these hallowed halls," Randy concluded.

Everyone got up to leave. "Thanks, Eric, for putting up with us," Albert added. "Yeah, Eric. Nice idea," Lenny agreed.

"So long you guys." Eric gave a quick wave as they left. Then he closed his room door, changed for bed, and wondered himself to sleep.

VI

Ro had written to Eric several times since transferring to Yale. He wanted Eric to visit, and early in the spring semester they settled on the first weekend in March. Eric now had the Ford wagon for debate trips, and after attending his only Friday morning class, he started down 290 to the Mass Pike west, then to 84 south into Hartford, and onto 91 all the way to New Haven. Eric was excited to see Ro again and to take a first look at Yale, but he felt a shade of uncertainty about meeting Ro's new friends. In his letters, Ro spoke of the high-powered minds and international backgrounds of many new acquaintances—an opera buff, a couple of math-science whizzes who were trading ideas about Einstein's equations, and one English student who felt sure that his recent critical essay on *King Lear* was the best short piece anyone had ever written about the play. Yale students were the offspring of diplomats, university professors, and US Senators. If St. James had even a few such progeny, they kept awfully quiet about it in the dorms.

Religion at Yale, Ro commented, was either "high church" Christianity, scholarly Judaism, or aggressive unbelief. "A typical Eli," Ro had written, "is the cool young atheist who has 'freed himself' from theological hang-ups. At St. James, Catholicism is mainstream, though because of that not always much more than nominal. Here, to be religious at all is almost countercultural. You're an object of curiosity and maybe of amusement." Ro said that a couple of times he'd found himself defending some Catholic doctrine he wasn't very sure about just because a clever agnostic was tearing it apart. So Eric wondered how amusing *he* would be to Ivy League skeptics. The less he said, the better maybe. And would his old chemistry with Ro still be there at all?

He exited 91 and looked for Whaley and Whitney Avenues. When he found them, Ro was at the corner beyond the light. They spotted each other quickly and waved. Eric pulled to the curb, and Ro jumped into the front seat.

"Eric, I'm so glad to have you here," Ro said in his almost formal way.

"Me too, Ro. Tell me where to go." Ro gave directions, and soon Eric pulled the car into a tight side-street parking space.

"This will be all right for now. I'll think about where you can move to later. Let's go in. This is Trumbull House, where I live and have most of my classes."

So Ro and Eric headed into a vaguely British-looking building that reminded Eric a little of parts of the Harvard Yard, but without its secluded feeling—closer to the traffic and commotion of New Haven than Harvard seemed to Cambridge. Ro brought Eric up to his suite—an arrangement of shared space that looked much more adult than St. James dorm life. He showed him an available bed and an empty bureau. Once Eric had his things arranged, the two would take a walking tour of Trumbull and nearby places. So they did. At Mory's, they had a vegetable dip and soft drinks while Ro told some of the lore of the place. Eric had heard the Whiffenpoof Song without having any context for it.

"So those poor little lambs doomed from here to eternity drank here," Eric joked.

"Very good. True enough." Ro smiled in agreement. Eric thought of Delaney and Sanderson, whose theological skepticism would hardly get noticed at Yale. At St. James, they were the house agnostics and the objects of offbeat fashion.

"The funny thing is," Ro's voice brought Eric back, "Harvard and Yale began as church schools to train colonial ministers. Ministers and every other type of cleric still get educated here in the Divinity School, but the rest of Yale is steeped in secularity."

"A den of heathens, you mean."

Ro laughed again. "A very comfortable den, Eric. Let's not forget." Ro then saw someone he knew.

"Shelby, sit with us for a minute. Eric, this is Shelby Chandler, a grad student in literature—and philosophy, right?" Shelby bowed with amusement. "Eric Malone is visiting from St. James College." Hellos followed as Ro told each friend about the other. Shelby was a third-year grad student that Ro had met at a Newman Center mass.

"St. James?" Shelby said. "A very good school." He tried to avoid any hint of irony. "I had a friend from Groton who went there. An English major. He's at Oxford now."

"I'm an English major," Eric said cautiously.

"Oh, really," Shelby answered. "I'm combining comparative literature and philosophy, though I'd combine them better if I could master German." Shelby shrugged at the futility of such a project. *If only we could all master German*, Eric thought but said nothing. Ro explained that he'd met Shelby at the Newman Center because Shelby had decided last semester to attend at least once every sort of religious service he could find affiliated with Yale.

"Yes," Shelby explained, "I've been to the Newman and Hillel Centers, the Luther House, the Buddhist and Zen Buddhist services, a Quaker Meeting, the Unitarian Church, and the Hare Krishna celebration. I'm still looking for others." He paused and started to laugh. "A strange hobby, isn't it?"

"So what have you liked?" Eric ventured.

"Well, I grew up Episcopalian but without much real belief, you know. It was more of a cultural thing for my dad, though Mother liked to read the Bible on her own. Anyway, I guess the Unitarians and the Buddhists of the non-Zen variety interest me most. They have a large-mindedness and an openness to science that other religions don't seem as comfortable with." Eric sipped his ginger ale.

"I think it's interesting," Ro offered, "that Shelby would be so deliberate about trying to get a sense of each tradition."

"Yes, it is," agreed Eric. "The options are simpler at St. James."

Shelby smiled. "The Episcopal and Catholic traditions are so close, of course. I find great beauty in some of the Catholic rituals and in the precision of its dogmas. All those Marian titles and patron saints of this and that. And the religious orders! Jesuits, Franciscans, Dominicans, Benedictines. Not to mention the institution of the papacy. I mean, what other church has anything like it, really?" Ro and Eric nodded silent agreement.

"You could say, I think," Shelby continued, "that Catholicism is in some ways the Hinduism of the West. The Hindus have all their gods and goddesses, Vishnu's avatars, and every sort of little

ceremony, and the Catholics have saints and angels, litanies and votive candles, rosaries and novenas. In a purely aesthetic sense, they
are the world's two most ornate religions."

"I suppose that's right," Ro agreed.

"Then the reformers arrived. The great simplifiers. Luther and
the Puritans in the West, who have mellowed all the way into Unitarians. And the Buddhists in the East seeking to break the cycle of re-
incarnations. Today the Dalai Lama and the Unitarians are probably
as comfortable with each other as the Krishnas and the Catholics
should be." Shelby rested. Ro and Eric both laughed.

"Not too sure about the comfort level on the Catholic side," Ro
countered as Shelby smiled.

"You should be a comparative religion major," Eric suggested.

"Well, sorry if I go on a bit much about it. I do find it fascinating and a literary gold mine as well." Shelby ordered a white
wine. Eric and Ro kept to their soft drinks. Eric smiled to think
that Shelby's notions of Hindu-Catholic compatibility had never
come up at St. James Sodality meetings. He decided not to attempt
explaining what Sodality was, though Shelby would probably have
been interested.

"So," Shelby changed subjects, "you're here for the weekend. Are
you thinking about coming to Yale?"

"No," Eric said. "Ro just wanted me to see what he's gotten himself into."

Shelby laughed. "A veritable temple of secularity, not to mention a heathen's den, despite the minority report I've just given you,"
Shelby said in mock seriousness. "Beware, my Catholic friend, beware . . ." Eric smiled and said he would be careful. The three decided
to have supper at Mory's, after which Ro and Eric said good-bye to
Shelby and headed back to the suite in Trumbull.

"I'm glad we ran into Shelby," Ro said. "He's a great example of
the comprehensiveness of Yale. I mean, he dabbles in religion, studies literature and philosophy in several languages, and is a wit on top
of it all."

"Yes, I liked him a lot," Eric agreed. "How old do you think he
is? I couldn't tell."

"Oh, maybe twenty-five. But he sounds like forty or fifty with all he knows."

"On his way to becoming a Dr. Johnson," Eric suggested.

"Right. That's a good comparison. A young Dr. Johnson."

"Richard Pendleton's probably the only person he'd find to talk to at St. James," Eric added.

"Oh, I don't know about that," said Ro. "There are plenty of smart guys at St. James. There's just not the same pleasure in having knowledge. Guys there sort of hide their intellectual interests. The official Catholicism suppresses, I don't mean forbids, but discourages much contrary inquiry. And sports and partying tend to replace the intellectual debates that go on here."

"Yes,' Eric answered, "though we have our little pockets of academia. Since I've gotten rid of the three languages, I've loved being an English major. Cahalane's Shakespeare is a feast."

"Oh, yeah," Ro agreed, "he's incredible. I had him for the James Joyce elective. 'Womb to tomb' he'd say of Joyce's comprehensive vision of life. I'm so glad you've been freed from the 'infamous three' at last," Ro concluded. The conversation wound down as Eric and Ro agreed about the niches of excellence at St. James and the vast menu of Yale. For now, they sensed, each of them had what he needed.

For the rest of his weekend visit, Ro took Eric through several libraries and museums in a quick sampling of Yale's riches. At the school bookstore, there was no end to the titles the Yale faculty had published. At St. James, a student might learn about breakthroughs in science or the latest scholarship in history and literature. At Yale, he could study with many of the leading scholars themselves. "Yes," Ro amended, "but he could also drift away and get lost in the breadth of opportunities at Yale. St. James takes students by the hand and gives them a good education in a strong but circumscribed curriculum. At Yale, a student needs to know what he wants or he might get lost in the abundance. But if he does find his way, the possibilities are endless."

"Well," said Eric as they headed back to his car, still safely in the same parking space, "you don't seem to be drifting."

"No, I'm very happy here so far. It is a bit heady and I don't know yet how it will change me, but I was ready for it."

"Thanks for giving me a glimpse."

"Eric, thank you so much for coming here. I wanted you to see what my new life is like."

They shook hands. Then Eric started the car, waved to Ro, and drove out of New Haven and back to Worcester again.

THE BIG POND

I

Spring warmed the Worcester hills, and the end of Eric's junior year fell like soft rain on the groves and flower beds of the campus. At last Eric made the Dean's List in his sixth semester. The luxury of available time even lured him to on-campus movies and into more dorm talk than ever before. "College" had finally begun. Then suddenly it was half over.

In early May, Eric found a letter in his mailbox with the return address of St. Joseph's High School in Shrewsbury. He opened it and started reading a note from Brother Samuel, the school's long-time speech and debate coach. Before leaving for the army, Roger had suggested to Brother Sam that Eric might consider being the debating coach for the school in his senior year. Sam was nearly seventy now and had employed Roger as unofficial coach for several months before his army life began. A younger voice appealed more to high school students, and someone in touch with current debating trends could give more practical advice. There would be a stipend, though Sam wasn't sure yet how much. Eric would need a car to get from the college to the high school and to drive students to tournaments, but St. Joe's could reimburse him for gas. When Eric phoned Mom about the possible job, she was encouraging. With Dad's old station wagon now available to Eric, it could all work out, but should he do it? Why give up all the afternoon and weekend time he had just gained by not debating? Would his grades fall again? Would high school debaters take him seriously since he would only coach them for one year? He could leave well enough alone and keep enjoying the breakthroughs of his junior year. He turned everything over for three days before he phoned Brother Sam to say yes.

So he committed to another season of debating after about twenty months away. He met briefly with Sam and five of the older debaters within a week of taking the job. It went well. The debaters were already making research plans for the summer, and Eric got a probable tournament schedule to help him plan for the varsity and novice debaters. He could expect as many as twenty guys to come out in the fall—so different from those first two years at Kenton with four speakers and Brother Daniel. But he *had* to keep his own school work on track and find the time to read the literature that he craved much more than debate research. All these thoughts gave Eric an edgy feeling about his final year at St. James as he left the campus for the summer.

I I

A few day trips to the beach, some free summer reading, and a little debating research too quickly passed the summer of '66 for Eric. Soon he was back at St. James for the last time to do those senior things that gave order and hid uncertainties.

Sodality had been one constant from his Kenton years. As a senior, Eric agreed to be the Instructor of Candidates, which sounded a little pretentious but was simple enough. He talked to some new freshmen members several times about reading Ignatius's *Spiritual Exercises* and about the annual retreat. He encouraged the guys to get involved in the "social apostolate" of community service projects in the Worcester area, which they wanted to do anyway. At the Monday night meetings, he heard Fr. Latourette's opening prayer-sermons and participated in discussions of faith. Sometimes the quiet statements of belief or doubt from classmates moved him. Folk masses with guitars and tambourines were still a fresh alternative to organ music and a parish choir. Yet the post-Vatican hopes were already fading, and the need for *personal* renewal filled more sermons than words about Church reform. Eric read Teilhard de Chardin and Protestant theologian Paul Tillich with great interest, yet he did not mention them at Sodality functions. They would sound like distractions from the Ignatian agenda. The Church had a way of smothering criticism in paternal hugs or sacramental silences from which it was hard to shake free. "We are the Body of Christ; you are the sinner in need of reform," it seemed to say, wordlessly. Eric decided to take the best from Sodality but look for more candor elsewhere.

Still, at the Sodality retreat in late September, Fr. Lionel was eloquent on the Gospels. One afternoon he spoke about the woman at the well, whose turbulent life (and five husbands) Jesus already knew and to whom He offered living water. "I see you are a prophet," Lionel quoted her with a smile. "Don't we all want to change the subject when someone looks too deeply into our souls?" Of this Samaritan woman's quick departure from the disturbing Galilean, Lionel concluded, "No wonder she forgot her bucket," and there he ended his Gospel commentary. The retreatants sat in silence for several minutes and tried to imagine such a moment for themselves. How would their lives be transformed by a voice from within and the offer of "living water"? No character in literature ever spoke as Jesus spoke in the Gospels, Eric thought. So far as he knew, no prophet of another religion had either. And yet the silences were long as he waited for the sound of that voice or something like it. God always seemed to throw Eric back upon himself, and the lightning never quite struck. What else did he expect? Something he could not explain.

When the young men went back at their own discretion to their rooms for a scheduled "time of prayer," Eric wandered through the double glass doors of the retreat house living room and out onto the lawn that skirted the patio above the beach on the Gloucester coast. He walked along a narrow gravel border of tiny pebbles and occasional larger stones. Among a clump of shrubs he found a broken tree branch an inch thick and a yard long. It was remarkably straight, and when Eric broke off the remains of three tiny branches from it, he smiled to see a stick-bat in his hands. He gathered a small pile of stones near his feet, spread his batting stance on the carpet-like lawn, and looked down at the boulders that bordered the beach and the sea. No one walked the chilly shore just then. One by one, Eric took up stones with his right hand, tossed them straight up, and batted them toward the beach. A few he narrowly missed or fouled off, but catching a rhythm he hit most squarely and watched them fly off and leave little dots on the sand below. After awhile, he moved toward a new supply of stones and continued for who-knew-how-long, tossing and swinging and following through and watching the arc of his blows like imaginary doubles into the gap or undeniable home runs. A few times a quick gust stopped him in mid-swing or broke up his contact, like a wicked curve ball or strange knuckler he'd never seen before, but mostly he kept a steady flow of hits toward the outfield until he felt satisfied and finally a little tired. Then he hurled his bat end-on-end toward the dots he had made in the sand. At last, he walked back inside and up to his room and saw no one on his way.

When the four-day retreat ended and everyone filed onto the bus for the ride back to St. James, Larry Donovan, the new Sodality prefect, sat down by Eric and flashed a smile.

"I saw you make some pretty good swings yesterday," he teased in a low voice.

"Oh, yeah," Eric said with a slight flush. "I just needed a break, I guess."

"I wasn't the only one watching either," Larry added with a brief laugh.

"God," Eric answered, "I didn't think anyone would see."

"Or hear?" Larry wondered as Eric wiped a hand across his face. "More like Yastrzemski than Williams, I'd say, but pretty good." Eric slumped in his seat. Fathers Latourette and Lionel sat together three seats behind Eric on the other side of the aisle and probably hadn't heard the whispered conversation. No one else ever mentioned Eric's retreat house batting exhibition.

* * *

A few weeks after their retreat in mid-October when the foliage was peaking in the White and Green Mountains and spreading south by the day toward Worcester, Ed Delorean, the Sodality's off-campus

195

contact person, and Larry explained plans they had made for a weekend retreat, or a hiking pilgrimage more exactly, with the women sodalists of Ave Maria toward the Chapel in the Woods, an outdoor Jesuit center in the forests of central Massachusetts near the New Hampshire border.

"We will leave early Friday morning for Donnelton, meet the women there, and walk on Friday and Saturday morning to the chapel," Ed explained. "The walk is about forty miles along country roads and some hiking trails. Friday night we will all camp at Austen State Park. They have some shelters for bad weather, but it'll be more fun to set up tents and sleeping bags for the night."

"HOW many are GO-ing?" Fr. Latourette asked.

"About eighteen girls and twenty of us, so far. I'll call Gennessa tonight—she's their prefect—and get a final count. I have a handout for everyone with suggested supplies and food to bring. We've got a permit to light one common campfire on Friday night, but we'll need to be careful about the dry conditions."

"What happens when we get there?" someone asked.

"Fr. Latourette," Ed nodded toward him, "will say mass at the outdoor altar. We're also encouraging everyone to read the scriptural passages we've copied and to do at least four journal entries along the way. We can share some of those Friday night and at the mass on Saturday."

"For sure," spoke up Jackson Craig, a senior who'd helped plan this event with Larry and Ed, "this will be a big improvement over our usual Sodality meetings."

Everyone laughed, including Latourette. "Not TOO big an imPROVEment," Father joked. "I'll be checking those TENTS for the Holy SPIR-it!"

To which Jackson cried out, "We must follow wherever the spirit leads. Amen, brothers!"

Three days later, the guys, with Latourette and Lionel as chaplain/chaperones, gathered after dawn near the Fenton Hall loop to board a bus for Donnelton, where they'd meet the Maria women and start their walk.

The morning was chilly but soon warmed. A few guys lowered some windows, and a breeze refreshed the bus as they rode into the countryside west of Worcester and then north for thirty miles. At a country store in Donnelton, the Ave Maria bus had just arrived. The two drivers checked directions and then drove toward the town park about two miles away. There the coed pilgrimage would start.

Near noon, after an outdoor lunch at the park, everyone began the hike toward the Chapel in the Woods. Eric did not recognize any of the Ave Maria girls, though several guys knew many of them from school dances or through community service projects. He and Larry Drexell started walking together and were soon talking with two girls named Janet Dumont and Ellen de Vita.

"I'm really glad we could all do this together," Ellen said.

"Yeah," Larry agreed. "Looks like we have good weather for it, too."

"The foliage is beautiful already," Janet said as she looked around. "It'll probably get even better as we hike more into the woods."

They all talked intermittently as they walked and took occasional sips of water from their canteens. Delorean and Donovan walked at the front with Gennessa and a few other girls, and they sometimes shouted back directions or information to the group. The two priests, dressed in jeans and flannel shirts, hiked just in front of Eric's group and talked with three Ave Maria girls and a woman professor who worked with their Sodality. An hour or so into the trip, everyone climbed a gradual embankment and then walked along a ridge overlooking a valley of small farms and a town off to the north. The wind increased, and most hikers put on the jackets or sweaters they'd attached to their packs.

"Let's stop over there for a break," Ed Delorean called back and pointed toward a clearing a few hundred feet away. There they sat and stretched their legs. Some lay back on the wild grass and closed their eyes.

"Have you hiked much before?" Janet asked Eric.

"Some. I was a Boy Scout for a couple of years and we went on several camping trips. I don't think I've hiked for forty miles. Anyway, we're keeping an easy pace so it shouldn't be tough."

Janet smiled. "No, I don't think so. I haven't hiked at all in New England, so this is beautiful for me."

"Where are you from?"

"Ohio. Just outside of Cleveland."

"How did you find out about Ave Maria?"

"My aunt and uncle live in Brockton. I looked at small schools in Ohio, but . . . I wanted a little space between me and home, so my aunt took me to some schools here that she knew about. Then Ave Maria gave me a partial scholarship, so here I am. What about you?"

"I was a high school debater, and I attended tournaments at St. James as a junior and senior. I guess that got me hooked."

"Are you still in debating?"

"No. I had to let it go when my grades dropped. But I am just starting to coach a high school team. Can't keep away from it for long, I guess."

"Really? You're the coach! I never did any public speaking. That must be hard."

"It can be at first. Once you do it a little, you get more confident. If you win, anyway."

"Did you win a lot?"

"Actually, yes. I kind of surprised myself that I was pretty good at it."

"Pretty good?" Lenny Drexell interrupted. "This guy won a bunch of trophies."

"You did?"

"Yeah, I did." Eric smiled to think about it.

"Well, I'll be careful not to get into an argument with you," Janet said with a grin. Eric laughed self-consciously.

"OK, everyone"— they suddenly heard Delorean's voice—"we need to start hiking again. Austen State Park is seven or eight miles ahead, and we should try to make it there before dark." The hikers gathered their things and helped each other with packs. Soon the group of forty-five was on its way through a more heavily wooded area and down along a stream toward an outcropping of granite. The rocks held the day's heat that the hikers felt when they braced themselves against the boulders and moved along a narrow creek bed, then across an old wooden bridge and into an open meadow. Up ahead Ed and Larry turned to face everyone. "Just beyond those hills off to the left," Larry called out, "is Austen. So we're almost home for the night. Is everyone doing OK?"

Several shouts of "yeah" and "fine" reassured the leaders, so they waved their pilgrims forward for the last part of the trek. Now Ed and Larry dropped back among the hikers and assured each little cluster that the day's effort was almost done.

"How do you guys like playing Lewis and Clark?" Jackson said for everyone to hear. Ed laughed and just waved aside the question with his hand.

"Actually, Lewis here has been working closely with Sacajawea," Larry joked and drew a chorus of knowing laughs and some sarcasm about how tough the wilderness can be. Gennessa was still walking up front and didn't hear the jokes, or pretended not to.

When they arrived at Austen, the dusk was thickening, so the leaders urged everyone to set up tents and sleeping bags for the night. The guys' and girls' tents were arranged in wide semicircles with the campfire site between them. Soon the leaders had a small fire going and then built on it. In the firelight, Ed asked everyone to do a journal entry, their second of the day, with scriptural readings from Genesis or Exodus as prompts. Eric read over one of the Genesis passages, which he'd never thought about before: "Yahweh God planted a garden in Eden which is in the east, and there he put the man he had fashioned. Yahweh God caused to spring up from the soil every kind of tree, enticing to look at and good to eat, with the tree of life and the tree of the knowledge of good and evil in the middle of the garden. A river flowed from Eden to water the garden, and from there it divided to make four streams" (Genesis 2:8–10).

Eric wrote that they had all seen a part of God's garden on their hike today and that they belonged in this natural setting, like Adam and Eve. He added, though, that nature was a gift *with conditions attached* and not entirely to be taken at face value. Not all the trees were equal, as the identities of the two special trees showed. So he assumed that our response to nature was supposed to be *guided* by God's intentions and was not just a matter of our own feelings about it. But he wondered what it meant that the tree of life and the tree of the knowledge of good and evil were not the same tree. Later, around the campfire, after several hikers had read their journal entries on the Bible text they had chosen, Eric read his without comment.

At last in the dark, everyone went to the tents to sleep, and the camp leaders doused the fire and broke it apart. In the morning, the hikers ate quick breakfast snacks, broke camp, and began the last few hours of their walk under clouds and a light wind. The foliage was brilliant, the more so near noon when the clouds broke and sunlight streaked through breaks in the trees.

"Wow! Isn't this great," Janet said to Eric.

"Yes. I'm glad we're getting some sun through these leaves."

They hiked on with occasional bulletins from Larry and Ed about how well they were doing and how close their destination was, though Eric felt that each part of the hike now took a little longer than the leaders estimated. A few rabbits scampered for cover in the distance, and once Eric was sure he saw a snake move among some fallen leaves. Then at last, over a final ridge, everyone could see the entrance sign for the Chapel in the Woods. A few cheers broke out. All the hikers were glad to lay their packs down at last near the same two buses that were waiting in the parking lot beyond the outdoor altar.

Soon Fr. Latourette was saying mass and Fr. Lionel preached as the girls and guys sat around in clusters. Eric watched the communion host being raised at the consecration and felt a different sense of the Eucharist in this open-air setting. Bread and wine, from the earth and made "by the work of human hands," was now sanctified in the nature from which it had come, and not with church decor all around.

When the mass ended, the students said good-bye to each other with numerous hugs. Waiting in a short line to board her bus, Janet turned and said, "Eric, I enjoyed meeting you. Hope I'll see you again. And I liked that question you asked about the two trees in Eden."

Eric smiled. "Too bad I don't know the answer. Hope we meet again, too. Bye."

After the slightest hesitation, they both boarded their buses and then waved to each other through the windows as the buses pulled away. But they had not traded phone numbers, and neither one saw the other again.

I I I

When his senior courses began, Eric could hardly wait for the first classes. Fall semester seminars in Chaucer and in Dryden, Pope, and Swift, both with Dr. Jared Winston, were like prologues for the courses he'd just finished on Shakespeare and the Romantic Poets. Winston lived up to his reputation around the seminar table. His inclusive humor relaxed everyone, and his quick understanding of each student's interests guided all to the best paper topics. Winston's round face, wide frame, and perpetual smile made him a genial Chaucer and an engaging, less acerbic Jonathan Swift.

The meticulous Dr. Morris Benacht took his students through eighteenth- and nineteenth-century English novels over two semesters. While Eric never finished the longer novels, he immersed himself in the worlds they depicted, most especially in Henry Fielding's hilarious *Tom Jones* brimming with characters like Squire Allworthy and Reverend Thwackum.

A political science elective in the government and politics of the Soviet Union, taught by a visiting Russian lecturer, resonated unexpectedly with Swift's political satire in *Gulliver's Travels.* Yet the most expansive and at the same time almost meditative course of that fall was Phenomenological Existentialism with Professor Carl Seth, an Oppenheimer look-alike with similar intellectual power. Dr. Lund's sophomores were now Seth's seniors, eager for more philosophical frontiers. Lund had stopped with Jacques Maritain. Seth now ventured into the secular waters of Camus and Sartre and then, for comparisons, on to Gabriel Marcel, a "Christian existentialist" if there could be such a thing. Dr. Seth asked in his soft voice whether morality and freedom could exist without God, without a theology, and what such an ethic would be like. In the French Resistance, he explained, atheists and believers had fought together against the Nazis in a stark boot camp for post-war philosophy and radical theologians. The abyss of Fascism had changed everything for those who had dared to stare into it.

Unlike Lund, Seth was no intellectual chameleon. He was always himself, thinking out loud as students overheard him, then asking from them the same vulnerability. Some classes sounded to Eric like the unscripted prayers of seekers asking their questions—more important somehow than any answers. Lund had publicly dazzled; Seth intimately mesmerized.

Whatever Ro might be finding at Yale, Eric felt transformed by the intellectual menu at St. James. The Catholic college umbrella was a wide one with room for radical questioning even of itself, he dared to believe. "Christian existentialists" and "secular humanists" vied for loyalty in the readings and in those belief-and-doubt debates in the nerdier corners of the "animal corridors." Such questioning seemed more fundamental than issues of liturgical reform or even ecumenical agendas for Catholics and Protestants, or for Christians, Jews, and Muslims. Buddhist and Hindu ideas had not quite arrived at St. James that fall, but Eric felt sure that they were on the way. In one dorm session, George Delaney teased with an agnostic smirk, "If God can be a woman, why can't priests?"

"I don't know," Eric took the bait, "but if God is 'spirit' and neither male nor female, why are we who are made in *His* image saddled with sexuality?"

"No bad-mouthing sex in my dorm," George's roommate Jeff Sanderson solemnly warned.

"Sorry." Eric smiled in apology.

Far from the free-thinking covens of the caf and the dorms, the Sodality was a divided forum with post-Vatican II reformers, social action types who mostly avoided theological debates, and a few more prayerful guys who sounded like future priests. When Eric and several other sodalists attended a "Church in the World" conference cosponsored by Catholic U and Georgetown in DC, they met the famous radical Jesuit Don Burleson. As the opening-day workshops ended, Don (as he said to call him) asked a small group of guys back to some friend's apartment. Around a living room coffee table, Burleson said a freestyle mass that included some spontaneous prayers and sliced Italian bread for the Eucharist. "Here is the early 'house church' of the first Christians," Burleson gestured with conviction at the improvised liturgy. The collegians nodded assent, though later they wondered to each other what Paul VI and his Curia would say to Burleson's enthusiasm for "primitive Christianity" over Vatican ceremonial correctness.

"Won't he get in trouble if he keeps doing that?" Larry Donovan asked later.

"What would Latourette think?" Eric wondered. "And why did he invite us but not Latourette to this private mass?" No one ventured the obvious answer, but Eric recalled a month earlier when Latourette had cautioned that the new vernacular mass would be watched closely by the Vatican because "abuses" could creep in now that the universal Latin text was gone. And no one wanted to guess what Jesus, who presumably spoke little Latin, might think of all this liturgical debate. Even church issues were getting existential for Eric as philosophy and politics kept poking their way into theology.

I V

Debating at St. Joe's began abruptly with a couple of organizational meetings in September, a few practice debates, and then the first tournaments in October. A dozen freshmen came out, and eight of them stayed well into the year and made a good core of novices that Eric could coach and critique. Three sophomores, two juniors, and a senior quickly became a two-tiered varsity team, with various partners for four-person tournaments and two clearly superior switch-side debaters, Joel Warren and Anthony Bellanger. Of them, Eric had the uneasy impression of self-directed, whiplash intellects. They tried to be deferential, but they had their own motivations and plans. They had already surpassed anything Eric had done as a researcher (Roger had taught them well) and had set their sights mostly on college switch-side tournaments that Eric had rarely entered from Kenton. He could advise them about delivery and time use and about learning to dismiss some second-rate arguments they still felt compelled to refute. At the highest levels of evidence, analysis, and case-building, however, they essentially coached themselves. They came to appreciate Eric's acceptance of that fact and treated him like a manager-consultant. He saw to their scheduling details and occasionally had an opinion on substance, but he mostly let them soar, and occasionally fail, as they did in a hectic, unforgettable year. "Small pond" successes had no appeal for Joel and Tony.

At the end of long debate afternoons, Eric usually drove Joel to his home several miles from the school. As they talked intermittently, Eric glimpsed the toss-off wit and adolescent intensity that often hovers at the apex of high school achievement. Ambition, insecurity, confidence, and single-mindedness swirled in a volatile solution capable of brilliant strokes and ill-advised overreaching. Joel and Anthony were higher-stakes players than Eric had ever been. They often revised Affirmative cases and experimented with new approaches to evidence. They "sacrificed" some tournaments to "target" others and floated trial balloons. Eric had tried to win everything he entered and let each success create the next goal. He hadn't known enough about the greater world of East Coast high school debating to dream of winning specific "big" tournaments or to plan any sort of a "run" at a national title. Neither had Brother Daniel, Eric thought now. It was all fresh and new, and every win was a thrill. Not so for Warren and Bellanger, who had great partner chemistry from the start and bigger, more precise ambitions than either Brother Sam or Eric fully knew. As senior and junior partners approaching the peak of their powers, they knew that this was the year to leave a mark. Only "the big pond" interested them.

With the hints of glory that Joel and Anthony might achieve as part of Roger's coaching legacy, Eric quickly decided that the core of his job was helping all the *other* debaters in greater need of coaching and strategic advice. So he spend the first weeks showing the freshmen what he could and learning the strengths and weaknesses of the three sophomores and the other junior. He let natural partners work together at first. Later he made changes when better combinations emerged. He tried to reward diligence in research and practice debates, and he discouraged any tendency to coast. Five of the new debaters dropped out by Thanksgiving, as expected, but the core that remained were dedicated workers often eager to debate "over their heads" to get better faster.

After some early successes at nearby tournaments in Worcester and Shrewsbury, Eric had a full slate registered for the U Mass Tournament in Amherst. The four-person novices were 4–6 and the varsity 5–5. Not bad, Eric felt, in mid-November against a wide field of good schools. In the switch-side varsity, Joel and Tony went 7–1 in four rounds of two ballots each. With semis and the final round ahead, they were confident. Yet against a strong St. Peter's High team in the semis, they sounded flat and tired. The lost all three ballots. Everyone tried to cheer them up on the way to the car, but they were annoyed with themselves at letting a winnable title get away. Not even speaker and team awards to Joel (Third Best), Tony (Second Best), and Third Best Team interested them much. "St. Peter's will hear from us again," Tony vowed quietly. Joel nodded as they slumped into the backseat of Eric's Ford wagon. Eddie Gillette and Eldon Biranchi sat in front with Eric. Junior Tom Travecci drove the trailing car full of freshmen and sophomores, and the debaters' caravan found its way back to Shrewsbury.

* * *

Union College in Schenectady (a four-person varsity tournament) was their first out-of-state drive and overnight stay of the schedule. The debaters left school an hour early on Friday, and Eric helped them load research file cabinets and overnight bags into the back of his wagon. Gillette took shotgun, and the others filled the backseat. Eric drove from Worcester onto the Mass Pike west on a breezy November Friday. For twenty minutes, Eddie selected radio stations and made changes as the boys wanted. Soon, however, debaters' repartee took over, and the radio was just background noise that no one listened to or would agree to turn off. Eric always liked quiet drives with no radio when he could watch the scenery and let his mind wander. No such luck with a car full of high school wits.

And so it began. A few early jokes and tolerable puns were actually pretty funny, Eric thought. Good for the guys to keep sharp while forgetting all about UN peacekeeping. But as the hours and the miles passed into western Massachusetts and across the New York line, the punning . . . never . . . stopped. As the laughter rose, the humor fell and every conceivable wordplay found instant voice.

Joel and Tony mocked other drivers and passengers, their cars, their probable (and impossible) lives, and every remotely suggestive road-side ad. Then Eddie and Tony ganged up on Eldon ("All Done B. Yankee" and "Elder By Ranky"). When Eldon managed only a soft fart for a comeback, "moon river" and "gas tax" insults bludgeoned him until, wet-eyed with laughter, Joel suddenly realized that Coach Eric had said absolutely nothing for more than an hour. Soon he was excoriated as "witless in Gaza" and "tongue-tied in Tibet." A highway Buddha turning the wheel of fortune on a long drive to nowhere. The coach of wordless wisdom. And on and on.

Eric smiled and then laughed but grew weary of it all. No one, he thought, not even Jonathan Winters at his most outrageous, could be funny every second. Humor, like people, needed to breathe, but his crew of comedians left no joke untold, no pun untried, and no bad pun unexplained. It was like a rash that no ointment could soothe, or a plague that would stop only when it ran out of victims—or in this case, when they got to Union College and unloaded their things into dorm rooms—one of which was for Eric *alone*.

"We'll meet for dinner in a half hour, guys." Eric waved them away as they jabbered with each other. He opened his room door, listened to the silence for twenty seconds, dropped his bag to the floor, and lay back on the bed with eyes closed and a weary half-smile on his face. If he ever had sons, would they be like this? Roger had been an inveterate punster with them, and now Eric had inherited their obsession, along with their brilliant minds and research energies.

Their dinner at a nearby Italian restaurant that night was remarkably calm, Eric thought. Eating was a merciful interruption to talking. Not even a chubby waitress with a slight lisp set them off, though Joel and Tony eyed each other knowingly every time she returned to their table. Virginia Woolf had urged "A Room of One's Own" for every creative woman. Eric was glad to have the same luxury tonight for other reasons. Tomorrow they would all debate, he would judge other debates, and the "Punic Wars," as they christened them, would pause—at least until their drive home, all four hours of it.

The tournament itself was a tightly scheduled five-round affair with the winner decided on records and points without a title round. The two teams each went 4–1, expected for Joel and Tony but a strong showing for Eddie and Eldon. The four were named the Fourth Best Team, and Joel and Tony got certificates as among the top ten speakers. Not all they wanted, but not bad.

"So how did the new arguments work out?" Eric asked Tony as everyone looked over the ballots.

"OK. We could have explained better how we'd get regional alliances to help fund UN troops, I guess."

"Well, you can fine-tune that before the next tournament," Eric said with instant regret as Joel immediately provided an illustrative and prolonged tuning fork hum, to everyone's laughter. Eric laughed too, but for another reason. Sometimes that was his only cover. They all piled into the car, and the comedic frenzy of the ride home began at once. No one even asked for the radio, though Eric now almost wished for it.

* * *

Two weeks later, over the Thanksgiving break, the same four debaters entered as two switch-side teams in the Boston College Tournament. Eldon and Eddie were a strong 4–2, and Joel and Tony finished with 5–1. When the final four teams were announced, however, three of them also at 5–1, St. Joe's was not included. A check of the total points during the semifinal debates revealed that Joel and Tony had outscored the last qualifying team by two points and should have replaced them in the semis. With the round already underway, however, the tournament hosts felt they could not correct the mistake. Eric didn't argue the point, and Joel and Tony just shrugged reluctantly. Near-misses and now an arithmetic mistake had frustrated them in three successive tournaments. Yet with many more ahead, they looked forward and busied themselves with refining arguments and evidence. Eric liked that resolve in them, even as he regretted their close calls. They were better than their record and everyone knew it, so the vagaries of early tournament results did not bother them—or so they decided. Success would come if they just kept giving themselves chances.

"Let's send BC a calculator when we register for next year's tournament," Tony offered magnanimously.

The novice debaters kept doing well in Worcester-area tournaments that sometimes declared no winner but just recognized the leading teams and speakers. Eric enjoyed their growing self-reliance and their eagerness to help each other with arguments and evidence. He smiled sometimes to hear their occasional "great discoveries" that were already old news at the varsity level, but no matter. Insight and originality were always relative. An awkward freshman might suddenly craft an argument as well as any senior and then recoil from his success until he could get back to that level again. And the weekly feedback of tournament ballots with judges' comments guaranteed both forward momentum and the quick bursting of wishful bubbles.

"Well, *that* didn't fly," Jack Mazilli said loudly as he looked over a losing ballot in the backseat of Eric's wagon.

"What didn't?" Eric asked.

"We tried to say that UN troops could use the same tactics they had in Indonesia for situations in Africa. The judge just wrote 'Asia and Africa—apples and oranges.'"

"Well, the nerve of that guy," Eric teased. "Nit-picking about cultural differences on separate continents!"

Mazilli's partner Henry Chester tossed his hands in mock exasperation. "Where do they get these judges? I'm sure you'd never write 'apples and oranges' on a ballot, Mr. Malone."

"Never," Eric answered solemnly, and the car full of freshmen all laughed.

"So what do you think you should do the next time?" Eric asked in a minute.

"Rearrange the produce," little Patrick Hurley shouted, and Mazilli bumped his shoulder in support. Eric loved these little guys. Nothing bothered them for long.

"Slice and dice," Chucky Gillette, Eddie's little brother, blurted out to keep the banter going. A chorus of groans filled the car as they headed back to Shrewsbury.

"We got sliced and diced," Mazilli conceded and put the ballot away.

"Well, show that comment to Joel and Tony and see if they've got some better evidence you can use about regional differences," Eric concluded. They all agreed. Minutes later Eric pulled into the St. Joe's parking lot where various parents awaited their sons, these four-month freshmen debaters.

V

The varsity four had one more New York tournament scheduled in early December. Then they'd take the Christmas break and use some of the time to prepare for the Dartmouth College tournament, the first big event of the second semester. So off they drove on another Friday toward the Hudson River palisades and Hendrick Hudson High School in the river town of Montrose, south of FDR State Park. Joel and Tony and Eldon and Eddie would be switch-side teams against another strong New York/New Jersey/New England field. Across the barren December terrain of western Connecticut they rode on I-84 through Hartford, Waterbury, and Danbury and then into New York toward Montrose, not far from West Point. The usual chatter prevailed, but this time Eric tuned most of it out and realized instead that half of his senior year was over. What door would open next when debating days and college years were done?

Suddenly Eric veered left to avoid four cars stopped in the breakdown lane to sort out their accident. Police had already arrived. A teenage girl and her mom talked with a cop and huddled together. Three other police took information from the driver of a pickup and a well-suited guy staring at the dented trunk of his Buick. In a few seconds the scene was behind them. Tony thought the whole thing was somehow artistic, but the others mocked his insensitivity.

"No, listen," he persisted, "a sculptor could do it. The women stare terrified as their car rushes toward the Buick and the truck. We see the cars and their trapped drivers just before impact."

"And call it 'Three Coins in the Fountain,'" Eddie cut in.

"No," waved off Tony, "though not bad. Call it—'Debating.'"

Everyone broke up laughing, and Eric's shoulders slumped a little as he smiled.

"Wait," Joel said quickly, nodding toward Eric. "Let's call it— 'Coaching.'" More laughter.

"Thanks for the honor," Eric offered, and then he plunged into their game. "I'd call it 'Inherently Relevant,'" a debating cliché for which they often ridiculed each other. Just this once they loved his joke and laughed wildly. *Everything to excess*, Eric thought, *in the teenage maelstrom.*

"I can't believe he said it," Joel gushed to the others, and they bumped and slapped each other in the endless hilarity of boys.

Having made his mark, Eric risked no more shots but retreated to his thoughts, while the four joked on about everything and nothing. This half-year had been good at St. James and fun with these zany young wits all around him. Somehow he had found time for both debating and course work. Long afternoons and weekend debate trips still left him energy for Chaucer and Swift. He always did the crucial readings, though never all the assignments, and somehow he wrote the papers. He had little time now for movies or dorm talk, but that was just a one-year tradeoff. The St. James debaters even asked about his coaching and shared his pleasure at the progress of the guys. He had agreed to be the college Freshman Debate Coach, though that really meant only three or four meetings with new debaters. He gave what advice he could without saying much about his own departure from the team. High school coaching gave him some legitimacy with them; it was an option they respected. Maybe they'd even do it themselves someday after all their college trophies were won.

* * *

As Eric drove on toward the Hudson River, he screened out the relentless chatter of high school punsters and thought about his senior year so far. With a car on campus at last, Eric had even been to the Miss Worcester Diner a few times for braised beef and veggies or a late-night omelette. The Polish cook kept recommending his "impeccable sausage," and Eric sometimes complied. Who worried about indigestion and lost sleep in the diner's irresistible aroma?

In October, Dr. Killian had nominated Eric for a Woodrow Wilson Fellowship. Nothing came of it, but the thought was still sweet to a flunker of French less than two years before. Now he was about to make the Dean's List again and had graduate school in mind. Cahalane, Winston, and Sousa had agreed to write his recommendations. At the counseling office, he read about various PhD and master's programs in English. This year's courses were good, but the glow of Shakespeare and modern playwrights from his junior year lingered. Yeats, Synge, O'Casey, Shaw. Some sort of research and teaching of them? A play he might even try to write? He wasn't sure, but the options were appealing. Whole new worlds waited for him. Hadn't others dreamed these dreams before? Yes, and look at them now: Cahalane, Winston, Sousa, Michaelson; the philosophers Lund and Seth; even Benacht and his two centuries of novels that no one could finish. He respected the devotion of Jesuits like Latourette and Lionel and those pillars of the college like Harrington, O'Connell, and Regan, yet compared with his free-thinking lay professors, these priests seemed too cautious—Jesuit organization men committed in advance to whatever Rome decreed, the diocese ordered, or the college decided. A vow of obedience, they called it, but didn't Catholicism need more creativity at last and less obedience?

Oh, once in a while a ripple of change caught hold. That fall, Latourette and a few Sodality guys had felt a brief surge of activism on the oddly paired issues of liturgical reform and Christian burial rites. They had drafted a letter to all American bishops—soon to meet in conference—and asked all the Sodality leaders, Eric among them as Instructor of Candidates, to sign it. The letter urged more support for vernacular liturgies and culturally diverse mass rituals "in fostering this vital evolution in Christian worship" and also asked for support for "inexpensive burials of Catholics" and simpler requiem masses to "relieve mental anguish and the financial burden involved" for grieving Catholics. The letter even requested that St. James be designated as a "liturgical center for experimentation" to pursue such changes. Whose language that all was, Eric didn't know. Latourette's, he guessed. Yet none of it would really matter. The Council of Bishops never answered. Only a few chastening letters arrived from older Catholic laymen to caution against tampering with "holy liturgies" or presuming to "pressure" America's bishops. It all seemed like jousting with the wind while more immediate on-campus issues and more important wartime politics remained "prayed over" but scarcely addressed.

Even Latourette soon conceded that nothing would come of their activist gesture.

Was that what the priesthood would be like? Rare bold gestures and frequent retreats? Eric wanted more freedom than such a life would allow, more chances to think and travel, read and write, and see where his choices led without preconceived destinations. A post-Vatican II malaise had taken hold, he thought. Every change was now too risky. A life of prayer and the sacraments seemed a tepid response to a nation at war and a church still in need of change. At least the Burlesons of the Church were not tepid, but their priesthood was always a battleground. How did they stand it year after year?

Eldon's voice cut into Eric's thoughts. "Coach, could we take a bathroom break at that diner?" The others teased Eldon about his bladder but were glad enough to stop. They got cokes, and Eric ordered a hot tea to go.

"The old folks like tea," Joel explained.

"You'll be old someday too," Eric countered from the far side of twenty-one.

* * *

Back on the road, Eric thought again about next year. He'd picked out English programs that seemed to suit him, though he suspected that once he enrolled his literary passions might change.

"In your personal statement," Dr. Winston had cautioned, "don't sound too sure of what you want to study. Don't sound like you're saying 'John Synge forever,' but show them that you expect your focus to develop." So he had tried to write his essay that way while letting his current enthusiasms come through. With the aid

of some catalogues and a few suggestions from a counselor, he'd selected schools and gotten the applications done. Who would take
him—a Dean's List student now but a C+ struggler in his French-
Latin-Greek years? After Kenton, he had applied only to St. James,
gotten in, and gone there. He had liked the ease of that, but for grad
school he made a list with everything from realism to fantasy on it:
Southern Illinois University, Delaware, Ohio State, BC, Yale, Brown,
Cornell, Wisconsin, and Harvard. Harvard, he laughed. Well, it's
just down the pike, as Dad reminded him often about BC. Yeah, but
it might as well be on Mars. Anyway, let them say no. At least he'd
get one letter from Harvard in his life. And where could he imagine being? The Midwest, especially Wisconsin, sounded interesting.
A leap at least as big as he'd taken from Kenton to St. James? No,
bigger. Would he get lost at Ohio State? Did he even want to go
there? Brown and Cornell he could imagine. Harvard and Yale were
whims. Would Ro still be at Yale, and how strange would that be if
they ended up together in that bigger universe Ro had chosen? He
hadn't mentioned his Yale application to Ro. No reason to unless he
miraculously got admitted. The BC and Southern Illinois applications were for master's programs, the others all PhD's. Eric thought
he wanted the doctorate but figured he should have a couple of MA's
in the mix. They might fit him better—and they might accept him!
Money could decide everything anyway. If he got a TA or a scholarship, he could go; if not, how much more could he ask of his parents?
Where would he be in September, not ten months away?

As the news from Vietnam got worse, his own prospects kept
getting better. Could that continue? First-year graduate students
were still deferrable from the draft, but that policy could change at
any time. Were his academic dreams and the wartime realities about
to collide? And what would he do barely into a degree program if the
draft called him? What should he do anyway about this misguided
war? Maybe he was simply afraid of risk, of an early death. Sure,
who wouldn't be? All advice seemed conditioned by people's own
experiences. Veterans were patriotic. WWII had to be won, they'd
say, and who could disagree? Korea had contained Communism and
so would success in Vietnam, they might add. At what cost in life,

money, and moral standing for America in the world, he wondered, but he rarely argued.

He and Dad would talk about the war sometimes at home when Eric came down from his room to see the late news. Eric still loved those nights, but he was cautious when the talk veered toward religion or politics. The war troubled Dad, too, because of its setbacks and endless costs, but not fighting for America was beyond his imagining. Dad had been 4-F in the 1940's—some nervous condition that Eric never got clear about. When his friends joined the army, Dad was frustrated that he could not be with them. Being safely at home while friends fought Hitler was troubling to a young man whose Irish immigrant grandparents had arrived in 1870, whose father was born two years later and had grown up full of Democratic politics and American pride. Eric agreed with his dad's concerns, but he said nothing of his more radical thoughts about American "save the world" imperialism. Dad thought policy failures were just honest mistakes, or incompetence at worst. Eric was more suspicious. Shouldn't the Vietnamese decide for themselves whether Ho Chi Minh should be their leader, Communist or not? Eric never asked Dad that question. And what would his father think if someday his son did something unpatriotic?"There's a sign for Montrose," Joel announced, pointing. Eric's long introspection was over.

"OK." Eric turned left onto a smaller road and suddenly noticed the sloping hills that anticipated the Hudson River cliffs. At last they pulled into the high school lot, registered, and got their dorm room keys for the night. They all had a quick dinner and went off to separate quarters. Eric caught some TV news—too much Vietnam again today. He turned it off and started to read Fielding's *Joseph Andrews*, then put it down. It wasn't the book for tonight. The wind swayed the trees and lifted the remains of autumn leaves across a parking lot and onto the campus lawn where they found companions in a dead flower bed or hung helpless in some bristly stubble.

The morning saw the familiar weaving of debaters and judges between rooms and among a small cluster of buildings to start each round of debates. When it all ended, Eric and the four guys assembled in the school auditorium to hear results and pick up ballots. Six-

and-two would probably be needed to qualify for the semis, but the boys were 5–3 (3–1 for Joel and Tony, and 2–2 for Eddie and Eldon). At least they could get a mid-afternoon start on the trip home. Hours later he had left them all off and arrived at last outside his dorm.

"How was it?" Zack asked when he entered their room close to ten o'clock.

"Five-and-three. We missed the semis by one win. I was hoping this time that Joel and Tony would have a shot, but not quite."

"Don't they get bored debating the same thing all the time?"

"Maybe sometimes, but the arguments always take new twists, and new evidence emerges. And sometimes a kid is eloquent and it has a sort of beauty, you know?" Zack flashed one of his side-angle smiles at Eric.

"I guess you'd have to be there," Eric conceded with a traceable grin.

"I suppose," Zack shrugged and turned back to his economics text. Soon Eric was in bed, and Zack draped a sweatshirt around his lampshade to shield the light from his roommate while he read on silently.

V I

The first semester ended in a flourish for the debaters with a 16–0 sweep in two novice/intermediate tournaments in Worcester. If Joel and Tony had not quite arrived, the underclassmen were soaring. St. Joe's could be a debate power for several years to come.

"Great job you and Roger have done for these boys," Brother Sam said energetically. The two shook hands before Eric rode away from St. Joe's and onto the familiar stretch of I-495 between Worcester and Lowell. Sleet peppered the windshield for several miles until the clouds broke to the east and the sun gave an austere December comfort. Home felt good again in its muted way.

These would be quiet holidays, Mom announced. Dad had been tired lately and just needed to relax. The Harrigans wouldn't come for Christmas dinner, but the Malones would make a quick visit to them afterward. Betty was home from college, and she and Marsha listened to Christmas records in the living room. Betty rocked slightly in an easy chair and chewed her tongue in that odd way she had. Marsha had gotten off the phone with a high school friend and wanted to go out, but Christmas Eve was a family night. She could call Julie in a few days, Mom assured, when both girls had spent holiday time with their families. At dinner, Dad asked how the debaters had done lately.

"Very well," Eric said. "The novices are so quick to pick up ideas. They've won all their debates in the last two tournaments."

"Well," Dad offered, "I'm sure the coaching has something to do with that."

"No doubt," Betty cut in, half teasing. Mom offered everyone more bread and beef stew. Marsha jumped up quickly to answer the ringing phone.

"Tell them you'll call them back later," Mom advised.

"I know," Marsha answered in a bored tone. Pie and ice cream for dessert kept everyone eating quietly. Then plates were cleared, and Eric said he wanted to take a quick walk.

"Now?" Mom wondered. "Well, all right, but don't be long. Bundle up. It's cold out there."

"OK, Mom."

It was cold but windless under a clear night sky. Eric walked to the end of Berenger Street and then left along East Merrimack by the bank of the river. Through the skeletal trees he saw streetlamps and houselights on Christian Hill above the opposite shore. No people or cars passed as he stood in a wooded patch between houses and looked up and down the river. A hot-drink, fireside Lowell night it was, so he turned and headed home. Alone in his room before eleven he finished reading "The Dead," Joyce's last story in *Dubliners* with its lyrical ending of snow falling faintly upon the living and the dead. He bundled up in bed and scanned the familiar ceiling marks and room shadows. God was generous enough, he thought, as sleep closed in, but couldn't He be less subtle on this *too silent night* before Christmas?

WINTER RITES

I

The air warmed after New Year's Day, and the shroud of December snow seeped away along sidewalks and into gutters. The icicles finally fell from the back of the house where tall trees and the garage blocked out most sunlight. On the brighter front side, the ice and snow were nearly gone. Water flowed down Berenger Street toward East Merrimack and the river, which swelled from several days of thaw. Then the weather turned cold again but stayed dry. The soft snow on the side lot refroze and crunched underfoot to form precise footprints. Eric had walked a wide oval around most of the lot and could still see his tracks three days later from the windows of the sun porch that formed an L with his bedroom.

The school break had over a week yet to run. Brother Sam was covering a couple of tournaments in the Worcester area so Eric could stay home until college classes resumed. Sixty-seven still sounded strange, and Mom laughed that she had already written 1966 on two checks before correcting herself. "Where does the time go?" she wondered aloud. Eric nodded and kept reading in an easy chair in the living room. Betty had returned to Maryhill College in Tarrytown on the Hudson, and Marsha was reluctantly in class again at Lowell High. Dad had gone to the office after rising a little late for him—eight thirty. Mom was vacuuming the living room rug to catch any fragments of Christmas after the tree had been dismantled and the stray packaging cleaned up a few days earlier. Just after noon, the doorbell rang. It was Wednesday, January 11, 1967. Mom opened the door.

"Why, Fr. O'Neill. Good to see you. Come in."

"Thank you, Marian." Eric looked up from his book and then stood and gave the priest a quick handshake.

"Still home from college, Eric?"

"Yes, I've got eleven more days."

"Not that you're counting," Fr. O'Neill joked, and Eric smiled. The priest put his hat down on the front hall desk not far from the door and cleared his throat. Eric saw a shadow of worry cross his mother's face.

"Is anything wrong, Father?" she asked. A midweek visit from a parish priest seemed strange.

"Well, nothing serious, I'm sure, Marian, but Vic was at the rectory this morning talking with the pastor about Fr. Eric's situation and he had a slight weak spell. He sat down for a minute and drank some water. Then, just to be sure, you know, we walked him across the street to the hospital. He complained of a headache, and they decided to admit him."

Mom's eyes seemed to well up for a moment, but then she asked in a steady voice, "How long ago was this?"

"Less than an hour. Once we got him admitted, I came here to tell you."

"Yes. Thank you."

"I could give you a ride down if you want to see him."

His mom hesitated. Eric watched her. "No," she said finally, "not yet. Eric, I think you should go see him first and let me know how he's doing. If I come in so soon, he'll think we're worried. Let's find out more before I see him."

"OK, Mom," Eric said and went upstairs quickly for his wallet and keys.

"I'll be here with your mom till you get back," Fr. O'Neill said.

"All right, Father. I'll just see how he is and come back soon." Eric went out the back door and started the car. He drove along East Merrimack Street toward St. Benedict's Hospital, an old brick building behind the Assumption School and a block from the granite fortress of the parish church. Adjacent to the church was the rectory where his dad had just been. Fr. Eric, Eric's uncle and an Oblate priest, had not been himself physically or emotionally for four or five years now. He often seemed lethargic, had gained weight, and was not anything like the energetic teacher of literature and Oblate administrator that he had been at the seminary and in the Provincial house. Now Dad was interceding again to see whether his brother should stay as a curate at Assumption or be transferred to the Oblate Novitiate in Tewksbury, a seminary and retirement house for priests. No one seemed to know what had happened to Fr. Eric, not yet sixty. A mild stroke? A slight head injury in a car accident back in '62? A nervous breakdown? Whatever it was, Eric's uncle still had full use of his limbs and was mentally aware. "Nervous breakdown" seemed a strong term for the sort of malaise that had sapped his energy without any obvious physical disability.

So Dad was talking it all over again with the pastor. How much his father took family matters to heart Eric knew from years of overheard conversations. Since the early '50s, Dad had recovered from two ulcer surgeries, had almost quit smoking, and, with much less stomach lining to absorb food, had lost at least thirty pounds from his peak weight. But his anxiety about family problems never went away. Eric had always thought it strange that as the youngest of seven siblings, his dad was more like the older brother seeing to the needs of the others. Without knowing more than sketchy details sometimes, Eric resented that his family seemed to lean so much on their youngest brother. Why didn't they take care of their own tax problems or business disputes or parenting troubles?

Eric parked the wagon, his debate-mobile, in front of the rectory and walked toward the hospital emergency entrance. Dad always seemed to be intervening in some situation and bringing common sense to it. Eric smiled a little at his righteousness. A son protective of his father? Yes. After all of Dad's earlier sicknesses, he needed to take care of himself more now. He'd heard Mom say to him with irritation that he was being pulled in too many directions. As an only child, she had none of the pleasures of a big family and none of its tensions, either.

Dad couldn't turn off his concern or his willingness to help. Sometimes Eric thought that his father was almost too smart for his

own good. Not book smart always but people smart. Yet how could
you criticize him for that? And no one could change him anyway.
So the various family issues lingered and subsided, only to heat up
again when a new crisis arose, such as Fr. Eric having another "bad
week." And what would Eric find now inside the hospital? A tired
man needing a few days off was the best he could hope for.

At the front desk a nurse directed Eric to the second floor where
the surgical recovery unit linked with the intensive care wing. Eric
knew little about hospitals despite his visits to Dad's rooms as a kid,
but neither of those names gave him any comfort. Too impatient for
the elevator, Eric bounded up the stairwell and onto the second floor.
In the distance, he saw an attendant in white wheeling a man into a
semiprivate room. He approached and recognized his father lying on
the portable stretcher. The attendant, a male nurse, smiled and said
that he would return in a few seconds to help his father into a bed.

"You can talk with him briefly," the nurse said, "but he needs to
rest."

"Of course." He turned to Dad, who looked up at him with a
half-smile and then closed his eyes for a moment. Eric wondered
what to say and finally just spoke.

"So you had a weak spell? How do you feel now?"

"Oh, all right. I have a little headache." His father turned his
body a bit more toward Eric and adjusted the pillow under his head.

"With everything else going on, this is the last thing we need,"
his father uttered with a mix of frustration and exhaustion. Eric put
his hand across his dad's wrist.

"Well, you'll just have to slow down and let somebody else take
care of . . . things," Eric chose his words carefully.

Dad smiled at Eric's advice. "I guess you're right. Is your mom
here?"

"No. Fr. O'Neill came to the house to tell us. Mom wanted me
to come in first and see how you are. She'll be by later once I go
home."

"Very good," Dad said approvingly, as if talking about someone
else's illness. He appreciated his wife's discretion and his son's willingness to be the first to the hospital.

"You tell your mom that I just had a little weak spell"—the phrase was beginning to bother Eric, as if it was hiding something— "and I'll be all right," his dad said with as much assurance as he could. "I'll be all right," he repeated to himself.

"OK, Dad. I'll go now, and Mom will see you soon." He squeezed his father's right wrist, and the patient gave a little wave of his left hand. He sank back into the pillow as if to sleep. As Eric was leaving, the nurse returned with another attendant. They nodded to Eric and wheeled his father toward the bed to lift him into it.

* * *

Eric drove home and blocked the numbness in his brain by focusing on the traffic and the barren winter trees. Dad's words were upbeat. He always made the best of everything, or tried to, but his eyes were heavy and his movements slow. Appalling thoughts intruded, but Eric quickly brushed them away. Turning onto Berenger Street, he noticed that Fr. O'Neill's car was gone.

Mom asked about Dad's appearance and about the nurse's comments. Had any doctor said anything? Not to Eric. She decided to heat some soup for a quick lunch and made Eric a tuna sandwich. They sipped tea, ate quietly, and were soon finished. Marsha would be getting a ride home from school with a classmate in a couple of hours.

"I'd like you to stay here until she gets home. I'll call Aunt Emma and see if she can come to the hospital with me. Then if we get any more news, I'll call you from the hospital."

So a plan was in place. His mom always liked being organized, and that seemed especially important now. No need to overreact. Just be flexible for whatever might happen. Marian made the phone call. Aunt Emma would be glad to go with her. Emma had not known that Vic would be talking with the pastor about Fr. Eric today. She wasn't aware of anything new about her brother's condition, though she had her doubts that he should continue as a parish priest when he lacked the energy to say regular Sunday masses or to visit sick parishioners. Not driving anymore made him dependent on other priests or on family members. Yes, she knew that Vic had not been feeling well himself lately. Of course, she would help Marian any way she could. Both thought that Vic's illness was probably just from stress. Marian hoped that the Oblates would transfer Fr. Eric to the novitiate soon. Emma agreed, though you couldn't ever tell priests what to do or speed up their decisions. Should they say anything to Fr. Eric about Vic? No, they agreed. He couldn't do anything anyway. No need to worry him since Vic would be fine with some rest.

Eric passed his mother still talking on the front hall phone and went upstairs to continue reading Hardy's *Tess of the d'Urbervilles* for his nineteenth-century novel class. He sat on the bed with his pillow propped against the bed frame. Downstairs his mom finished her call.

"Eric, I'm going to pick up Aunt Emma and go to the hospital. You wait here for Marsha, and I'll call you with any news."

"OK, Mom," Eric said, then hesitated. "I'm sure Dad will be all right," he blurted out.

"Yes, I'm sure he will," she answered. He heard the back door close. A few more pages into the novel he put it down and looked out into the backyard. The barn behind the side lot was a dingy grey with peeling paint and a few cracked wood panels. Why didn't they paint it or tear it down? The neighborhood had long ago ceased to be farmland. Funny how people held onto relics like that shabby barn, or did they just stop seeing them after so many years?

Eric moved to his desk and grabbed his new copy of a baseball encyclopedia. He scanned the career records of some of the greatest players once more. Some stats towered over all the others. Ruth's homers, Cobb's batting average, Johnson's strikeouts. No one would ever match those records. Then he remembered that Spahn and Feller had both lost years of playing time in World War II. Maybe they would have approached Johnson's strikeout mark. Ted would have hit another 150 homers or so with the five years he'd missed in the military. Then he'd be second to Ruth and way ahead of everyone else, though Mays was on his way to six hundred or more. Imagining "hypothetical careers" was a baseball fantasy game for the winter months until a new season brought him back to today's stars and to whatever shape the pennant races took. The Sox had finished a dismal ninth in '66. Eighth place was no longer the cellar in the expanded ten-team leagues. Frank Robinson's Triple Crown last season and all that Baltimore pitching had so far outclassed Yaz and the Sox that nothing much better seemed likely for Boston in '67. Eric took refuge in baseball history and in other team's prospects, since the Red Sox just kept spinning their wheels. The Lead Sox, one sports writer had called them. Had any other franchise wasted so much great hitting with so little consistent pitching? Hard to imagine that before 1920 the Sox had won all five of their World Series. Cy Young and later Babe Ruth had pitched for them then. Speaker, Hooper, and Lewis ruled in the outfield, and Boston was baseball crazy. Eric closed the encyclopedia. Those pages could carry him away all afternoon if he let them. So could the baseball photos he had saved from magazines for several years and stored in a large box, someday to be arranged in a scrapbook that he was forever reorganizing in his mind.

"Hello! Anyone home?" he heard Marsha come in.

"I'm up here."

"Where's Mom?"

"I'm coming down." He met Marsha in the living room. She put down her schoolbooks and thumbed through a record rack looking for something to play.

"Mom's with Aunt Emma at the hospital," Eric said. Marsha turned from the records and looked at him.

"Why?"

"Well, Dad had a weak spell"—that phrase again—"and they're checking him out."

"Oh," said Marsha with wide eyes and a serious look. "What happened?"

"He was at the rectory talking with some priests about Fr. Eric"—Marsha nodded at the familiar scenario—"and he felt faint. They got him over to the hospital and checked him in. He says he'll be OK."

"Did you see him?"

"Yeah. Mom had me visit first. Now she and Aunt Emma are trying to find out more."

"Do you think . . . ?" Marsha began and stopped.

"I don't know. He looked tired and moved slowly," Eric paused. "He said he had a headache. I wish he didn't have to worry about Fr. Eric so much."

"Right," Marsha agreed. "That situation never gets any better."

"Mom will call us or just tell us any news when she gets back."

"OK," Marsha said abstractly. She went to the kitchen, scanned the refrigerator, found nothing she wanted, and returned to the living room. She picked out a Broadway show music album. As he started back upstairs, Eric recognized the music from *South Pacific*. He opened the novel at his bookmark and resumed reading. He was almost two more chapters along when the phone rang. Before he could get to it in the upstairs den, Marsha had picked up downstairs. He listened.

"Oh . . . when? What are they trying to do? Oh . . . yes. OK, we will, Mom. Bye." Marsha stood still at the phone for a second and looked up at her brother, who had walked around the second floor landing and now looked down at her from the top of the stairs. Her face was a little flushed, and she didn't speak for a moment.

"Daddy is not so good. Mom wants us to come to the hospital."

"Damn!" Eric heard himself say. Marsha gave him a startled glance. "All right," he recovered. "I'll get the keys." They drove together to the hospital without saying a word.

* * *

When he arrived near the hospital entrance, Eric found parking more difficult than earlier. Impatiently, he pulled into the Assumption School's paved playground and decided that with school out he could stay there. As he and Marsha walked toward the hospital entrance, Eric noticed a cream-colored Chevy sedan in front of the rectory. That was Uncle Ted and Aunt Sarah's car. Had they been called already about Dad?

This time Eric took the elevator with Marsha to the second floor. The doors opened onto the corridor perhaps a hundred feet from the room where Eric had last seen his father. As he and Marsha approached the room, a patients' waiting room diagonally across the hall came into view. All at once, several relatives' faces looked up at Vic's children. Aunt Emma came forward between them and hugged each with one arm. She took them to empty chairs along the waiting room wall and sat between them. She had a tightly wound tissue in her right hand, and her eyes were red.

"Your mother is talking with the doctor now. She'll be back soon." Aunt Emma breathed deeply and continued. "Your dad has some internal bleeding in the brain. They've put him on an IV and given him some pain medicine, but they're not sure where exactly the bleeding is or how to stop it."

"Is he conscious?" Marsha asked.

"A couple of times we've spoken to him, but then he will fade or"—Aunt Emma choked up briefly but continued—"he seems to be in some pain." She looked up. "Here's your mother."

Marian came into the room with a doctor, who smiled quickly to everyone and then returned to Dad's room. Mom had been crying but did her best to greet Eric and Marsha. "The doctors have made a couple of calls to brain specialists in Boston to see what they suggest. They are trying to relieve the pressure from the bleeding. Let's just say some silent prayers for now."

Marsha hugged her mom, and the two began to cry softly. Eric looked around the room at the stunned and grieving faces—Uncle Ted and Aunt Sarah and their daughter Alice Mary; cousin Jerry McCarron, the funeral director at Malone Funeral Parlor since Uncle Bill had retired; and there, in a chair at the corner of the room, Fr. Eric with Fr. O'Neill sitting by him. So they had told Fr. Eric after all, or maybe Fr. O'Neill had told him. Eric walked around to everyone and received their handshakes or a touch on the shoulder. "We're praying for him, Eric." "The doctors are doing all they can." Eric nodded and said thanks a few times. Aunt Sarah hugged him with her thin arms but could not speak.

Slowly Eric made his way over to his uncle. "Hello, Fr. Eric," he said and offered his hand. His uncle took it and looked at him with moist eyes and a vacant face. "This is quite a shock," he said slowly. Eric felt a pang inside for his uncle, so much of his own life gone already, now coping with the possible death of his younger brother, two weeks short of his fifty-fourth birthday. Eric swallowed hard and took the priest's hand in both of his own. Then he walked back toward his mother and found a seat beside Marsha, who held her mother's hand across the arms of their two chairs. Everyone waited now in a vigil with only one likely ending.

Soon after five o'clock, Mildred, Ralph, and George Harrigan arrived. All had gotten off work early as soon as someone had called them. They greeted everyone quietly, and Mom explained to Mildred what had happened since noon. Nurses occasionally went to and from Dad's room, but an hour or more passed with nothing new. Jerry McCarron stepped out briefly and returned with sandwiches, coffee, and soft drinks for everyone. Close to seven o'clock, Dad's oldest brother Uncle Bill and his wife Aunt Bob arrived. They nodded to the rest and then sat by the Harrigans. A hospital volunteer brought in four folding chairs for any late arrivals. Tissues and tears, mumbled prayers, quiet sobs, and brief words of tentative hopefulness marked the different ways his family dealt with uncertainty and grief. Eric felt numb again. He was too stunned to know what to do or say. Was this it? Would Dad leave them with hardly a good-bye? What would happen without him was too strange a question for Eric to face. The suddenness of it was senseless.

Around seven thirty, a different doctor entered the waiting room. "Mrs. Malone, may I speak with you for a moment?"

"Certainly, doctor." Mom rose and walked away with him to a private office. A few minutes later, she returned with the doctor and sat by her cousin Mildred, who had been like her sister since childhood. The doctor looked around the room and everyone quieted. He was perhaps thirty and new to most of the family, though Jerry McCarron knew him and virtually all the doctors at St. Benedict's Hospital.

"Mr. Malone has been in and out of consciousness," he spoke to everyone. "We are doing our best to make him comfortable. The . . . pain relief (Eric thought he avoided saying morphine) has seemed to work, but the . . . internal bleeding . . . continues. I think it best, if you would like, to enter the room in small groups just for a few moments each. Maybe he will be able to hear you or say a word. You are all welcome to stay, but we are not likely to have any further news about his condition for some time." The doctor nodded to everyone and walked back toward his office. Eric knew that they were all being asked to take a final look at his father and then to leave if they chose to. So they did. In threes and fours they went to the foot of Victor Malone's bed. Some said a few words to see if he could hear them. Twice Eric thought from the waiting room that he might have heard a murmur of response, but he wasn't sure. The relatives all hugged or said good-bye to Mom, Marsha, and him as they exited the room and left for home. They would be in touch tomorrow.

"Jerry," Aunt Emma said to her son, "I'm going to stay with Marian tonight."

"All right," Jerry answered. He then looked at the Malones and said almost formally, "God bless you all," and he left.

With everyone else gone, the three of them now entered the room with Aunt Emma. Dad seemed to have his back slightly arched under the bedclothes—or were those pillows supporting him? Eric wasn't sure. He breathed slowly for a time, then more haltingly, and then calmer again. After five minutes he opened his eyes and seemed to recognize his family.

"We are right here, Vic," Marian said softly. A young nurse was standing by the bed. She had occasionally wiped Dad's brow and face with a damp cloth. In a moment of alertness, Dad looked toward her and mumbled, "I think my wife is jealous." Everyone smiled at Victor's final joke.

"God bless you, Daddy," Marsha said, touching his hand. "Good kids," he seemed to say to no one in particular and then closed his eyes. The family stood by him for a few more minutes and then returned to the waiting room. Marian now cried quietly on Aunt Emma's shoulder. Marsha sat by herself, and Eric stood and looked up at the colorless ceiling. He sat down again and had his head in his hands for a few minutes when the nurse came from the room and beckoned them all to return. Now Dad had a round plastic tube in his mouth and sucked air through it in short gasps. His eyes were closed as if breathing could be his only thought. A different nurse entered and checked his pulse and wiped his forehead and hands. She watched him for a long moment and then gestured to Mom to indicate that she wanted to draw the curtain around the bed.

With her hands, Mom took the hands of Marsha and Eric. "Let's go," she said. Aunt Emma followed them back into the waiting room. Five minutes later, the young doctor came along the corridor with Fr. Galligan, the pastor. Both nodded to Marian. Eric saw a small clerical bag the priest carried and knew he was there to give Dad the last rites. When that was done, he came into the waiting room and hugged each of them.

"What a wonderful man," he managed to say until his voice began to crack. "God is surely waiting for him."

"Thank you, Father," Marian said with dignity.

"Please tell me if I can help you in any way," the pastor added and said good-bye.

Mom sighed deeply and sat once more. Three minutes later, the young doctor emerged from the room and approached them.

"Mr. Malone is gone," he said quietly. "We did all we could for him."

Thank you, doctor," Marian answered as the doctor took her hand, nodded awkwardly to them all, and left. The three women hugged each other, and then his mom came to Eric and gave him a careful hug. While she did, he looked over her shoulder at the wall clock and noticed the time: four minutes after nine. Only nine hours had passed from the first warning to the end.

11

Aunt Emma stayed with Marian through that weekend. Jerry called a couple of times and visited once to talk over plans for the wake and the funeral. What flowers did they want? What church music would Vic have? Any preferences for his appearance in the casket? His mom got through these discussions well enough, almost needing them to keep going. Between such planning times and the light meals she took, her grief came in tearful spasms. She retreated to her bedroom then with Aunt Emma and a couple of times with Marsha. Mildred visited on Thursday afternoon and left a chicken dinner and two pies for them all. When Mildred left, his mom turned to Eric. "George has arranged to take tomorrow off and has offered to pick up Betty in Tarrytown. I'd like you to go with him."

"OK," Eric agreed. So they left early Friday morning in George's Oldsmobile. They would drive to Maryhill College and back the same day to get Betty home as soon as possible. The three Harrigans, single all their lives, took an interest in the Malone kids as godparents and as unofficial uncles and an aunt. Like others in his parents' generation, they had learned the fine art of parlor conversation where silences were impolite and ought to be filled. So now as Eric and George rode west away from the Boston commuters, George made small talk about the weather and the traffic and the places they passed on the road—a restaurant he liked, a hotel where the Harrigans had once spent a vacation weekend years before. Eric managed the polite minimum of responses until George finally sensed that he didn't want to talk very much and the conversation stopped.

When they arrived at Maryhill, Betty was waiting at her dorm entrance with three bags. Eric and George put them in the trunk, and the three started promptly back east toward Lowell. Betty asked a few questions about the funeral timetable, and Eric told her as much as he knew. Dad would be waked at Malone Funeral Parlor, then the funeral mass at Assumption Church, and finally the burial at St. Patrick's Cemetery. Grampa Harrigan had been buried there six years before. Betty did not ask about Dad's sudden illness, and Eric was relieved not to go over all that now. She could learn every detail later from Mom and Marsha. Better not to discuss all that with George, who would comment too much. When they stopped for a snack and bathroom break west of Hartford, Eric offered to drive, but as expected, George said no. He and Betty should just relax. That was fine. He had offered anyway.

Once home, Betty felt the force of her mom's grief. Mom had been the only child of Irish immigrants and had grown up in the 1920s and '30s. She had spoken to Eric in brief, unguarded moments of her father's fruitless strike as a railroad worker in '24 and of the need to "play quietly" in their upstairs flat, lest she upset the tenants below. No one could risk losing good tenants, her mother had reminded her often. The so-called Roaring Twenties had been no part of Marian's life. All that was for rich people with more money than brains, she had quipped, though Eric wondered if she weren't a little envious of all the fun that others were having (if people believed the papers). She had never been poor or without security exactly, but poverty, like New Deal promises of prosperity, was always just around the corner for Marian and her parents. Only the war had replaced that fear with something worse. The three Harrigans' brother Phil had enlisted in the army days after Pearl Harbor and been sent to Italy. He came back as the casualty of a military vehicle accident in Anzio in late '44. Not a combat death, but what did the details matter when a brother was gone? Marian's four cousins were now three, and with Ralph and George also in uniform, who could be sure of that number?

Marian had drawn closer to her cousins during the war, and when Vic Malone proposed to her, Mildred Harrigan was happy to be the maid of honor on September 20, 1944, the thirty-third anniversary of her own parents' wedding. Vic's large family, his business success, and his gregarious personality had banished the shadows of earlier years from Marian's life. Yet Vic's health had become a constant question, and Eric remembered several hospital visits for his dad's two ulcer surgeries. Now, after years of better health but frequent anxiety about family problems, Vic Malone was suddenly gone. Marian's happiness, long awaited and carefully nurtured, was abruptly snatched away.

Eric could put all that together as a backdrop for his mother's tears, but such tears themselves he had never seen before and had no words or gestures to soften them. Aunt Emma and his sisters knew more about that—women knew more, he assumed. So Eric kept busy, ran errands, found polite words to say, and otherwise kept to himself. The details of his father's last days reran through Eric's mind like scenes from a complicated movie before the film had abruptly broken. Every detail now seemed portentous or ironic. The little tensions between them over Vietnam battle news or church issues suddenly felt vapid and barren. Why hadn't he found some way to talk with his dad about father-and-son things more immediate than the world's turmoil? Well, he hadn't, and nothing could be done about it now. Eric's sense of what mattered had all the gaps of a fledgling mind formed by too many books and too little else. Had his dad been waiting for something more from his son when the wait was ruthlessly terminated? Or maybe his father had more important things to think about, like the well-being of his brother the priest.

After much planning, the wake was upon them. More people knew his father in more ways than Eric could imagine, and the line was long for most of the two-day wake. Jerry had taken care of every detail—a professional in charge of his own emotions so that others could cope with theirs. And Jerry was directing this funeral of his youngest uncle at least twenty years too soon. The tight lines on his face told the story.

The stream of dark-clad mourners continued through the first afternoon and evening. Only on the second day did the numbers subside. Eric took in the fact that all of Dad's siblings and most of his cousins were older than his father. This death had stunned them. It verged on cruel—a young man with three children. Eric felt tightness in his throat for them. Several times he came almost to tears at the tears of others, yet it was all too strange for very clear emotions. He hardly knew what to feel.

When Eric's dentist, the unrelated Dr. Herbert Malone, took his hand, Eric prepared for another polite exchange, but Dr. Herb looked straight at him and said quietly, "You know now what you need to do, don't you?" Eric nodded, not quite sure what the question meant until the doctor said firmly, "Then do it," and moved along toward Marian. Slowly the dentist's point dawned on Eric—to be a man now for his mother in whatever way he could.

Several visitors later, Eric smiled shyly to see Mrs. Albert Belisle approaching him. She had already been crying, and she moved beyond Eric's outstretched hand into a firm hug for several seconds. "It is so hard for you young men to lose your fathers so early," she said, and Eric recalled that Ro's dad had passed away from cancer while he and Ro were still freshmen at Kenton. "I so enjoyed your dad," she added. Ro stepped forward and gave Eric a quick handshake. "We will be in touch," Mrs. Belisle promised as she turned toward Eric's sisters and his mom.

Eric had been to more wakes than most of his friends and had heard the familiar consoling phrases again and again for every possible circumstance—from the passing of Grampa Malone at eighty-four to the shock of his father's death at fifty-three. He even dimly remembered the wake of his cousin Theresa, age eighteen, who had died in a violent auto accident when Eric was just eight. His parents had let him say a quick prayer then at the kneeler in front of the closed casket and had taken him home soon after. Betty and Marsha had not gone at all.

"He looks so peaceful. Jerry did a wonderful job," Uncle Bill said to Eric's mother as Eric returned to the receiving line.

"Yes, he did," Marian answered. "Vic always liked that suit, and the rosary beads were a souvenir of Fr. Eric's twenty-fifth anniversary."

"Oh, yes," Uncle Bill remembered. At seventy-two, Uncle Bill was several years retired as the funeral director of Malone Funeral Parlor. He had embalmed and laid to rest two generations of family members and hundreds of Lowell residents and other family friends since he was just a young funeral director in the new business that Grampa Malone had funded back in '23.

"I'll never get used to this," Uncle Bill said to Eric's mom. "God wanted him. That's all we can say," Aunt Bob added.

Fr. Eric came with Fr. O'Neill and the pastor on the second afternoon of the wake. At a time when the line of mourners had thinned, they approached the casket and greeted Eric and his sisters before speaking to Marian.

"God bless you, young man," the pastor said to Eric, who thanked him. Fr. Eric could not quite speak to his nephew and namesake but only placed his hand briefly on his forehead as if in silent blessing.

* * *

When the calling hours ended, Fr. O'Neill led the family and some mourners in the Sorrowful Mysteries of the rosary. He concluded the five decades of Hail Mary's with the Hail Holy Queen prayer. Eric remembered that these priests were all Oblates of Mary Immaculate, to whom Marian devotions were important. Like many guys his age, Eric had gotten away from saying the rosary. Rote prayers seemed deadening to him in all the post-Vatican II liturgical reforms. Yet around his father's casket to hear about twenty voices saying the "Our Father's" and "Hail Mary's" together had a unifying impact that silent, solitary prayers could not. When they had finished, the three priests and the other visitors left. Eric, his sisters, and his mother knelt before Dad's coffin one last time for a brief prayer. His mother touched her husband's hand softly and then stepped away. Jerry now came forward and closed the casket. The funeral procession would begin from the funeral home at nine in the morning.

At the altar the next day, Fathers O'Neill and Galligan con-celebrated this mass with Fr. Eric and another older priest seated to his right. "Immaculate Mary," "Holy, Holy, Holy, Lord God Almighty," and "How Great Thou Art" reverberated through the church during different parts of the mass as a solitary cantor sang them. After the Gospel reading on the resurrection of Lazarus, Fr. Galligan gave not really a eulogy (Mom wanted nothing too elaborate) but some thoughts on the passing of Victor Malone.

"Such losses test our faith," he said, "because they are by earth's standards so untimely and so sudden. In these kinds of events, God gives us no warning, no time to prepare. Of the end of the world, Jesus said, 'You know not the day, nor the hour.' So it is as well with some of the greatest losses of our lives. God's plans and His timing remain a mystery to us. And yet if we are always ready, as Jesus also told us to be, we can face the worst that this life forces upon us without losing hope. We know from his generous and faithful life that Vic Malone did not lose hope. We are confident today that he was as ready as any of us can be for God's sudden call."

Eric looked toward Fr. Eric, who stared at the floor without expression.

233

"Some of you know," the pastor continued, "that Vic was taken ill while at the rectory talking with Father O'Neill and me. Even then he was seeing to the welfare of others." Eric looked again at Fr. Eric, whose face did not change. "That was Vic Malone's way. His wife and children, his family and friends, were always more important to him than himself. So today, let us be full of hope, even in our sadness, for God knows all the good that Vic did and tried to do. We can be confident that He has taken this faithful servant unto himself."

When the mass ended, Eric walked slowly down the aisle with his family after the casket. He looked beyond the reserved family pews toward the back half of the church. Several neighbors and some old high school classmates were there. Among them he noticed Joel and Tony with Brother Sam. They had come all the way from Worcester to attend the mass. Eric caught their eye and nodded to them. Outside at the hearse, Jerry supervised the return of all the family members to their limos, and the final motorcade from the church to the cemetery began.

Where Appleton and Central Streets meet in downtown Lowell, stood a corner soda fountain and sandwich shop, Mello's Café. Eric's dad had sometimes gone there in the early evenings or on a day off for a milk shake and snack and the company of business friends and other locals. As the funeral procession approached, Eric saw the lights on in the café but no one seated at the counter. Then he looked to the sidewalk in front of the café. He counted eighteen people standing in single file along the curb, the men with hats off, to say farewell to Victor Malone. Eric gave them a quick wave, and his mom smiled broadly to them. Some nodded or waved quickly, but most stood at attention until the cars had passed. Nothing in all that long day affected Eric so much as that tribute from his dad's everyday friends. Instead of dressing up and being all but invisible at the church, they had chosen to honor him where they knew him best.

The procession continued along Gorham Street past St. Peter's, another old Gothic church. Then it passed by the bar that Grampa Malone had owned maybe sixty years before (now closed at this morning hour) and finally turned right into St. Patrick's Cemetery. The grave had already been dug into the hard ground before the

Harrigan-Malone headstone. The bearers, all Dad's brothers and nephews, took the casket toward the gravesite and laid it down on a cleared spot surrounded by some flowers from the wake. Fr. Galligan said the formal prayers commending Eric's dad to the earth and to heaven. Fr. Eric stood by him but did not speak. The mourners formed a wide semicircle in the cold January air. Eric saw their breath among the overcoats and scarfs. A thin layer of snow remained on the ground and along the tops of some of the gravestones, and the hard New England earth in stony silence took back one of its own.

Swift Passages

I

Final semesters fly by like the ends of long road trips, or they linger like unwanted leftovers. Eric's days raced along through a strange new stillness. On his ride back to St. James, his brain teemed with conflicting thoughts. Much was the same. Everything was different.

Dad had provided well enough to assure Eric's tuition and other expenses. Like a good insurance man, he had taken care of first things first. His business was still there, and Mom had expressed mixed feelings about whether to sell it or to run it herself. She'd been a legal secretary before her marriage, and she had plenty of business sense. Perhaps she wondered if Eric wanted to inherit the business, though she hadn't asked. Eric doubted he'd be much of a businessman. He smiled to imagine himself sneaking hours for novels and philosophy books when he needed to be reviewing the accounts receivable or advising home sellers and buyers to change their bids. He couldn't envision doing all the social things his father did routinely, enjoyably. With his worldview secure (Roman Catholicism via the Jesuits), Dad had turned his practical mind toward succeeding in the world. His business had expressed the best of himself, and Eric couldn't duplicate that. Vic had been worldly wise so that Eric could have the luxury of speculation, though his father had not really planned it that way. "We send you off to college," he quipped once, "so that you can come back and tell us what narrow backs we are." Eric shook his head in disagreement, but he had no easy comeback. Everything he thought to say sounded vaguely ungrateful. Another conversation he could not do over.

Whatever he would decide about the draft and the war, Dad would not be there to support or to criticize. Eric was on his own now; it was liberating and scary. Before that crisis arrived, he would be busy again with spring courses, including a different one called History of Modern Art. More visual, less verbal—a good thing for him. He'd have Cahalane again for Modern British Poets. Could the old spellbinder be as exciting there as with Shakespeare? Maybe not. He was a hard act to follow, even for himself. Anyway, getting into new readings and new writers would distract him from father-less solitude. So would the second half of the debate season. The Dartmouth tournament was next, another big chance for Joel and Tony.

Stubborn winter would fight off spring until it no longer could and the days would warm intermittently until, as Mom liked to say, it was suddenly 98 degrees one May afternoon and the summer heat had arrived. Then he would graduate—to what and to where? What would that June day be like without Dad? Another ordeal for Mom, but she'd get through it as she came through everything in recent days. Private tears and public smiles.

For now, it was enough on a cold Saturday at dusk to park near a new snowbank behind his dorm and walk alone up to his room. Zack was gone till tomorrow night. Then the dorms would fill up again with all the reassuring craziness that made the stillness feel almost normal.

11

The debaters were awkwardly deferential when Eric met with them on a Wednesday after school to talk about the Dartmouth tourna-ment. No one knew what to say beyond the familiar phrases of con-dolence: "I'm sorry about your father." "Thanks." "It was a nice ser-vice." "I appreciate your coming."

Brother Sam was a little more effusive. He asked briefly about the illness and then regretted the loss of such a young father. "We never know what God has in mind. I will keep your dad in my prayers."

"Thank you, Brother." Eric parted with a brief handshake and moved along the corridor to the English classroom where the debaters waited.

Joel and Tony had some new quotations to copy onto file cards. Rather than a full-scale practice debate, they thought that tomorrow afternoon those going to Dartmouth for the four-person varsity event could quiz the two of them about the new sources. It would do the questioners good, too. So the next day, when everyone had read all the new cards, Joel and Tony quoted them to support specific points about UN peacekeeping troops and then Singletary, Hendley, Gillette, and Trevecci (replacing Biranchi for this tournament) asked quick questions of the two. For about forty minutes, the exchange was lively, and Eric only suggested an occasional tightening of a question or an answer. Joel and Tony, for all their verbal agility, had a tendency to treat all challenges equally instead of dismissing an irrelevant point or an unsupported objection. Today they were better about that, and the questioners were picking up details about the new sources by challenging them.

"We need to leave about six thirty Saturday morning, guys, so everyone try to be here before that," Eric said finally. They nodded and then smiled or groaned when Tony pursued a laborious joke about sleepy, predawn birds outmaneuvered by zigzagging worms.

"Deftly put," Joel ridiculed his partner, and Eric waved them all out of the meeting. Bad jokes were an ironic sign that the guys were ready, Eric thought on his way back to St. James.

The Saturday morning ride from Worcester to Dartmouth was cold, clear, and surprisingly quiet. Trevecci drove Hendley and Singletary, while Eric had Gillette, Bellanger, and Warren with him. The guys mostly chatted with less than the usual energy. These birds weren't hunting any worms yet. Eddie Gillette searched the radio for a few minutes and then turned it off. He looked out at the morning-lit mountain ridges and at all the road signs for the small towns between Concord and Lebanon along I-89.

At last the stately austerity of the Dartmouth campus surrounded them as they carried their file cabinets into a dorm foyer, checked in, and got their first-round assignments. Four rounds with two ballots each would take the debaters into mid-afternoon. Then all but the two finalists of the switch-side tournament would be free to head home in the winter dusk. Some unfamiliar New Hampshire and Vermont high schools were in the mix, together with the usual powers from greater Boston, New York City, and upstate along the Hudson. Some had arrived on Friday and stayed in hotels, while others had driven as far as Eric and farther.

The Dartmouth tournament was a midwinter showdown to launch the second semester and to identify some contenders for the Nationals in Atlantic City. Yet the tournament itself, like all debate tournaments, was a mysterious affair with no results until the end as teams and coaches-turned-judges worked their isolated debates with hardly a spectator. Rumors were intriguing but unreliable. Judges, Eric included, made no direct comments and kept their judicial deadpan almost intact. Debating was like waiting for the jury in a courtroom, only here there were no clues from jury requests for evidence or from a juror suddenly excused. Debating was about arguing and waiting—arguing all day and then waiting for all the verdicts at the end. Only in eliminations rounds, if a tournament had them, did the leading teams have much of an audience. Then their strategies and key evidence became more public, and nimble changes in tactics could be crucial from one round to the next.

At Dartmouth, the four-person tournament had no title round. Wins and points would be decisive. In the switch-side division, the two best teams by record first and then points would face each other in one championship debate. By then, secrecy mattered less since no debates would follow. And on a cold winter's Saturday in New Hampshire, most eliminated teams would have a warm dinner and head home. The final two contenders would be talking before teammates, some tournament hosts, and seven neutral judges. Competitive fire would be fighting off mental exhaustion in each debater's mind: I want to win—I just want to eat and go home.

When the four-person results were announced, each St. Joe's team was 2–2. *A good effort*, Eric thought, *in a tough field*. Then the switch-side results came. The day would be longer as Joel and Tony had swept to victory on all eight ballots. Today, they had hit the mark and they knew it. Perhaps thirty debaters and a handful of coaches stayed to see the final round against Xaverian Prep, a strong New York City school. Eric usually took debate notes on loose-leaf sheets folded into four columns for the four speakers, but this time he had brought an artist's sketch pad and used it to make more elaborate flowchart notes with arrows between the columns to link each speaker's comments on similar topics. In a good debate with few gaps in coverage by any speaker, the flowchart could look like a complex maze of abbreviations, arrows, and check marks. The whole debate was there on one page. So it was for the St. Joe's–Xaverian debate.

Despite the long day, both teams were sharp, but Joel and Tony synthesized so well in their rebuttals and distinguished quickly between solid opposing points and less credible ones. Not a second seemed wasted, and when they were done, Eric's flowchart told him that they had won. Five of the seven judges agreed. Joel and Tony had broken through at last. From now on, other schools would take more notice of them. All their research, and maybe even Thursday's question-and-answer exercise, had put them over the top.

The ride home, after a happy dinner together in Hanover, was a celebration. No one cared that they would arrive in darkness and not finally all be home until after nine p.m. Joel and Tony had won at Dartmouth!

Two weeks later at the Catholic Prep four-person varsity event, Joel and Tony wanted to spread their strengths, so Eldon (back in the lineup for Trevecci) paired with Joel on the Affirmative, and Eddie and Tony took the Negative. Against a familiar greater Boston field, they rolled to a 6–0 record. Then Eldon and Joel won a unanimous 5–0 decision in the championship round. Two wins in successive weeks! All the preparation was working at last, and the "partner chemistry" was becoming more adaptable. Eldon and Eddie were now an outstanding varsity team themselves—and only sophomores.

A week later, these four and Eric drove south for the next big college switch-side tournament at Georgetown University. This event drew schools from nearly the whole East Coast. Debate powers from Pennsylvania, Maryland, Virginia, and farther south attended, along with the familiar Northeast schools and a few from as far west as Ohio and Michigan.

For some affluent debate schools, their schedules looked like a college football team's with weekend after weekend booked and a big travel budget available. Georgetown was another key lead-up to the Nationals in May. This time, the guys resumed the usual pairings with Joel and Tony together, and Eddie and Eldon as a second varsity entry. When the regulation rounds ended, Eldon and Eddie were 4–2, and Joel and Tony, with a 5–1 mark, were among the "sweet sixteen" to make the octofinals. There they beat St. Brendan's Prep, three ballots to none, but in the quarterfinals they lost to an unfamiliar Pittsburgh Central Catholic team, one ballot to two. The Pittsburgh debaters went on to win the Georgetown tournament. Still, Eric was excited at this three-tournament run: two wins and a top eight in three successive weeks. God, these guys were good! Next up, after a weekend off, was the "hometown" college tournament at St. James.

Back home in Mullane Hall ("Superdorm" the guys dubbed the giant new building), Eric lay awake thinking of these rising debate stars and of himself about to be a judge at his own college's tournament where he'd been a nervous young competitor just a few years earlier. With Dad gone, he felt suddenly older—a college senior and high school debate coach, soon a college graduate and a grad student himself, maybe even a new teaching assistant somewhere. His roles were changing faster than any wisdom he had gained to cope with them. Or maybe Dad would say, "Don't get a swelled head, Eric, but you're smarter than you think. Now don't forget what I told you about the swelled head."

I I I

Another "leadership role" suddenly fell to Eric when Fr. Lionel asked if he would be one of the three general secretaries for the college's annual Faculty-Student Conference that happened to be scheduled for a nondebate weekend. The chaplain's office, the Sodality, and the student government were cosponsoring a school-wide discussion of three topics about college life: the general academic scene, the specific academic scene, and the cultural and social scene. One hundred thirty students, faculty, and administrators had been divided into thirteen discussion groups to consider a series of subtopics—or to develop some new ones—under these three headings. A "state-of-the-college symposium," Fr. Lionel called it with a quick grin, not wanting to sound pompous. Each general secretary received reports from the thirteen groups and synthesized them into a written report. Fr. Lionel then interviewed the three on campus radio to get their sense of what the participants had said. What was the pulse of St. J in late January of '67?

Eric sat in the waiting room of the college radio station adjacent to the school theater and one floor above the administrative corridor that everyone called Mahogany Row. Secretaries Jack LeBeau and Melvin Reich, both juniors, were being interviewed before him. All three would have about fifteen minutes each with Fr. Lionel to answer questions and to offer conference feedback. A radio played the live broadcast in the waiting room, so Eric heard the first two interviews as he skimmed through each of the reports. When his turn came, he would know what to say and what little glitches to avoid on the air. Or would he? He didn't feel nervous, though who could be sure of that? His debate tournaments had never been broadcast.

The first two segments of the conference agenda had suffered from overlap as participants slipped too easily between general and specific academic issues. Anyway, the results suggested more conflict than agreement. Could some of these people—students, faculty, and administrators—Jesuits and lay people—be talking about the same school? St. James curriculum was too secular. No, it was too Catholic and not diverse enough. What exactly was the college's educational mission anyway? To train young Catholic leaders? To produce "men for others" with a commitment to service? Maybe it was just to educate the next generation of doctors, lawyers, and businessmen with some overlay of social conscience. Conference comments often sounded like point-counterpoint. The professors were highly qualified but too preoccupied with their disciplines and rarely available to students beyond the classroom. The students, except for a handful of true scholars, were apathetic, sports obsessed, and not interested in any deeper interactions with professors. The campus was too isolated from other campuses. Why didn't we do more with nearby colleges and universities? But who really had time for that when homework piled up? Some wanted more pass-fail course options for electives to encourage exposure to new disciplines without the pressure of grades. And wouldn't more students from diverse backgrounds—other religions and races, and women—deepen the classroom experience? But we can't be everything to everyone and should try instead to be a better men's Jesuit college instead of chasing after new identities. Did it all sound like the pouting of the privileged? Time for a good dose of *Summa Theologica*, Dad might have said.

LeBeau spoke in as neutral a voice as he could manage. Father Lionel tried to lighten the mood with an occasional joke or an interesting follow-up question.

"Jack, what do you think about all those college identity comments, and just how widespread do you think the discontent is?" As Jack slowly pieced together an answer, Eric imagined who had raised some of these issues in the conference workshops. Faces came to mind. Recalling the Jesuit education of Dad's time, some Jesuits and older faculty had probably sounded the traditional themes. Sanderson and Delaney had both managed to get picked for different conference groups. Which one of them, Eric wondered, had LeBeau been quoting when he said pointedly, "One student argued forcefully that St. James should just become a public university and maybe merge with Claraton or another nearby school"? Relentless Delaney, probably. Did he or Sanderson really think that after more than century of Jesuits on the hill, the college would just wipe away its past and become something completely new? No. They knew better but were having too much fun being provocative in a much bigger forum than a dorm room rant.

"Thank you, Jack," Fr. Lionel said at last. "We certainly have plenty to ponder from your comments. Now we welcome Mel Reich, who will comment on his Specific Academic Scene report."

Mel tended to ramble more than Jack, and pretty soon Eric had the sense that every topic had merged into every other. Mel also editorialized on the points he favored despite Fr. Lionel's efforts to bring him back to his actual notes. Mel said that at St. James academic excellence too often meant good test scores and grades rather than original thinking or creativity, that too many students from Jesuit or other Catholic high schools produced a sameness in many classroom discussions, that a more open admissions policy would bring more non-Catholics, nonwhites, and—at last—women to the campus, and that "many students" (he asserted) wanted better library facilities at the college.

"Does that mean more books or more lounge chairs?" Fr. Lionel quipped.

"Both," Mel answered directly as Fr. Lionel laughed softly into the mike.

Mel continued with what sounded to Eric like his own personal wish list, though several of the items were printed in Mel's written report—a college press, a writer-in-residence program, the elimination of "faculty deadwood," a faculty advisory system for students, and more.

"Well," commented Fr. Lionel at last, "some of those things might require much greater resources and the transformation of St. James into a larger university, don't you think?"

Mel wasn't sure, though he felt that many conference participants were open to such significant changes at the school.

"Thank you very much, Mel, for your work on this report. And now we will hear from senior Eric Malone on the cultural and social scene at St. James."

Eric nodded to Mel as he left and then sat down at a small table opposite Fr. Lionel. Microphones on either side of the table awaited their discussion. Eric placed his report on the table and hoped he could find specific marked passages if he needed them. He had not quite understood why Fr. Lionel had asked him to report on the social workshops. He'd never even been to a campus dance and was hardly a social notable (or a "culture vulture," as classmate Charlie Danison had once proclaimed himself). He was only available at all because no debate tournament was scheduled for this weekend. So here he was, a wallflower scoring a dance contest. By now, Fr. Lionel had heard about all sorts of conference "concerns," actual or alleged, so Eric tried to stay close to his notes in answering each question.

"Eric, what would you say were the dominant ideas coming out of your workshop groups?" Fr. Lionel began.

"Well, one was a strong preference, though not unanimous, for coeducation at St. James. Eight of the thirteen groups favored it, and seven of those were unanimous."

"What were their reasons?"

"Some groups said that social life seems 'artificial' and 'programmed' at the college. Women on campus would mean a more natural social life. The males would learn to treat women as persons rather than as objects. Some also said that female competition would improve male academic performance and make the whole college stronger."

"Were there any negatives to that change?"

"Yes. A few groups saw coeducation as possibly cutting into alumni support by ending the male tradition of the school. Also, many guys now enrolled here might not have been admitted if women had been competing against them."

"Can you determine any leanings by the faculty or students specifically on this question?" Fr. Lionel asked with a half-smile.

"Not really. Maybe we could assume that students support coeducation most, but no group actually said that."

"OK. What other issues were important?"

"Many felt that dorm life currently is deficient or worse. Four groups suggested integrating the dorms across grade levels to break up the worst behavior within classes. Two mentioned some kind of 'house' system of dorms based on a theme, such as foreign language dorms or science-math dorms. Each could have a dorm council that would plan activities and have some authority to monitor dorm behavior."

"That's very interesting. Did anyone think such a system would weaken class unity?"

"No one said that. Many seem to think that dorm life now is pretty bad—a 'horror show' one group called it—" Fr. Lionel laughed but said nothing"—so that class unity is more of a drawback than an asset, at least in the dorms."

Fr. Lionel took a deep breath and paused. "Well, that's certainly not the intent of the current system. I recall when classes had some pride in their dorms and even decorated hallways for Thanksgiving and Christmas. I guess we can't expect that anymore."

"I don't think so," Eric agreed.

"What else did you find?"

"Several groups wanted increased faculty-student contact, but no one seemed sure how to achieve it. Four groups did mention these Faculty-Student Conferences themselves and said they'd like to see more of them. One group even thought that some sort of ongoing committee could meet monthly to come up with recommendations for the student government and the administration."

"Would there be enough interest to sustain that, I wonder?"

"I don't know. No one actually volunteered to do it." Eric and Fr. Lionel both laughed.

"Eric, did you find any discussion of Christian spirituality as part of the campus culture?"

"Yes. Five groups talked about that, though their views were divided. Some felt that the innovations in the liturgy—guitar masses and so forth—had strengthened student involvement. Two others saw more activity in community service projects in Worcester as a good sign. But many felt that only a minority of students were very committed either to Christian liturgy or to social action. Most students are seen as preoccupied with studies or with partying in various forms. Some groups even wanted longer 'parietal hours' to allow students to have female guests in dorm rooms and lounges until later. And three groups felt that the school should be less concerned with drinking as such but should punish *bad behavior* from drinking more forcefully."

"All of that sounds pretty familiar," Fr. Lionel said flatly. "A lot depends on what kind of campus life people want."

"Yes. I think most groups felt that college life here is better than it was a year ago but that many students don't really know what to do with more freedom, even when they get it."

"Of course. That's always a basic question. What is freedom for? Well, Eric, thanks for your insights on these issues."

"Thank you, Father." And the broadcast ended with Fr. Lionel's familiar sign-off.

IV

To Eric, the Faculty Student Conference had settled somewhere between a wish list for the college's future and an indecisive griping session. With just a few months until graduation, Eric cared more about the realities than the wishes. He wanted to finish well and then take his next step. First-year graduate students continued—for now—to be deferrable from the draft. Eric wanted graduate school in any case, but now he had an added incentive. He could buy some time for deciding what to do about this war that wasn't going away. "The troops will be home by Christmas" sounded like media and Pentagon dreaming. "Which Christmas?" became the mocking follow-up. Meanwhile, despite all the conference criticisms of dear old James, Eric still loved his course lineup.

Dr. Winston's Dryden, Pope, and Swift seminar had given way to the Age of Johnson. Early on, Eric wondered how exciting a course built around a literary critic could be, but the depth of Johnson's judgments and the quirky pathos of his personality, especially as pictured by his perpetual chronicler James Boswell, soon caught hold of Eric's imagination and gained his respect. Here was the greatest encyclopedic mind of the era, one of the greatest in history. How could one man have done all that massive reading and then have evaluated it with such consistency and precision? If his Augustan aesthetics struck Eric as too conservative, the sheer size of Johnson's mind more than compensated. Dr. Winston had even prayed for the soul of Dr. Johnson at a campus mass one day. "I feel great affection for him," Winston explained to about thirty attending students and a few faculty members, "and I pray that he will finally have the happiness that eluded him in life." What could anyone say but "amen"?

Cahalane was deft and witty again in Modern British Poets, but he could not have the sustained impact from poet to poet that he had achieved through two semesters of Shakespeare the year before.

In The Nineteenth Century Novel, Dr. Benacht lectured precisely about Dickens and George Eliot, though Eric could never finish their tomes and felt a bit cheated, as if the course was just a preview of readings he would get to later—in some imaginary year when he would just read novels. After the excitement of Lund and Seth in philosophy, Eric's final philosophy elective, The Philosophy of Man, disappointed him. This standard survey course never had the "cutting edge" feeling of Lund or the almost mystical intimacy of Seth's meditations on Existentialism. Courses could be valuable without being magical, but once he'd been to the mountaintop, Eric wanted to go there again.

Maybe the most uplifting experience in Eric's final semester was Fr. Scanlon's History of Modern Art. With frequent slide lectures, Scanlon traced the evolution of art from stately classical balances to medieval religious otherworldliness and on to the humanistic explosion of the great Renaissance painters and sculptors. What a pleasure to view such visual riches nearly every day and to learn about some techniques of composition and perspective that the artists had used, and often invented! Eric enjoyed Scanlon's wit as well. This celibate Jesuit had not an ounce of shyness about the nudity of Renaissance art. No reason he should presumably, but Eric had never heard a priest speak so frankly about artistic sensuality. Those slide images would linger, Eric guessed, long after he'd forgotten all but a few literary texts. The goodness of human bodies was a nice counterpoint to all the Catholic abstractions about spirits and souls and the invisible "presence of God" that theology proclaimed. Like the Romantic poets who had sought the divine in earthly beauty and sensuous imagery, the great artists and sculptors pursued a transcendent sensuality where body and soul came together. The "image and likeness of God" might include the heroic physiques of Michelangelo's "scandalous" Sistine Chapel with its rejection of medieval modesty. Not even popes, apparently, could argue with bodies like those. Perhaps God wasn't as buttoned-up as theology taught. So Eric's thoughts went that spring, from art class to the campus trees and flowers that marked the end of another New England winter.

By the time spring weather took hold in April, Eric's graduate school applications had brought their results, and decision time had arrived. Harvard, Cornell, and Yale had denied his applications for an English PhD. Brown, Wisconsin, Delaware, and Ohio State had said yes. Two MA applications had also been successful, South Illinois University and Boston College. Of them all, only BC had made the further offer of an English TA with full tuition remission. That letter had arrived in the last week of March and required an answer by April 4.

So there it was. Brown and especially Wisconsin appealed most among the doctoral programs. What would life in historic Providence or "radical" Madison be like? And then, there was Dad's school in beautiful Boston, where Eric had spent little time for someone who'd grown up thirty miles away. A master's program was less of a commitment than a doctorate, and with the draft looming, Eric considered that he might *finish* a master's before having to make a decision about military service, but he probably could not complete a PhD and might not return to it once he had left. BC would cost nothing, and Mom would have no more financial pressures from him after all the St. James tuition that Dad had paid.

When he'd shared each application result with Mom, she had said little, perhaps *hoping* but careful not to influence *his* decision. Shouldn't he stay nearby so soon after Dad's death? Wouldn't a master's be a better option just now? And Boston! Whatever Madison might offer, who could want more than all the ethnic and cultural riches of the Hub, as the Boston papers loved to call the city? He typed a quick answer and put it in the mail. BC it was. Wouldn't Dad be gratified that Eric had finally seen the light? He called Mom and told her of his choice. She kept her approval restrained, though Eric imagined that she was more pleased than she admitted. He would pursue a master's at BC and become a teaching assistant, his first classroom teaching. How long he might be there was beyond his control, so he did not talk with Mom about that. One rite of passage at a time was enough.

249

AT THE BRINK

I

Debating, like any competition, has its rhythms and momentum shifts. After their three-tournament run of Dartmouth, Catholic Prep, and Georgetown, Joel and Tony had a letdown at the St. James Tournament with a 3–3 mark. Eddie and Eldon stole that show at 5–1. No one took home any speaker awards, but Eric felt good that the B team could sometimes be as good as the A team often was. Joel and Tony, though disappointed, explained that they were trying some new arguments, particularly on the Affirmative side. Like athletes restless to improve, they tinkered with familiar arguments to catch opponents off guard. But excessive innovation might trouble a debate judge as well. As with some new routine in ice skating or gymnastics, too much newness in a debate tournament could seem eccentric and unconvincing. Then judges would deduct points.

So, the St. James Tournament ballots drove home the risks of "high roller" strategies for Joel and Tony, and for Eric as well. These two were risk takers whose real goal was to compete at the Nationals. Other victories along the way were fine, but merely winning did not interest them much. For Eric, who had never debated at their level, the priorities had been different. The brand new Kenton Academy debate team savored every victory and valued all tournaments nearly equally. They gave each debate everything they had. They did not "experiment" or sacrifice one tournament for the sake of a bigger one. Kenton's sudden success in eastern Massachusetts four-person tournaments seemed to validate that strategy. But to break into the

New York and Mid-Atlantic "big leagues" of high school debating, they would have to master the two-person, switch-side format and produce reams of unanticipated evidence. They would need to sound more like junior lawyers and not just natural orators working from small boxes of file cards.

High school debating had ended for Eric before he ever reached that higher level. Looking back, he doubted that "junior lawyer" debating was something he had ever wanted. Teams with long debating traditions and a dozen researchers to feed evidence to the best speakers could debate like that. The Yankees and Dodgers could play like that. Big ducks on big ponds, as Brother Sam loved to say. Eric had been a big duck on a small pond. So he helped Joel and Tony where he could, but the two coached themselves, especially in the weeks before the Nationals.

Eric also knew that after graduation he would leave debating behind because he wanted other things more. The point was to make *this* year the best it could be. That meant bringing along a deep field of rising debaters and pretty much leaving Joel and Tony alone. So he did. After a less successful outing, he would just ask them what had not worked and what they thought of doing about it. He never told them what to do. Roger had brought them to the brink of great success, but Eric never had Roger's authority with them. That was fine. In fact, Joel and Tony seemed grateful that Eric took on a supportive rather than a directive role with them. When they "failed," it was *their* job to figure out why. Thus Eric was learning all the delicate chemistry of high school boys with huge talents and fragile egos.

At the next two important switch-side tournaments, Joel and Tony kept experimenting. The Xaverian Prep Tournament in New York City and the college event at Seton Hall would have been big victories for any team, but Joel and Tony were 2–4 and 3–2, respectively. It was now the first week in April. The Nationals began on May 4.

On the "small pond" of the Worcester Diocesan Championship on April 8, Joel paired with Eldon on the Affirmative, and Tony with Eddie on the Negative side. Together they took second place with a 6–2 record, and Joel and Tony each won Best Speaker trophies.

The "big ducks" still ruled, and Brother Sam was pleased with the speaker awards. Joel and Tony smiled politely and continued making their own plans. This second-place finish had qualified them for the Nationals, which was all that mattered to them.

"I don't think we want to enter any more tournaments this month," Joel announced to Eric at their next Wednesday afternoon meeting.

"Oh," said Eric slowly. "Do you think that preparation time is more valuable now than more debating?"

"Exactly," answered Tony. "Besides, we're hosting a lot of good schools here in three weeks. We can hear some their latest stuff and then work to answer it."

"Since we won't compete in our own tournament," added Joel, "we won't be tipping anyone off about new ideas."

Eric smiled. "But don't you think these other schools know all that, too?"

"Oh, sure," Tony shrugged. "Everyone does extra things for the Nationals, but still it won't hurt to hear them without having them hear us a week before Atlantic City."

"OK," Eric said. "So what about the C.W. Post switch-side tournament?"

"Eddie and Eldon have been saying that they want a break to catch up with schoolwork. Let's just send somebody else," Tony suggested.

Eric thought for a few seconds. "I could take Hendley and Singletary as a switch-side team. That would be a big chance for them. Besides, they were 2–1 at the UNH switch-side last weekend while you guys were conquering the diocese."

Joel laughed, and Tony struck a Crusader pose, imaginary spear in one hand, shield in the other.

"Infidels out of Jerusalem!" Joel shouted.

"Kill a Commie for Christ!" Tony yelled.

"Wrong century," Joel corrected him.

"Same attitude," Tony countered.

"All right," Eric agreed as he waved off their jokes. "You guys and Brother Sam can plan the tournament, and I'll take Ricky and Burt to Post. They can be the headliners for once."

11

The C. W. Post switch-side tournament and a nearby one at St. Louis High School would end the debating schedule for St. Joe's. All that remained was their own event on the 29th and the Nationals on May 4–6. Though a switch-side event, Post drew at best a moderate field of New York and southern New England schools. Some of the best would come to St. Joe's event instead, and others, like Joel and Tony, were off the circuit to prepare for the Nationals. So Eric thought that Ricky Hendley and Burt Singletary might have a winning record at Post, though probably nothing spectacular. As sophomores, they had emerged more or less as St. Joe's third varsity team. Ricky had a tendency toward a monotone delivery, and Eric had tried to coax more expression from him. However, he was well organized and managed to leave no argument unanswered. Burt tended to ramble around the issues more, but he often had original ideas if the judge could find the right spot for them in his debate notes. Burt also spent spare moments in debates browsing through the file box to read the latest entries. He was becoming an evidence hound. As important, Ricky and Burt liked each other and liked debating together. That mattered a lot as young debaters built their confidence. In their unspectacular way, they could be quite good—the sort of team that impressed no one until a judge looked over his notes to find that they had covered every opposing point. These two had also taken quickly to the switch-side format, unlike most young debaters who wanted to succeed on one side first before risking the other. At a tournament like Post, of course, no one feared Ricky and Burt because no one had heard of them. So the element of surprise could be an asset.

The tournament unfolded and Eric did his judging, had lunch with his pair of sophomores, and then finished the two early-afternoon rounds. Post had the odd format of five switch-side rounds, meaning that each team debated on one side once more than the other. Semifinal and final rounds would follow, with no team taking the same side twice in a row. At the tournament assembly to hear the final four teams announced, Eric waited with his team. Four teams had all finished with 4–1 marks, and Ricky and Burt were one of them. Eric shook their hands as Ricky smiled shyly and Burt pumped his fist and tapped a little drum roll on his file box until other debaters looked at him and he stopped.

In the semifinal round, Eric watched with growing amusement as Ricky and Burt were their usual pesky selves on the Negative side. Their opponents were two senior girls from a St. Dorothy's school somewhere in the Hamptons (Eric had not heard of the school or seen these girls at any tournament). They tried to sound superior to mere sophomores, but they could not shake them. Hendley and Singletary won a split 2–1 decision and were now in the final round! Eric wished that Joel and Tony had come along to share a laugh at this unlikely result. If two debaters could resemble a pair of dogs who wouldn't let go of a bone, Ricky and Burt did.

In the final round, they took the Affirmative side, and from the start Eric had a good feeling. Ricky managed just enough animation in his First Affirmative speech to sound alert and confident. Their opponents were a girl and boy pair from St. Brendan's, though not the school's first or second team. Still, Brendan's was Brendan's, and the pair attacked the St. Joe's case pretty well, Eric thought, until Burt began unveiling unfamiliar quotations from somewhere deep in the file box. Some new Joel and Tony material, Eric assumed. The new evidence seemed to shake the Brendan's pair, who retreated into standard arguments. Though Ricky showed his fatigue in his rebuttal and became repetitive, Burt in the final speech of the debate kept pointing out ideas and evidence that the Negative team had not answered. As he finished, Eric leaned back in his cushioned auditorium chair, looked up at the ceiling, and almost laughed out loud. These two nobodies had just won themselves a tournament. And so they did, by a 2–1 decision.

"You guys were great," Eric said in the car as he patted each one on the shoulder. "Wait till St. Joe's hears about this!" That ride home was one of the sweetest for Eric all season.

Hosting a debate tournament for any school was easily more nerve-wracking than competing in one. Hundreds of details had to go right for everything to happen on time. But Brother Sam, Joel, and Tony had planned well. They invited the schools, prepared the ballots and purchased the trophies, handled the questions about accommodations from visiting teams, and then calculated the results very carefully. A couple of ten-minute delays were the only hitches—nothing compared to what Eric had seen at some tournaments. All Eric did was offer a few welcoming words and then let his debaters serve as the tournament staff. And what a tournament it was! Several top schools came, a sign of their respect for the St. Joe's debaters. When the four-round switch-side event ended, some of St. Joe's best rivals were all over the leader board, like a golf tournament led by Palmer, Nicklaus, and Player. On won-lost record and points with no elimination rounds, the top four teams were these:

1st—St. Brendan's (A)
2nd—St. Francis Prep
3rd—Melrose Academy
4th—St. Brendan's (B)

And the top four speakers were familiar names from the same leading schools:

1st—David Townsend, St. Francis Prep
2nd—Katie Fitzhugh, St. Brendan's (A)
3rd—Isaac Burnside, Melrose Academy
4th—Roy Donaldson, St. Brendan's (A)

Here was a preview of what Joel and Tony would probably face on the next weekend in Atlantic City. Without actually sitting in on any key debates, the two hosts had heard plenty about what the top teams were saying. Whether it would matter or not, they felt good about their strategy. The big ducks were ready for the biggest pond of all.

IV

Eric had never been to Atlantic City before. As they drove toward the hotel, the early May sun and salt aroma hinted of summer days ahead. They pulled into the Clarendon Hotel, checked in, and looked over the tournament program handed to every arriving team in the hotel lobby. Eric remembered his Nationals trips to Miami in '62 and Pittsburgh in '63. He had not flown to a debate event before, and both trips had a big-time feeling for a kid who'd never been farther from New England than his one trip to DC as an eighth-grade graduate. Tony and Joel were not so easily impressed. Tony waved freely to every rival he spotted. Joel was quieter, and when both got settled in their room, they quickly turned to the business of reviewing some new evidence until Eric knocked on their door and walked with them to the opening banquet in the huge Clarendon dining hall.

At dinner, the prearranged seating had St. Joe's at a large round table with debaters from Ohio and Kentucky. None of the Kentucky kids had ever been to New Jersey. The Ohio debaters from Cincinnati Catholic had made the Nationals in '65, just missed in '66, and were now back for a second time.

"How about you?" their coach asked Eric.

"This is our first time."

"That's exciting. Congratulations," said a religious brother of maybe forty, and then he paused. "Oh, I'm Brother Conrad." He offered his hand.

"Eric Malone."

"You look young to be coaching these debaters."

"I'm a senior at St. James in Worcester, Massachusetts."

"Ah, yes. A fine school. Do you debate there?"

"I did for a while. Academic pressures forced me to stop as a sophomore."

"It can be demanding. Well, good luck to you tomorrow," Brother Conrad offered, "unless, of course, we face you."

Eric smiled. "Good talking to you."

The banquet guests drifted off toward their rooms. Joel and Tony spotted some familiar rivals in the lobby and stayed to talk with them. Eric waved to them all and headed out onto the Boardwalk for a look at the ocean and the people on this mild May night. It was almost over. All the meetings and practices and rides to tournaments and returns home in the darkness were done. Only this weekend remained. In his one year as a debate coach, his team—or the team he accompanied anyway—was at the NCFL tournament. He glanced at two pretty girls walking toward him and looked away as they passed. A thin crescent moon was dim near the horizon. He walked by other hotels with their restaurants and bars. On the beach a group of kids in T-shirts and cutoffs played twilight volleyball without a net. Two boys maybe ten or eleven tossed a baseball between them while their parents sat on a blanket and looked at the surf. The tide was rising. A half-mile or so beyond the Clarendon, he turned and started back. People of all ages, some with dogs and one Oriental-looking woman with a parrot sitting on her shoulder, kept him interested. He nodded to a few and said "hello" a couple of times. The Asian lady did not answer his greeting, but the parrot did.

Atlantic City was a heightened version of Hampton Beach. It was already lively in early May. He imagined July nights along the Boardwalk, then turned and headed between some outdoor restaurant tables toward the Clarendon archway with its large white anchor and nautical decor. In the lobby, he stood briefly and looked around. Joel and Tony were gone—to relax with some kids, he hoped, rather than planning last-day strategies. A few people sat at the bar and a second round of diners, or maybe the third, looked over menus. It was sometime after eight, though Eric saw no clock and wore no watch. He was turning toward the elevator to go up to his room when he caught a side glimpse of Joel at the far end of the lobby and half-obscured behind some decorative plants. He was talking to someone that Eric couldn't see. As he moved toward them, Tony saw Eric first.

"Look who we found?" Tony gestured toward a man with his back to Eric.

"My God, Roger Preston!" Eric exclaimed and the two shook hands. How long was it since he'd seen Roger? About two years, he guessed.

"What are you doing here?" Eric asked.

"Well, Eric," Roger was all hands as he talked, "I came to see a dynasty in the making," nodding toward Joel and Tony. Eric still had a puzzled look on his face until Roger explained.

"I'm stationed at Fort Dix. They gave me a quick leave to see some weirdness called debating. I'll be here right through the championship round," Roger teased.

"We'll blow you a kiss from the podium," Tony promised as they all laughed. No one doubted that he would. The four talked for a few more minutes, and then Eric excused himself to go upstairs. A half hour later he heard Joel and Tony coming into their next-door room. Roger Preston at Fort Dix! Where else had he been or would soon be? At least he'd get to hear Joel and Tony debate. Eric was glad to see Roger again at last and to have him here to support his two star debaters. They had to feel better knowing he was nearby. So did Eric as random memories of debates with Roger flooded back. Settling into bed with the book he'd brought along, Gene Smith's *When the Cheering Stopped* about Woodrow Wilson and Versailles, he could hear the muffled voices of Joel and Tony in their familiar cadences of question and answer, statement and rebuttal. Whatever happened, he thought, this tournament would be a spectacle, a vanity fair of high school debating's best hoping for some moments of glory. He was happy being part of the scene once more.

* * *

The National Catholic Forensic League Finals was a tournament heavy on judging. All teams debated for four switch-side rounds with three judges in each, or until a *second* loss eliminated them. From won-lost records and then speaker points on their twelve ballots, the top sixteen teams faced off in the octofinals with the winners advancing to the quarters and semis until the top two teams debated for the national title. *May Madness*, Eric thought, *without the frenzied crowds and media publicity*. More like a verbal chess tournament with the pieces as ideas and quotations. From all over the country, the geeky researchers and eloquent persuaders poured out torrents of words, and the judges took flowchart notes to record every lapse and eloquent flourish that tilted debates one way or the other.

Eric had a full day of judging ahead, but Roger was free to wander from debate to debate, slipping in or out between speeches or at the five-minute recess before the rebuttals. He could follow Joel and Tony all day, but he'd rather hear some of their work and then check out other contenders. He knew many coaches and would surprise them by appearing now at the Nationals after so long out of circulation. Here was an old ballplayer suddenly back in the stands to see what the new kids could do. A debate aficionado.

So it began. Two rounds, then lunch, then two more. At lunch Eric did not see Roger but caught up with Joel and Tony. They felt good, as their familiar banter proved.

"I carried him all morning. Dead weight," Joel moaned.

"Ha!" exclaimed Tony, like a Renaissance noble suffering the impudence of a peasant. "Who was it that started confusing Nicaragua with Nigeria? Must I pack an atlas for quick reference?" Eric laughed and wished them luck for the third and fourth rounds. So far they'd faced unknown teams from Texas and Wisconsin. Nor had Eric judged any of the more familiar East Coast schools. The tournament wizards must have arranged for geographic diversity in these early rounds. Later, between the third and fourth rounds, Eric spotted Roger on his way from a debate.

"How's it going?"

"Fascinating," Roger assured him. "I heard about half of Tony and Joel in round one and then found the St. Francis Prep team for rebuttals. They were killing some Negative team from Georgia. How about you?"

"I haven't judged any familiar teams yet. I'd say they've all been pretty good, but I haven't heard anyone that Joel and Tony couldn't handle."

Roger laughed. "Let's hope it stays that way. See you after the fourth round."

"OK." Eric found his fourth debate room and sat down toward the back center of a hotel suite rearranged and refurnished for debaters. He turned over his art pad and readied another sheet with four speaker columns. The Affirmatives were already setting up at a table to Eric's right. They printed their names on a small blackboard mounted to the left of their table and wrote across the top, "Collingwood Academy, Chicago." Eric knew of their strong reputation but had never heard them at a tournament. A minute later the Negative team arrived—Fitzhugh and Donaldson from St. Brendan's, the runners-up at the St. Joe's tournament a week before! So at last Eric would judge a familiar competitor. The other two judges sat near the opposite corners of the room. When all three had filled out their ballots with the debaters' names and readied their flow sheets, they nodded to the debate timer, who signaled the First Affirmative speaker to begin.

Eric thought about what every judge looked for as the debate began. A good First Affirmative speech should introduce the topic briefly, cite some problems with the present system, present the Affirmative plan to solve those problems, and argue for the benefits of that plan. The speaker might also compare the plan favorably with the status quo and its *inherent* problems and even anticipate some Negative team objections. The goal was to sound clear and coherent without revealing too much of the Affirmative team's strategies and evidence base too soon. Then the Negative team needed to show that the Affirmative plan would not work, was no improvement over the status quo, and had some *inherent* flaws of its own. Beyond that, a debate could hinge on the quality of each team's research. Who had the better data, the more convincing expert opinions, and a fuller knowledge of the history of the issue? This year's topic concerning the powers of the UN Peacekeeper forces invited consideration of various world "trouble spots" where UN troops from various countries had either succeeded or failed. Cold War history since WWII mattered, as did a good sense of geography. One should be careful not to confuse Nicaragua with Nigeria (Eric smiled again at Tony's joke).

By all of these standards and more, the Collingwood–St. Brendan's debate was a good one, the best Eric had heard that day. Here were two teams that would require all of Joel and Tony's talents to beat. Well into the rebuttals, Eric had not made up his mind. He took notes rapidly and used arrows and check marks, pluses and minuses, to denote coverage or advantage and disadvantage, respectively. In a good debate, each speaker would tilt the scales toward his or her team, and the seesaw would continue until someone made a mistake. A small flaw like an unanswered question, a bit of doubtful logic, or a factual error could make the difference. Eloquence mattered, too. Were the speakers efficient and competent, or even compelling and passionate? And did partners work together, or was one carrying the other? At last, and by a narrow 47–45 score, Eric decided that St. Brendan's had won this debate. He was sure that this Brendan's team would make the elimination rounds. Collingwood might as well, even though they had lost his ballot. They were too good to lose more than a few. He sealed the paper into the attached envelope and handed it to the timekeeper, who collected all three ballots and returned them to the tournament tabulators.

Eric felt mentally drained. A close debate always stretched and tired the mind. And when it was the fourth of the day, any judge would be ready, like the debaters, for some comic relief. He knew that Joel and Tony would provide it. The hyper-rationality of debating almost forced competitors into after-hours absurdity. No one could be that serious indefinitely. Yes, a confident debater could risk a quick joke or wordplay in competition, but in the best debates there hardy seemed time for levity, unless the joke also clinched an argument.

Eric stretched his neck left and right, rolled his left wrist around, and flexed his writing fingers. Ink stained the outer edge of his writing hand as it always did when he'd written for a while with his cramped, over-the-top style. He closed up his art pad and made his way back to the dining hall. Had he just judged the last debate of his life? If Joel and Tony made the elimination rounds, Eric could not be in the pool of judges any longer. So he hoped it was so. He was ready for all that intense effort over several years to be done.

"How was it?" Roger asked, approaching Eric from behind as coaches and debaters began to gather.

"I judged Collingwood and St. Brendan's. A very good debate. I thought Brendan's won but not by much. Who did you hear?"

"I listened to the main speeches for Georgetown and Xaverian Prep. Then I found Joel and Tony in time for their rebuttals. If they've been that good all day, they are not done yet."

"All right!" Eric said confidently. He and Roger sat at a dining table and looked around for several minutes until Joel and Tony finally returned and found them.

"What did you think?" Joel asked Roger, obviously referring to the fourth debate.

"I just heard the rebuttals, but you were both solid."

"Yeah," said Joel, "I think we won the first, second, and fourth debates. We weren't as sharp in the third one against Collingwood Prep."

"Oh, I just finished judging them against St. Brendan's," Eric answered. "Brendan's won my ballot but narrowly."

"How many ballots could a team lose and still make the eliminations?" Tony wondered.

Roger responded. "I'd guess two at most and probably only one. Very few schools will be 12–0 in this field, but the best won't lose more than a couple of ballots." Everyone thought about that. Joel and Tony went to get sodas at the refreshment table, and Roger used the bathroom. Eric sat alone and watched tournament officials drift in and sit down at the head table. Many had not returned yet. Then the tournament chair, a Dr. Creighton from Villanova Prep, stepped to the mike. "Folks, we should have the tabulations finished in about another ten minutes. So relax and we'll be with you as soon as we can." By now, the dining hall was nearly full of debaters and coaches. The room seemed tired, and the buzz of conversation was low. Everyone waited.

After what seemed more like twenty minutes than ten, three more tournament officials entered. One passed several papers to Creighton and pointed out some details. The two whispered for several seconds, and then Creighton approached the mike again.

"Ladies and gentlemen, we thank you for your patience. As you know, the top sixteen teams will advance to the octofinal round. We have determined those teams based on ballots won first, and then on speaker points to break ties in won-lost records. Five teams had 12–0 records, six more teams were 11–1, and seven teams were 10–2. All of the 12–0 and 11–1 teams will move on, and five of the seven 10–2 teams will advance. Which five of these we have determined from total points scored on the twelve ballots. So that we do not prejudice any judging in the elimination rounds, we will announce the top sixteen teams in alphabetical order. We will not indicate each team's record. Of course, the judges for these advancing teams will not be eligible for any further judging. The specific matchups, the judges for each debate, and the locations of the debates will be posted tomorrow morning by eight thirty a.m. right here. The octofinal round will then begin at nine a.m." He looked around the room and smiled. "So, are you ready?" A collective "yes" rose from the audience.

"The sixteen octofinalists in alphabetical order are as follows:

1. Archbishop Stevens High School
2. The Assumption School of Dayton
3. Assumption Prep of Miami
4. Boston College High School
5. Canisius Academy
6. Georgetown Prep—"

"No Collingwood," Joel whispered to Tony. "Maybe we beat them." Tony nodded and kept listening.

"7. Holy Family High School
8. Loyola Academy of Chicago
9. Mission Hill Prep
10. Pittsburgh Central Catholic
11. Regis Prep
12. St. Brendan's High School
13. St. Francis Prep
14. St. Joseph's Academy of Philadelphia—"

They all looked at each other. Could there be two St. Joseph schools in the mix?

"15. St. Joseph's High School of Shrewsbury, Mass.
16. Xaverian Prep."

Roger gave Tony a sudden hug. Eric shook Joel's hand. "Yes!" Tony exclaimed and hit the top of his file cabinet with his right hand.

"Way to go, you guys," Eric said as the meeting broke up.

"Congratulations," David Townsend of St. Francis Prep called from three tables away.

"Thanks. You too," Tony answered. "Maybe we'll meet again."

Townsend just smiled and nodded. A few other debaters from the "sweet sixteen" shook hands with each other, or shouted congratulations to friends from other schools. For most, of course, the tournament was over, though nearly all would stay for the awards banquet on Saturday night. Why hurry out of Atlantic City in May?

* * *

In the morning, Joel and Tony arrived with Eric at the dining hall shortly after eight o'clock. A complimentary breakfast awaited the debaters and coaches. A few minutes later, Eric saw Roger across the room talking with two coaches. He then turned and headed toward the St. Joe's group.

"Hey, guys," Roger smiled. "I hear the debates will be posted in a few minutes." As he spoke, a tournament official pinned a schedule to the bulletin board by the head table. Tony jumped up and went over to check. He came back and announced: "We're Negative against Assumption of Dayton in room 207." They all picked up their things and went off to their octofinal debate. Eric had brought his art pad but would not bother to use it now, unless some detail from yesterday's flowsheets might be worth a quick reminder to Joel and Tony.

The Assumption debate was closely argued in a packed room. Eric and Roger sat by the far wall away from the door. Maybe thirty people had crowded in using extra folding chairs. At the recess, Roger said he was going to check out a few other debates and would be back before rebuttals ended. Eric nodded. He looked around the room at the mix of familiar faces from several schools. Was anybody "scouting" here and reporting back to his or her school? No one could really control that, but the odds of being able to use some "inside information" at this point were slim since no one knew who their next opponent was or even which side they would take. Usually the sides alternated from round to round, but if two winners had just been Affirmative, say, a coin flip would determine the Negative team for the next debate.

Eric had never been very sharp about tournament intrigue. Roger was better at collecting tidbits of speculation, which was why he liked to wander in this situation when he had no judging duties. As Tony started the final Negative rebuttal, Roger slipped back into his seat. He leaned toward Eric and whispered, "The second speaker for Xaverian has a bad cold. He may not be able to continue, and they're trying to find out if they can substitute someone from the team."

"God, what a time for that," Eric answered, and Roger nodded. When the Assumption debate ended, Eric and the others walked back to the dining hall to await the octo results. In about fifteen minutes, Dr. Creighton announced them, this time indicating the victory margins. St. Joe's had beaten Assumption, 2–1. Congratulations now were brief, and the quarterfinal assignments followed quickly. Joel and Tony would be Affirmative against Loyola of Chicago in room 125.

The quarterfinal debates were even more crowded, and tournament volunteers brought more chairs to each of the rooms. Roger decided to wander off again and came back in the middle of Tony's Second Affirmative speech. "St. Francis looks pretty good early against Mission Hill," he whispered with a smile, like a bookie giving a sports tip.

"No surprise there," Eric answered, and they both turned their attention to Tony. Eric felt fairly confident about this debate, particularly when Joel used some UN reports to great effect in his rebuttal. Loyola's Second Negative had their team's final rebuttal, and he gave one of those breathless summations of the whole debate that impressed some judges, like a steamroller on the move or a tennis star covering the whole court. Tony stayed right with him in his own rebuttal, however. It could still go either way

Back in the dining hall, Creighton soon had the results. Once more, Joel and Tony had won a split 2–1 decision. How good were these guys against the best competition? Eric began to think that they could beat anyone. Joel was thoroughly and deeply analytical. Tony was all that, with quick flashes of wit as well. It was all up to them now. Eric and Roger were along for the ride.

Then Creighton's assistant chair, Mrs. Powell from Cleveland Academy, stepped forward to announce the semifinal schedule.

"St. Francis Prep, Affirmative, vs. St. Joseph's High, Negative, in room 130.

BC High, Affirmative, vs. Pittsburgh Central, Negative, in room 204.

And after the semifinals, we will meet in the auditorium to the right of the dining hall"—she gestured that way—"to announce the results and have the final debate. We will also have a lunch break before the final round. That debate will begin at one thirty p.m. Good luck to all the semifinalists."

So it was St. Francis Prep one more time! The runners-up in St. Joe's own tournament last week would now face off against their hosts and rivals. *That means St. Brendan's is out*, Eric thought with surprise. Eric didn't know much about the current BC High or Pittsburgh Central teams, except that Joel and Tony had lost to Pittsburgh at Georgetown. But St. Francis was familiar territory. This could be the debate of the year. If Joel and Tony could win this one, why not everything? Who was any better every week and every year than St. Francis?

As both teams were setting up in front of the room, Tony turned to David Townsend and shook his hand.

"I guess you were right about meeting again," David smiled.

"Good luck," Tony answered.

"You too," said David, and the contest was on. Sensing the importance of this debate, Roger decided to stay put. As spectators moved to get seats, he and Eric were separated and ended up sitting twenty feet apart with four or five people between them.

The St. Francis debate was everything that Eric and Roger expected. Townsend had sometimes been the First Affirmative and then given the last rebuttal of the debate, but during the season the pair had switched off with Orlofsky delivering the opening speech. Townsend would still have the final word in rebuttals, however. Joel and Tony knew all about David's powers of summation. To win the debate, they would have to be clearly in the lead before Townsend's final speech. A tie by then would end as a loss.

True to form, St. Francis's Affirmative case had a couple of interesting changes from what Eric had heard before. But Joel and Tony were ready. Their innovative research led to the use of some sources that Eric, and he hoped the St. Francis pair, had not heard before. Still, at the recess following the four main speeches, Eric felt he could throw a blanket over the four speakers, so close were their performances. The final Townsend rebuttal looked ominous now. Joel and Tony must do *something* before then to counter it. What that could be Eric didn't know. Eric glanced back at Roger, who gave a little shrug to agree that this debate was tight.

In the first Negative rebuttal, Joel went to work on a couple of sources that Orlofsky had quoted. These statements were dated 1963, but Joel cited 1966 material suggesting that these same foreign policy specialists had changed their thinking. Eric felt hopeful. Orlofsky countered that the later quotations referred to different political conditions and did not actually contradict the 1963 ideas. What would the judges think? Tony added some fuel to this fire by confirming another change of heart by another key St. Francis source. "If experts can rethink their views," Tony argued, "no one should base important policy decisions on outdated analysis."

Eric smiled. In his biased heart, Joel and Tony now had the edge at just the right time. Townsend's final rebuttal was another tour de force, but he never quite untangled the matter of sources that had reversed themselves. Whatever the result, here were Joel and Tony at their strategic best. The St. Francis team had to be feeling nervous.

Several minutes later in the Clarendon auditorium, Mrs. Powell again delivered the results. BC High had beaten Pittsburgh Central, 3–0, and St. Joe's had defeated St. Francis, 2–1. Now David Townsend offered his hand, and so did Orlofsky. "That was brilliant," David said, "and too late for us to figure out a good answer."

"Good luck in the final, guys," Orlofsky added.

So they had done it—come to the brink of a national champion-ship! The title debate would be a Massachusetts showdown between St. Joe's and BC High. Roger and Eric congratulated Joel and Tony and then just looked at each other with a "Can you believe this?" glance.

At lunch, Tony was hungry and dug in. Joel was quieter and ate less. Both had to be tired by now, but the BC High team would be as well. Eric's guys had not faced them all year, though they knew that BC could debate with anybody. Soon everyone assembled in the auditorium. The four finalists shook hands, and Dr. Creighton came to the podium. "In the national championship debate," he began, "St. Joseph's of Shrewsbury, Massachusetts, on the Affirma-tive will face Boston College High on the Negative. Good luck, gentlemen."

Three hundred people all but filled the auditorium as the de-bate began. Even a few hotel guests had wandered in, curious to see what "debating" was all about. They stood close to the exit and left discreetly after the First Affirmative speech. Debating was obviously an acquired taste. Eric and Roger sat next to each other on the right side of the central aisle about ten rows back and almost directly in front of Joel and Tony. Each pair of debaters shared a table with file cabinets and a few magazines and books obscuring the legal pads on which they scribbled quick notes.

Joel's First Affirmative speech was clear and well-paced, though maybe not as animated as it could have been. Dan MacGregor, the first Negative speaker, moved directly into a critique of the Affirma-tive plan and seemed effective to Eric without being overwhelming. MacGregor raised some budgetary questions about how UN mem-bers would fund troop movements, particularly in multiple trouble spots at once. Suppose member nations were reluctant to contribute. When Tony responded, he argued that any nation willing to provide UN troops had every incentive to fund them as well. "Nations find ways to meet the needs of their own troops," Tony asserted, then paused. "The French, for instance, have always moved their troops by taxi service." Laughter broke out in the audience and even the BC debaters smiled, conceding to Tony the best joke of the debate. Eric and Roger just shook their heads and smiled at Tony's irrepressible confidence. *We're all right so far*, Eric thought.

In his Second Negative speech, Michael Leonard turned from financial issues to the politics of UN operations and raised some complicated questions about achieving cooperation between Americans and their European allies, who were often rivals as well. "He's good," Roger whispered to Eric as the speech ended and the debate recessed for five minutes.

"Another close one," Eric said.

"Yeah," Roger agreed. "At this level no one is going to blow an opponent away. Everyone is too good."

In the rebuttals, each debater reasserted his side's core ideas and hammered away at the opponents' evidence. All were effective, but Joel seemed a bit tired to Eric in his delivery. They must all have been feeling the strain of the Nationals and of the whole, long season. When Joel finished, Eric felt that Leonard's political analysis still needed more attention. Leonard then gave the final Negative speech. He pointed to deep tensions among the Western allies and noted that even short of using their UN veto power, the Soviet Union and China knew how to drive economic wedges between the Western powers, especially in the matter of sending troops and money to faraway places where they were hard to sustain. "America's experience in Vietnam, even as we speak, underlines such difficulties. The Affirmative plan," he concluded, "optimizes the assets and minimizes the problems of Western nations in sustaining UN efforts. That is just a little bit naive."

Leonard sat down abruptly, as if leaving the judges, and Tony in the final rebuttal, to face that stark truth. Eric hoped that Tony had one more compelling rejoinder in him. He was good. He gave examples of successful UN actions and reasserted the ties of the Western democracies. "Their common interests against Soviet and Chinese expansion will assure their cooperation at crucial times," he argued.

As Tony finished, Eric wondered if he had done enough. They all waited while the three judges completed their work, sealed their ballots, and handed them to the debate timekeeper. Dr. Creighton and Mrs. Powell took the ballots into an adjoining room and emerged a few minutes later. Then Creighton spoke.

"Ladies and gentlemen, let me first ask for a round of applause for our finalists, who have given us an excellent debate." The audience responded vigorously, and all four of the debaters smiled.

"These decisions at this high level of competition are always difficult," Creighton resumed, "but we finally have to decide. By a 2–1 vote, the judges have awarded this year's national championship to Boston College High School." As applause resounded, the four debaters all shook hands. Joel looked particularly sad, while Tony tried to seem more upbeat.

"Well," Roger said to Eric, "they had an incredible run and gave it everything."

"They sure did," Eric agreed. Eric approached the debaters first. "Guys, it was a great debate and an amazing tournament."

Tony nodded and Joel said, "I'm sorry for you. We wanted to win it for you."

"For me?" Eric answered. "You two have accomplished more than I ever did. No need to be sorry about anything." Roger shook each debater's hand and said he was proud of them. He then walked over to the BC table and congratulated the winners. "An outstanding debate," he assured them.

"Thanks a lot. St. Joe's is a great opponent," Michael Leonard answered.

The tournament banquet that evening was a lavish affair with an excellent menu and plenty of relaxed talk among the debaters and coaches. Joel and Tony had mostly recovered from their disappointment and were sociable with everyone. They still got some congratulations for their second-place finish from many debaters and coaches. Both, of course, were among the top ten speakers. They also received a certificate as one of the five 12–0 teams after the four preliminary rounds. All of that was fine but secondary, because the biggest prize had eluded them by the narrowest of margins, a few points on each of the two ballots that had gone against them.

Roger had to leave that night to get back to Fort Dix. He hugged each of the debaters again.

"Keep in touch. Stay safe," Eric managed to say as he shook Roger's hand.

The debaters' ride back to Worcester via the New Jersey and Connecticut turnpikes was subdued. Tony and Joel talked briefly about a couple of moments in different debates, but neither mentioned the final round. They didn't want any more analysis of that. At St. Joe's, Joel and Tony's parents were waiting along with Brother Sam. The second-in-the-nation news thrilled them all, and the debaters patiently received another round of congratulations.

"What a great job you have done," Brother Sam said to Eric.

"I'm so proud of them. They've reached a level that I never did."

"Well, thanks so much for your efforts," Brother Sam concluded.

Eric drove back to St. James. He lay back on his bed reliving it all for more than an hour. Zack was still out somewhere. Second at the Nationals! Joel and Tony would always have that, and so would he— and Roger especially, who had primed them for it. His own debating days were over, Eric knew. He wanted something different from all the hair-splitting intensity, despite the gratification it had given him. An amazing year was ending, and who knew what was next?

V

The end of the debating season meant four free weekends for Eric until graduation day in June. As courses wound down, he also found more time for free reading. Religion, literature, and politics, as always, held the most interest. Sometimes they interconnected in unexpected ways, especially as his thinking grew more speculative. He still felt the beauty of Catholic rituals, but the rule-bound morality and authority-laden structures of the Church were more troubling and distant from him. John Robinson's *Honest To God* and James Kavanaugh's *A Modern Priest Looks at His Outdated Church* were among the "bad influences" he indulged. After so much hope for change, the message seemed to be that nothing really important *could* change in Rome. Graham Greene's dissolute priest in *The Power and the Glory* had clung to a sacramental theology that transcended his personal unworthiness. On the other hand, Stephen Dedalus in Joyce's *Portrait . . .* had let go of a strident Irish Catholicism and embraced an aesthetic spirituality, a priesthood of art. Eric was no Joyce, but he shared the writer's amusement at a heaven that promised "eternity in the company of the Dean of Studies." The artist, the writer, the politician, even the theologian needed room to breathe. Paul Tillich advocated *The Courage to Be,* and Eric wondered if he had it.

Roger would end up in Vietnam. Ro would graduate from Yale and then what? The Peace Corps, he thought, somewhere in French-speaking West Africa. The class of '67 had celebrated its Hundred Days Party in February and later its milk-throwing in the cafeteria. Eric had stood on the fringes of the first and skipped the second. Were these their idea of freedom? They'd call him a nerd or worse if he bothered to criticize, so he didn't bother. Sodality's final meetings were good for the friendships there and for the warmth of Fr. Latourette, but their spiritual austerity no longer held him. What exactly do you want, confused young man? It was true. He could more easily say what he did not want.

Thoughts of the priesthood had lingered since high school, as they had for many Catholic school guys, but suppose he followed that path only to find Church politics, patriarchy, and secrecy—Vatican secrecy—more than he could defend? If Jesus had been transparent, shouldn't His Church be also? He knew why various Marian apparitions had produced warnings for the world. The world was full of brutality, neglect, and greed. But why were there no supernatural warnings for the Church? Was God content with hierarchical authority and ecclesiastical complacency? Were sacramental and moral rules really enough get souls into heaven? Was God the great record keeper? Eric smiled to imagine all the varieties of Christians jostling for position at the Second Coming and finding themselves less righteous than they supposed. And where would he be in the melee?

One of Eric's bad habits, he knew, was keeping too much to himself. A good spiritual advisor would surely have talked him through all of his confusions and sent him on his way to become a Jesuit. No thanks. Not *that* way, at least. If he ever chose the priesthood, it would be a much reformed priesthood he would choose. Otherwise, he would risk a freer kind of goodness. And what about the women he had never given the chance to know him for fear of losing them, or losing himself in their expectations?

Mom came to the graduation where valedictorian Richard Pendleton spoke about the possibilities of mind and of life to his classmates, who admired his mind without ever, most of them, coming anywhere near it. Maybe Eric should have sought him out a few times and asked what he thought it was all about. Would Pendleton have laughed, or said kindly, "Well, Eric, that's something you have to figure out for yourself. But don't worry. All the necessary ingredients for happiness are at hand"? Yes, he'd have said something like that if Eric had ever asked.

Mom observed what a smart young man this valedictorian was. Eric agreed. Then Governor Vincenti spoke, a Massachusetts Republican full of practical but somehow unexciting advice.

Classmate Jack Brewer shook hands with Eric after the ceremony and took a picture of Eric and his mom. He'd spent time with Eric intermittently at the college, but today he was somehow drawn to him. Was Jack also sensing the lost opportunities of college life? All the good people one never quite knew? Or did he just want a friendly face today? Come to think of it, where was *his* family? In Dad's absence, Eric had his mother at least.

* * *

The day was good when college ended, and Eric drove his mother home and talked briefly with her and wondered during the silences if his life to come in Boston would somehow unlock secrets that college life had never quite revealed.

Late in August, Eric rode again with his mom. This time she drove him toward Chestnut Hill. She would leave him off at the room he had rented in a comfortable old house on Com. Ave. near BC and a short walk to the green line that would link him to the city of historic patriots and of endless ethnic life.

As they cruised along Route 9, they came to a rise in the highway. There, emerging above the curtain of trees for several alluring seconds, the whole skyline of the Hub rose up. In the afternoon sun the buildings had a reddish glow, and Eric stared at them until the highway descended and the green curtain again obscured the light and the journey continued, but still the red-glowing city kept drawing him in.

CPSIA information can be obtained
at www.ICGtesting.com
Printed in the USA
FFOW02n0944291015
18137FF